GAMES OF ROME

To my darling Amelia,

May our phalli
always have wings
and fly high!

All my love

J.P.

GAMES OF ROME

DOMINUS: BOOK 2

BY

JP KENWOOD

Dedication

For my wonderful editors, **Molly Beakers** and **June E. Rigby**. Thank you both for all of your feedback, patience, and humor, and for helping to make this a better story. And for my brilliant cover artist and dear friend, **Fiona Fu**. Many thanks also to **Catherine Dair** for her beautiful, bespoke map of Rome.

Warmest thanks also to Pd Singer, Elin Gregory, and all of the wonderful friends, fellow authors, reviewers, and especially the readers who have supported me.

Special bleating thanks to **Michelle Robinson** for naming Gaius's onery nanny goat.

Author's Note

Games of Rome is the **second** book of my erotic m/m alternate history saga, ***Dominus***.

These are NOT stand-alone stories.

The **first** book in this saga, ***Dominus***, is available at Amazon Worldwide. The French translation of ***Dominus*** can be found at Juno Publishing.

While many details in this saga are historically accurate and tied to major historical events and prevailing cultural attitudes during the reign of the Emperor Trajan (AD 98-117), the twisted tale and the main characters are entirely fictional. The names, characters, and incidents are products of the writer's imagination or have been used fictitiously and are not to be construed as real. Any resemblance to persons, living or dead, actual events, locale or organizations is entirely coincidental.

Please note that some historical facts and dates have been changed to suit the alternate history plot. For example, according to the relatively scant ancient sources, Publius Aelius Hadrianus (Hadrian) did not return to Rome after the Second Dacian War. Other details, especially those regarding the ages of the sexually active characters, have been altered from ancient norms to comply with modern sensibilities. All major characters in this story are 17 years old or older.

Advisory

This work contains sexually explicit scenes as well as graphic language and violence and may be considered offensive to some readers. Intended for adult audiences only. **Not intended for anyone under the age of 18**. Please store your files where they are inaccessible to under-aged readers.

General notes on Roman nomenclature

The names of the characters, especially the Roman characters, in this story can be challenging at first, so here's a quick summary of how Roman names worked. In the Imperial period, Roman male citizens most often had three names (*tria nomina*). Our protagonist, Gaius Fabius Rufus, is a perfect example of typical Roman male nomenclature.

The **first name** (*praenomen*) was used only by those most intimate with the man—his family, his lovers, and his very close friends and most trusted clients. There were a limited number of Roman male first names, and many first names were very common. Gaius was an extremely popular first name, as were Lucius, Marcus and Publius.

The **second name** (*nomen*) indicated the man's family or *gens*. It denoted either the family into which he was biologically born or the family that adopted him. Gaius Fabius Rufus hails from the Fabii family or the Fabian clan, one of the oldest and most esteemed patrician families of Rome.

The **third name** (*cognomen*) is akin to the modern notion of a nick-name and was either given to the male child by his family or chosen by the man himself. In public life, most men were referred to by either their first and family names (Gaius Fabius) or their family name and nick-name (Fabius Rufus). Many famous historical figures are familiar to us today by their nickname, such as Cicero (Marcus Tullius Cicero). Gaius Fabius Rufus's nickname, given to him at birth, means 'red-haired.'

Roman women did not have a first name (*praenomen*) nor did wom-en take their husbands' family name when they married. Instead, women received the feminine form of their father's family name (*nomen*). Thus, Gaius Fabius Rufus's wife, Marcia, hails from the Marcii clan, another old and distinguished founding family of Rome. Lucius Petronius Celsus's daughter was named Petronia after her father's clan. Some women were also referred to by their nicknames (*cognomina*).

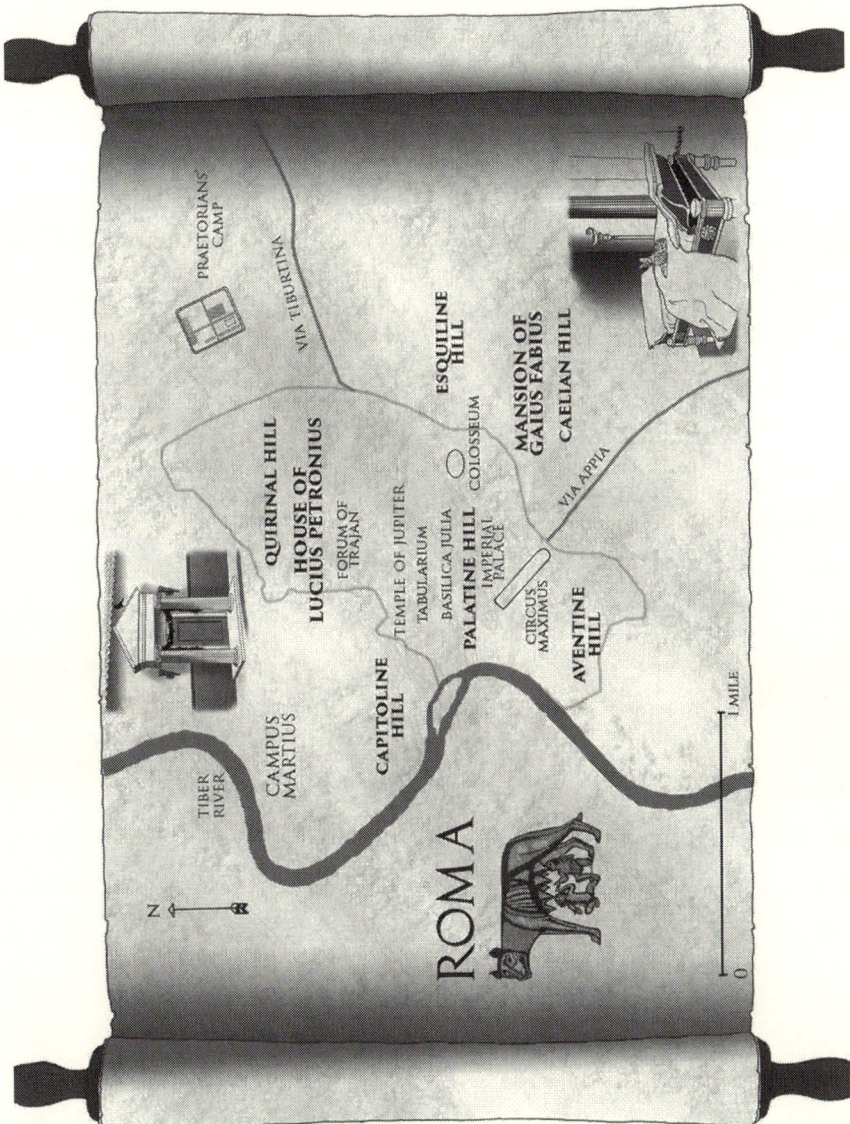

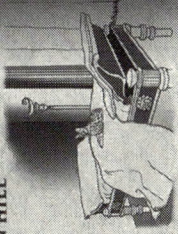

PROLOGUE

AD 2010
Piazza della Rotonda, Rome

S WALLOWING MY LAST SWIG of beer, I stared off into space while shadows slowly enveloped the columnar façade of the Pantheon. Since late morning, I'd been sitting outside the cafe, jotting down memories of that summer three years ago. I set my glass down and rubbed my tired eyes when two tourists stopped in front of my table and blocked my priceless view. Arguing over where to sit, the couple finally settled into the metal bistro set next to mine and ordered from the overpriced menu.

He was decked out in typical, brash Americana: a baseball cap, a silver football jersey, and brand new jeans barely held up by a black belt with a fancy brass buckle the size of a saucer. His buxom wife—I assumed they were married—wore a pink 'I heart Roma' t-shirt, the words grotesquely stretched across her enormous breasts, along with flower-patterned capris and lime-green plastic sandals. After our surly waiter dropped off their expensive sodas, the guy downed his entire glass in three gulps and leaned back, his bulky legs splayed as if his scrotum were the size of a small country.

"*Magrippa* something *coster* something *feck it*," he drawled in a heavy accent. "What do those letters up there mean, Loretta?"

"The guide book says a Roman general named Agrippa—you see his name on the building—made this monument two thousand years ago, Roy, and it's still standing. Isn't that neat?"

I ground my teeth. Say nothing. Do not correct. Do not engage.

After opening my journal, I pushed my wire rim glasses up my nose, slithered down into my chair like a pathetic antisocial worm, and pretended to write something, anything to avoid getting trapped in a conversation.

"It looks like a bank. Does that book of yours say if it was a bank?" The guy belched.

"It's an ancient Roman temple with a huge vaulted ceiling made of solid concrete. It says here we should go inside and see the dome, Roy."

Roy grunted, apparently either unimpressed or disinterested in learning anything more about the ancient crown jewel of the eternal city. "Where's the Vatican? I came to see St. Peter's, and we're leaving tomorrow."

She reached into her purse and pulled out an unwieldy, wrinkled map. Once she'd shaken it open, his wife wiggled on her narrow reading glasses. "Looks like the Vatican is right around the corner across the river. Before we head over there, I want to get some postcards from that souvenir stand, Roy."

She didn't give him a chance to object; Loretta was out of her chair and flip-flopping her way across the piazza before old Roy knew what had happened.

"More damn postcards," he muttered and ordered a second drink. After vigorously readjusting and rubbing his balls, the guy leaned over to read my writing.

"What the hell does that say? Peppermint prick? But hey, you speak English!" Flashing a friendly smile, he stuck out his paw. "Name's Roy Robinson. Me and the wife are on one of those all-inclusive bargain tours. We were traveling with Loretta's sister and cousin, but the girls got sick as dogs and flew home. We leave on a bus for Florence tomorrow. We've already seen London, Paris, and Madrid."

I took a deep breath and closed my notebook. Staring at his package-scratching hand, I introduced myself as normal people are supposed to do. "Hi. Charlie Hughes. Sorry for not shaking your hand, but I have a bad cold."

He dropped his arm and scooted his chair back as if I had the plague. "Nice to meet you, Charlie. Where you from?

"I'm originally from New York."

"Dangerous city. Never been there. Are you here on vacation too?"

"Business."

"Yeah? Us Americans work until we drop dead. Hey, have you been inside that building? Is it hot and packed with people just like the rest of Rome?" he asked, pointing to the Pantheon.

I nodded. "It can get crowded, but it's nice and cool inside. You should check it out. The interior of the Pantheon is impressive and well worth a visit." And then my big fucking mouth betrayed me. "Your wife's book is wrong, though. Agrippa didn't build it."

"Huh? But his name's up there in huge letters: MAGRIPPA."

"Marcus Agrippa didn't build that structure. Another man at a much later time commissioned the Pantheon and put Agrippa's name up there as a kind of tribute to him."

"How do you know that? Are you one of those tour guides I see everywhere carrying around those little flags on a tall sticks?"

"Not exactly. I'm sure they make more money than I do."

"But you know all this boring history stuff, right? So, who built it?"

I crossed my arms and exhaled, figuring I might just as well regurgitate a big load of history vomit all over Mr. Itchy Sac. "The Pantheon was built by Publius Aelius Hadrianus, better known today as Hadrian, emperor of Rome from 117 to 138 AD. However, some people have suggested the building was started earlier by Trajan and his architect, Apollodorus."

"Huh? How the hell do you know that?"

"The bricks used to build the Pantheon date to the second century AD."

His eyes glazed over; Roy downed his second soda and tilted his head like a puppy. "See now—I've never heard of any of those fellas or any stories about bricks." He glanced at me suspiciously and scoffed. "Listen, if an official travel book that cost me twenty bucks says Magrippa built it, and his name is on it saying he built it, then he must have built it. Who cares about some stinking bricks? Maybe you should buy a guide book or find a new job, Charlie."

He stood up and dumped a pile of change onto his table. "Loretta! I want to see the Pope!" he shouted as he elbowed his way past the pedestrians and disappeared into the crowd gathered to enjoy the lamp-lit view of the towering ancient façade and the summer evening's mild air.

"Bye, Roy. Say hi to the Pope for me, buddy." I shook my head and opened my notebook, cursing under my breath. As I looked down at my scribbled recollections, Roy's remarks reminded me of the nagging reality that had kept me awake too many nights for the past three years.

Just like my unplanned, idiotic conversation with Roy, history was a series of chance circumstances and random accidents. Inscriptions in stone might survive, even the misleading ones like the Agrippa inscription on the Pantheon, but in truth our collective memory was as fragile as a butterfly's wings. For millennia, countless people have lived and died and been forgotten. Long ago, history's winners decided which people would have a lasting voice, which stories the future could and wouldn't remember.

And why the hell hadn't Hadrian put his name up on the Pantheon anyway? There were theories that he was too humble to take credit, but I doubted that. We'd probably never know his real reasons, just as old bearded Publius had probably intended.

Just as we'd probably never know who'd once owned that incredible ivory-handle dagger.

Despite every piece of evidence our team had uncovered during five seasons of digging out on the Tiburtina, we still had few solid clues as to what had happened at our Roman villa. We'd discovered two well-preserved skeletons and a unique ceremonial dagger, but we still hadn't formulated a convincing hypothesis. Only one thing was certain as far as I was concerned; that underground corridor where we'd found the bones was haunted.

~

15 JULY 2007

WHEN WE LEFT THE restaurant, I had the scrap of paper with that handsome guy's phone number carefully tucked into my front pants' pocket. It was well after 23:00 when we finally arrived at the excavation site; the usual bustling traffic that clogged the modern Via Tiburtina during the day had dwindled down to one or two cars and buses. After Stefano parked his battered red Fiat along the side of the road, he unlocked the high security gate and we turned on our flashlights before scrambling up the path that wound its way to the top of the weed-covered slope.

"Shit, it's dark. Not even a scrap of moonlight."

"New moon tonight, *caro*," Stefano explained.

"And here we are in the middle of the night breaking into ancient Roman ruins to crawl down a hole and visit two creepy skeletons.

Whose idea was this, anyway?"

"Charlie, I need to examine that pile of architectural debris."

"I hope you find whatever it is you're looking for because I'm not sneaking around in the dark like a criminal again. Wait, what was that sound?"

"Could be ghosts." Stefano chuckled, but quickened his pace. "There are thousands of ancient burials along these roads."

"Yeah, I know. Rome's suburbs are one big spooky graveyard."

Louder than the first, a second rustle shook the thorn bushes clustered along the sides of the dirt trail. I redirected my flashlight's beam to scan the vegetation when a strong gust whipped through the spindly branches of the olive trees behind us.

"I think it's just the wind," I suggested without conviction.

"Probably, but it could be *cinghiali*. Do you have a weapon?" Stefano asked while he picked up a large stick.

"What? A wild boar?" I patted all of my pockets, knowing damn well I didn't have a knife on me. I pulled out my bulky keychain. "The only weapon I've got is an old bottle opener from my trip to Acapulco."

"When did you go to Mexico?"

When the pricker bushes moved again, we took off and hightailed it up the low hill, glancing back to be sure some vicious pig with deadly tusks wasn't on our heels. At the top of the ridge, Stefano and I found the opening to our three-meter deep well hastily covered with planks of plywood. The winds were picking up, blowing the thin sheets of wood like sails as we took turns pulling them off. Letting out an irritated sigh, Stefano beamed his flashlight down into the well.

"At least the ministry left behind a sturdier ladder than our old wooden contraption."

Not appreciating my attempt to lighten the mood, my colleague grumbled, "Our contraption was handcrafted by a highly-skilled, octogenarian artisan. That piece of shit is made of cheap aluminum crap. Wouldn't last one field season, if that."

"Are you sure we should do this?"

"No." Stefano adjusted his scarf over his mouth and nose, and rested his foot on the third rung. "It won't take long, Charlie. I just need to examine that debris pile before the ministry changes the locks. Humor me. Here—put on this dust mask."

After Stefano reached the bottom, he held the ladder while I climbed down into the hole. We squeezed through the opening in the wall of our medieval well, and shimmied down the substantial slope of the debris pile, landing on the floor of the underground Roman passageway. The air clouded with dust; my partner immediately got to work inspecting the heap of stones mixed with other construction refuse. Like an idiot, I walked into the blackness of the corridor, the beam from my flashlight dancing across the Roman walls as my hand trembled.

"Shit!"

"What is it, Charlie?" Stefano asked without looking up.

"Argh! I walked right into a massive spider's web!" I screamed, flailing my arms around, trying to pull off an invisible sticky net of yuck.

"You'll survive. Just five more minutes here, ok?"

"Asshole," I mumbled as I approached the skeletons. Apparently untouched, they were lying side by side on the brick floor just as we'd left them, but the dagger was gone. "Our ghoulish friends are still here, but the ministry took our dagger, Stefano."

"I'm not surprised. It's the most spectacular and valuable artifact ever found at this site," he grunted before standing up. "I think I know why our well diggers couldn't see the skeletons."

"Why's that?" I asked, turning my flashlight towards him.

Stefano lifted up a thin, broken triangular brick. "This debris pile is made up of imperial period bricks—given the shape and quality, I'd date them to the second century. The side walls of this corridor are built from different materials; those walls date at least two hundred year earlier. Check the construction surface of that back wall for me, ok?"

I sidestepped the skeletons and focused the flashlight's beam on the far wall. "Yup, the brickwork here is second century too, just like your debris pile. So, let me get this straight. We have an underground corridor built much earlier during the Republican phase which was then substantially altered during the second century."

Still clutching the brick fragment, Stefano strolled over to stand beside me. "Our anonymous villa owner must have remodeled this long passageway, dividing it up into rooms. But there's no doors or other openings to allow access to this space as far as I can tell."

"Could they have turned a section of an old corridor into a storage space or cistern?"

Stefano tossed the broken brick; it landed on top of the debris heap with a ping. "*Si, che è possibile.* But there's no evidence for a piping system or waterproof concrete on these wall surfaces, so even if it was supposed to have served as a water storage tank, it wasn't finished."

"And two people died here."

"Or their bodies were carried here along with that priceless dagger." Stefano lit a cigarette and inhaled. "So, here's an idea: that debris pile was originally one of our Roman remodeler's wall additions built during the second century. Let's imagine that newer wall collapsed not in antiquity but sometime during or after the eighth century. There's regular seismic activity in this region, so an earthquake could have toppled it under the right conditions. That would explain why our well medieval diggers didn't see the skeletons—the second century wall was still standing when they accidently broke open that hole, blocking any access or views to the passageway behind it. They only saw the Roman wall, never knowing the corridor existed just on the other side."

"That also could explain why the medieval diggers patched the hole in the first place. They thought they could salvage their well."

"It's possible." He threw his cigarette down and ground it out with his boot before throwing his hands up and shrugging. "But it's only a guess, Charlie."

I jumped out of my skin and nearly pissed my pants when a loud noise resembling a growl echoed through the darkness.

"Jesus Christ, what the hell was that?"

"I don't know." His eyes wide, Stefano's normally confident voice cracked. "And I don't want to find out. Let's go."

Stefano was halfway up the metal ladder with me right behind when something cold and strong gripped my left shoulder and squeezed. It felt like a hand—a big fucking hand.

I squealed.

"Are you all right, Charlie?" Stefano's panicky voice boomed down from the surface.

The phantom or whatever it was released its grasp and whispered into my ear. As soon as I'd thought I understood the garbled words, I didn't. I couldn't speak or catch my breath, but thank fucking Jehovah my feet cooperated. Dashing up the ladder's rungs, I tumbled onto the ground above the hole, my glasses knocked askew.

"Did you hear that?" I asked, straightening my lopsided frames before removing my dust mask.

"No, I didn't hear anything after that bizarre animal noise. What was it?

"I'm not sure." I rose to my knees, and rubbed my bruised elbows. "Something spoke to me, I think. Something human."

"Maybe one of our skeletons came back to life." Shaking his head, Stefano chuckled as he extended his hand. "That's enough creepy thrills for one night, my friend. Get up and let's get out of here. It's late, and we have the information we came for. Let me buy you a nightcap."

"I'll need three. Shit, I need an entire bottle of booze."

He patted my back as we headed down the path. "We'll start with one and go from there, *si*?"

Scratching my ear, I turned back to look at the well disappearing in the distance behind us.

"Deal."

1

AD 107
Lucius Petronius's house, the Quirinal Hill, Rome

Gaius stood outside the entrance, his fists clenched and his feet planted wide. Perched on the tiled roof of Lucius's home, a lone crow flapped its wings and squawked as if mocking his battle-ready posture. After retrieving a stone lying on the curb, he looked up, poised to hurl his missile at the pesky bird when he saw them.

Two torches in iron brackets hung high on the wall on either side of the grand door.

Both were unlit. Extinguished. Never again would their flames signal Lucius was alone and waiting, his gorgeous body free to defile. No more sneaking in for those risky but satiating afternoon fucks. No more sucking and kissing and rimming in the baths. No more forbidden games in the garden.

"Put an end to this dishonorable dalliance with Petronius Celsus!"

The emperor's command during that palace dinner was direct and unequivocal. Gaius had acquiesced like a dutiful auxiliary soldier following a centurion's orders. He'd ended the long-standing affair with his occasional lover and dearest friend.

Shit, the Lion of the Lucky Fourth was little more than a spineless coward. A mouse. Before he died, had Luc forgiven him for abandoning their bittersweet, illicit passions?

Gaius Fabius Rufus would never know.

And now the massive oak door through which Gaius had passed many times loomed in front of him, taunting him with its indifferent permanence. Heavy pine garlands drooped low, obscuring the white marble doorframe, their branches threaded with wilted red roses and the black ribbons of death. As he raised his fist to knock, heartache sliced through his chest. Gaius slowly lowered his arm and massaged his aching brow.

Before making the dreaded climb to the top of the Quirinal hill, he'd ascended the steep and sacred Capitoline slope. At the altar in front of the Rome's greatest temple, he'd sworn an oath to almighty Jupiter. An oath of vengeance.

He would exact revenge, but now was not the time for war.

Now it was time to confront the awful, inescapable truth.

Time to say farewell.

"Commander? Are you all right, sir?"

"Announce our arrival, Maximus."

After he'd stepped back from the door, Gaius tossed the rock to the ground and gazed down the length of the curved, paved street. The painted plaster walls of the neighboring posh homes, with their colorful flowers cascading down from their high terraces, seemed less vibrant than they had in the past.

Lucius Petronius was dead, murdered in the prime of his life.

Who was to blame? Those nefarious spies from the palace, the envious bastards in the Senate? Of course, there was Luc's greedy widow, Aurelia, to add to the long list of suspects. And what if, gods forbid, his fellow ward—his little brother, his Greekling—was involved in this heinous crime?

Shit.

Gaius rubbed his whiskered chin and exhaled. "Varius, take two men to the back gate and make damn sure no one leaves this estate without my fucking permission."

"Yes, Commander."

After Max lifted and released the stout iron knocker three times, the door slowly opened, creaking on its metal hinges. A guard with a familiar face nodded and welcomed them into the vestibule.

"Greetings, Commander Fabius. We've been anticipating your arrival, sir."

Gaius patted the man on the shoulder before turning to address Maximus and his two guards. "Stay here—all of you."

Having left everyone behind in the entrance hall, he walked alone down the dimly lit corridor to the atrium. In that formal gathering hall, he would find Luc's corpse washed and dressed in a formal crimson-striped toga and laid upon an elevated funerary couch with his feet pointed toward the street. A golden crown of laurel would encircle Luc's dark hair, the coin to pay the ferryman of Hades already tucked in his mouth. Tall candelabra would stand at the corners of the couch, the air thick with the pungent smoke of fragrant herbs. Luc's once handsome face would be ghostly pale, his bright grey-blue eyes closed for eternity.

Lucius was dead.

Gaius paused to sniff the air. Where was the smell of burning herbs? Where was that unmistakable stench no amount of incense could mask?

He quickened his pace until he was jogging over the threshold to the stately atrium.

The hall was empty. No couch, no candelabra, no corpse.

"What is the meaning of this?" Every word was a struggle as if the wind had been knocked out of him. "Where—where is Lucius?"

"I'm afraid you're too late, Commander."

Draped in dark mourning robes, she stood off to the side with her arms crossed and her right hip cocked, a satisfied sneer twisting her severe features.

"What did you…?" His voice cracked. "Where is Lucius, Aurelia?"

"We burned his corpse in Mars' field yesterday. The omens were favorable and the kindling lit well. The gods seemed quite pleased."

Biting down hard on his lower lip, nearly drawing blood, Gaius collapsed against one of the massive columns bordering the shallow pool in the center of the room. "He's gone?"

"Lucius has crossed the River Styx, and you failed to arrive in time to bid a proper farewell to your dearest friend."

Heartless bitch.

"We traveled from Campania as quickly as possible, but several roads were washed out and impassable. I hadn't anticipated you'd have the audacity to complete his rites before I returned to Rome."

"I postponed the funeral for as long as possible, Commander Fabius. My poor, dead husband's body laid here in the atrium for nine long days. The summer's heat and dampness took their toll. You should know I consulted with Empress Plotina on the matter of his funeral. The palace granted me permission." With a grimace, Aurelia inhaled through her pointy nose. "I've had the slaves ventilate this room all morning, but the fetor of decay still lingers, doesn't it?"

Gaius dug his fingernails into the fabric of his tunic until they gouged his thighs. How easy would it be to wrap his hands around her bony neck and snap it like a twig?

Twirling the fringed edge of her robe, Aurelia sauntered across the atrium. "The funeral procession through the Forum was magnificent. Members of the Senate bore the gilded bier on their shoulders and our consul, Minicius, delivered a laudatory eulogy at the Rostra. I hired the most renowned undertaker in Rome to arrange the details:

twenty-four professional mourners and a crew of talented trumpeters. We sacrificed a bull *and* a sheep in addition to the pig. I spared no expense, and the populace enjoyed a generous feast. The entire city will remember my devotion to my dear deceased husband for many summers to come."

The smugness on her face morphed to fear when Gaius took two steps toward her. "If you had anything to do with this…" After circling her, Gaius stopped and glared, his lips inches from Aurelia's terrified, rodent-like eyes. "If you were involved in Luc's murder, Aurelia, I will not stop until I see your callous corpse crisp on a pyre of rotted wood."

"I had no part whatsoever in Lucius's death! I loved my husband. Why would you believe otherwise?"

"What I believe isn't fucking relevant. Not legally. Tell me, have you also had the gall to unseal his will?"

"Commander, I'm fully aware the disclosure of my late husband's final testament requires all six witnesses to be present. Lucius's brother boarded a ship at Piraeus. Titus Petronius is sailing to the capital from Greece and, assuming the winds are favorable, he should arrive soon. My late husband's youngest brother, Gallus, attended the funeral and was most benevolent to me." Aurelia swallowed hard and continued. "And *you* are the executor of Lucius's testament. The magistrates would never unseal his will without your consent."

Gaius smiled although his eyes remained cold and hard. He stepped back and held out his hand. "Give me his ring. It's mine to safeguard until his final testament is read before the witnesses and the people of Rome. Perhaps, if the gods have any blasted sense, he will have left you nothing save the rags on your back."

"My husband was noble and generous. He would never…" Aurelia coughed softly into her fist before stammering, "Did—did Lucius

15

reveal his bequests to you?"

He gritted his teeth at her stall tactic. "Surrender Luc's fucking ring. Now!"

Aurelia scurried over to the bronze chest in the far corner of the atrium and retrieved the sacred token of Lucius's identity and judicial rank—his unique gold signet ring decorated with an oak leaf.

"I pray this thing curses you as it did him." She pressed the ring into Gaius's open palm. As Gaius closed his fingers around the gold band, a boisterous commotion erupted from one of the corridors off the atrium. From the shadows, Varius hauled a man into the center of the hall. The fellow thrashed, pulling out of the veteran's grasp.

Gaius slipped Luc's large ring onto his middle finger. "Well, what do we have here?"

"We found this gentleman hiding by the back portal, Commander. It appears he was trying to leave the premises undetected."

"Sneaking about like a sewer rat?" Gaius grabbed the man's clean-shaven chin to get a better look at his pockmarked face. "Ah, it is you, Victorinus. I thought I recognized you. Why, for shit's sake, has a member of the emperor's guard sequestered his sorry arse by the back exit of Lucius Petronius's home?"

"I..."

"Yes?"

"I'm—I'm on assignment. I was told to guard the grieving widow, Commander Fabius."

"Dressed in commoner's clothing?"

"I was ordered to be, well, furtive. Sir."

Gaius narrowed his eyes as he pointed at Aurelia. "You were instructed to leave the palace to protect this pitiless wretch?"

"Yes, sir."

Gaius scratched the dense, itchy golden-red bristles now blanketing his jaw and neck. As was customary, he hadn't had a shave since he'd first learned of Luc's murder. Fucking stubble was driving him mad. Even when he was on campaign, Gaius always preferred to keep his face clean-shaven, but he'd relented and allowed his aggravating beard to grow. Bloody tradition and all that.

"I'm not sure I believe our friend's far-fetched tale, my dear Varius. What do you think?"

"I've never known a praetorian to be charged with protecting a citizen, Commander. Discreetly or otherwise."

"Neither have I." Gaius crossed his arms and sneered. "May I assume our esteemed Emperor Trajan will corroborate your incredible claim, guard?"

"The Praetorian Prefect gave the order, not the emperor." Victorinus glanced at Aurelia and cleared his throat. "Sir."

"How lovely. I must remember to thank our most thoughtful Livianus when I next see him at the palace. Varius, escort our furtive guest to the front door for a proper departure. I wish you good health, Victorinus."

The guard nodded sheepishly. "Farewell, Commander Fabius."

While Varius shoved the smaller man towards the exit, Gaius shook his head. These recent praetorian recruits were fucking imbecilic, the whole lot of them. And the Prefect of the imperial bodyguard, Livianus, was a despicable, sycophantic boar. He'd never understood why Marcus had promoted the goon to such a prominent position.

"Commander?"

"Yes, Maximus?"

"Sir, my apologies for the interruption, but..." Max whispered into Gaius's left ear, "Bryaxis, sir. I can't find him anywhere."

"That's most curious," Gaius mumbled before thundering over to

Aurelia and grabbing her by the folds of her dress. "Where is Lucius's Caledonian?"

"What?" She squeaked.

"Luc's concubine, Bryaxis. What have you done with his pleasure slave?"

"When that insolent slut dared speak its mind at my poor husband's deathbed, I had it beaten and locked in the library. That was quite a while past. It may be dead." She raised her eyebrows and shrugged. "I might have forgotten to feed it."

"That slut is under my guardianship now. You'd better pray he's not dead."

"Your guardianship?"

"Lucius and I signed documents, Aurelia—legal and binding. I'm now the guardian of his personal slaves until his will is read, and I had better find them all alive."

Turning to deliver instructions to his veterans, Gaius noticed Max staring at the floor, his strong arms hanging limply at his sides. Max and Bry had been close once.

Not lovers, though they knew every inch of each other's bodies.

They'd been more akin to brothers.

Friends brought together by the Fates.

"Maximus?"

Max looked up, and tears spilled over his cheekbones.

"Collect yourself and follow me to the library."

Max wiped his face. "Yes, sir."

Together they walked down the passageway, Max lingering two steps behind his patron.

"Maximus, I will see Bryaxis receives a proper burial."

After a moment of silence, Max answered, "When he was a child in the northern wilds of Caledonia, Bry survived far worse than a flogging and a few days without food, sir."

Gaius stopped and turned around, reaching up to brush the back of his hand along Max's jaw. "You two shared much over the years. I will take care of Luc's slave, no matter what his condition."

"Bryaxis is alive, sir. He's strong."

Gaius flashed a weak smile. Max's loyalty to those he loved never wavered, did it?

"I do hope you're correct, but don't mistake my intentions. I will do what I must, whether he's alive or dead, but not because of any affection for Bryaxis. I've never cared for that disrespectful, spoiled whore. But I will fulfill my duties because Lucius and I swore an oath many years ago to protect each other's families. The documents were designed to give each of us the necessary legal authority during those days before our respective testaments were unsealed. I will protect Bryaxis because it is my duty to my dead friend."

Gaius gnawed on the inside of his cheek and looked away.

"I confess I'd been the one who'd suggested the contract to Lucius since the odds were I'd perish on the battlefield long before he died. I needed to be sure my family—you and the boys and Zoe—that you would all be protected after my death. Lucius agreed, and we signed the papers."

Gaius took a deep breath to try to ease the ache in his chest. All this would have been much simpler if only he had perished first. "Come, Max. Let's find Bryaxis."

The library was located off a grand corridor on the western side of the estate. It was a large square room with enormous windows and cupboards stuffed with correspondence, accounts, and legal records. The library had been Luc's pride and joy, his oasis from the political tempests of the courts. And it was the perfect private place for a quick fuck over a table. Gaius knew every piece of furniture in that damn room.

When they arrived, they found the door handles secured by a thick chain and a sturdy iron lock. The entrance resembled that of a prison rather than a sanctuary for study or secret afternoon trysts.

Gaius gripped the chain with both hands and rattled the doors. "Bryaxis! Answer me, slave!"

No sound except his own pulse thumping in his ears and Max's labored breathing.

"There's no time to persuade our uncooperative bitch to hand over the key, assuming Aurelia even knows where the fuck it is. Find something to remove this chain, Maximus."

After Max had run off in the direction of the gardens, Gaius leaned on the door, his forehead pressed against his forearm. He slapped the wood panel with his palm and yelled, "Bryaxis!"

The muffled rumble of thunder shook the walls. Another violent summer storm was swooping down on the city.

"Bryaxis, fucking answer me!"

Soft, high-pitched cries drifted through the dark corridor to Gaius's right. A flash of lightning momentarily brightened the hallway, quickly followed a louder thunderous boom.

"Commander Fabius?" Euphronia trembled as she rocked back and forth, tears streaking her full face, her bright hair a mess, and her arms wrapped tightly beneath her sagging breasts. By the gods, the woman looked as though she might faint. "I knew—I knew you'd save us, sir. I prayed to the goddess every morning and night."

Gaius rushed over and embraced her; he buried his face in her disheveled curls and inhaled the savory scents of the kitchen.

"Euphronia, are you hurt?"

"I—I am alive." She nodded towards the library door. "That evil woman locked Bryaxis in there after Dominus died. I managed to smuggle in some water for him on the second day. She discovered my disobedience and had me caned."

"She did what?"

Euphronia paused to catch her breath. "I heard—we all heard a terrible scream yesterday before the funeral. Oh, Great Mother! Oh, Cybele! What has that woman done to Bryaxis? He's never hurt her. My poor boy would never injure anyone." She beat her pudgy hands against Gaius's chest in desperation.

"Hush, Euphronia." He grabbed her wrists, gently but firmly. "Maximus will be back any moment with something to break the chain. Be strong for me—for Lucius. Are you listening to me?"

Euphronia took a deep, cleansing breath as she pushed two damp strands of hair off of her face and stood a bit straighter. "Yes, Commander."

"You're under my protection now. Lucius and I made arrangements long ago. As soon as we get Bryaxis out of there, we're leaving."

"Dominus showed me the contract, sir. But..." Euphronia wiped her eyes. "How can I leave? I've lived here nearly all my life. This house is my home, where I watched our three young mischievous masters grow into honorable, fine men. So many memories..."

"Look at me." He gently lifted her face. "Lucius Petronius is gone. There's no master here to protect you. Your home—and Bryaxis' home—is with my family until Lucius's testament is unsealed."

Euphronia sucked in her plump, tear-drenched lips before nodding. "Yes, sir—but what about the child? What will happen to Dominus's daughter?"

Gaius blinked and swallowed.

"I don't know. As soon as Titus Petronius arrives from Greece, Lucius's testament will be read in the Julian basilica before the inheritance magistrates. The custody of Petronia and the ownership of this estate will be known then."

Their moment of solemn silence was broken by Max's holler.

"Commander!" Max charged down the corridor, huffing and puffing, a gardener's hatchet in his hand.

"Break the chain, Maximus."

After two blows, the chain crashed to the floor.

"Euphronia, fetch some broth from the kitchen."

"Sir?"

"Now, woman!"

After she'd hastened off, Max asked, "Do you believe he's alive, sir?"

"From what she just told me, Bryaxis was alive yesterday. He may no longer be, and if that's the case I don't want her to see whatever we find in there. Remain here and make sure Euphronia doesn't enter until I give the word. Understood?"

"Yes, Commander."

Gaius pushed the door open and stepped inside the library. It was pitch black, and like a field following a battle the air reeked of urine and blood.

"Bryaxis? Where are you?"

Feeling his way from a table to the cupboard to another table, Gaius padded toward the windows when his left foot bumped against a lump on the floor.

"Shit."

He carefully stepped over whatever it was and opened the shutters wide. Menacing, grey-green clouds filled the sky, but the impending downpour hadn't yet begun to fall. Faint light crept into the library, enough for Gaius to see Bryaxis curled up in a ball, naked and unconscious. A puddle of dark blood stained the floor near the slave's bent legs.

"Bryaxis," he whispered and crouched down when another flash of lightning lit the space. The slave was breathing—shallow and faint, but he was alive. Gaius gently rolled him over onto his back. A bloody mess of bandages covered Bry's groin.

Gaius lowered his head and looked away. "Fucking unholy Furies."

Another crash of thunder followed by another blue flash of lightning.

"Commander?" Max's normally strong voice was barely audible.

"I told you to stand by the door, Maximus."

Gaius pushed the fringe away from Bry's face and brushed his hand across the lad's whiskered cheek. "Bryaxis is alive, but…" Gaius nodded towards the bloodied cloth dressing. "He's been castrated."

Max stumbled backward. "What?"

"He's lost quite a bit of blood. Dispatch one of my veterans to the home of my physician. Instruct him to transport Archigenes here immediately. Tell him to carry the old Greek coot on his damn back if need be. Then retrieve a clean cloak or blanket or whatever the fuck you can find and bring it to me quickly."

"He's…" Max choked on a sob. "Bry's been castrated?"

"By Hercules, Max. Move! And whatever you do, do not allow Euphronia to enter this room."

Gingerly, Gaius carried Bry over to the nearest couch and set him down. His long body was lighter than Gaius had expected.

Starved and dehydrated, no doubt.

Unprotected.

He'd been too late—too late to honor Lucius, too late to protect Luc's boy from harm.

He'd failed his best friend, again.

Gaius sat down on the edge of the couch and stroked Bry's unwashed hair as the heavy storm clouds rolled through the afternoon sky. From this high vantage point up on the Quirinal, the silhouette of Jupiter's enormous temple was visible in the distance, dominating the tempestuous horizon.

"I promise you, Luc—they will pay. All of them. As Jove on the Capitoline is my witness."

～

SLOUCHED FORWARD, HIS ELBOWS resting on his thighs, Gaius sat on a bench in the same garden where, not long ago, he and Luc had dined and laughed and fucked. Flooding the gravel-covered ground, heavy sheets of rain soaked his shoulders and back. He looked down at the puddles lapping at his feet. In a few more moments, the rising water would cover his worn riding boots.

Gaius buried his face in his hands and cursed the gods. He cursed his dead, disgraced father, Quintus.

Cursed himself for his failures.

The doctor, Archigenes, had already come and gone. The old man, whose spot-covered hands trembled from age, had inspected the Caledonian's wounds and applied clean bandages. The physician had concluded a professional must have been hired for the gelding. Not the cleanest of cuts, but expert enough to not kill the slave.

Bryaxis would recover, at least physically.

Once this damn storm passed, they would leave this fucking tomb of a house. A cart had been prepared to transport Bryaxis to Gaius's home; he was too injured to hike up the Caelian Hill to Gaius's estate. Luc's gelded slave would share the ride with his former master's legal documents. As instructed, Gaius's veterans had packed all the papers from Luc's library and office into wooden crates. That irreplaceable slew of letters, books, and ledgers might hold clues to solving his murder. And Gaius wanted them, so he bloody well took them.

Fuck Aurelia.

Euphronia had also gathered some items, including her favorite cooking pots and spices. They weren't her property, of course, but he'd told her to take anything she wanted to bring to his home.

All of them—Bryaxis, Euphronia, her kitchen girl, and a few more of the long-time household servants of the Petronii family—all of them were now his responsibility until Luc's testament was unsealed and its contents read.

It was a burden, but one he would bear for Lucius.

He'd sworn an oath.

"You're still here?" she shouted over the downpour from underneath the shelter of the portico encircling the garden. "I'd thought you'd left long ago."

Gaius scowled at her as raindrops dripped from his lashes.

"You fucking mutilated Bryaxis!"

"Nonsense. Given many men's carnal preferences these days, that whore is worth more gelded than intact. Don't you dare accuse me of devaluing anyone's property, Commander. The magistrates would laugh you out of the basilica."

Damn it, she was right. Coldhearted to be sure but, unfortunately, she was correct. In the eyes of the courts, castration would be judged as a valuable modification for a pleasure slave. For shit's sake, pretty slave boys were losing their testicles left and right these days. Even Publius had voiced his disgust over this popular trend, but no one— not even the emperor—had done a damn thing to curb Rome's growing lust for eunuchs.

"Lucius would be furious you gelded his boy!" he shouted over the noisy downpour.

She laughed. "My beloved but rather possessive husband had ordered his slave's castration. He'd left detailed instructions, of course. You know how lawyers are—or were."

"You're a fucking liar."

"I can show you the letter if you like. Aren't you the slightest bit curious what I did with—?" Aurelia smirked as she curled her right hand to form a cup in front of her crotch. "Them?"

"No."

"Just as my husband stipulated, I had the slut's balls placed in a sack and then I threw them up onto the pyre. Its filthy plums crackled as the flames consumed them. Now my dear Lucius can squeeze his concubine's testicles for eternity, and you might have a eunuch to sell for profit if my late husband bequeathed his slave whore to you in his will. It's an old eunuch, but it should still fetch good coin at auction. So you see, Commander Fabius, everybody wins."

She wiped her hands on her dress. "I believe it's time for dinner. Would you care to stay and join me? I'll have a servant fetch you some dry clothes."

Gaius pushed the saturated clumps of hair away from his eyes. He could barely see her through the wall of rain.

"I will destroy you."

"What? Speak up! I can't hear you."

He rose and marched over to the covered passageway, every muscle in his body taut with fury. He wrapped his left hand around her throat and pressed his thumb pad into the hollow below her larynx; her clammy skin shivered under his threat.

"If I discover you've conspired to murder your husband, I will destroy you, Aurelia. I will cut off your vicious head and shit down your neck. And if I learn that adulterous louse of a Praetorian Prefect assisted you, I'll eliminate Livianus as well. There will be justice for Lucius."

"I was not involved," she croaked.

Gaius released her throat; his scowl slowly morphed into a maniacal grin. "Please forgive my boorish manners, Aurelia. Before we depart for the Caelian, I'll instruct Euphronia to prepare a heaping plate of her best fare for you. I know where Lucius stored his arsenic. Would you care for a farewell meal, you heartless gorgon?"

Massaging the red mark on her neck, she spat back, "Lucius never loved you."

"Varius, hurry up and get those damn wagons ready!" He shouted before storming off, his sodden travel clothes dripping all over the black and white mosaic floor.

⟶⟫⟫⟫✦⟪⟪⟪⟵

2

S EVERAL SMALL BLUE FLOWERS on a large rosemary bush had miraculously survived the violent summer storm. She reached out and gently brushed one with her fingertip as though she were afraid it might disintegrate. Max crossed his arms behind his back and cleared his throat before announcing his presence.

"Greetings, Domina."

"Maximus!" She spun around, her long golden earrings dangling back and forth. "You've made it to the Caelian, at last."

Her voice sounded tired, but Domina's smile was as bright and genuine as ever. Unlike Bryaxis, Max had never had any reason to fear his master's wife. Truth be told, he adored this petite, attractive brunette woman from that very first day she joined the family. She had a spine of steel, tempered by an understated dignified nature. Fortuna had smiled on him—on the entire household—that day seven years past when Commander Fabius wed Marcia Servilia.

"Where is my husband, Max?" Marcia stood on her toes in an attempt to see the entrance to the garden over his broad shoulder.

"The commander is in the vestibule delivering instructions to his veterans, Domina."

"I imagine he's been planning revenge from the moment Apollodorus delivered the awful news." When she took one of Max's hands

28

between hers and sighed, Max raised an eyebrow and nodded. His patron's wrath had been palpable for the entire laborious trip up the Via Appia. For much of the journey, Commander Fabius had ridden alone some distance ahead of the architect's posh travel wagon. Whenever Max happened to be within earshot of the general mutterings, he'd heard anger-filled promises to Lucius Petronius, oaths to find and kill his murderers.

The peaceful gurgling of the fountain in the center of the plantings in the herb garden was muffled when the commander barreled in, growling a string of curses. His wet clothes clung like a second skin to the solid curves of his muscular body. After he stripped off his cloak and threw it over an evergreen bush, an elderly steward tiptoed over with a folded bundle of dry garments. Commander Fabius snatched them, approached his wife, and lifted her hand to kiss it. "Greetings, Domina."

Her forced smile couldn't disguise her grief. "Gaius, I'm…"

He pressed his forefinger against her lips and turned his attention to Max. "Maximus, see that Lucius Petronius's servants have adequate accommodations. And tend to Bryaxis. He should wake soon."

~

AFTER MAX BOWED AND left, Gaius peeled off the rest of his sodden clothes. Naked, he carelessly dropped them to the ground before pulling a freshly laundered tunic over his head.

"I was too late, Marcia," he lamented as he adjusted the ivory folds.

"I do wish you'd stopped here before traveling up to the Quirinal. I would have warned you. Please know I did try to convince Aurelia to delay the funeral until your arrival, but Plotina…"

"Yes, Aurelia told me all about our dear Plotina." He gave Marcia a peck on the cheek and sat down on the nearest bench. "That fucking bitch made sure to inform me she'd received permission from the Empress."

"I visited their home and paid our respects, Gaius. And I must admit the funeral was indeed magnificent—a most worthy celebration of Lucius's status and achievements. He has..." She paused. "Lucius had many friends."

"And at least one deadly enemy," Gaius muttered in a raspy voice as he leaned back against the painted wall surrounding the garden. "Were you aware Aurelia had his beloved whore castrated?"

"Immortal gods!"

"She claimed Lucius had ordered his slave's testicles sacrificed as offerings at his pyre." He added with disgust, combing his fingers through his messy damp curls before scratching his scalp.

"Is *that* what she threw into the flames?" Marcia covered her mouth with a loose fold of her light flaxen dress before asking, "Lucius would never have wanted such a barbaric thing, would he? I realize he was often selfish when it came to that boy, but..."

"She's a lying cur, Marcia. Aurelia claimed she had a letter from Luc instructing her to do so. If the damn thing exists, it's a fucking forgery. For all his faults, Lucius Petronius was a decent man. He'd never have ordered a castration. And, if my suspicions are correct, she's fornicating with Livianus, the Praetorian Prefect."

"Adulterous cow. Do you suspect Livianus was involved somehow?"

"He's near the top of a very long list of suspects, Marcia." He patted the bench cushion.

She sat down next to him and squeezed his knee. "Gaius, I am so terribly sorry. I know how close you and Lucius were all these years."

Gaius closed his eyes. "If it takes the rest of my life, I will find the bastards who murdered him."

They were both quiet, lost in thought until Marcia sighed. "When you do find them, the magistrates will show no leniency."

"I don't plan on affording those lawyers the luxury of a delivering their self-serving speeches during some farce of a trial, dear wife." Gaius turned to look at her. "By Jupiter's staff, I swear I will kill Luc's murderers myself with my damn sword. Slowly, painfully, and most certainly without any bloody mercy."

"Gaius, that's vengeance, not justice."

He grabbed her chin; his fingertips pressed into the flesh beneath her cheekbones. "Don't quibble with me over petty semantics. Luc's murderers will die. Do you understand me?"

"Yes, Dominus." Her calm tone failed to hide her resentment. "I understand quite clearly."

He released his grip and gently caressed the skin he'd abused. "A loyal and discreet wife is a precious gift."

"Then you are a most fortunate man, Gaius Fabius," Marcia hurled back. She stood up and tossed the loose folds of her mantle over her shoulder. "You stink. The steward has prepared your baths. Wash off the filth of your travels and perhaps your precious wife might join you for dinner, dear."

~

MAX PICKED UP THE strip of cloth soaking in the cool water, wrung it out over the wooden bowl, and pressed the damp rag against Bry's forehead. The ferocious thunderstorm that had drenched the city earlier provided little more than a brief interlude from the heat. The sweltering humidity had returned, hanging heavy in the air of the spare room in the slaves' quarters.

"There, that's soothing, isn't it?"

Bryaxis lay on the bed, silent and unresponsive. Max was growing nervous; Bry needed to come round soon. The old Greek doctor had warned them not to let him sleep for too long.

"Bry, wake up. C'mon, love."

Max shook Bry by his shoulders until his eyelids fluttered. He moaned; gods, he sounded weak.

"Wake up, old friend."

Bryaxis cracked open his lids and tried to prop himself up on his elbows. Squinting, he scanned the room. "Where am I?"

"At Commander Fabius's estate on the Caelian."

"The Caelian? Why?"

"You've been—" Max wasn't sure what word to use. "Hurt. A doctor inspected the wound to be sure it hadn't become foul. He changed the bandages. You'll be fine."

"Oh gods, I wasn't dreaming? It wasn't a nightmare?" Shaking, Bry ran his hand down his abdomen until he touched the soft wad of cloth. Suddenly, he rolled onto his side and wretched over the edge of the mattress. Max held the rag underneath Bry's mouth; strings of saliva dripped down his chin.

With a groan, Bryaxis collapsed back on the bed, covering his eyes with his hands, and cried, "They cut off my balls!"

"Bry, I…" Max stumbled over his words. "Listen, you're lucky to be alive."

Bry grabbed hold of Max's thick forearm for support as he tried to sit up again. "Please, Max."

"What do you need? There's fresh water in this jar. Here, let me…"

"I don't want any fucking water!"

Max kneaded his face in frustration and asked, "Then what can I do? Tell me."

"You can kill me. Or just give me a knife. Please. I can't... I don't want to be here. Not like this. Not without Lucius."

"I can't do that. I'm sorry."

Bryaxis lay back down and turned his head to the side; a stream of tears flowed down the side of his perfectly straight nose while more tears stained the tan pillow.

"Leave," Bry whispered.

"You need water. And you haven't eaten in days. I'll have Euphronia prepare you some food."

Bry glanced up through the tears. "She's here?"

"Yes, they're all here: Euphronia, Daphne, and many of the other servants of Counselor Petronius's family—your family. Everyone's alive and under Commander Fabius's protection."

"Fabius owns me now?"

"The Commander is guarding you until Counselor Petronius's testament is read in the courts."

Bry nodded and winced. "Is Domina here as well?"

"Gods, no. The commander despises her. He's furious she performed the funeral rites for your Dom before he'd returned to Rome."

Bryaxis bit the inside of his cheek. "Domina said Lucius had instructed her to geld me as part of his funeral celebrations. She fucking laughed while those brutes held me down." He licked his chapped lips and lowered his voice. "I don't understand, Max. Lucius said he loved me. Why did he order me castrated?"

"I don't know. But it's over, and you're safe here. Do you need more elixir for the pain?"

"No."

Bryaxis closed his eyes.

"I can't feel a thing. I'm numb. If you won't help me die, fucking leave me alone."

Max extended his hand. "I won't abandon you. I'm getting you some food, and you will eat it. Sit up. That's an order."

Through his tears, Bryaxis snorted in disbelief. "An order?"

"I'm a freedman, Bry—I outrank you. Now sit up."

～

SIDE BY SIDE, THEY turned the corner and ambled down the next length of the covered portico. The marble columns flanking the walkway were bathed in the rosy golden light that often washed over the city shortly before dusk in the summertime. The glow of the waning sunset reflected off the stone, transforming the stubborn puddles of rainwater into pools of glimmering amber.

Marcia slipped her arm through the crook of Gaius's elbow. "That meal was divine."

"Euphronia is the best cook in Rome. Be mindful not to boast about her skills when you visit the palace. If Plotina learns of her talents in the kitchen, our empress might compel us to sell Euphronia to her. Understood?"

Marcia squeezed his arm and chuckled. "I won't say a word. And speaking of slaves that should not be discussed at dinner parties, your blonde breeder is faring well."

Shit.

He'd completely forgotten about Zoe. When they'd arrived at the southern edge of the city, he'd sent Zoe and Callidora straight off to the Caelian in Apollodorus' wagon accompanied by two guards.

"It was an arduous trip from Puteoli. Are you sure she's in good health?"

Marcia squeezed his bicep harder, digging her nails into his skin. Despite her placid, stoic demeanor, she resented the impending arrival of his slave bastard. "Zoe is fine. She was exhausted from the journey, but she's well. I assigned her and Callidora adjoining rooms in the girls' quarters. Melissa is keeping a watchful eye on her. If something worrisome occurs, my pet will inform me immediately."

Gaius smiled half-heartedly but looked straight ahead.

"Then you agree with the plan I'd detailed in my letter?"

"Scheme is the more appropriate term, don't you think? Yes, I agree. Only the gods know how tricky this might be, but it will be worth the risk if Zoe gives birth to a boy. We'll need to convince the court—or should I say, Empress Plotina—that the child is mine. If we're successful, the emperor will certainly name you his successor to the throne." She pulled him to a stop and asked, "Gaius, the baby is your child, correct?"

Unblinking, Gaius stared into her suspicious hazel eyes. "Yes, the child is mine," he replied. "Has my physician examined Zoe yet? He owes me a barrel of favors for the generous stipend I've granted him for years."

"Archigenes is scheduled to visit after Lucius's will is read in the basilica. Given that Zoe is well, I thought it best to focus our energies on one task at a time. Can we trust your Greek doctor with our gambit?"

"If he dares open his mouth, I'll cut his tongue out right before I slit his fucking throat. He may be half senile and decrepit, but Archigenes is no fool."

"Gaius, if members or staff of the court were complicit in Lucius's murder, this could be dangerously complicated."

"I'm well aware of the perils. While I'm ferreting out the murderous snakes slithering about the palace, what will you be doing, besides feigning pregnancy?"

"I think it's best if I handle our dear adulteress, Aurelia," she replied, a sparkle of mischief twinkling in her eyes. "Do I have your permission, Dominus?"

Gaius kissed Marcia lightly behind her ear and murmured, "Eviscerate her."

~

JUST BEFORE DAWN BROKE, Max picked up a small lamp and made his way through the hallways to Commander Fabius's suite. The bronze panels of the enormous door to his bedroom were decorated with sculpted scenes from Virgil's epic masterpiece. Even from a distance, he recognized two episodes from the famous poem: Queen Dido's suicide and the hero Aeneas' defeat of his rival, Turnus. When Max had been a young cock warmer, his auburn-haired master had recounted the poet's stories of ill-fated lovers, wars, and the whims of fortune. With a glimmer in his eyes, the general had described exciting tales of deceit and vengeance and suffering inflicted by heartless gods. "And so was the violent birth of our great empire," Commander Fabius was prone to jest sarcastically at the conclusion of each story.

Sweet recollections of much simpler days.

Max wiped the grin off his face before approaching the entrance. Two stout guards wearing helmets and armed with short swords stood at attention in the vestibule on either side of the stately portal. They nodded silently and allowed him to pass without question; everyone who lived or worked at the Caelian estate understood Max's unique and privileged status.

Expecting his patron to be awake as was his habit, Max knocked on the door. He winced when the light rap of his knuckles echoed much louder than he'd anticipated.

"Enter."

The commander lay stretched out on the plush mattress of his enormous bed; folds of ivory-colored bed linens were bunched casually over his lap and legs. With an unrolled scroll in his right hand, he stroked the large spotted cat sitting by his side. Lucius Petronius's gold signet ring on his middle finger flashed in the flickering light of the lamps.

"Look, Pyramus. We have an unexpected guest, my dear puss."

The African feline blinked lazily, extending its front legs before meowing its bizarre exotic cry.

"Greetings, Commander."

"Greetings, Maximus. It's rather early for a visit."

Max drank in the vision of his near naked former master lying on the bed in front of him. Feeling overdressed, he fidgeted with the hem of his short cloak. "It is early, sir. My apologies, but I wanted to ensure you have everything you require before the day's activities begin."

Gaius's dimpled grin brightened the low-lit room. "Tending to my morning desires is no longer your duty, although I do appreciate the sentiment. Look here—I have a good book to read and a content companion purring by my side. What more could a man possibly need?"

When the commander tossed the scroll onto his bedside table, Pyramus jumped down and crept under the bed. Gaius pulled back the covers to reveal long, wavy locks of brunette hair spread like a feathery fan over his bare stomach. He gently tapped her bare shoulder. "Wake up, nymph."

The slave girl groaned softly before lifting her head to look up at his face. "Greetings, Dominus."

She had a flirtatious accent. Arabian, Max guessed.

Gaius carded his fingers through her thick mane. "You, my dove, were a most pleasant diversion, definitely worth a second taste. I'll enjoy you again before I depart Rome, but for now you may return to your quarters."

She smiled and slid off the bed, her olive skin glowing like polished bronze. When she spotted Max standing near the foot of the bed, the curvaceous young whore picked her dress up off the floor and hastily covered her naked body.

"This is my client, Maximus." Gaius informed her before he sat up and leaned back against the wall, crossing his arms behind his head. "He and I have matters to discuss. Leave."

She nodded nervously and struggled to dress as she padded out of the suite. Gaius tilted his chin and sighed in contentment.

"A new sprite Marcia recently purchased. She's enthusiastic and exceptionally limber. My wife does have excellent taste."

Max glanced over his shoulder to watch the girl glide out through the door. "She's graceful. What's her name, sir?"

Gaius paused and then confessed with a smirk. "I haven't a fucking clue. Tell me, how is Bryaxis?"

"He's—well, he's…"

"Alive," Gaius stated flatly. "And damn fortunate to be so. He'll adjust, Max. Give him time."

"Yes, sir." Max placed the small ceramic lamp on a table. "Bryaxis has requested an audience with you, Commander."

"I'll speak with him after my morning salutations," Gaius replied and yawned.

"Yes, Commander."

As Max turned to leave, Gaius blurted out, "Despite a good, satisfying fuck, I barely slept at all."

"Has your insomnia returned, sir?"

Gaius covered his crotch with the folds of the blankets. "That bloody curse rarely gives me peace. But this was different. His anger haunted me throughout the night."

"Sir?"

"I felt nothing when he died, Max. Nothing. But here in Rome I can feel the heat of Lucius's wrath boiling over."

"You and Counselor Petronius were close friends for many years, sir."

"Yes, we were. And now he's dead and his spirit is furious." Gaius rubbed his face and sighed. "Max, pour us some wine. There's a smooth Spanish nectar in that jug on the table."

"May I ask a question, Commander?"

Gaius laughed. "There's no need to ask for permission, Max. You're not a slave. When we're alone, you may speak freely."

"Thank you, sir. Could you appease his spirit with sacrifices at his tomb?" Max carried over a silver cup of Spanish grape and handed it to his patron.

"Perhaps. I intend to ride out to his sepulcher this afternoon to offer libations and share a meal with my old friend."

"I'm sure Counselor Petronius's spirit would enjoy that, sir."

"One can only hope. Luc was always a finicky son of a bitch when it came to food and drink. Max, pour some wine for yourself and sing me a song to soothe my troubled mind."

When Max hesitated, his lips parted in surprise, Gaius reassured him. "It's a request, not an order, Maximus."

"Sir, I…"

The commander hadn't asked him to sing in years.

"Did you lose your mellifluous voice when I freed you?" Gaius chuckled as he raised his cup, took a gulp, and placed the vessel on the table. "Sing me something in your native language. I confess I've missed your lovely serenading almost as much as I've missed pummeling your fit ebony arse."

His face warm, Max smiled and swallowed a hefty drink of wine before he put his cup down to unclasp his cloak and loosen the fabric of his tight collar.

"It would be my pleasure, sir." He cleared his throat and began to sing. Low and hoarse at first, but gradually his voice smoothed out to its mellow, melodic charm.

Gaius closed his eyes and whispered, "Ah, yes—so damn tranquilizing. I don't believe I've heard this song before."

Max sang the haunting lyrics to an old tune his dear mother had often sung to him and his younger siblings. After he sang the last word of the poignant final line, Max hummed softly until his voice faded to silence. Just when he was convinced the commander had dozed off, Gaius opened his eyes.

"Max?"

"Sir?"

"What was that song about?"

"It's an old ballad, sir. Two lovers from enemy peoples ignore the threats of their fathers and meet in secret every night to share their passion."

"Forbidden love, then?" Gaius held out his cup, and Max filled it with more undiluted wine.

"Yes, sir. At the end of the song, the young couple flees the security of their homes and run off into the vast emptiness of the desert, never to be heard from again."

"Then it concludes on an optimistic note."

"Optimistic, sir?"

"In the end, the lovers are alive and together, yes?"

"I've never thought of it that way, but I suppose that song does have a hopeful ending, sir."

A few more moments of quiet passed. Max settled into a chair while Gaius stared at the stucco ornaments decorating the high vaulted ceiling of his suite.

"I know why Lucius is angry."

"Sir?"

Gaius guzzled more wine before he explained, "I've forsaken him."

"I don't understand, sir. How, if I may ask?"

"I failed to protect his family," Gaius declared, though Max could sense there was more troubling his patron. Gaius fidgeted with the bed covers until he finally exhaled and confessed, "And I've allowed my heart to be enchanted by a fucking barbarian."

Gaius took a small sip of wine and smiled. "If he were still here, Luc would judge my infatuation as a form of temporary madness. He would laugh at me for this foolishness. I can hear him now." He lowered his voice to mimic the counselor's deep baritone. "Gaius, have you handed your besotted heart to that furry wolf pup? Have you lost your fucking mind, soldier?"

Max's brow furrowed. He'd suspected Paulus had fallen for the commander, but he hadn't realized Dom had feelings for the Dacian.

Gaius chuckled as he rubbed his brow. "By Hercules, this lack of sleep has me blathering nonsense. Ignore my ramblings. And thank you for the song, Maximus."

"I'm pleased it gave you comfort." Max paused before suggesting, "Commander, do you believe Counselor Petronius's spirit could be…"

Gaius arched an eyebrow and waited.

"Perhaps his ghost is upset about Bryaxis. Perhaps he…"

"Shit, Bryaxis was there." Gaius threw off the bed covers and jumped to his feet. "Ram a satyr's fat prick up my arse! How, by the gods, could I have been so inattentive?"

After Gaius pulled his tunic over his head, he yanked his curly hair free from the neck hole. "Aurelia had said Bryaxis was present at Luc's deathbed, and I fucking disregarded the only useful and likely truthful bit of information that harpy shared."

He drained the last of the wine from his cup. "I need to speak to Bryaxis now. Guard!"

One of the sentries rushed into the room, the hilt of his sheathed sword firmly in his grasp.

"Commander?"

"This morning's salutations are cancelled. Tell the steward to inform my clients I'm unwell or some other rubbish."

After the guard left, Max asked, "May I join you, sir?"

"Why?"

"Bry's demeanor tends to anger you, sir. He's hurt, but he's still the same cheeky, brazen lad he's always been. Bry's confused and upset, sir. He may say something inappropriate."

"For fuck's sake, Maximus, I don't intend to strike him." Gaius pressed his lips together as he slipped on his shoes and buckled his belt. With a heavy sigh, he opened the door and marched down the corridor. When Gaius reached the corner, he turned and added, "Join me if you wish, but do not interfere."

"Thank you, sir." Max jogged to catch up.

"I need Bryaxis to tell me everything he remembers from that night. He may have heard information concerning Luc's killers." Gaius patted Max's cheek and smiled. "And I *can* control my temper when the situation warrants, Maximus. You better than anyone should know. Our mischievous Nicomedes still has his impudent balls, does he not?"

3

GAIUS FABIUS'S MANSION, THE CAELIAN HILL, ROME

"**B**RYAXIS!"

Jolted out of a deep slumber, Bry grimaced as he rolled off the bed and dropped to his knees more gracefully than Gaius had expected considering the concubine's injury.

"Commander. Fabius. Sir," he uttered between drowsy wheezes.

"Get up and sit on the bed, slave."

With effort and another grimace, Bry pushed his tall frame up and carefully lowered his hips onto the thin mattress. Clenching the bedcovers until his knuckles turned white, he stared at the floor while Gaius dragged a tall-backed wicker chair close by the bed.

"Look at me, Bryaxis." Gaius scooted the chair forward. "Fucking look at me!"

Despite being bloodshot and swollen, Bry's golden-green eyes burned with feisty resilience—the haughty self-confidence Gaius had always resented; the brazen fire Lucius had always adored.

Gaius cupped the slave's scruffy chin and lifted his face for inspection. "His color is better. You've proven yourself a capable nurse, Maximus."

"Thank you, sir," Max acknowledged over Gaius's shoulder.

"Bryaxis, you were present at Lucius Petronius's deathbed, correct?"

The lad blinked once, slowly. "I was there from the moment they carried Dominus into the atrium. He was in agony and covered in blood. Sir."

Gaius rubbed his face and took a deep breath. "Was he able to speak? Did Lucius say anything?"

"He thanked me for loving him. And for allowing him to love me."

Gaius swallowed the ache assaulting his heart. "Anything else?"

"Dominus made me promise to tell you…" Bry's pained voice trailed off.

Gaius sat back and crossed his arms; a thousand possible confessions flew through his mind, but his gut told him none included the word, love. "Go on."

"He wanted you to know he'd never intended to get involved. He said he'd had no choice. He demanded I beg on his behalf for your forgiveness, Commander."

"Those were his exact words?"

"Yes, sir. Dominus said, 'Tell Gaius that I'm so sorry.'"

His fingers curled into fists, Gaius stood up and left the room to regain his wits. After a few deep breaths, he turned around and went back into the small cell.

"Did he reveal anything more, Bryaxis? I was told his two estate guards who'd survived the attack saw nothing and know nothing. Did Lucius recognize his assailants? Did he give you any damn clue as to what nonsense he was involved in?"

"No, sir. He could hardly speak. He was in terrible pain." Biting his full lower lip, Bryaxis glanced to the side before asking, "Do you forgive him?"

"How can I fucking forgive him for some transgression I know nothing about?"

After he'd sat back down, Gaius tapped his fingers on the arms of the wicker chair, waiting for his anger to cool. He needed a strategy.

"You've fulfilled your promise to your master. Now I must fulfill mine. And to do so, I need your assistance."

Bryaxis stared at the two signet rings adorning Gaius's fingers—his lion band on his right ring finger and Luc's oak ring on the middle finger of his left hand. The Caledonian looked at Max for reassurance before he asked, "You need me, sir? I had expected to be sold."

"That might happen, slave. We'll learn your fate when Lucius's testament is read in the courts. In the meantime, I've a task for you. All of Luc's papers and books are here in crates stored in the room next to my office."

A slight smile curled the corners of Bry's chapped lips. "Domina allowed you to take his papers, sir?"

"I forgot to ask for permission. Listen, you will go through his documents—every letter, every fucking ledger, and legal paper—and read them carefully. There isn't much time until Lucius's will is unsealed."

"If something seems amiss or noteworthy, should I set it aside for your eyes?"

"Yes, exactly. You were his assistant. You'll spot any discrepancies more quickly than I could. Do you remember the conversation in the garden the last night I'd visited the Quirinal and..." Gaius arched one brow.

"Do you mean the evening you and Dom shared me for dessert?"

"Yes. When I first arrived, you were concerned about Lucius's mood. Do you recall that?"

"I remember you slapped my face, yes." Bry closed his eyes and took a deep breath. "I remember Dom mentioned an embezzlement case—some funds missing from the imperial purse. I believe he was reviewing the palace ledgers in his library the morning of the day he was murdered. Sir."

"Start with those ledgers. Lucius was fond of scribbling notations in the margins in Greek. You can read Greek, correct?"

"Yes, sir. I've mastered both languages. I'd read Sappho and Meleager to Dominus regularly."

"Our counselor always had a soft underbelly for love poetry." Despite his smile, Gaius ground his teeth to stay in control. He'd saved every damn one of those love poems Luc had written for him back in Athens; they were still sitting in a neat bundle in a box tucked away in his office. Luc's gold ownership chain and those sappy verses and faded memories were all that remained of their reckless youthful passion.

Gaius startled out of his bittersweet reverie when Bryaxis hacked into his fist. The slave coughed once more, softer, before delivering a line of Greek verse to showcase his proficiency. "I run to you as the traveler runs towards the shade when scorched by the sun."

"A fine example of Theokritos' mawkish drivel. I've never been a devotee of that Sicilian poet, but your pronunciation is passable. For a Caledonian wretch," Gaius scoffed as he stood up.

"Perhaps you'd prefer a rousing war speech from Thucydides instead, sir?"

Cheeky shit.

"Save the recitals for another time. And lose the fucking sarcasm. You'll start reviewing Lucius's records tomorrow morning. For now, my freedman will help you wash up and shave off those scraggly whiskers. I've grown a beard of mourning in honor of Lucius, but slaves are not permitted such privileges. Maximus, he'll need clothes more suitable for travel. Be sure he has a summer cloak."

Max stepped forward. "Are we leaving Rome, Commander?"

"Unless the Fates decide otherwise, we're fucking stranded here for the foreseeable future. But we are making an excursion this afternoon."

"May I ask to where, sir?"

"We're traveling to the tomb of my dearest friend, Lucius Petronius Celsus, to pay our respects and offer all of the proper sacrifices. You will have an opportunity to say your final farewells, Bryaxis. Lucius would have wanted that. He would have demanded it."

Bry opened his mouth as if to ask a question but instead looked at the floor and spoke in his most deferential tone. "Thank you, Commander Fabius."

Despite Gaius's grumblings all these years, Lucius had trained Bryaxis well.

With one foot near the threshold, Gaius turned around and clapped his hands together. "By bloody Tyche, Fortuna has presented us with a fortuitous opportunity! I'll bring along the rest of the family. We'll assemble the entire household and my veteran clients and, together, we'll travel in solemn procession to Luc's sepulcher on the Via Tiburtina. It's well past time the noble Fabii put on a fucking public spectacle worthy of our illustrious ancestors. What do you think of my idea, Maximus?"

Taken aback by the question, Max sputtered, "It's—it's a splendid suggestion, sir."

With a sly grin, Gaius marched into the corridor and hollered, "Varius!"

Moments later, the disfigured veteran lumbered down the hall. "Yes, Commander?"

Gaius barked orders over his shoulder as he trotted towards the atrium. "Tell the staff to prepare a feast—our finest wine and three plump sacrificial hogs—and order the hands to hitch the horses and oxen to every damn cart and travel wagon I own here in Rome."

"Understood, sir." Varius panted as he tried to keep pace.

"And then send word to my veterans. Tell them to gather where the arches of the aqueduct cross the Tiburtina at the marble gate of the Divine Augustus. We'll meet you there for our march out to the mausoleum of the Petronii. And Varius?"

"Sir?"

"Fetch my parade armor."

"Your armor, Commander?"

"Be sure my breastplate's spit and polished. I'll cover it with civilian garb as tradition requires until I cross the sacred boundary. And Varius?"

"Sir?"

"Bring extra swords." Gaius pointed to the stone floor. "There are murderous vermin crawling through the fucking sewers beneath our feet."

Varius took off for the kitchen while Gaius turned down another short hallway leading to the atrium. There he found Marcia and two of her girls lounging on couches, their heads close together as they whispered, deep in conversation.

Marcia hushed them and nodded to her husband. "Good morning, Dominus."

"Greetings, my dear."

"I trust you had a pleasant night."

"She was most pleasant." He pointed to her slave girls. "There's no spare time for sitting about the hall, muttering trivialities. We've a busy day ahead of us. Every girl of this household—every kitchen slave, every damn chamber servant, and every bird in your delectable flock—will dress in her finest garments. Tell your nymphs to be prepared to dance. We're taking a trip."

"A trip? To where, Gaius?"

"Have you looked outside, wife? The sun is shining, and the summer breezes are tolerable. It's the perfect day to enjoy the green fields bordering our capital. We'll travel through the city on our way out to the suburbs. Make a bloody show of it." Gaius lowered his hands and dropped his comical tone. "The entire family is traveling to the Tomb of the Petronii—for a fucking picnic. Let's move!"

~

THE OLD FORUM, ROME

WRAPPED IN A VOLUMINOUS summer cloak to conceal the bronze armor strapped to his torso, Gaius rode at the head of an impressive column of vehicles. The long line of carts and wagons, all draped in festive festoons, carried Marcia, Bryaxis, Euphronia, and most of Gaius's domestic slaves. In front of him, a regiment of attendants on foot carried long poles topped by colorful banners fluttering in the warm midday breezes. Musicians played tubas while Marcia's girls, twirling about in their swirling dresses, chimed their finger cymbals in time with the procession's thumping march. Behind Gaius, astride horses and surrounded by armed guards on foot, Max and Varius rode side by side. In his booming voice, Varius prattled on about another one of his bloody war adventures; no doubt Maximus was trying his best to appear interested in the gruesome particulars.

Gaius chuckled under his breath. He was tempted to silence Varius, but the old veteran was a damn fine storyteller.

His large retinue of riders, footmen, and wagons slowly passed beneath the towering facades of the marble temples crowding the Forum along the paved road of the Sacred Way. When the parade approached the rows of shops near the basilicas, groups of citizens and merchants stopped their animated conversations to watch the procession. A few people applauded with boisterous whoops and hurrahs; most froze, mouths agape until they were forced to step aside to get out of the way. It wasn't every day Gaius Fabius Rufus paraded his entire household through the fucking center of Rome.

As they trekked past the high podium of the shrine of the Divine Twins, an attractive harlot pushed her way through the crowd and stepped out into the street. She hoisted her skirt high above her bare hips.

"Might a lady interest you in a quick screw, Commander?"

With a broad smile, Gaius shouted back over the noise, "Should Fortuna someday abandon me, my dear, you'd be the first street trollop I'd fuck!"

The throng of onlookers cheered.

"Toss her a piece of brass, Maximus."

The prostitute caught the shiny coin before it had a chance to hit the ground; after she'd bowed with gratitude, she grabbed her bush of dark pubic curls and made a gesture so lewd even battle-hardened Varius flushed bright red. Gaius tossed his head back and cackled with delight before kicking his horse forward.

A short distance beyond the temple, a middle-aged man dressed in a striped senatorial toga and a broad-brimmed sun hat grabbed the arm of his slave as they both shuffled to get out of the path. Gaius signaled his parade to stop.

"Gaius Plinius Secundus, you filthy equestrian! Why is our noble friend puttering about the Forum in this midday heat? Shouldn't you be dining and bathing in leisure at one of your many country villas?"

"Gaius Fabius! Alas, court business has me trapped in this marble inferno. I see you've marshaled an impromptu parade through the center of Rome. Most impressive, sir."

Gaius dismounted his horse, rushed over to the slight fellow, and pulled him into an embrace tight enough to dislodge his sun hat. "By

Hercules, it's been far too long since I've seen you, Pliny."

"It has, my dear Gaius." Pliny wriggled out of Gaius's arms, straightened his hat, and boldly tapped Gaius's chest. "You're wearing a metal breastplate under that mantle. Preparing for battle, General?"

"It's my parade gear. My family and I are headed out to the suburbs to pay our respects at the Tomb of the Petronii. Lucius would have wanted me dressed in my best ceremonial armor for the occasion. And such good fortune to run into you since now you will join us. Maximus! Dismount that beast and lead it over here for our dear and most honorable Senator and counselor of the courts."

"Gaius, I have obligations." Pliny protested with a wave of his hand as Max slid off the horse's back.

"Rubbish." Gaius's smile hardened to stone. "You have obligations to Lucius Petronius—and to me. Here, let me give you a good shove up, old boy."

After landing in the large saddle with a thud, Pliny lost his balance and nearly fell off.

"Despite your equestrian rank, you're not much of a horseman, are you?" Gaius joked as he lifted himself back onto his tall chestnut steed with his attendant's assistance.

"I'll have you know, my dear Commander, I am in fact a most accomplished rider," Pliny countered as he took hold of the reins. "Gaius, all jests aside, I am deeply sorry about the death of your dear associate."

"Lucius Petronius was your friend as well, was he not? Let's enjoy a leisurely journey out to the cooler air of our verdant suburbs."

Gaius guided his mount until it pressed against the shoulder of Pliny's borrowed horse. "While we ride, you will tell me all about this intimate bash of yours—the dinner party you hosted, the last affair Lucius attended before he was murdered. I want every damn detail,

Counselor."

Pliny removed his hat to wipe his brow. "Yes, Commander."

After they'd nudged their horses to a slow walk, Gaius asked, "What food did you serve that night?"

"Pardon me, Commander? Did you just ask what food was served?"

"Yes, and I want particulars. Make my fucking mouth water."

After he'd put his hat back on, Pliny scrunched his brow. "Well, if I recall correctly, my cook prepared a delicious menu: roasted hare with sweet fig sauce, fish from my pools baked in tender vine leaves, lentils with lemon and coriander, chickpeas in saffron, and the most exquisite dried pear pudding. Not a palatial feast, I admit, but the ingredients were fresh and succulent. My esteemed guests were pleased."

"You have a keen memory for minutiae, Pliny."

Pliny delighted in the compliment, as Gaius knew he would. Flattery from a superior was a treasured commodity for lower born aristocrats like Gaius Plinius Secundus.

"You are too kind, Commander Fabius, but thank you. I have always prided myself on my talents for recollection."

"Given your sharp mind, then, you should have no issue recounting that night's conversation. I already know who was there. Tell me what your guests discussed."

"Most of the evening was spent listening to a formal reading. I'd invited one of Quintilian's pupils—that Juvenal fellow—to present some of his satirical writings. He told this story, Gaius, about an enormous fish, a monstrous turbot with spikes for scales. It was quite an amusing tale. Alas, he's a verbose man, deft but indefatigable. My esteemed guests had little time to converse about court gossip, let alone matters of state."

As they passed the high walls of the Vestal Virgins' urban residence, the arcades of the towering Flavian amphitheater rising above the rooftops to the east, Gaius asked, "And when they did have time, what did they discuss?"

"Since my party was a select gathering of the most learned men of Rome, our colleagues carried on conversations in pairs. Lucius occupied a couch with Publius Aelius Hadrianus. He was Publius's invited guest, though of course I would have invited Lucius myself had Publius not done so. Such a bright fellow our Lucius was. Such wit. I'll miss him terribly."

"As will we all. Considering how long you and Lucius had served together on the emperor's courts, I'm surprised you two didn't discuss your current judicial cases. Did Lucius mention anything to you about the embezzlement situation he'd been charged to investigate?"

Pliny lowered his volume. "Embezzlement? No, he never mentioned anything of the sort. Why, by Jupiter, wouldn't he have told me?"

"I don't know. Perhaps someone advised him to be discreet."

They traveled north-east of the amphitheater and ascended the slopes of the Oppian Hill, riding past the bustling construction site of the emperor's new bath complex—a deafening cacophony of hammers striking metal, saws slicing through wooden beams, and foremen cracking their whips and screaming orders at the gangs of slaves. When the clamorous commotion was behind them, Gaius turned in his saddle. "Pliny, exactly what did my dear brother and Lucius Petronius chat about that night?"

"I fear I only heard bits and pieces of their conversation. Publius Aelius was complimenting our dear associate most audaciously, as I recall."

"He was flirting with Luc?"

"I would never make such an inflammatory accusation, but much wine was consumed."

"Pity you didn't hear more. With whom did you speak?"

"I spent far too much of my energies conversing with our consul, Minicius. By Minerva's spindle, he's a most vapid man. He prattled on and on about his accomplishments, how quickly he'd ascended the offices—his usual asinine gloating. I pretended to listen, but I may have nodded off once or twice."

"Minicius is a dullard, as is that satirist twit you invited to recite. I've heard Juvenal deliver his daft poetry twice now—and I've suffered through that ridiculous fish story. He's an imbecile, daring to suggest publicly that Roman men shouldn't bed lads," Gaius spat in disgust. "That bloody moralist won't ever receive patronage from our dear, lad-loving Emperor Trajan. Juvenal will be lucky if he's not exiled. What happened at the end of the dinner?"

"Nothing out of the ordinary. In fact, Lucius departed when the desserts were served. He seemed bored, anxious to get home."

"Perhaps he was embarrassed by Publius's fawning, or desirous to get back to his bed warmer. His concubine is here, you know—in the wagon back there with my household servants. I'm guarding him until the courts unseal Lucius's testament."

"It was considerate of you to bring the slave along and allow it to pay its respects to its former master."

"I'm a fucking paragon of virtue, my dear Pliny."

They both fell into that comfortable, genuine laughter only close friends dare to share.

"We'll discuss this party of yours again, Counselor. I expect I'll be in Rome longer than I'd care to be." Gaius raised his hand; the procession slowed to a stop to allow a file of supply wagons loaded with timber to cross the road. "You'll join me for dinner on the

Caelian. Lucius's cook is in my custody as well; she'll prepare the finest meal you've ever tasted. Perhaps the atmosphere will spark some additional memories of that evening."

"It would be a great honor to dine with you, Commander."

"I can't guarantee the most intellectually stimulating dinner conversation, my dear Pliny, but I can promise you no one will be fucking murdered." Gaius lowered his arm and kicked his horse. "Forward!"

4

WHEN THE PROCESSION REACHED the aqueduct on the eastern outskirts of the city, Gaius's veterans joined the parade and followed the slow moving wagons past the rows of cypress trees lining both sides of the paved road. Between the trees, funerary monuments of all shapes and sizes stood crowded together close to the curbs, while behind the trees sprawled the vast parks of aristocrats' suburban villas. Generations of the dead mingled with the living along stretches of the consular highways of Rome.

As Pliny babbled on about something or other, Gaius closed his eyes and inhaled the cooler air lightly fragranced by the evergreens.

"So will you assist me, Gaius? Will you speak with him?"

Annoyed, Gaius turned to the lawyer. "You're disturbing my peace, Counselor."

"My apologies, but will you please urge Tacitus to reply to my letters? He listens to you. He was your pedagogue, after all. You see, Gaius, I'd sent him some of my writings before the festival of Ceres and I've heard nothing. It's been over two months now and not a single comment from him."

"Do you smell that, my dear Pliny—that delicate spice of cypress? It's much more pleasant than the heavy blanket of juniper and pine choking the air of the Dacian forests."

Swaying back and forth in the saddle as his horse ambled down the basalt pavers, Gaius closed his eyes again. His mind drifted off to memories of marching through the rocky Carpathian Mountains with his legions, felling trees and building forts, bridges, roads—anything to conquer those Dacian savages. In those dark, primeval forests, wolves lurked in the shadows, vicious beasts that were nearly invisible but always there.

He glanced over his shoulder to study the rugged faces of the veterans who'd followed him into battle and survived those brutal wars fought so far from home. He'd lost many soldiers, many loyal friends. Thousands of brave Roman men had given their lives to acquire a fortune of glittering Dacian gold.

As the lawyer continued to prattle on about his writing rubbish, Gaius combed his fingers through his curls and mumbled, "Thank the fucking gods we won the damn war."

Pliny paused his yammering and raised his palms to the sky. "Let us praise almighty Jupiter for granting us glorious victories! Praise our triumphant Emperor, Marcus Ulpius Traianus! The Dacian scourge no longer menaces our empire and his games promise to be spectacular." Pliny dropped his arms. "You'll be here for the festivities, Gaius, won't you?"

"Your gift for hyperbole is admirable, but the Dacians were never a serious threat, merely a costly and time-consuming nuisance. And, of course, I'll attend the triumphal games, but they won't be held for another year or more. Marcus wishes to showcase his grand structures during the celebrations, but the renovations to the great circus aren't finished and the construction of his enormous forum and his imperial baths are both behind schedule. The emperor may desire to conduct his triumph before winter arrives, but his building projects are formidably ambitious. For all his talent, Apollodorus is not a fucking magician, Pliny."

"Apollodorus is a skilled and experienced engineer. I, for one, would never wager against his punctuality."

"He's a mortal man, subject to the whims of our capricious gods. And even if by some miracle every supply ship arrives from the stone quarries without incident, the cranes can't lift marble blocks in the damn rain. I'd wager it'll be a year or three before those buildings are completed, although I doubt Marcus has enough patience to wait until the final stones are in place."

Gaius swatted a large mosquito buzzing around his face. "I see the noxious marsh pests have already invaded the capital. By Pollux, I despise Rome this time of year. Nevertheless, I will remain here and scour every block until I find Lucius Petronius's killers. Trust me— there will be nothing left of them to burn on the pyre when I'm finished."

After they'd passed the second-mile marker, the silhouette of a large domed tomb rose above the trees. Pliny sat straighter in his saddle and pointed. "There it is! What a noble tomb for such an accomplished family."

"It's too bloody ostentatious for a plebian mausoleum, no matter how distinguished the Petronii imagine they are."

Gaius swore under his breath, chagrined by his callous insult, and said, "Forgive my arrogant barb, Pliny. Despite your plebian ancestry, you and Titus Petronius are most honorable men."

"Thank you, Gaius, but I prefer to note my equestrian rank, not my plebian lineage."

Gaius flicked his hand with a dismissive huff. "Equestrian, plebian—it's all the bloody same. Your clans achieved political influence only after Rome's founding families had already won the critical battles."

"The struggles between the well-born families and the plebian clans ended ages ago, Commander. Together, plebians and patricians have ruled, fought, and fornicated for generations. But fear not—at the end of the day, you will always be a patrician prick, my dear Gaius."

When Gaius didn't laugh, Pliny's right eyelid twitched.

"I suppose I deserved that, but you've seen me in all my naked glory at the baths." Gaius lifted himself from his saddle and grabbed his crotch. "You must admit my patrician cock's a noble shade of crimson."

Pliny exhaled in relief, rubbed his eye, and snorted. "Yes, a most high-born Tyrian purple indeed! You should have that engraved on your tomb, Commander: Here lies the porphyry patrician prick of Gaius Fabius Rufus."

"Ha! Brilliant suggestion, but why do we bother? Our stone memorials are doomed to crumble to dust. It will be the historians, like our dear friend Tacitus, who will determine our legacies, Pliny."

"And, I fear, our careers," Pliny griped. "What about the accolades of the Roman people, Gaius? Surely the populace's adoration will live on forever."

"The proletariat is a cesspool of fickle bitches with bottomless stomachs, my good friend. We placate them with free grain, bloody spectacles, and drunken feasts. They stay satiated, and we remain in power. And that strategy will always succeed until…"

"Until?"

"Until the barbarians storm the gates and learn to master the games of Rome."

Gaius collected the reins and said, "And when that day comes, my dear Pliny, let us pray we have a loyal and well-equipped army willing and able to defend our noble city. Our soldiers will stand as the stalwarts of Rome's dominion, not the filthy urban mob or those crusty old fucks in the Senate, present company excluded of course. Now, excuse me."

Gaius waved for the parade to come to a halt while he unclasped the gold brooch pinned to the front of his mantle; the dark blue folds fell to the sides, revealing his polished bronze breastplate decorated with griffins and winged Victory figures arranged as pairs on either side of a war trophy. After he'd pushed the excess cloth of his cloak over his shoulders, Gaius turned to Varius.

"Stay here while I ride ahead. Proceed at a slow march only after you see I've reached the tomb."

"Yes, Commander."

With a nod, Gaius kicked his chestnut mount to a canter and rode over a mile down the road to the entrance of a large brick structure half-sheathed in polished marble slabs. Withered roses blanketed the ground, the debris of the recent funeral celebrations. He dismounted and grabbed a handful of the wilted red petals, slowly spreading his fingers until the flowers fluttered to the ground.

"Greetings, Lucius Petronius Celsus. Finally, I've arrived to say farewell, share some damn fine wine with you, and sacrifice sows in your honor. You've only just left this world, and already I miss you more than I can bear, Luc."

After he'd pulled his indigo cloak over his head in the manner of a priest's cowl, Gaius wiped his nose and approached the entrance of the tomb.

"Your tardy soldier made a vow of vengeance before thunderous Jove. Don't laugh, Counselor—perhaps the heartless bastard listened. Justice will be served, Luc. I promise you Rome will never forget you, nor will I. Your whore tells me you've asked for my forgiveness, but I pray one day you will forgive my failures." He caressed the bronze door and whispered, "Please forgive me, Luc."

Gaius squatted and touched the grey marble slab set into the earth, its polished surface pierced with a pipe in the center. From a leather pouch attached to the red sash tied around his breastplate, he pulled out a small silver flask. Slowly, he poured a thin stream of wine into the lead tube snaking its way underground to feed the dead.

"I offer your thirsty spirit this Chalkidian grape, the same wine we'd enjoyed back in Athens all those years ago. Drink this nectar of our carefree, salacious youth and find everlasting peace, *Erastes*."

After the last drop had fallen into the pipe, Gaius sat on the ground, legs crossed with his elbows on his knees. The cicadas in the surrounding trees chirped as he stared at the sculpted metal plaques attached to the pediment above the tomb's doorway: an owl and an olive branch—the symbols of warrior goddess Minerva, the patron deity of the Petronii.

That virgin hag hadn't protected Lucius either. They'd both failed him.

Fuck, his head hurt. Everything hurt. Even the normally dulcet song of the cicadas pissed him off.

"Quit that fucking racket!"

The cicadas' chirping grew louder.

"Insolent buggers."

A ghost of an ache tingled in the fingertips of his right hand. He extended his arm in front of him, palm down. The tremor was slight, barely noticeable, but he felt the faint the spasms, the subtle warning signs he'd grown to fear since childhood.

After swallowing a small but potent dose of Calli's disgusting potion he always kept stashed at the bottom of his travel pouch, Gaius grimaced at the bitter taste as he shut his eyes and balled his hand into a tight fist. It would not happen. He would not allow it. He would not thrash in the dirt, slavering like a rabid dog in front of his entire household. He would not surrender to the dreaded affliction.

Gaius dug his fingernails into the damp skin of his palm until he drew blood. "I curse you, Harpies of the lunacy. Be gone! Leave me be!"

He squeezed his eyes, unfurling and closing his fist slowly. The spasm faded and disappeared. All was quiet. Even the cicadas stopped screeching. Moments passed, and the low rumble of the approaching wagons grew louder, frightening a mourning dove perched in the nearby bushes. The white bird cooed as it flew up into the pine trees. When the procession pulled to a noisy stop at the assembly area in front of the mausoleum, everyone remained in their seats and waited.

Gaius took a deep breath, wiped his bloody hand with the edge of his dark cloak, and rubbed his eyes.

The cicadas' cacophony returned.

He rose to his feet and signaled his household to disembark and join him. The crowd quickly took their positions before the entrance to the mausoleum, the veterans standing at attention in formation, the slaves dropping in unison to their knees. At the back of the crowd, Marcia's girls, accompanied by the musicians, sang a somber funeral hymn in rhythm with the insects' renewed chirping.

Poor, distraught Euphronia. There she knelt, wailing as she pulled her saffron-colored locks and beseeched her great goddess. Gaius would ensure she was well taken care of, no matter what Luc's final testament dictated.

But what was he to do about the castrated Caledonian?

Dry-eyed and stoic, his hands clasped firmly over the small of his back, Bryaxis knelt with elegance as he mouthed silent prayers for his murdered master. Gaius suspected he already knew what Lucius had determined for Bryaxis in his will. He would have done the same for his boys.

Marcia strolled over to her husband, followed by an attendant waving a large fan of feathers. "Greetings, Dominus. You look pale. Are you ill?"

"I'm perfectly fine." Gaius curled is injured right hand into a fist to hide the cuts. "Was your trip comfortable, Domina?"

"Most pleasant. By gods, the Petronii have built themselves an awfully grand tomb—a bit too grand for their status, perhaps." With her hands on her hips, Marcia carefully studied the assembly of household servants and soldiers. "Gaius, all of Lucius's slaves are displaying proper hysterics, except for that one. Do you see how he's not sobbing? That's most disrespectful."

"Ignore him, Marcia."

"You're not going to reprimand Lucius's catamite for disregarding custom by refusing to mourn openly? His behavior is downright blasphemous."

"I said ignore it, wife. Luc's slave has been punished enough, for fuck's sake." Gaius turned and shouted, "Varius, take ten men and fetch the swine! Be sure to observe the proper handling of the sacred beasts. The rest of you begin preparations for the sacrifice."

As the servants dashed about, arranging stools, tables, jugs of drink, and serving dishes, a covered litter carried on two gilded poles by six guards approached the tomb from the opposite direction of the Tiburtina.

Gaius removed his hood and shielded his eyes. "Marcia, is that who I think it is?"

"Your grandmother," she answered flatly.

"Shit." He rubbed the bridge of his nose and pinched it. "You invited Avia?"

"I dispatched a courier to her estate with an invitation to join us.

She's frail and won't be on earth much longer. Besides, it's a family gathering, and you know how she loves a feast."

"She will fucking skin me alive for not visiting her since well before the last war."

"You've been negligent. I thought it time you two reconnected."

"Why is it Roman women insist on meddling in their husbands' affairs?" He groaned and offered his elbow.

"We are the mortal daughters of our vindictive divine mother, Juno. Imagine what horrors I could concoct if you were ever unfaithful to me." She countered with a smirk and took his arm.

"Are you still harboring ill-will towards our fair Vibia Sabina?"

"Gaius, your entanglement with Sabina happened before our marriage. The pitiful girl is married to Publius now. But if you're asking me if I trust our delicate imperial flower, your first love, my answer is no. I would be lying if I said I did."

"I never loved Sabina."

"She loved you. She still does." Marcia stopped and asked, "Gaius, have you ever truly loved anyone?"

Without responding, he grunted and pulled her forward as they approached the litter. The well-dressed attendants carefully lowered the ornate couch to the ground. When the tallest of her guards held back the ivory curtain, she emerged in all her patrician magnificence.

Avia looked well considering she'd survived seventy-five summers. Although her short frame was thin, her tawny hair now stark white, and her once beautiful face wrinkled like a dried plum, her light amber eyes still twinkled with the vitality of a young girl.

She straightened her bulky silk dress and declared, "So gracious of you to wait for my arrival, my dears. What a marvelous day for an outing."

Gaius spoke softly into Marcia's left ear as he nodded toward the litter. "I adore this woman. She protected me as much as she could during my frightful youth. And I cherish you, Marcia, but I will never give you anything more than I already offer. It's best for you to remember our marriage began as an amicable and mutually-beneficial political arrangement."

"And you should take comfort in knowing I've never wanted anything from you but your respect, Gaius."

"Don't dare surprise me like this again if you wish to keep my fucking respect. Understood?" He marched over to his grandmother and bowed his head before he kissed her hand. "Greetings, most beloved Avia."

She jerked out of his grasp and clenched his bicep with her bony, weathered hand. "I should cuff you right here, in front of your veterans and your slaves. Would serve you right! Does the Lion of the Lucky Fourth think himself too grand to pay a visit to his poor old grandmother? Is Memmia Cornelia now unworthy of the dutiful respect of her damn grandson?"

"My apologies, Avia. I was preoccupied." He leaned down and pulled back his auburn curls to expose his left ear. "Strike me in public for my crimes. I deserve it. I'd expected far worse than a blow to the head."

She reached up and pinched his earlobe until he winced. "It's early. I reserve the right to punish you more severely after we eat, you cheeky sprog. You always were trouble, Rufus." Together, they turned to greet Marcia when she came forward.

Memmia extended her hand. "Greetings, my dearest Marcia Servilia. Your complexion is radiant. The suburban winds agree with you."

Marcia bowed as she pressed the elderly woman's angular knuckles to her forehead. "Thank you, Avia. We're pleased you could join us for this somber occasion. Such a tragedy."

"Indeed, the best men of Rome are often taken from us far too soon."

They both stared at Gaius, who merely raised his hands and shrugged before he wrapped his arm around his grandmother's shoulders.

"Avia, let's move over to the shade. You look parched. We've brought our best Falernian. Come." Gaius insisted as he led her over to a serving table under a cluster of chestnut trees. "Ah, see? It's much more refreshing beneath this canopy of leaves. May I pour you some wine?"

She nodded and pointed. "By Castor—is that young Plinius over there? I haven't seen him in ages. The poor lad has lost much of his hair, hasn't he? No wonder he wears that ridiculous brimmed hat."

Memmia took the cup from Gaius's outstretched hand and lowered her voice. "Listen, Gaius, I've heard you put on quite a spectacle today, parading your guards through the Forum. What, in the name of Zeus, was the purpose of that reckless display? And why are you wearing armor? Are you deliberately trying to anger the emperor? Is my foolish cousin, Tacitus, whispering fantasies of revolution in your ears?"

Exasperated, Gaius took a deep breath and explained, "First of all, this is my parade armor, not my field gear. I've donned my ceremonial breastplate to honor the spirit of Counselor Petronius, not to inflame the palace. And Tacitus is not your cousin, Avia. You may share the same family name, but he's not a patrician. He's descended from a far less noble line of the Cornelia family."

"Armor is armor, Gaius." Memmia scoffed. "You're fooling no one, certainly not me. And Tacitus is a better man than most of the patrician Cornelii boars of late I've had the misfortune to know. If I say he's my cousin, you will not correct me, Rufus."

"Fine." Gaius waved his hand in surrender before continuing, "Second, neither Tacitus nor I believe in some farcical return to the days of the Republic. You know exactly what I was doing—demonstrating to all of Rome that I intend to find Lucius's murderers whatever the cost. I have the means and the swords to insure justice is served, whether our esteemed Emperor cares to assist me or not."

"By our holiest gods, Gaius! Is that what you believe? You think Marcus has no interest in avenging this horrendous crime? He treasured Lucius's talents and loyalty. Marcus Ulpius Traianus will hunt down those criminals, whether you throw a childish tantrum through the Forum or not, you daft turnip."

"It wasn't all that long ago Rome's Forum was filled with armed men fighting for justice. My grandfather—your esteemed husband—fought valiantly alongside the Divine Vespasian's allies. Was he throwing a childish tantrum?"

"Your grandfather was an honorable man but an impetuous idealist. Do you truly wish to return this city to the chaos and bloodshed of civil war? Stop behaving like a spoiled stripling and visit the palace as soon as we've completed the rites for our poor Lucius."

"I will call on the emperor tomorrow," Gaius growled as he crossed his arms.

"You, Gaius Fabius, will pay your respects to our revered Emperor today. Go to the palace and grovel at Marcus's feet if you must. Considering the grievous circumstances, he might forgive your puerile behavior."

"Yes, Avia." Gaius capitulated as he studied the fluttering silver undersides of the chestnut tree leaves. "I seem to be asking damn near everyone for forgiveness these days."

"Perhaps the gods will grant it. It's important to mind the counsel of your elders, Gaius, especially guidance from your grandmother." She shook her skeletal finger in his face. "I survived far worse nightmares than you could ever imagine. Remember what I have sacrificed for this family."

As his amber eyes softened with affection, Gaius uncrossed his arms to lightly stroke her painted cheek with the back of his hand. "I remember you were my light of hope during my wretched youth. You taught me who I was, who I was obligated to be. I will be forever grateful."

Memmia covered his hand with her slender fingers and squeezed. "We survived those wicked tests of our fortitude, my strong boy, and for that we both must give praise to Fortuna. We've persevered through adversity, and we've triumphed because we are Cornelii."

Gaius chuckled as he leaned down to lightly peck her on the other cheek. "I am a proud son of the Fabia clan, Avia."

She swallowed another gulp of wine and exhaled. "Ah, but you are also a Cornelius, a noble family certainly equal in achievement to the great Fabii. Remember that it was the Cornelii who led Rome's legions into battle against the Carthaginian viper and razed their wicked city down to the infertile African sands. Remember, Gaius, *all* of your esteemed ancestors are watching you."

Memmia drained the last of her drink and sighed as she fussed with her cumbersome robes. "I often thank almighty Jove for blessing you with robust Cornelian testicles, Rufus. You certainly didn't inherit your grandfather's flimsy, freckled Fabian balls. Now light the cooking fires, refill my wine cup, and sacrifice the blasted pigs. I'm old, I'm famished, and I want some damn pork."

～

GAIUS FABIUS'S SEASIDE VILLA, CAMPANIA

ALLERIX AWOKE BEFORE DAWN, roused from sleep by a vivid fantasy. His dream had been deliciously real—the wet warmth of the Roman's mouth covering his naked body with demanding kisses, bruising his skin.

So damn real.

He'd even sat up and checked his thighs and hipbones for bite marks before collapsing back onto the mattress.

As the first rays of light crept in through the window grate, he lay there on his bed, restless and randy and thirsty. Soon, another hot day of raking out the stalls and feeding the horses would begin. Rubbing the twisted rope of silver around his neck, Alle stared at the ceiling and counted, again. Still nine wooden beams—no more, no less. Nothing had changed; he was still a captive trapped far from home. Absentmindedly, he ran his fingertip over the inscribed words on the bronze fugitive tag and shut his eyes.

Paulus. To be returned to the house of Gaius Fabius Rufus.

He was no longer a free man; he was property. A war trophy of the general who had destroyed his people, owned by the man to whom he'd willingly surrendered his body. But Allerix had surrendered much more than his flesh. He was losing focus on his plan for revenge.

Shit, he couldn't stop thinking about the bastard, and now he was dreaming about his possessive, intoxicating touch?

What was this madness?

How, by mighty Zalmoxis, had the Roman pierced his heart? How had he found the chink in the armor Alle had crafted when he was a boy—an invisible shield of distrust to preserve his dignity and protect him from his half-brother's hatred and his father's disappointment? The bastard must be a powerful sorcerer, or perhaps he truly was the red-haired daemon Dacian mothers had long taught their children to fear.

Allerix lifted his finger off the metal tag and slowly traced patterns through the drops of sweat pooled in the clefts of his taut abdomen. He was smoldering from the inside out. He closed his eyes tighter and imagined the commands dripping like drops of honey off the Roman's long tongue.

"Surrender to me, cub. Obey your master."

With his pulse thumping in his eardrums, Allerix flipped over onto his stomach. He clenched the thin bed sheets with both hands and squeezed the folds, imagining they were the Roman's fiery copper locks tangled between his fingers. When he buried his damp scruffy face into his lumpy pillow, memories of that lavender-perfumed water in those luxurious baths filled his nostrils. Grinding his throbbing prick into the mattress, Alle writhed and rocked up and down on his small lonely bed.

"Fuck."

He needed more. He needed release. Allerix rolled over on his back and brushed his hand down his torso to grip his engorged shaft. He pumped hard and fast before pausing to pinch the sensitive skin below his wet slit; a desperate guttural groan burst from his lips.

It wasn't enough. He needed him—his mouth, his hands, his undeniable heat—but the Roman was hundreds of miles away pining for his dead lover.

He arched his back and spread his knees apart; the cool morning air tickled the whispers of dark curls below his balls. Moaning softly at first and then louder, Allerix watched his left hand pump fast, sliding his dark foreskin up and down, until the head of his cock glistened. As he teetered near the edge, he reached down with his right hand and pushed two fingers through the tight ring of muscle. Almost. Fucking.

There.

"I surrender, butcher!"

"Butcher? Shit, does Dom know you call him butcher?" Nic asked in his familiar flippant tone from the doorway, and Allerix's hard penis shriveled faster than a startled eel as he quickly pulled the bed covers over his exposed and painfully unsatisfied lust. "I'd offer you a helping hand, Dacian, but it appears you have the basics figured out. You do know there are dildos in the small cupboard in the common room, right? Lots of sizes."

"What—what are you doing here?"

"I've brought some wine leftover from the morning sacrifices. I thought we'd share these dregs before chores." Nic held up a plain ceramic jug and arched both of his shapely dark blond brows. "Well, to be honest, I brought it up here for me to savor alone before work begins, but your lewd moaning was too hard to resist. Dom must adore your fucking hot whimpering. Sorry to interrupt your wank. Carry on."

"No, no. It's all right." Allerix sat up, wiped his sweaty face, and asked, "You have wine? Come on then—share. I'm parched, and you owe me now."

The rosy glimmer of the sunrise reflected off the sea and lit up a corner of the small room.

"Budge up," Nic ordered as he hiked up his green tunic to sit down. With a grunt, Allerix scooted over to make room on the narrow mattress for his fellow pleasure slave. Nic's lips were stained red from wine, and his long flaxen hair, loose and messy, hung down past his shoulders. The blond always looked as though he'd just been relentlessly fucked over a table.

While Nic handed him the jug, Allerix fought the words but they spilled out to betray him. "How much longer before the Roman finishes honoring his dead friend and returns home?" he asked, before guzzling a healthy swig.

Shit, he sounded like a love-struck maiden.

"That Roman is *Dominus*, Dacian. I thought you were getting better with proper address. And why do you care when Dom returns? Do you miss him?" Nic puckered his tinted lips in a mock kiss as he poked Allerix's shoulder. "S'all right, though. We all miss him. It's fucking boring doing nothing but chores. Even Atticus gets restless, spending his free time tossing off his wrinkled old pickle. Did you know that perverted badger has scrolls of brothel drawings stashed behind the cupboard in his room?"

Allerix laughed. "You must miss Max."

"I miss him more than anything," Nicomedes replied softly with a tender smile. "Dom and Max will return soon, but they can't leave the capital until Counselor Petronius's will is unsealed and read publicly in the courts. Dom said he'd be home near the Kalends. That's less than—" Nic counted on his fingers. "Ten days."

"Ten days," Alle repeated.

"I'd wager Dom is counting the days as well. He despises Rome in the summertime. Dom says it's too bloody hot."

Allerix handed the wine jug back to Nic. "Have you been to Rome?"

"Never, and I don't ever want to go there—Rome's packed with thieves and murderers. Max says the capital is worse than Neapolis, and Neapolis is a sewer." Nicomedes tossed back a gulp, wiping the burgundy drops off of his smooth chin. "Simon was born in Rome, but Dom sent him down here before his balls dropped."

"So Max is the only one who's been to Rome?"

"Yes. When he's not on campaign, Dom keeps his favorite close by his side." After he'd offered Alle the wine jug, Nic scooted down towards the foot of the bed and rested his cheek on Alle's chest. "Max used to be Dom's favorite, but you know that, right? Max lived at Dom's house up in Rome, and Dom took him to parties at the palace. Dancers and acrobats and…."

"And soup served in tortoise shells. I remember. Why didn't Dominus take Simon on this trip?"

Nic glanced up and smiled mischievously. "Our curly-haired nit isn't the favorite anymore." He ran his hand down Alle's side and squeezed his knee through the bedcovers. "Dom's fancies you more, Dacian. It's your heavy-lidded, seductive eyes and that arrogant, pouty mouth, not to mention your perfect arse." Nic reached up and rubbed a shiny strand of Alle's mane between his thumb and forefinger. "Your hair's getting longer. I can braid it with ribbons if you like."

"I'm not a prostitute." Allerix scowled. He placed the empty jug on the small side table and lifted up his slave tag. "I'm a prisoner of war."

Shaking his head, Nicomedes playfully tugged Alle's black chest hairs. "I'm fond of you, Dacian—you're beautiful and feisty and all furry—but you're a collared runaway slave, not a war prisoner. You're fucking lucky to be alive. But I still say you'll be Dom's favorite bed warmer once he comes home. I see how he looks at you. We all do. If you're lucky, Dom might take *you* to Rome someday—that is if you ever learn proper behavior and all."

Alle bit his thumbnail. "Is there a formal ceremony or something?"

"For what?"

"For being named the favorite?"

Nic laughed so hard snot bubbled out of his nostrils. "Shit, no! It's not like when a slave is freed. There's no official audience with the property magistrates. There's no arcane ritual or floppy freedom cap. You're still a fucking slave."

"But how will I know?"

Nicomedes shook with hysterics again before he wiped his eyes. "Do you expect the herald to announce it from the rostrum? You'll know when it happens—Dom will call you to his bedchamber, fuck you hard but sweetly, and afterward he'll gift you a special token. Atticus, who spies on bloody everyone around here, will inform Max and Max will tell us. And then you're officially Dom's favorite cock warmer. At least, that's how it happened with Simon. The little twerp received two gold bangles that night."

"I've seen them," Allerix mumbled. "Simon treasures those bracelets."

"He'll get to keep his baubles and some delicious memories, but he'll no longer enjoy a privileged place in Dom's bed." Nic licked the dip of Alle' breastbone and grinned. "Because you'll be there."

As Allerix silently mulled over Nic's explanation, Nic rolled onto his side and propped himself up on his elbow. "Let's talk about something more interesting like cock sucking. Max says you're nearly as talented as me. He said you do this flicking motion with your tongue that's bloody sinful. Now, I squeeze my cheeks, and..." Nic rested his palm on the bedcovers hiding Alle's hardening dick. "Pity we can't share our fellatio secrets."

"Not without the Roman's permission." Allerix protested and half-heartedly pushed Nic's hand off of his crotch. "My prick is not getting locked in a cage."

Nicomedes leaned forward, his lips hovering close to Alle's mouth, and stroked his own blatant erection. "You know there are cages designed for pleasure, right? Years ago, after Theodorus was sent to Rome, Dom gave Max this cage for Saturnalia shaped like snarling sea serpent. He showed it to me. It's solid gold with red rubies for eyes and pearls for teeth."

More blood rushed to Alle's groin. "Besides trinkets, does the favorite get any *real* power?"

Nic laughed again before dropping his voice to a sultry hush. "The favorite boy spends most nights in Dom's bed, drinking his wine and tasting his mouth and whispering desires and counsel into his ear. That's power, right?"

Allerix stifled a groan as he shuffled his bum under the bedcovers to try to hide the bulge of his now raging erection.

Nic smiled knowingly and purred, "You do know we're allowed to pleasure each other with our hands, right?"

Allerix nodded and licked his lips. With an exasperated huff, he threw off the blanket. "Nic, please toss me off. I'm so fucking horny."

"See! You're already demanding naughty favors like a true, spoiled favorite, although you have better manners than most."

As the tip of his tongue poked out from between his shiny, flushed lips, Nic reached down and caressed Alle's full balls until Allerix wriggled and groaned. He wrapped his fingers around the base of Alle's cock and squeezed hard before stroking his length.

"Faster," Alle pleaded as he watched Nic's expert machinations tease pearls of juice from the slit of his prick. Alle arched his neck back until his chin pointed to the ceiling. He swallowed and closed his eyes.

"Are you thinking about Dom?" Nic teased as his tempo sped up to a furious pace, his talented hand twisting and pulling Alle's shaft. "Are you pretending this is Dom's hand pumping your cock?"

Alle gasped and knocked the wine jug off the table. It fell to the stone floor with a loud crash.

"You want to be Dom's favorite, don't you?" Nic teased. "You want him to take you to parties and spank you pink in front of his friends and fuck you senseless over a couch, don't you? Come on,

Dacian. Give it up. Surrender to your master."

"Shit, yes!" Allerix screamed, as strings of hot seed spurted out, landing all over his stomach and chest. His entire body shivered with relief; panting, he covered his eyes with his forearm. When his breathing slowed, Alle turned his head towards the doorway and opened his eyes.

He was standing in the shadows at the threshold to Alle's room, his green eyes glowing in the dark like those of a deer in the woods. Alle booted Nic off the end of the bed and sighed. "Simon."

Simon said nothing. He covered his mouth with the back of his hand and turned to run down the hall, the pitter patter of his bare feet gradually fading as he bounded down the staircase to the common room. Spewing a string of curses, Nic picked himself up off the floor and chased after him.

"For fuck's sake, we were just having a lark. Don't be a jealous little twat, Simon!"

After Nic had left, Allerix fell back down and pulled the crumpled bedcovers over his spent and sweat-drenched body. As he stared at the ceiling once more, the pang of guilt in his gut boiled over into anger. He raked his fingers through his thick hair, scratching furiously until his scalp burned.

He had to focus; he had to clear his mind of these fucking distractions. He couldn't feel anything for the Roman. No passion, no guilt—nothing at all.

Alle sat up, jerked the cushion out from underneath his head, and punched it over and over until he was forced to stop to catch his breath.

"I—I will be the butcher's favorite, Simon. I have no option. Either I'll be torn to shreds by beasts in their arena, or I kill their king and earn immortality. Either way, I will die. But I'll do everything in my fucking power to die honorably."

With tears streaming down his flushed cheeks, Allerix lifted the pillow to his face and whispered, "Hear me, my gods. Guide me through this treacherous passage to my eternal salvation. Grant me the wiles to win the Roman's trust. I beg you to blind him to my games, I implore you to make Gaius Fabius Rufus mine to seduce, mine to betray."

A strong beam of light streamed in and he closed his eyes. The cruel summer sun had climbed higher in the morning sky. Somewhere outside, a cock crowed to celebrate the beginning of another scorching, humid day. Another day, far from home.

Another day alone.

Alle threw off the blankets one last time, and stood up, stark naked and resilient and exhausted. It was time for Allerix, second son of Thiamarkos, collared property of Gaius Fabius, to get dressed and go to the stables to shovel shit.

→→》》》❯━❮❮❮《《←←

5

"DACIAN! SIMON! TIME TO eat!"

Allerix tossed the last forkful of hay onto the pile and wiped his brow with his forearm before taking a long swig of cool water. His shoulders ached, and the muscles along the backs of his arms were sore. He'd hauled countless buckets of water to the troughs, mucked out every one of the stalls, and restacked mountains of scattered hay. It was backbreaking work, but at least he'd sleep well tonight. Day after day of physical labor in the humid heat and bright summer sun was transforming Allerix's alabaster body, distracting his troubled mind. The terrifying nightmares of his capture and rape in some distant field were less frequent now.

Allerix, second son of Thiamarkos, was healing.

When Nicomedes hollered a second time, Alle propped the wooden handle of the rake against the wall and ran out through the open barn door. The sun had passed its zenith in the sky; Plautus should have plates of food waiting for them in the common room.

"Did you stack the hay properly?" Nic sounded more bored than concerned as he untied the leather band at the base of his thick blond plait and shook his wavy hair loose.

Allerix fell into step beside him. "Yes. I finished my chores, and I'm hungry."

"After our morning playtime, I would expect you'd be bloody starving." Nic jested before he furrowed his brow and glanced over Alle's shoulder. "Where's our little twat gone to, then? I thought he was with you."

Alle's stomach grumbled. "He was at the stables earlier, but he left. Do you think he's still angry about…?"

"Nah, I talked to him. It was just a fucking hand job, after all. I promised to pull his pecker tonight." Nic winked and turned back towards the stables. He cupped is hands over his mouth and screamed, "Simon! C'mon now, it's time to eat!"

From somewhere in the distance, they heard a faint but surly voice holler, "I'm busy!"

Nic raised an eyebrow before clutching Allerix's elbow and dragging him back down the gentle slope and past the barn to a patchwork of animal pens at the far end of the stables. In one fold, ten or so colorful goats with long hair and curved, twisted horns mulled about, each one wearing a thick leather collar. Allerix touched the heavy silver torque around his neck before shielding his nose from the stench.

"What in the name of the most holy Penates are you doing, Simon?" Nic asked with amused curiosity.

Close to the hindquarters of a white goat in the near corner, Simon squeezed the swollen teat of the albino nanny until milk streamed into the wooden bucket. "What does it look like I'm doing?" Simon pushed his curls away from his face and looked up. Anger burned in his young eyes. Alle doubted Simon's resentment had anything to do with a meaningless hand job. Simon wiped his brow and explained, "Plautus said that if we return to the stable house without fresh goat milk, we won't get fed."

"Plautus can't deny us food without Dom's permission, can he?"

Nicomedes wondered, rubbing his chin.

Simon shrugged. "I could use some fucking help."

Nicomedes raised his hands in protest. "I am not going anywhere near those filthy beasts. This tunic was laundered just yesterday." He lifted the fabric and sniffed. "It still smells fresh."

Allerix exhaled. He was famished and tired. "I'll help you, Simon."

Nic patted Alle on the back. "Well, aren't you a charitable fellow. Go and fetch a milk pail from that stack over there." Nicomedes scanned the small herd, clearly looking for a specific target. "And Dacian, you see that brown and white one by the tree? She's older and slow, but she's Dom's favorite bitch. Her name is Terentia. Dom says that nanny produces the best milk. Start with her, but don't squeeze too hard, right?"

Allerix nodded and wriggled out of his work boots. With a bucket and a generous handful of grain, he pushed open the gate and stomped barefoot through the sludge to the opposite end of the pen. It hadn't rained in days, but the lingering mud, combined with goat shit and piss, squished through his toes like sticky raisin pudding.

"I'd wager you've milked many a goat, peasant," Simon sniped over his shoulder as he took hold of the nanny's other teat.

"No, I haven't. Where I'm from, girls tend to these animals."

"Well, now you're the goatherd maiden, barbarian," Simon spat back, his tone wavering between indifferent and caustic. Simon was changing as well.

Cautiously, Allerix walked up to Terentia. The nanny goat cried and eyed him, her black rectangular pupils widening with distrust. He patted her flank and offered her grain while he reassured her. "Easy there, old girl. I won't hurt you, I hope."

With an eye on Simon's machinations, Allerix crouched and took hold of one of Terentia's teats. Her udder was swollen like a satyr's wineskin before a holiday feast. With a firm grip, he rolled his fingers down the length of the gland; a thick stream of milk squirted into the wooden bucket. Wide-eyed with delight, Allerix exclaimed, "It worked!"

Lounging on a bench outside the pen, Nic hollered. "That's a fucking milk goat, you furry twit! It's supposed to work!"

Wearing a satisfied grin, Allerix rubbed his hands together as he prepared to tackle the other teat. Suddenly, the old nanny took a step to the side, bleated and kicked him in the chest. More shocked than hurt, he fell backward into the squishy ooze.

"Argh! What did you do that for?" Allerix yelled at the animal as he pulled himself up from the slime and wiped his mud-coated hands on his short tunic. "Fucking disgusting."

Off to the side, Simon snickered while Nic cackled until his laughter dissolved into a coughing fit.

Allerix planted his hands on his hips. "I'm going to milk you, Terentia, and you're going to cooperate. No more daft shenanigans."

As he turned around to retrieve the bucket, Terentia squared her shoulders, lowered her head and butted the easy target that was Allerix's perfectly round, mud-covered bum. He was launched face first into a deep pool of slimy manure. Dazed and humiliated, he rolled up onto his knees and spat out a glob of muddy saliva.

"Enough playing with the goats, Dacian. Finish the job!" Nic barely got the words out before he doubled over. Simon pressed the back of his hand against his mouth and laughed so hard that his brunet curls bounced.

"You think this is funny?" Allerix asked before he rose to his feet and coughed up more mud.

Simon stood up. "It's bloody hilarious. Dom would laugh his balls off if he could see you now, all covered in shit—his poor little peasant knocked on his arse by that mean old nanny goat."

Allerix sloshed through the muck until he was within an arm's distance of Simon's shit-eating grin. "I'd offered to help you with this chore, Simon, and this is your gratitude? Finish milking your bitch before I knock that ingrate smirk off your face."

"Well, well—the Dacian has a nasty little temper." Simon snorted before he rushed forward and stiff-armed Allerix back two steps. "You don't order me around." Simon stormed over until he was in Alle's face. "You're a savage, an animal. You should have died in the war along with the rest of your heathen swarm."

Confused by the commotion, most of the goats meandered aimlessly around the pen, bleating loudly, while three smaller nannies huddled together in a corner. Allerix rushed forward and shoved Simon, hard; Simon nearly fell backward over one of the wandering beasts.

Alle clutched Simon's forearm and pulled him close. "You know you're right, *pup*. I should have died." He snarled before releasing his harsh grip.

Nicomedes walked over to the fence and yelled, "Lads, lads—no fighting now!"

"Let them fight."

Out of nowhere, Felix and Plautus sidled up on either side of Nicomedes and rested their elbows on the wooden railing. "We haven't enjoyed much entertainment around here lately. Let the baby bed warmers settle this spat with a bit of wrestling." Felix cupped his hands and shouted, "You *can* wrestle, can't you, Dacian?"

"A wrestling match?" Nic asked.

"Why not? What prize should we award to the victor, my dear Plautus?"

Plautus chortled and raised his hand like an official at the start of a circus race. "The winner of today's match will get an extra serving of the midday meal *and* a full cup of wine."

"Let's see you grapple like Olympians, whores! Tunics off or no one wins any wine!" Felix shouted with lusty glee. As if Nic were invisible, he leaned over him to talk with Plautus. "Might as well enjoy some flesh, right?"

"I prefer ladies' bosoms, my dear Felix, but what's the harm? Besides, the scoundrels have already ruined those clothes."

"Exactly—what's the harm? Get naked, pretty boys! Care to make a wager, my old friend?"

Plautus eyed the slaves over. "It's a fairly even match though the Dacian seems to have bulked up, hasn't he? Hmm. My coin is on the barbarian, tricky bastards they are."

"Excellent. I'll take the curly-haired Greek faun. Begin the games!"

With his eyes fixed on Allerix, Simon stripped off his tunic and threw it towards the fence. Rage twisted Simon's face, a rage born from fear and sorrow. Simon had already lost, and he knew it.

Allerix peeled off his shit-soaked tunic and spread his arms wider, wiggling his fingers. "Come at me then. Let's see how a pampered Greek slut fights."

They circled each other, weaving through the roaming goat obstacles. When the path between them cleared, Simon crouched and rushed forward. He tried to wrap his arms around Allerix's waist, but Alle jumped to the side. Simon stumbled, bumped his bum into another large goat, lost his balance, and fell into a pile of manure.

He propped himself up on his elbows and snapped. "Is that how Dacians wrestle? By cheating?"

Alle laughed. "That was a perfectly legal evasive maneuver. Here, take my hand, Simon."

"Sod off!" Simon pushed himself up onto his knees and paused to catch his breath. Just as he appeared ready to concede defeat, he jumped to his feet and dashed forward, grabbing hold of Allerix's wrist, twisting his arm until Alle fell to his knees in the slop.

"Where's your fucking evasive maneuver now, barbarian?"

"Simon," Allerix spoke softly. When Simon leaned down to listen, Alle grabbed him around the neck with his free arm and flipped Simon over on his back into the muck with a splash. He crawled over, pressed down on the smaller boy's chest with his forearm and growled. "I had a sadistic bastard of an older brother, Simon. I know how to defend myself. You're going to get hurt."

"Fuck. You." Simon rammed Allerix in the balls with his knee. A flash of blinding white light and excruciating pain ripped through Alle's body. He fell over in agony, both hands cupping his battered groin. A collective groan of sympathy rose from the crowd of spectators, which had grown to include several curious field hands.

Trying not to vomit, Alle raised his shaking hand and extended his finger to flash the surrender signal. He gasped, "I yield."

"Yield?" Simon pulled himself up out of the mud and moved back. "You're can't fucking yield. Get on your feet and fight me!"

"Simon, I don't want to fight you. I don't want their shitty wine. I only want to go home."

Simon dropped and straddled Allerix's abdomen. Face to face, their noses practically touching, he took hold of Alle's silver collar and yanked it. "Bollocks! You don't want to leave. Why would you leave when Dom's gifting you precious tokens of his affection like this costly antique necklace?"

Struggling to breathe, his testicles throbbing in pain, Allerix tried to squirm out from under Simon's weight but he was pinned. "Tokens of his affection? Are you mad? It's a fucking slave collar. I'm a piece of property, a disgrace to my people. There's no honor in being his slave whore."

Simon's lips quivered and his face turned red as he pressed his palm against his chest. Tears streamed down through the mud, creating stripes on his young cheeks. "This—what did you call me—this *pampered Greek slut* is a beloved and valued servant of the Lion of the Lucky Fourth. Dominus counts on—no, he treasures my obedience and my loyalty. I have a purpose, a family, and a home. I have cartloads of fucking honor, savage."

Simon released Alle's collar, rose to his feet, and hissed as he kicked a heavy spray of mud at Allerix's face. After he'd raked his slime-coated curls back with his fingers, he straightened his posture, lifting his chin, and picked up his bucket half-filled with milk. He headed toward the stable house; wet clumps of lumpy sludge slid down the channel in the center of his naked back. Simon paused before the throng of onlookers to place the pail on the ground and bowed.

"I do hope you enjoyed the match, sirs. Here's your fresh milk, Plautus, sir. There are splashes of mud in it, though. Now if it pleases you all, I'd like to wash off this filth before the midday meal."

"Bloody good show, lad! Off to the baths with you, then. You earned that wine—two hefty cups, I'd say." Felix clapped like a drunken, giddy buffoon as Plautus picked up the bucket and shook his head before tottering to the kitchen. The field slaves glanced at each other and silently departed for their midday feeding.

Still winded and in pain, Allerix struggled to sit up. Nic strolled over with an old, frayed horse blanket and wrapped it around his torso. Alle opened his mouth to protest but stopped.

"Are you all right?" Nic asked as he dabbed splotches of mud off Alle's face.

"I'll live." Allerix touched his aching groin and winced.

"We'll find you another tunic—a better one—and don't be too angry with Simon. The lad's a dreamer, and he's beginning to realize his dreams will never come true. It's sad to watch, but it was considerate of you to let him win, Alle."

"You just called me by my real name for the first time." Alle forced a smile as he readjusted the dusty cloth around his filthy torso "I didn't let him win, Nic. I was a fool to think he'd fight fair. Simon's one cagey, angry little shit."

"Simon's a survivor. We all are—so far. By the gods, you stink. Here, let me help you up." Nicomedes smiled, extending his hand.

Grunting and groaning, Alle slowly pushed himself up to his feet with Nic's assistance. He was fucking hungry, but first he needed a bath. Allerix, princeling of the house of Thiamarkos, had a pair of bruised balls and a load of goat shit lodged up his royal bumhole.

～

THE IMPERIAL RESIDENCE ON THE PALATINE HILL, ROME

GAIUS ASCENDED THE FINAL treads of the broad marble stairs; with each step, the hobnails of his leather soles clattered across the polished stone. Colorful veined slabs and gilded bronze ornaments covered every dazzling surface of the enormous entrance to the palace. Rome wallowed in her obscene wealth, celebrating and reinforcing her ubiquitous power with grand edifices sheathed in marble and gold. And no ruler of Rome—not even the Divine Augustus—had ever amassed such omnipotent imperial authority as had Marcus Ulpius Traianus. He was a living divinity and a triumphant hero—the man who ruled all other men. Thank the gods Marcus was also a relatively just emperor and a fair son of a bitch.

When Gaius had returned home from the tombs out on the Tiburtina to bathe and change into his civilian clothes, he sent word ahead to the palace to inform Emperor Trajan of his impending visit. Marcus didn't appreciate surprises. The emperor would be waiting for him in the imperial audience hall. If his former guardian received him from atop his elevated gold and ivory throne, Gaius was in deep shit.

He wiped his sweaty palms and steadied his breathing. So many memories of his childhood days as Marcus's ward he wished he could erase from his mind forever. The fear and the loneliness and the resentment he'd harbored all those years spent far from home. When Gaius reached the spacious landing, he scratched his scruffy beard, rearranged the folds of his toga over his left arm, and took a deep breath.

Time to swat the hornet's nest.

"Lo! Halt in the name of our most revered Emperor Trajan."

The Praetorian Prefect, Tiberius Claudius Livianus, along with twenty armed men of the Guard, marched onto the wide landing with their hands on their sword hilts. Several of the younger helmeted soldiers were little more than babies, their faces discolored by pimples and their wide eyes wary from inexperience.

"There you are, Livianus. I want to thank you for stationing one of your men at the home of Lucius Petronius. We wouldn't want anything to happen to the counselor's bereaved widow, now would we?"

Livianus's eyes twitched. "Commander Fabius? I didn't recognize you with the facial hair, sir. I wasn't aware you'd scheduled an audience today."

"I'm in fucking mourning for my dead friend, Prefect. And apparently you haven't been given access to all of the emperor's correspondence. One wonders what else slips past your notice."

"Are you certain our esteemed Emperor is expecting you? I'm quite confident I would have been informed, Commander."

Gaius's false smile disappeared as he gripped the handle of his dagger through the heavy wool of his toga. "How confident of that are you, exactly?"

"For the love of all that is sacred, Livianus, step aside and let my noble brother pass!"

In his colorful, gold-threaded garb, Publius sauntered out of the doorway to the left of the landing. With his typical flourish, he ambled over and snarled into Livianus's ear. "Should the Fates spare us from untimely deaths, you do realize either Gaius or I will be the next emperor of Rome, don't you? Livianus, my dear boar, you've managed to piss off the both of us."

Gaius chuckled. "How very imperial of you, Publius. I'm impressed."

"But did I intimidate you, Gaius?" Publius jested, his arms outstretched for a hug, as the crowd of guards parted to clear the way.

Gaius walked past them without so much as a glance and pulled his thespian brother into a tight embrace. "I'm bloody shaking in my boots."

After a long hug, Publius placed one hand on his own heart and the other on Gaius's shoulder. "My despair over the death of our dear associate, Lucius Petronius, can not be measured. By the gods, I was with him, laughing and sipping some fabulous wine only moments before he was cut down in the street."

"So I've heard. We will capture the criminals who murdered Lucius, Publius. Of that, I can assure you. There are many candidates I could name off the top of my fucking head." Gaius raised his brows before addressing the Prefect, "Livianus, were you born in Spain like my ward brother and our noble Emperor?"

"I'm Italian, a proud native of the district of Latium."

"Ah, then we're practically related. I was born in Rome, as were my ancestors. What is your birth town in our fair Latium?"

Livianus puffed his chest out. "Tusculum, sir."

"Lovely place—fertile and most scenic. And you grew up there?"

"Until I came of age and was sent to Rome to begin my career in the army, sir."

"Then, as a fellow native son of Latium, you should have no trouble understanding this." Gaius raised his right hand, lifted his middle finger, and twisted and jabbed his wrist in a most indecent manner.

"I believe all soldiers, especially those of us from Latium, understand that particular gesture, sir."

"Excellent. It happens to be one of my personal favorites." Gaius curled his fingers into a fist. "If you ever block my path again, Prefect, I'll yank those shiny insignia baubles along with your fuck ugly head out of your ignoble arsehole. Understood? Dismiss your men!"

Livianus narrowed his beady eyes and replied, "Yes, Commander."

"Enough small talk with the help, Gaius. Come, the emperor is waiting for us." Publius seized his arm.

"Us?"

"He sent for me—his messenger interrupted a lovely massage—after your request for an audience arrived. I love your beard, by the way. Are you keeping it after the mourning period ends?"

"No."

"Pity. It's spectacular—all coppery and thick and curly. I'm bloody envious. Listen, I'd heard reports of your spectacular parade through the city this morning. So sorry to have missed it, Gaius. Care to tell your dear brother the purpose of your visit to the palace? Another misguided performance, perhaps?"

"I'm here to take it up the arse and have my ear chewed off if I'm lucky."

"You're the favorite of Fortuna. You are always lucky, brother."

Together they walked down the length of towering vaulted corridor, its floors carpeted with colorful pictures in mosaic: heroic myths and hunting scenes and gods frolicking with mortals. Six older

Praetorians greeted them at the entrance to the imperial audience chamber and opened the massive bronze doors nearly two stories high.

"Commander Gaius Fabius Rufus and Legate Publius Aelius Hadrianus, Caesar!"

As the doors closed behind them with an ominous bang, Gaius exhaled with relief. Marcus was not seated on his throne; he was standing by one of the windows overlooking the palatial gardens. The emperor smiled and waved them to enter.

"Greetings, Caesar," they mumbled simultaneously as they bowed.

"Caesar? By bloody Jove's randy cock, when my boys refer to me by my most formal title within the walls of the palace, there must be trouble. And look at your whiskered face, Gaius. Now both you and Publius are bearded little bastards. Let's retire to the couches, lads. Phaedimus, my sweet, bring us wine."

While Marcus reclined on his side, Gaius and Publius sat on an adjacent couch, hip to hip, their hands buried in their laps. They acted more like remorseful scamps awaiting the paddle than two grown successors to the purple.

The young attractive steward, Phaedimus, deposited a platter with a silver pitcher and cups on the low marble table; a rosy-cheeked slave boy wearing a scandalously short tunic sampled the drink and then poured the wine. After Marcus brushed his hand over the curve of his cupbearer's exposed prepubescent bum, he handed Gaius a silver drinking vessel and asked, "So tell me, what the fuck did you think you were doing this morning, Commander Fabius? I assume you're here to clarify the intent of your actions."

"I led my family out to the Tomb of the Petronii for sacrifices to honor my dead friend, Caesar."

"Seems harmless enough. So why was it I'd heard you'd put on a pompous show of force down the damn Tiburtine road? And will you stop bloody calling me Caesar!"

"Yes, Dominus." When Gaius paused to choose his next words, Publius nudged him with his elbow and spoke up.

"Father, I'm certain Gaius meant no offense. A procession of one's household out to the suburban tombs is certainly not treasonous."

"What a curious circumstance we have here. Normally, Gaius is the one defending your questionable behavior, Publius."

Gaius coughed into his fist and declared, "I demand justice for Lucius Petronius Celsus, sir. I intend to use all of my authority to apprehend his murderers."

"You demand? Your *authority*, Gaius?"

Marcus slowly rose to his staggeringly lofty height and looked down on them both. "Have those scarlet bristles sapped the sense from your mind? How dare you suggest I have no intention of capturing Lucius Petronius's murderers! My men are scouring this city, day and night. As we speak, my spies are investigating every person who may have been involved in this crime. What more would you have me do?"

"Authorize me to hunt down the vermin, personally. My esteemed Emperor."

"And allow the leader of the Lucky Fourth and his veteran clients to prowl the streets of Rome with their swords drawn? I need you on the battlefield, Gaius, not recklessly slicing your way through the wretched urban mob."

"The wars are over, sir."

"War is never over, my fierce, whiskered lion cub." Marcus reached down and ran his hand through Gaius's amber locks. He tugged on a clump of Gaius's curls; Gaius blinked and folded his hands together over his crotch as the Emperor continued. "We shall use this brief interlude in the fighting to celebrate our great victories, replenish our legions, and stockpile sufficient supplies for the next campaign. We will return to the glory of the battlefields soon, Commander Fabius."

"And peace affords us time to embellish our capital with splendid shrines to the gods as well." Publius interjected a tad too enthusiastically, but Gaius was grateful for the change of topic. He'd be damned if Marcus made him cower like a helpless boy. Not again.

Never again.

"Have you reviewed my latest designs for the Forum temple, Father?" Publius asked.

"I gave them to Apollodorus to evaluate," Marcus replied with blatant disinterest as he slowly removed his hand from Gaius's hair. "Now listen to me, both of you. I will find Lucius's killers—and when I do, they will be publicly executed in a most gruesome manner after a fair trial. We have laws, for shit's sake! Lucius Petronius understood that. He was a man of the law."

Marcus marched to the nearest window, pushed aside the curtains, and sighed. "I adored that handsome young man. He had brains, wit, and noble bearing. I'd once asked his father to surrender guardianship of him to me. He was just a small Cupid of a lad, but even then I recognized Lucius Petronius was special. Unfortunately, his old man denied my request, and I was in no position at that time to force his hand."

Gaius and Publius stared at one another in disbelief.

Publius mouthed, "Did you know?"

Gaius pressed his lips together and shook his head. Thank holy Vesta and all her maiden priestesses that Lucius's father had been a responsible head of his household. The thought of Lucius as a bright-eyed innocent under the lecherous thumb of Marcus sent a shiver down Gaius's spine.

Gaius cleared his throat and insisted, "Lucius had no interest in the throne, sir. He could barely hold a sword, and after he was thrown from his horse—"

"A strong emperor doesn't need to engage in hand to hand combat, Gaius. He merely has to pay his soldiers handsomely and on time. It's only foolish pugilists like you and I who insist on participating in the bloodshed."

Marcus turned around and swallowed a deep draft from his cup.

"I am sponsoring gladiatorial contests in honor of our esteemed Lucius tomorrow. You will both be in attendance at the great amphitheater, as will your wives. Afterwards, we'll sacrifice two prized bulls to Jupiter and Mars and enjoy a festive family feast here at the palace. Guaranteed fun times for all. Have I made myself clear?"

"Yes, Caesar."

"Good." Marcus leaned down and blew his nose into his slave boy's sleeve. "It's past time for my bath. You two bewhiskered scoundrels may leave."

Gaius and Publius bowed once more before exiting the hall; together they trotted side by side down the cavernous hallway.

"Did it please you to utter the offense of treason, little brother?"

Publius's mouth fell open. "I was defending you, Gaius."

"Of course you were. Tell me, what do you know about the substantial coin missing from the imperial coffers?"

"I only know Lucius had been charged to investigate the thievery." Publius scampered to keep up. "Nothing more."

"The subject never arose during your coquetry with our dear counselor at Pliny's dinner party?"

"No, it did not. And, despite what you may have heard, I wasn't flirting with Lucius. Gaius, if you think for one moment you're going to accuse me of being involved in his murder, I will—"

Gaius stopped and grabbed Publius's blond beard. "You will fucking what?"

"I will—I will not defend you before Father anymore," he stammered in a surge of choppy syllables.

Gaius snorted and stepped down onto the broad landing. "I don't need your inept protection, princess."

"I will tell him about your affliction."

Gaius spun around, his eyes narrowed like dagger blades. "Did you just threaten me?"

"If you dare accuse me of involvement in this most egregious crime—a crime of which I am completely innocent—I will inform our father that his precious lion cub suffers from the dreaded lunacy."

Gaius slowly stepped back up onto the floor of the hallway and squeezed Publius's face between his hands. With a dimpled smile, Gaius purred, "Your allegiance is most valuable to me, little brother. Gods willing, one of us will indeed rule our great empire, so be damn careful not to rattle my cage. This lion cub doesn't forgive empty threats as easily as Marcus does. Now excuse me. I have an appointment to meet Cornelius Tacitus at the archives. Stay out of trouble. I shall see you and your lovely wife in the morning for a glorious day of blood and gore."

Through his squished mouth, Publius gurgled, "We look forward to spending our day with you and our graceful sister, Marcia Servilia."

"You're endearing when you capitulate." Gaius kissed Publius's forehead, gently patted his sweaty cheek, and stormed down the steps.

When he was halfway down the first flight of stairs, Publius shouted, "You're an unbearable, arrogant fucker, Gaius!"

"Lick my patrician arsehole, Greekling." With a broad smile, Gaius raised his middle finger and flashed the soldier's salute.

6

The Tabularium, Old Forum, Rome

G AIUS LOWERED HIS SHOULDER and shoved the jammed door open
with such force it hit the brick wall with a bang. At the far end
of the archive reading room, his former mentor didn't move.
Hunched over a long wooden table, Tacitus was either engrossed with
his research or he'd become harder of hearing. Probably both. Gaius
coughed loudly into his fist before announcing his presence.

"Greetings, *magister*."

Tacitus turned around, his grin stern but affectionate, and ambled
over to embrace him. The historian's gait was less steady than the last
time Gaius had seen him. Close in age to the emperor, Publius
Cornelius Tacitus was still a cantankerous crocodile, but he'd lost
much of his exuberance.

"Gaius Fabius! You're late, my son. Not that I'm surprised since
you never were the sort of pupil who arrived promptly for his
lessons."

"I may not have been your most punctual acolyte, but I was always
your favorite," Gaius retorted, squeezing the older man's shoulders.

"Yes and indeed you still are. It's marvelous to see you back in
Rome, although that red fur on your face is most disconcerting. Do
shave it off after the mourning period like a proper Roman."

"I intend to, sir."

"Marvelous. For a moment there I feared you were going Greek on us like your foolish bearded brother." Tacitus shook his head as he grabbed hold of Gaius's hand. "My condolences on the loss of your close associate, Lucius Petronius. He was a just and moral man."

Gaius nodded in gratitude. "He will be missed. I've come straight from the palace, hence the unavoidable delay." Gaius tugged on the fabric of his formal attire. "And the rare sight of this soldier clad in a cumbersome toga. Our esteemed Emperor sends you his kind regards, sir."

With a skeptical sigh, Tacitus lowered his voice. "I sincerely doubt that. Marcus hasn't invited me to the palace for years. Did our great king admonish you for that parade stunt of yours this morning?"

"For the love of Hercules, is every soul in this city aware of my impulsive little procession?"

Tacitus sat down in the nearest chair, clasped his hands in front of his mouth, and mumbled, "That was the point, was it not, Gaius?"

"Subtlety has never been my strong suit. Fortunately, the emperor seems to have excused my rash conduct. You, however, should refrain from referring to our esteemed Emperor as *king*. Your mockery could prove lethal, *magister*."

Tacitus laughed; he'd lost two more teeth since before the last war. "Marcus tolerates my occasional outbursts of insolence as long as I stick to publishing my useless chronicles and avoid public life. Since he hasn't put a sword through me yet, I'm confident I shall live out my days growing more grey and feeble with each passing season."

Gaius strolled over to his former adviser and rubbed his head. "You were grey. You're now bald, my dear Tacitus."

Tacitus enjoyed a deep belly laugh and extended his arm; Gaius helped him rise from his chair.

"Congratulations on another successful campaign, Commander

Fabius. The Lucky Fourth has brought glory to our empire once again. I look forward to the triumphal games. But Gaius, why of all places did you wish to meet me here in the bowels of the state archives? We could be at my home, relaxing under the arbors by the fountain."

"Perhaps next time, sir." Gaius squeezed the small piece of papyrus in his right hand. "I'm here to review the registers of identified Dacian noble houses, the lists of the princelings killed or captured during the wars. I have a name which intrigues me, and few men know how to navigate these archives as well as you, sir."

"The Dacian registers? Those ledgers would be on the third floor, in the room at the far end of the hallway on the right. We'll use the stairs over there."

Tacitus pointed to a steep and narrow vaulted staircase connecting all five stories of the enormous depository building. Despite its colossal size, the Tabularium was packed to the rafters with senatorial proceedings, legal documents, and war records dating back to the early days of Republic. Thank the gods the Emperor had started construction on a new administrative center with additional storage spaces. Rome was bloody drowning in canisters of papyrus scrolls.

Gaius grabbed hold of the senator's slim arm and held fast. While he'd been away campaigning in Dacia, he'd received word from Rome that Tacitus had suffered a bad fall and was bedridden for weeks. The old bloke was damn lucky he hadn't split his fucking skull open.

They took the stairs slowly. It was an arduous climb, but together—step by cautious step—they made their way up to the third floor and down to the storage room.

"Over here, Gaius. The registers for the recent wars are arranged in two sections. The shelves up there hold the lists for the first war against the Dacian menace, while those contain the tallies for the second. Where do you wish to start?"

"The second war, first scroll."

"You know what you want. That should make our quest more expedient." Tacitus waved a finger towards the top shelf; the skittish archive slave scrambled up the ladder, took hold of the hefty bundle and carried it down before spreading the rolls out on the reading table.

Gaius rifled through the batch, searching for the tag attached to the first scroll of the alphabetized lists. "Here it is."

After he'd pulled a lamp closer, Gaius laid the crumpled piece of paper he'd brought from the villa on the table and smoothed the wrinkled papyrus. "Here's the name that interests me: *Allethodokoles*."

Tacitus chuckled and tapped the hastily written word. "That atrocious combination of letters is not a noble Dacian name, Gaius. It must be a false moniker of some insignificant pretender or a haughty peasant with starry-eyed aspirations."

"I suspect you're right. But let's have a look in any case, shall we?"

Gaius unfurled the scroll and scanned the entries in the neat list. No record of an Allethodokoles, as he'd expected. The fabricated name was fucking ridiculous. He traced his fingertip over the record of Dacian names. No mention of Allerix or his capture. He breathed a sigh of relief and asked, "Where's the last scroll for the second war?"

After he'd rummaged through the pile, Tacitus pushed the roll across the desk. "Here you are. What are you looking for now, son?"

"Nothing more than a hunch. Tell the slave to fetch the records for the first war while I review this list."

While Tacitus was delivering meticulous instructions to the archive worker, Gaius quickly unrolled the scroll and found what he was hoping to find—the name that had riled his raven-haired Dacian in the villa playroom.

Tarbus

First son of Thiamarkos.

Killed during the siege of Sarmizegetusa. Inked.

Ah! So this Tarbus wasn't Allerix's mysterious lover after all. He was Alle's older brother—a very dead older brother. And yet the mere mention of Tarbus's name had caused his cub's hackles to rise. This knowledge could come in handy down the road.

But if Tarbus perished during Rome's siege of the great Dacian capital, why the fuck hadn't he heard of this fellow? Tarbus was the son of a royal house, albeit a minor kingdom, and the attack on Sarmizegetusa had been carried out under Gaius's direct command. With his own damn sword, he'd cut down scores of Dacian fighters during those bloody days. What if he'd killed Alle's older brother? Would Allerix curse him or thank him?

Gaius scanned the names written below Tarbus but found no record for Thiamarkos. Alle's insignificant father must have either perished during the first war or was alive and hiding with the other refugees in the Carpathian Mountains. If the latter were true, it would explain Allerix's thirst for escape. As the details fell into place, Gaius licked his lips with satisfaction.

"Well, that was for naught," he complained as he quickly rolled up the record and shoved it under the bottom of the pile.

"Here is the first scroll from the first war." After Tacitus had handed it to him, Gaius pretended to review the names. No record of an Allethodokoles, of course, although there were at least twenty Alexandros characters listed. Dacian fathers must have once had lofty ambitions for their now defeated, disgraced dead sons.

"And again, nothing." Gaius dropped his head to exaggerate feigned frustration.

"There's one more, Gaius. An addendum to the registers for the second war this slave discovered shoved back behind the canisters. It's slim but here it is."

Just as Tacitus had warned, the supplement was thin and incomplete, but there he was.

Shit.

Allerix

Second son of Thiamarkos.

Captured pr. Kal. Iunius. No markings.

Gaius pressed his lips together. He'd been dining with Lucius on the evening he'd received word of Alle's capture from his agent. He burned that communication immediately after he'd read it, sharing its contents with no one, not even Lucius. But now here was this brief but official record of Allerix's existence—worse, his capture. This addendum needed to disappear as well. Should Gaius's ruse ever be discovered, Alle would be condemned to the beasts and the Lion of the Lucky Fourth charged with treason.

Scratching his scalp vigorously with his left hand to distract his companions, Gaius wrapped the slender supplementary list around his right pointer finger before he shoved it under the heavy folds of his toga. "There's nothing of interest in the addendum either. I fear I've wasted your valuable time, Tacitus."

"Nonsense. As long as you agree to escort me home and share a pitcher of grape with your old teacher, I'd say this venture was most successful."

"A brilliant proposal," Gaius replied while he assembled the messy pile of scrolls into a neater stack for the slave to return to the shelves. "This brutally long day has left me parched. I expect your best wine, my friend."

"Of course." Tacitus patted him on the back. "Only the best for my triumphant student."

They walked out, arm in arm when the archive slave spoke up.

"Sirs, I can't seem to locate the addendum."

Gaius turned and warned with a wag of his finger, "If the chief magistrate of the archives discovers any of those records have gone missing, it'll be your head that gets chopped off. I've heard he's a right vicious bastard who doesn't tolerate sloppy housekeeping."

The slave shut his mouth and nodded as he scooped up the unwieldy pile of scrolls. Gaius smiled; for slaves and freemen alike, self-preservation was paramount.

When they finally exited the arched entrance to the archive building and stepped out into the bright light of the Old Forum, Gaius touched the edge of the stolen papyrus. Before they'd left the storage room, he slid it into his scabbard alongside the blade of his dagger. With the record now in his possession, Allerix, second son of Thiamarkos, was all but erased from history.

Fuck the sacrosanctity of the archives. Fuck the law.

He failed Lucius, but—gods be damned—Allerix would not be shredded to bloody bits for the mob's amusement in the sandy arena of the amphitheater.

He would keep his Dacian princeling safe.

Unharmed and his alone.

Gaius wrapped his arm around Tacitus's spindly shoulders and exhaled before he mused, "Have you ever wondered what would happen if the state archives were ever burned to ashes, *magister*? I suppose it's a bloody miracle the records weren't destroyed during the great conflagration of Nero's tyranny."

"Fortunately that catastrophic inferno was extinguished before it could damage the archive building. For nine long days, the entire populace watched in horror as the flames engulfed much the city. I was still living with my family in southern Gaul during that hot summer, but the reports my father received from the capital were terrifying."

They passed a row of shops; the smell of freshly baked loaves and sweet pastries filled the air. If marble and gold were the emblems of imperial power, these delightful fragrances were the citizens' daily rewards for Rome's conquests. Victory in war brought not only peace and riches but also some fucking delicious bread.

Tacitus stopped at the last stall and purchased a honey cake. He devoured it in three bites while Gaius continued, "Nero's fire will not soon be forgotten, *magister*. But imagine, for just a moment, how simple it would be for our ancestors, our enemies—for us—to simply disappear from history in some frightful blaze. Poof!"

"You jest, Gaius, but pray to the almighty gods it never happens. We rely on the registers to preserve our accomplishments and safeguard the past. Recollection alone is far too fragile and capricious."

"Memory of our deeds will endure only as long as the papyrus scrolls survive the ravages of time. Perhaps that's why the old farts in the priesthoods exhort us to commission portraits made of bronze and stone."

Tacitus nodded, his face serious, when Gaius added with a smirk, "Future generations may forget our names and our accomplishments, but apparently they'll remember us by our unsightly heads." He playfully patted Tacitus's crooked back.

The bald senator chuckled as he wiped the yellow crumbs from his lips. "You are an incorrigible skeptic, my dear Gaius. I suppose, if the priests are correct, we ought to put on a damn good face for the sculptors. Posterity is a famously cruel judge."

"Don't worry others will judge your portrait statue by that mammoth proboscis of yours, my old friend. Everyone knows the noses are the first to break off."

~

THE FLAVIAN AMPHITHEATER, ROME

As THEY STROLLED PAST the guards standing at attention along both sides of the wide, vaulted passageway, a thunderous roar shook the travertine blocks of the great amphitheater. Ahead, a bright veil of fine dust clouded the arched opening leading to the open-air auditorium. All of Rome was here, each man assigned to a section and row according to his wealth and status. Their booming cheers signaled another death, another spectacle of slaughter.

Unfortunately, there was little time left to enjoy the cooler air and invisibility of the tunnel. A few more feet and he and his wife would ascend the staircase, step out onto the elevated platform, and wave to the throng before taking their seats in the imperial box. Gaius gripped Marcia's hand and pulled her to a stop.

"Are you feeling better?" he asked.

Marcia wouldn't look at him; she merely flashed a pained smile and nodded. Crowds made her twitchy, and she hated gladiatorial contests even more than she disliked chariot races. But it was time for his dutiful wife to push aside her distaste. It was time for her to perform—another unavoidable consequence of her marriage to Rome's second in command.

"It was the poached ostrich egg which upset your stomach. Damn things are too rich to eat for a first meal." He cupped her face with his hands. "We shouldn't be here long. At this late hour, only one or two combats remain. You'll have ample opportunity to lie down and recover in time for tonight's festivities."

"Are you upset we're late?"

"Why on earth would I be angry? Marcia, the less time I'm forced to spend with my family, the better. But I am very grateful you insisted on accompanying me."

Marcia smiled as she nudged him forward. "Of course I'm here. Marcus's games are in honor of our dear Lucius. It would appear unseemly to miss them, no matter how nauseous I may feel."

Gaius glanced to the left and the right. The Praetorians stood at attention in a straight line along the access corridor, their faces obscured by the shadows of their broad-brimmed steel helmets. The palace's lethal gang of obedient machines.

"Lucius despised gladiatorial spectacles. Now if instead the emperor had sponsored a theatrical festival with choruses of cherubic boys singing his praises in Sapphic meter? By the gods, Luc would have cherished such a celebration."

"I know, but the games are tradition," Marcia replied, fussing with her dress. "And I also know the Emperor will be most cross at our tardiness."

"Marcus will be irritated, and he'll grumble a bit, but nothing worse. Plotina, of course, will be apoplectic." He grinned and squeezed Marcia's hand again. "I'll handle it, wife. Try to relax and, if need be, avert your eyes from the arena."

They glanced at each other one final time before stepping into the bright, hazy sunshine onto a marble platform bordered by a bronze parapet.

"We've arrived between shows." Gaius tipped his chin towards the elliptical stage below. Weaving through pieces of shattered metal and wood, two attendants crouched as they hauled off an enormous battered fighter. The Thracian champion, holding his small rectangular shield high above his head in triumph, headed for the tunnel to the gladiators' nearby quarters. Gaius waited for the dwindling cheers of the audience to subside before he raised his hand, which encouraged an outburst of applause led by the veterans in attendance.

"They adore you," Marcia noted with little enthusiasm.

"Don't let the mob's insipid flattery fool you. Until Marcus makes a decision about the succession, I'm nothing more than another expendable soldier. Come, let's take our seats."

All the members of the imperial court were present, decked head to toe in their finest garb. Marcus and Plotina sat perched on their gilded chairs, front and center, surrounded by family, senior allies in the Senate, a high priest or two, and the chief court advisors. Publius was there, as were Pliny, and the consuls, Minicius and Senecio. Clad in a rainbow of bright fabrics, they prattled to one another like regal peacocks but not a single one of them had been born a patrician.

Rome's well-born families were dying off, slowly replaced by rich plebians and provincials.

And then he saw her.

She was seated on the other side of her husband.

Shit, he hadn't seen her in nearly two years; they'd barely spoken ten words since her marriage to his ward brother. Sabina wore a pale blue gown trimmed in gold and copper threads, her wavy blonde hair braided and tied back into an elaborate bun. She folded her hands and turned to say something to her pinched-faced mother, Matidia. Both women tried their best to pretend he hadn't arrived.

Her mother said something back, and Sabina laughed. Despite her mask of feminine propriety, anger flashed every time she moved her lips, a deep resentment born the day Plotina ended Sabina's brief and unofficial betrothal to Gaius.

Vibia Sabina, daughter of a dead former consul, had every right to despise all of them, including the Emperor, her great uncle. They all betrayed her, or so she often complained during those days after Plotina's grand announcement in the audience hall. But even clueless Publius would now be forced to admit the once scrawny, awkward girl had blossomed into a stunning beauty: high cheekbones, a rosebud mouth, lithesome curves, and those bright, clever eyes. What a bloody sham of a marriage. The girl deserved a more attentive husband than the Greekling.

Fucking meddlesome Plotina, forever spinning her web of schemes and fantasies.

"You're late, Commander Fabius," Marcus barked as they walked by, crinkling his aquiline nose in displeasure. Powerful gusts of warm wind blew overhead. The giant canvas awning—a naval engineer's ingenious invention to provide shade for the sweltering spectators—flapped up and down like the wings of some colossal vulture fighting to stay aloft.

Gaius paused and bowed. "Greetings, Caesar. We were delayed by unforeseen circumstances. Please, accept my apologies and—"

"I'm afraid it was my fault," Marcia interrupted, her voice cracking mid-sentence. "I fell ill this morning, my most esteemed Emperor."

Marcus rose from his seat and extended his hand. With genuine concern in his eyes, he asked, "My dearest child, is your health better now?"

"Much better, sir. Thank you for your concern."

With a wave of her hand, Plotina sighed in annoyance as Marcus sat back down. "First our fair Sabina and now you, Marcia? I once had hope the wives of this court would have constitutions as robust as their ambitions. Alas, you're both as fragile as glass vessels. Empty, brittle containers."

"I appreciate your heartfelt sympathies, my beloved Empress,"

Marcia replied with a sardonic smile.

Gaius covered his mouth to shield his grin and turned away. Down in the arena, the next four combatants circled the sandy floor, adjusting their armor and testing their weapons. As he and Marcia settled into their seats, the gladiators separated into pairs. On the left, a heavy-set Thracian brute swung his short curved sword with skill. His opponent, a paunchy middle-aged man, armed with the equipment of a Murmillo, sliced his long gladius through the air only to hit himself in his shin guard before tripping over his long shield.

"This should be fucking quick," Gaius grumbled.

"Care to make a wager, dear brother?" Publius inquired as he wiped is perspiring brow.

"No."

Publius groused. "You've become a right bore, Gaius. Who in Rome doesn't love a good gladiatorial fight?"

"War depletes most soldiers' interest in this choreographed slaughter—at least for those who've experienced the barbarity of battle first hand. But you wouldn't know about the horrors of hand to hand combat, would you?"

Publius turned his back in a huff.

"Brother?" Gaius paused and waited until Publius had turned to face him. "I've received several alarming reports concerning the conduct of your associates. Just yesterday, a group of your clients shouted disgraceful insults at my veterans who were simply strolling through Pompey's portico. Control your wayward ducklings, little brother, or I will."

Publius chuckled; his breath smelled like peppery cheese crusted to the sole of a beggar's foot. "Disgraceful insults? I'll have you know one of my loyal and most competent secretaries was stabbed to death three days past in one of the safer neighborhoods on the Aventine."

"By whom?"

"We don't know. Despite the new security patrols, this bloody city is as dangerous as ever. First Lucius Petronius and now my dear Myron. I'm wary of leaving the palace some nights." Publius scrubbed his flaxen beard before grabbing Gaius by the wrist. "I don't know who killed Lucius, or why. I assume his murder was related to his theft investigation, but the emperor deliberately barred me from all deliberations." Publius dropped his voice. "He wouldn't even divulge the specifics of the case to our beloved Empress. Marcus doesn't trust anyone."

Gaius grit his teeth. "Let go of my fucking hand, Greekling."

"Gaius, you must believe me."

"Lads! There will be no bickering between you two today. This a celebration."

In unison, Gaius and Publius turned to face their former guardian, the unequivocal ruler of the civilized world. Marcus tossed back a hefty gulp of wine before he smiled and raised his cup. "Let us enjoy the remainder of the games!"

A palace slave rushed over with a platter of full cups; they each selected a silver goblet for the salute. "To your generous celebrations, Caesar!"

Down below, their every move scrutinized by over fifty thousand pairs of eyes, the second pair of fighters tested each other's mettle. A lean-muscled Retiarius attempted to toss his unwieldy net over his foe, an ox of a Secutor. The armed bull stepped to the side and waited for the uncoordinated idiot to untangle his net from the prongs of his trident. Gaius leaned over and spoke sarcastically into Marcia's ear, "No expense was spared for this farce."

Marcia shrugged and exhaled a hushed chuckle. "Perhaps the organizers ran out of professional gladiators? I'm certain I've seen that portly one with the long sword in the Forum selling fabrics in the markets near the Temple of the Divine Augustus. Gaius, why is that fellow on the right with the net not wearing armor?"

"The Retiarius isn't permitted armor. According to the rules, he can use only the weapons of Poseidon and his wits if he has any."

"But the other man is so much larger and more heavily equipped. It seems an unfair match."

"Perceptions can be misleading, Marcia. If the Retiarius is quick on his feet, he can force that armored mule to chase him. It's as hot as a potter's kiln down there, and that gear is heavy. Should the Secutor become tired and winded, the Retiarius can simply ensnare him and finish him off with one clean thrust of his trident. That's if he has the skill, mind you."

"So there's a strategy to this madness?"

"Some might believe so. Our dear Publius finds these contests most riveting.

"What's your opinion?"

"These shows are nothing more than orchestrated and costly pantomimes designed to entertain the riotous proletariat and placate our pitiless gods." Gaius sighed and closed his eyes. The day wasn't half over. He still had to stomach this evening's dinner with his crazed family.

"Caesar, a message from the Praetorian Prefect." The imperial freedman announced with a quick bow before handing Marcus a sealed scroll. Gaius glanced over his shoulder. Where was Prefect Livianus? The serpent wouldn't miss an opportunity to sidle up to the emperor in front of such a large and adoring crowd.

"Who are you looking for?" Marcia asked.

"Livianus. He should be here."

"I doubt he's far. You did notice Aurelia, didn't you?"

"Where?"

"To your left, three rows up. She's sitting beside Marciana."

There she was, bouncing in her seat, babbling incessantly as her hands gestured with each witless comment. Aurelia's trapped companion, the Emperor's elder sister, Marciana, nodded in response every so often, a practiced smile plastered to her face like a well-worn comedic mask. Unlike Luc's despicable widow, Marciana was a virtuous matron: kind, generous, and perceptive. At fifty-nine years, she radiated a glow far brighter than her younger sister-in-law, the Empress.

Gaius faced forward and crossed his arms. "That bitch has some bloody nerve showing her weasel snout in my presence."

"Lucius was her husband. As his widow, Aurelia is expected to attend games in his honor. Be patient, Gaius." Patting the back of his hand, Marcia sighed when the official raised his hand to signal the start of the contests.

Contest was a generous description; slaughter would have been more apt.

The Thracian killed the rotund Murmillo with three precise stabs of his short blade. No mercy, no appeal to spare his life; the fabric merchant-turned-gladiator no doubt had cheated a good amount of coin from his customers over the years. The mob delighted in the criminal's gruesome but quick death. In contrast, the helmetless Retiarius faired better, for a while. The amateur net-thrower lasted two full rounds of sparring before kneeling to beg for clemency, which Marcus duly denied to the applause of the spectators. Presumably under orders to prolong the mob's gratification, the Secutor made slow and grisly work of Retiarius's execution.

"Fucking predictable," Gaius griped before covering his mouth to stifle a yawn.

Marcus leaned over. "If you'd arrived on time, you would have enjoyed the earlier combats, Commander. I enlisted the best professional fighters in all of Rome to honor Counselor Petronius. This morning's gladiators were highly trained and well matched. By the gods, their sword skills were truly heroic. I spared all of them, every single one." The emperor beamed as he sat back and slapped the arms of his chair with his palms.

Unblinking and stone-faced, Gaius stated flatly, "I've no doubt Lucius's spirit was most impressed, Caesar."

"Hmm? I do hope you are right, Gaius. Lucius Petronius Celsus deserves the grandest of spectacles." Marcus looked around for a specific servant and summoned him over. "I've arranged a special finale, a treat to celebrate the great achievements of our dear departed counselor of the courts."

Plotina furrowed her brow and asked, "Have you planned a surprise without my knowledge or my input, my esteemed Emperor?"

"It seems I have. Imagine that?" Marcus clapped his hands and yelled at the slave, "Inform Prefect Livianus it is time to sacrifice the heathen!"

"Yes, Caesar."

A sharp pain stuck Gaius's throat as if he swallowed a broken peach pit. These days, heathen was synonymous with Dacian.

Moments later, after the slaves had served more wine and scrumptious finger foods to everyone seated in the imperial box, Livianus emerged through one of the tunnels below. He waved to the crowd as he dragged a terrified scraggly youth into the center of the arena. Behind him marched ten soldiers of the Praetorian Guard. Working in prearranged teams, each pair of men struggled to hold onto the chains linked to the iron collars of five vicious but well-trained dogs of war. The massive beasts snarled and pulled and pawed the sand, hungry to feast on human flesh.

Marcus stood and extended his arm. "People of Rome! I offer a barbarian sacrifice to Jove and Mars for the continued good fortune of our great Empire and to honor the blessed spirit of our noble counselor, Lucius Petronius Celsus!"

A deafening roar of approval rose from the packed auditorium.

"Gaius, that barbarian is only a boy," Marcia objected in a quiet voice.

She was right. Naked except for a filthy frayed loincloth, the lad was too thin and too young to be a warrior. He likely hadn't even grown his first beard yet. He never would. The peasant boy wailed and struggled until he collapsed. Two arena slaves hastily strapped the wretch to a wooden stake.

"Prefect Livianus, tell us the name of this recently captured Dacian cur we offer to the ferocious canines of Mars!"

Livianus pulled out a piece of papyrus and read the letters silently to himself before hollering, "Alle-tho-do-ko-les, Caesar!"

At first confusion buzzed through the audience. The curious murmurs soon changed to hoots of laughter. It was a ridiculous fucking name.

Gaius choked on a swallow of wine and wiped his mouth. By Bacchus' drunken balls, the absurd name wasn't a fabricated alias after all. Did Allerix know this poor lad, Allethodokoles? Had they been friends?

Gaius cleared his throat and remarked, contempt dripping with every word, "Caesar, permit me to remind your greatness your laws permit public execution without trial for enemy royalty—royalty, as in barbarian kings and princelings. Surely you can see this frail creature is a low-born farmer's bastard."

"Your legal clarification is dangerously close to insolence, Gaius.

I'm perfectly aware of what my fucking laws require. The Praetorians' prison holds many captured Dacian swine of the royal variety. However, I've decided to save those animals for execution during our triumphal games. This unfortunate louse, be it princeling or peasant, must suffice for today's celebrations."

"Then let us pray almighty Jupiter is not offended by our miserly gift."

Marcus's grin tightened into a scowl. "Since you have taken such keen interest in this sacrifice, I award you the honor of signaling the release of the dogs, Commander."

"You are most indulgent, Caesar," Gaius spat back as he raised his right arm. He lowered it quickly; the guards moved the dogs forward. Wide-eyed, his skin pale and sweaty, the doomed Dacian waif screamed and thrashed and begged until he fainted.

Gaius raised his arm again and lowered it. The guards dropped the chain leashes. Two dogs charged and ripped apart the boy's abdomen. Another tore off his left leg but soon lost his bloody prize to an even larger dog. The most nimble of the beasts jumped up, grabbed the Dacian peasant by the throat, and chewed through flesh and bone. The lad's mangled head fell to the ground, a twisted expression of terror frozen forever on his young face.

Clutching her stomach, Marcia scrambled to her feet and dashed off toward the exit. Gaius didn't move. He couldn't move. The pungent stench of bile and urine, the ravenous growls of the dogs fighting for scraps—the horror of every gory detail mesmerized him.

Paralyzed him.

After a few more moments, the handlers hollered the command to return; the war dogs obediently trotted back, tongues hanging and tails wagging, their manes and muzzles soaked crimson.

Gaius blinked twice, slowly. The cheers of the bloodthirsty mob in the amphitheater became the cries of battle on some distant Carpathian hillside. He recalled those howls for mercy and desperate prayers to deaf gods. Roman swords pierced frenzied, half-clad Dacian fighters as lethal falx blades sliced off the heads and limbs of many of his soldiers. The green mountain grass turned muddy brown-red from the streams of blood, Dacian mixed with Roman, flowing down the gentle slopes.

A sharp blow to the back of his skull snapped him out of his ghastly flashback.

"Get up and tend to Marcia, you idiot! Can't you see she's unwell?"

He turned just in time to see her beautiful eyes narrow. Fierce and blue. Heavy-lidded but guarded. Except for their color, they resembled Allerix's hypnotic eyes.

Allerix.

Was he safe? Could Gaius protect him from execution? For how fucking long?

After glancing down at the arena one final time, Gaius turned back and opened his mouth to say something but there were no words. Sabina lowered her voice and pointed to the corridor. "Help your wife, Gaius."

In a daze, he rose to his feet, all the while never breaking eye contact with her. In a hushed voice, Gaius said, "We'll see you and your husband at dinner this evening. Farewell and good health."

Sabina scoffed and wagged her finger. "If Marcia is not feeling better, do not bring her to the palace. The poor thing is already humiliated beyond belief."

Gaius hurried to the tunnel where he found his wife leaning against the travertine wall, spit dribbling down her chin. A gaggle of palace slave girls held her up by her arms and wiped her mouth with a damp cloth. He rushed over and pulled her into an embrace. "Let's get you home."

Marcia sobbed, pressing her face against his shoulder. "Gaius, forgive me. I don't know what ails me. Oh, most holy, Juno—I shouldn't have consumed that wine!" She pushed back and heaved, regurgitating all over the front of his formal tunic.

Clap.

Clap.

After ordering the guards to escort Marcia outside, Gaius spotted the silhouette applauding in the shadows just inside the tunnel entrance.

Clap, clap, clap.

He squinted and yelled, "How dare you insult my wife! Who are you? Show your face."

Before he could move, Sabina stepped into the bright light cast by a torch affixed the corridor wall. "Gaius, I would never mock your bride. I've grown quite fond of Marcia, and that execution was most revolting. If I were ill, by the gods, I would have retched as well. I'm merely saluting her excellent aim. Vomit suits you."

As her rosebud lips stretched to a spiteful smirk, Sabina raised her right hand and flashed Gaius's favorite soldiers' salute. "Are you surprised I remember the crude gestures you taught me?"

"Not in the slightest." Gaius cocked an eyebrow and lowered his chin. "You were an eager pupil."

"And *you* are still a shameless, self-important prick. Thank the gods I never married you. And you look awful with a beard." She lifted the hem of her long dress, turned around, and strode back into the auditorium, hollering over her shoulder, "Bring a hearty appetite tonight, Commander Fabius! Rumor is the palace chefs are roasting a rhinoceros."

7

"WOULD YOU CARE FOR rhinoceros, Commander Fabius?" the pretty palace slave asked as he offered the tray, batting his dark blond lashes.

Gaius shielded his nose with the back of his hand. "Get that vile flesh away from my face."

"It's surprisingly delicious, Gaius," Marcia commented, before selecting another dark red, bite-sized piece of meat from the pile carefully arranged high on a silver platter. "It tastes like ox, but a bit sweeter."

As he studied his wife's fetching profile, Gaius pursed his mouth in disgust while she chewed the tough morsel. He waved his hand in front of his face and grumbled, "That might taste sweet, but it smells like ox shit. I am, however, pleased to see your appetite has returned with a vengeance."

Marcia wolfed down the gamey meat and snatched another warm slice of roasted rhino before the slave departed to serve Matidia, Marciana, and Pliny, who were lying on next couch.

"Thanks to healing Hygeia!" Marcia exclaimed and popped the bite into her mouth. As she munched, she mumbled, "Thanks to all the gods for my quick recovery after that debacle at the amphitheater."

Propped up on his left elbow, Gaius pushed a strand of brunette hair away from her hazel eyes with his right hand. "A long soak in a warm, fragrant bath followed by a dreamless nap cures many afflictions."

"We're all relieved you're feeling better, Marcia," Memmia interjected as she peeked over Gaius's right shoulder. "In the future, you must avoid the heat of the arena, dear girl. It traps the insalubrious African breezes invading our city this time of year. The baleful winds of cursed Carthage. Don't you agree, Rufus?"

Confident his grandmother couldn't see his face, Gaius rolled his eyes. "Yes, Avia."

She punched him in the shoulder. "Then why, by Castor, did you force your indisposed wife to attend the spectacles, you brute?"

"I did not force anyone to do anything. My wife insisted on attending. And Emperor Trajan made it quite clear our presence was mandatory. It was a direct order. You told me to grovel at his feet, remember?"

"Bah! Marcus and his foolhardy directives." Memmia pushed herself up; her aged joints cracked with every move. She smacked her lips and asked, "Where are those damn grilled oysters? Now those were tasty. I want more."

Gaius leaned back and joked. "Maximus, be a dear and fetch Avia some oysters before she withers away and starves to death."

With his hands crossed behind his back, Max fought off a chuckle. "Yes, Commander."

Before Max could trek across the dining hall, horns trumpeted the arrival of the imperial couple. Accompanied by six armed guards, Marcus entered first, wearing a long burgundy mantle over his cream-colored tunic. Plotina wore layers of blue and green fabric, her pile of curls pierced by gold hairpins, her neck and wrists dripping with gem and pearl-encrusted jewelry.

"Ah, the imperial couple has finally made their grand entrance. See how our modest Plotina demonstrates her efforts to curb ostentatious displays of wealth," Gaius murmured snidely to Marcia. She swatted his forearm but resisted the urge to laugh.

With her palm resting on her husband's outstretched hand, the Empress strolled through the room and surveyed each of the six couches like a hawk, noting who was present and where they sat. Gods help anyone who ignored her prearranged seating placards.

"Greetings, beloved family and dearest friends!" Marcus hollered as he guided his wife to their spots on the elevated dining couch of honor. "How's the fare?"

Pliny cheered. "Splendid and generous, as always, my esteemed and most victorious Emperor!"

"Fucking sycophant," Gaius muttered to himself. He glanced over at Apollodorus, who reclined alongside his beautiful wife, Helen, two couches away. Appy shook his head and flashed an exasperated grin. Even the Greek engineer found Pliny's blatant flattering tiresome.

Marcus chuckled. "I am pleased you're satisfied, Gaius Plinius. And how about you, our dearest Memmia Cornelia? You've traveled all the way from the suburbs to join us this evening. We are most honored. Are you enjoying the party?"

"I'd enjoy it more if that scamp over there would bring me those delightful oysters." Memmia playfully grabbed her bony neck and coughed. "And my scorched throat would appreciate a refill of wine."

Laughter filled the room, drowning out the sounds of the water splashing from the decorative fountains set into niches on the walls. Memmia Cornelia loved the attention; she always appreciated an adoring audience. With a smile, Marcus ordered the servant to rush to her couch with a heaping platter of shellfish and a full jug of drink.

While the guests nibbled the exotic array of meats, cheeses, and breads, entertainers performed for their amusement. Blowing mellifluous tunes through their panpipes, a troupe of dancing maidens skipped between the columns encircling the dining couches. Over in one corner, two massive dark-skinned Egyptians each held up a long metal pole; a duo of naked boys twirled around the rods in acrobatic wonder. In another corner, a costumed slave recited an epic Greek poem, but no one seemed to pay him much notice. Just inside the servants' entrance, a slave dropped a tray of figs and received three harsh blows from the chief steward. Marcus's personal attendant, Phaedimus, was nowhere in sight. Whores, even the most pampered palace bed warmers, were rarely allowed to attend formal dinners, and certainly not when Empress Plotina was present.

Although she sat on the opposite side of the intimate dining circle, Gaius could feel her judgmental eyes bore through his skin. Pompeia Plotina, the grand matron of Rome, the most powerful woman in the world. The indomitable queen of all bitches.

After placing his silver cup on the low marble table in front of their couch, Gaius scratched his nose. How old had Plotina been when his mother, Julia, abandoned him at Marcus's estate all those years ago? He was fourteen years old, still wearing his puerile toga. Plotina must have been fifteen. Perhaps sixteen? Marcus's new young bride had despised him from the moment they met. She still did, but her youthful beauty had long since disappeared. These days her garish cosmetics cracked at the corners of her mouth whenever she moved her lips. Plotina looked at least a decade older than her thirty-seven years. Meddling in Rome's political affairs had taken its toll.

Plotina rose from her couch, rearranged the folds of her intricately embroidered azure gown, and sauntered over. "How wonderful you're feeling well, Marcia Servilia. We are so pleased to see you've joined us."

"Thank you, Empress. I am—"

Before Marcia could finish her thought, Plotina turned to speak with Gaius. "Commander Fabius, trade seats with me. Our esteemed Emperor wishes to speak with you." It was an order, not a request. Plotina never asked for anything. She took.

"Of course, Domina."

Poking his yellowed teeth with an ivory toothpick, Marcus patted the couch cushion. "Sit down, Gaius. Did you try the rhinoceros? It's most memorable though the stench is rather repugnant." The emperor licked his gums with his tongue as he flicked the toothpick; a sliver of partially chewed meat landed on the colorful marble floor. "Listen, I've received word Titus Petronius has finally arrived in Rome. Now that he's here, Lucius Petronius's testament can be unsealed and read on the next auspicious day. According to both the calendar and my astrologers, that will be in two days time."

"Welcome news, Caesar."

Farewell and good fucking riddance, Aurelia!

Marcus continued, "And after the counselor's will is read before the inheritance magistrates in the Julian basilica, you will depart this city. Have your bags packed, and your horses saddled."

"Depart? But—but what about the murder investigation, sir?"

"From this point forward, I will supervise all aspects of the investigation. Go to your estate in Campania—go anywhere, as long as you stay far outside the boundaries of the capital. Be my guest and enjoy a relaxing holiday at the imperial villa on Capri, if you like. The flowers should be in full bloom."

"Why must I leave?"

"Your mere presence in the capital encourages your veterans to squabble. Their steadfast loyalty to you is commendable on the battlefield but not here in Rome. Today, while we were all enjoying the games at the amphitheater, a gang of your followers attacked two of your brother's clients. Witnesses claim both sides exchanged many slanderous insults. Fortunately, it was a brief skirmish, easily quelled, but worrisome nevertheless. A citizen died, Commander."

Gaius glanced over at Publius and swallowed. "My men killed one of the Greekling's associates?"

"No, thank Jove! The poor chap was an innocent nobody. The fight took place in front of that tavern your veterans frequent down by the riverfront warehouses. Appalling behavior. Have your men no discipline? I will not tolerate civil disobedience, Gaius."

Gaius exhaled and rubbed his face. "I will reprimand my clients, sir. Severely, I assure you. But I can't leave the city until Lucius's killers are caught and punished. I swore a sacred oath to Jupiter Almighty."

"I don't care if you swore an oath to every fucking god in the entire divine pantheon. You will leave Rome after the testament is made public. I will not have petty violence between your men and Publius's minions clogging the streets of our fair capital. Do you understand me, Commander Fabius?"

Stewing in silence, Gaius and Marcus stared at each other until Gaius whispered, "I will not leave. I swore a fucking oath."

His face beetroot red, Marcus stood and screamed. "You will do as I order, soldier! Otherwise, I shall have the Praetorians drag your arse out of Rome in iron shackles. And as for you?" Panting, Marcus shook his finger at Publius. All hushed conversations stopped. "You, Publius Aelius Hadrianus, will control your clients' wagging tongues. I want those murderers found, and I will not have you and your friends hampering my investigation!"

Publius gasped, glancing at Sabina for support. When she turned her back on him, he blubbered, "What—what did I do?"

"You did nothing, my dearest Publius." Plotina marched to Publius's couch and reached down to cup his bearded face. "Our esteemed Emperor simply asks you and your men cooperate fully with his imperial agents."

"We have cooperated, mother. Shall I be interrogated next, tortured until I make a false confession like some wretched slave? I was not party to any crime!"

"Enough! No one is accusing you of complicity, Publius, but you will do as I command. I am the fucking Emperor of Rome!" Marcus's snarl dissolved into a coughing fit. Plotina rushed to his side and took hold of his elbow.

"My most esteemed Emperor, please sit down. Undue aggravation is dangerous for your health. Remember what your doctor advised?"

Marcus slowly reclined on the couch, breathing hard and rubbing his chest. Plotina placed a plush pillow under his head and stroked his thinning hair as two slaves fanned him with palm leaves. When his breaths grew less labored, she turned to face Publius, who was now standing beside Gaius, arguing with him in a soft but incensed tone.

The empress screeched, "Stop quarreling, both of you! You heard our glorious Emperor's orders." She wiped her lips and adopted an artificially pleasant voice. "Let us all relax and enjoy the rest of this evening's festivities. It's a celebration after all. The chefs have prepared exquisite desserts."

"I do so love sweets," Memmia mumbled to Marcia, as Gaius returned to his spot on their couch.

"What, by gods, did you say to the emperor?" Marcia asked wide-eyed.

"Nothing. He claims I'm interfering with his investigation."

"How so?"

"By being in Rome. Apparently, a few of my idiotic clients roughed up two of Publius's associates today." Gaius shook his head and gulped down a giant swallow of wine. "A bystander was killed."

"What will you do?"

"What I've been ordered to do—leave the city in two days time."

"For how long, Gaius?"

"Until the emperor grants me permission to return. Marcus will arrest someone for Luc's murder, sooner or later. I'll come back to the capital for the trial if there is one."

"That could take months."

"Or longer. And all the while, Plotina will make sure Publius remains in Rome to dispense favors, sponsor festivals, and bribe informers. His prestige and authority with the proletariat and the Praetorians will strengthen. He'll be fucking insufferable."

"He's already insufferable."

"I won't be surprised if Plotina convinces Marcus to adopt him as the official heir before I return."

"Gaius, we can't allow that to happen." Marcia dropped her voice. "What about the baby?"

"At this particular moment, there is no fucking baby, is there?" Gaius sat up and rubbed his temples. "I have no options, Marcia. You'll send regular reports to Campania regarding Zoe's condition?"

Flabbergasted, Marcia exhaled. "Yes, of course."

"Who or what is this Zoe?" Memmia asked, but a rush of bustling activity quickly distracted everyone. Through the service door, a flock of slaves dressed as parrots flew into the dining hall. Each bright green bird carried a large golden dish of scrumptious desserts: fried cream cakes, cheese pastries, and bowls of spiced egg pudding, poached peaches, soufflés, and candied Syrian pears. With her skeletal fingers, Memmia snatched up one of every kind. The old bint suffered an insatiable sweet tooth.

"If you won't do anything to secure our future, I certainly will." Marcia hissed into Gaius's ear. Without warning, she sat up, cleared her throat, and stood. "My most honorable Emperor Trajan, may I say something?"

Another hush followed by whispers hummed through the hall. Marcia Servilia tended to remain respectably quiet at family gatherings.

"Of course, my dear. But I warn you—do not attempt to dissuade me. Your husband must leave Rome in two days. I will not change my mind." Marcus's tone was gentle but stern.

"Yes, Emperor Trajan. I accept my husband must depart the city for the sake of your investigation, but—but I would like to make an announcement."

Silence.

Tapping the edge of her gilded couch with her fingernails, Plotina cocked her head. "Yes? We're all waiting."

"The goddesses have blessed us." Marcia rubbed her abdomen and smiled. "Rome shall welcome a new member of our illustrious family shortly after the Saturnalia."

The blood drained from Gaius's face. He grabbed a fistful of the folds of his wife's dress and tugged, but she ignored him and continued, "I am delighted to announce to all present I am with child."

They hadn't discussed any formal announcement!

Not here at this disaster of a dinner. Not now.

Shit.

Their risky scheme to feign pregnancy and claim a slave's child as their own had become real. The most dangerous game of all had begun. Gods bloody help them.

Gaius released his grip on her dress and swore a string of curses under his breath as Marcus shoved Plotina to the side and jumped off his couch. "You and Gaius are having a baby? Thank Juno Lucina! Thank most sacred Fortuna!" He trotted over to Marcia and dropped to one knee, taking both of her hands into his. "You've been touched by the fecundity and grace of the virgin huntress, my daughter. You have been chosen to deliver Rome's future."

The emperor stood and lifted his palms to the heavens. "Thanks to omnipotent Jove and wise Minerva and torch-bearing Apollo and...." His somber prayers softened to giggles of joy. "And to all the other glorious gods of this great empire whose names I cannot recall at this wondrous moment! There's to be a grandchild. My grandchild!" Marcus lowered his arms and addressed his wife. "Empress Plotina, order the priestesses to make offerings of thanks at the altars every morning and evening until the next full moon." Marcus pulled Marcia into a cautious embrace. "You, dear girl, shall move into the palace for the duration of your pregnancy."

"You are most generous, my esteemed Emperor, but I must decline your kind offer. Our physician has advised me to retire to the Alban Hills. My health and the health of Gaius's baby would benefit from the cool breezes and salubrious air of my country estate near Lake Albano. With your permission, I would prefer to reside at my ancestral villa until my husband returns to Rome."

"Sage advice. Summers in Rome are plagued by pestilence. Of course, you may go to the Alban Hills, but I will require Memmia Cornelia join you."

Marcia glanced at Memmia, who was trying to shove an entire sugary pastry into her mouth. "You are most thoughtful, sir. I should also request Counselor Petronius's widow, Aurelia, accompany me. She's a pleasant companion and a witty conversationalist."

"Of course, of course!" Marcus turned and extended his arm.

"Gaius Fabius, come here. Your wife will stay at her Alban estate while you are away. I will dispatch my most trusted sentries to protect her during your absence. And my hearty congratulations, Commander." Marcus pulled Gaius closer and patted his back as he whispered into his ear, "Good work, soldier. I knew the Lion of the Lucky Fourth would sow his Fabian seed, eventually. I'll call you back to the capital when I have the murderers in custody."

Across the dining room, Publius's mouth hung slack while Plotina dabbed her perspiring brow as she tried to catch her breath. Sabina simply smiled and hoisted her silver cup in salute, shaking her head in amused astonishment.

It was now official: Gaius Fabius Rufus would be the first imperial ward to produce an offspring. If the child was male and survived, the contest for the throne was over.

"Congratulations, Gaius." It was all Publius could manage to grumble before he tossed back the rest of his wine.

Could this audacious scheme actually work?

"Thank you, little brother. We are most blessed. Behave yourself while I'm away on holiday, yes?"

Gaius turned around to find Maximus staring down into his eyes. With an incredulous smile, Max said, "A thousand compliments, Commander."

"Yes, well let us pray Fortuna, in her infinite wisdom, does not abandon us. Escort Domina and Avia back to the Caelian. Tell the staff to begin preparations for our departure to Campania. We leave Rome in two days time. I will return to the house tonight before the sixth hour. I expect the dessert I ordered will be waiting for me in my master chamber, yes?"

"Yes, sir. I procured a beauty whose appearance matches most of your specifications. But may I ask where you'll be in the meantime?"

"I must find Titus Petronius. The reading of Luc's testament will be pandemonium, as these public spectacles always are. All of Rome will be there, hanging like monkeys from the damn second-floor balustrades of the basilica. It will be a madhouse; Titus and I won't have an opportunity to speak privately, and I have instructions for him."

"Then you're headed to his estate on the Esquiline, Commander?"

"Gods, no. At this hour, I expect my former Tribune will be sharing war stories over cups of ale. I'm going to the docks."

Max protested. "The city is dangerous after dark, Commander. You shouldn't travel the streets alone without a retinue."

"I appreciate your concern, Maximus, but it's misguided." Gaius patted the ivory-handled dagger hidden under the heavy folds of his mantle and lifted the hem of his long tunic to reveal a second lethal blade strapped to his calf. "I'll be cautious; I'm not a lawyer. Tell Varius to meet me there."

"And where is there, sir?"

"Scrofa's shithole."

~

TAVERN OF SALVIUS SCROFA, ROME

HIS CLOAK COVERING HIS head, Gaius pushed open the heavy door and stepped over the threshold. A red ceramic cup flew through the dusty air, whizzing past his nose and barely missing his left shoulder before it smashed into pieces when it hit the adjacent wall.

"You swindled me, you cunt-licking fart!"

With one dark eyebrow arched, Titus grinned as he counted his pile of winnings. "Now, now. Watch your language, Blaesus. There are ladies present."

"What ladies?" Blaesus glanced up at the rickety wooden railing of the second-floor balcony. "All I see are money-grubbing whores with their tits hanging out."

The five men crowded around the table to watch the dice game laughed and slapped each other on the back as the plastered veteran, Blaesus, pleaded, "Io, be a sport and give us another chance then, sir. That's a month's wages. My wife will murder me if I return home with an empty purse."

Titus carefully picked through the stack before he tossed his opponent a shiny denarius. "I'll gift you this coin minted by the Divine Augustus—pure silver, not debased like the emperor's new specie. Now, you may thank me for saving your cuckolded balls." Chuckling, Titus pushed his chair back and crossed his arms. "And I do not cheat at dice, you filthy dog."

"You're a thief and a liar, Titus Petronius!" Gaius roared with a smirk from the doorway. The veterans seated at the wooden tavern tables stopped talking and turned as Gaius removed his hood, revealing his mess of auburn curls. The men all staggered to their feet and straightened their drunken postures. One spastic fool knocked over an entire pitcher of drink; the amber ale puddled in the wide cracks between the limestone floor pavers.

"Commander Fabius, sir." They saluted in near but not precise unison. Discipline had become lax.

Fucking peacetime.

Titus pushed himself up from his chair and bowed with an exaggerated flourish. "Greetings to our most victorious Commander, the illustrious conqueror of the dreaded Dacians. Ah, I see you brought your faithful sidekick. Greetings to you as well, Varius."

Varius lumbered over and offered his hand. "Greetings, Tribune Petronius. Welcome home, sir."

"Tsk, tsk. That's not quite right." Titus wagged his finger with the unsteady tremor of one too many drinks. "I am Governor Petronius now, the Senate's caretaker of our fair Achaea."

Gaius wrapped one arm around Varius's shoulder, the other around Titus. "Varius, the Senate shipped this shithead off to Greece after the last campaign. A promotion, they claimed. Our friend here has no doubt returned home laden with Eastern riches. Buy us all a round of drink, Tribune Petronius. Wait—make that two fucking rounds. Listen up, lads. I have an announcement. I'm going to be a father!"

Their cups raised, the veterans cheered as Gaius meandered through the groups and patted men on the back, addressing each fellow by name. When he reached the far table, Scrofa waddled over with a tray of cups filled to the brim with ale. Gaius lifted one for a toast. "To fruitful Aphrodite! May she bless us all with healthy boys and obedient bastards!"

"Blessed Venus! Mother of Rome!" everyone replied.

Gaius swallowed his drink in three gulps and belched. "Now, who here is responsible for attacking the clients of my unborn child's uncle?"

A rustle of remorseful murmurs as their shamed arses fidgeted in their chairs.

"There will be no more quarreling with Publius Aelius's men. That's an order. I have his assurances his associates will behave like the gentlemen they pretend to be. Understood?"

Affirmative grunts echoed through the room.

"Your behavior reflects poorly on us all. Thanks to your fucking recklessness, the Emperor has ordered me to leave the city. While I'm banished—temporarily, mind you—from my beloved Rome, you will do as I command." He stalked around the room, stealing swallows of ale from random cups. "You will stay home—and tend to your families—and fulfill your damn civic duties as proper, law-abiding citizens. Fuck whatever it is you fuck but stay off the streets. Understood?"

More nods and grunts.

"And if I send orders demanding action on your part, you will follow them without question. Obey me, and when I return you will receive your promised grants of arable land and donatives of silver."

"Yes, Commander!" The veterans answered as if they were a well-rehearsed chorus.

"Excellent. Bring that second serving of ale." Gaius tipped his chin towards Titus. "With our deepest gratitude to Governor Petronius, of course, the wealthy concubine of bountiful Greece."

With an ear-to-ear grin, Titus lifted his cup. "Congratulations on the splendid news, Commander Fabius. I must say it's good to be home."

Gaius wiped his mouth and sighed. "If only all the circumstances were joyous, Titus."

"Indeed, sir."

After he'd received another cup from Scrofa, Gaius waved Titus over to share a table with him near the hearth. When Varius plopped down onto a nearby bench, Gaius ordered the veteran to leave.

"A private conversation, then?" Titus asked as he pulled out a stool and sat down.

"Most private." Gaius paused and scrubbed his whiskered chin. "I need someone in charge here in Rome while I'm gone. My clients require supervision, and they respect you."

"Consider it done." Titus paused. "Commander, forgive my impertinence, but why has our esteemed Emperor Trajan ordered you to leave the city? From what I've heard, the fight today was little more than a foolish tussle. The Emperor's actions seem a bit rash considering the circumstances, no?"

Gaius furrowed his brow as he tapped the side of his drinking cup with his fingertips.

His elbows on the table, Titus leaned forward. "Who killed my brother?"

"I don't know, but they'll pay for their crime. This attack wasn't some random act of street violence; Lucius was murdered for a reason. I'm inviting Gaius Plinius to join me in Campania for a short stay. He knows more than he's revealed thus far."

"The lawyer?"

"I'd invited him and his wife to dine with us on the Caelian for a chat, but our twitchy senator claimed his spouse had suffered a convenient bout of dysentery. You must have heard our dear Pliny hosted the dinner party your brother attended on the evening he was killed. Luc was murdered a short distance down the street from Pliny's residence."

He tried to hide it, but Titus bristled at Gaius's affectionate nickname for his older brother. "Then it was an ambush. And what if Pliny refuses to share what he knows?"

"I won't give him that option. Pliny and I shall drink and dine under the southern Italian stars, during which time he'll tell me all about the whispered rumors circulating through the courts."

"And why would he do so?"

"Always with the fucking questions, Titus. Shit, you never change. He'll reveal what he knows because we'll be alone. Pliny loves and fears me—a powerfully persuasive combination. I'll intimidate the damn information out of him."

Titus rubbed his bloodshot, glassy eyes. "My poor brother. I can't believe Lucius is dead. I always thought I would die first on the battlefield."

"So did I." Staring at the swill in the bottom of his cup, Gaius said nothing. On the other side of the tavern, a group of veterans swayed back and forth, slurring the words of an old marching song.

"You're wearing his ring." Titus noticed.

Gaius glanced at Luc's gold signet ring on the middle finger of his left hand. Shit, he'd forgotten to remove it before he'd left the house that morning. He sighed as he ran his fingertip over the stamped image of an oak leaf. Luc was gone, but his token of authority had been with Gaius all day—in the baths, at the palace, at the amphitheater to witness that grisly execution of the Dacian peasant boy.

"I'm safeguarding Luc's ring until his testament is unsealed." Gaius balled his hand into a fist. "I swore an oath of vengeance before Capitoline Jove to find and destroy his killers, but I have another mission for you, one which requires persistence tempered by absolute discretion."

"Of course, Commander."

"Listen, closely. I need you to discover the names and the Eagle of a band of legionary scouts who were assigned to spy the perimeter of the Carpathian Mountains shortly after the end of the last war."

Titus narrowed his blue eyes; he had the same pattern of laugh wrinkles at the corners as Lucius. Gaius looked away and wiped his nose. Gods, he missed Luc.

"The Carpathians cover an enormous territory, Commander. Can you be more specific? Do you have a particular timeframe for when this scouting occurred?"

Gaius drained the last dregs and smashed his empty ceramic cup over the edge of the table, startling everyone in the tavern.

"Harmless accident, men. Back to your merriment!"

He burped as he bent down to pick up the largest piece of broken pottery. Gaius held the cup fragment in one hand and withdrew his dagger from its scabbard.

"These are the major peaks of the Carpathians, yes?" he asked as he scratched a crescent shape filled with triangles into the surface of the red shard with the point of his blade. "A few days before the Ides of June, a squadron of scouts patrolled here, along the eastern edge of the western valley below the southern spur. Find out who these scouts were and to whom they reported."

"They would have reported to a centurion."

"Exactly, but who? Message me details when you have all the names."

"Don't you also want to know what information these scouts collected?"

"I already know what they found."

Gaius pushed away from the table and stood. "Oh, one last thing. I need to know which bastard in this pisshole encouraged the men to fight my brother's twits today."

Titus surveyed the crowd of men and exhaled. "I'll find out who it was."

"When you do, flog our over-enthusiastic ruffian in front of the others. Scar him, teach him a lesson, but don't kill him. Murder is an offense to the gods."

Titus chuckled. "And a punishable crime, assuming our laws haven't changed during my short tenure in Athens."

"And that is why I have assigned this task to you, Tribune Petronius. You've always been most my competent and furtive hound." Gaius snatched Titus's cup of drink and finished it off before slamming the vessel on the table. "I'll see you in the Julian basilica for the reading of Luc's testament. Give my regards to your lovely wife."

"She hates you, sir."

"Antonia's an excellent judge of character. Farewell and good health. I'm must go now. I have a long-overdue reward waiting for me back at my estate on the Caelian." Gaius paused as he headed for the door. "And, Titus?"

"Commander?"

"It is good to have you home, Tribune."

8

"LET ME HAVE A look at you," Gaius ordered from his seat near the terrace of his master chamber. Leaning against the backrest of the chair with his legs spread wide, he untied the belt of his white mantle to reveal his conspicuous lust. He'd grown weary of Marcia's voluptuous nymphs, but there were no male pleasure slaves at his mansion in the capital. The streets of Rome, not to mention the palace, were too dangerous and unpredictable. Before the last war, he'd elected to house all his boys down at the stable house in Campania. With his full balls ready to burst, Gaius now regretted his cautious decision. Despite his simmering resentment over Marcus's orders to leave the city, he couldn't wait to get the fuck out of Rome and return to his lads and his picturesque seaside villa.

To Allerix, his beautiful barbarian enigma.

At least for tonight, Gaius could indulge his fantasies.

Standing by the light of the bronze candelabra, the dark-haired prostitute unclasped his hands, letting his lean arms fall to his sides. He lifted his cleft chin up high in the air to show off his attractive profile as he'd clearly been taught to do.

Max had chosen well.

The lad was about the same age and a close physical match: long legs; nicely muscled but not bulky; big brown eyes; a small curved nose and full, pouty lips. Perfectly androgynous, not that Gaius was drawn to delicately featured men, at least not until he'd laid his eyes on Allerix. The prostitute on display front of him was no spirited Dacian, however. This statuesque faun was a submissive treat available only to customers who could afford his services.

"What are you called, boy?"

"My name is Paris, sir." The high-priced whore spoke with a distinct northern Gallic accent. Not as melodious as Alle's singsong Dacian cadence, but still lovely.

"Paris, hmm?" Gaius stood up and walked behind the attractive lad to inspect his sleek physique from different angles. He lifted the loose transparent tunic off of Paris's left shoulder and then his right; the pale blue fabric fluttered down and pooled around the whore's ankles. Gaius drew his arm back and slapped his bum. Paris didn't flinch though his lightly bronzed skin quickly flushed bright pink.

"Firm and red—a ripe Trojan apple," Gaius noted, caressing the warm handprint he'd left on Paris's arse. With a chuckle, Gaius strode back to his chair, sat down, and spread his knees apart again. "Bring me a cup of wine and come kneel at my feet."

Paris glided over to the serving table and poured a generous serving of red wine into one of the sculpted golden cups. With a flirtatious sway to his narrow hips, he bought the cup to Gaius and dropped to his knees with his hands folded behind his back. The lad was graceful—not as graceful as Bryaxis, but impressively nimble.

After enjoying a healthy gulp, Gaius lifted the boy's face with his finger and offered him a sip. The liquid trickled down Paris's throat, rogue drops spilling from the corners of his luscious mouth.

Gaius ran his thumb pad over the mounds of the whore's wet lips. "Wrap your pretty mouth around my cock. Let's find out what three bits of silver buy these days."

Paris took his client's engorged length between his lips and swallowed him down his throat with ease. Gaius tipped his head back, closed his eyes, and imagined it was Alle sucking his prick. As he tangled his fingers in the prostitute's hair, he pictured Allerix's long black lashes, his shapely lips, his long fingers, and his ideal round arse. Gaius undressed the phantasm in his mind until Alle was kneeling at his feet, worshipping his thick vein with his hot mouth, moaning around his shaft with wanton desire.

"My beautiful, naughty warrior. Gods, your mouth feels divine," Gaius whispered with a grin. But when he glanced down, the prostitute's seductive moans morphed in his mind to terrified, guttural sobs. Desperate cries for help, agonizing screams for mercy. He saw Allerix choked by his silver slave collar as he thrashed against the bindings. With the imagined echoes of Dacian curses ricocheting inside his skull, Gaius envisioned a pack of monstrous war dogs ripping Allerix to shreds. Alle's royal blood sprayed everywhere, soaking every seat in the amphitheater and drenching Gaius's white toga in crimson.

"Sir, is there something wrong?" Paris asked nervously, after Gaius's prick went limp and slipped out of his wet mouth.

"By Pollux, what are these torments plaguing me?" Gaius covered his eyes with his fists and tried to ignore the ghastly images and sounds polluting his imagination, but it was futile. The harder he tried, the louder and more persistent the scene replayed over and over. He gripped the arms of his chair until his knuckles turned pale before he reached for his cup and threw it at the wall. The dregs of wine splattered blood red over the pale frescos.

"Stop!"

Gaius grabbed the whore by his black hair and pulled him up until he was staring into Paris's wide, unblinking eyes. "What fucking games are you playing, *căţel*?"

Baffled, Paris stuttered a string of incomprehensible protests as Gaius dragged him over to the enormous bed and threw him face first down on the mattress. Gaius's hand trembled as he wrapped his palm around his listless cock and tugged hard, pausing every so often to slap his flaccid prick against the firm curves of the prostitute's bum cheeks. But even the prospect of pounding that delicious arse wouldn't harden his uncooperative member. Frustrated, he stepped back and grumbled, "Leave."

With fear in his eyes, Paris peered over his shoulder and asked, "Leave, sir? I—I don't understand."

"Neither do I. Maximus! Get in here!"

Max opened the door and trotted into the bedroom. "Commander, is everything all right?"

Gaius pulled his cloak tight around his torso. "Have two guards escort this useless trollop back to wherever it came from."

Max jogged over and picked up Paris's gauzy tunic. As he dragged the naked prostitute towards the door by his arm, Max reassured his patron. "I'll have your coin reimbursed, sir."

"No, it's not the whore's fault. It's been a long abysmal day, and I've consumed too much drink. Just get him out of here."

Max carefully closed the door behind them while Gaius extinguished all but one lamp before he slumped back into his chair. In the spaces between the slender columns of terrace balustrade, a field of shimmering stars filled the late night sky. He realized the slim crescent of the waning moon would disappear before they set out for Campania. It would take longer to travel to Puteoli without moonlight, but they'd finally escape this marble sewer of politics and lies.

In less than two days, Lucius's testament would be unsealed, and his last words read out loud before all of Rome. Once that last rite was over, his dearest friend would fall mute to the perpetual silence of death as his spirit waited for justice—justice Marcus had greedily snatched from Gaius's rightful grasp. It was no wonder he was going insane.

And yet, in this raging storm of vengeance and feigned pregnancies and manipulation, all he could think about was Allerix. Gaius combed his fingers through his hair and sighed. "What the fuck is wrong with me?"

He needed to go home to his villa; he needed to finish this struggle. He would not allow the Dacian to haunt his dreams or cloud his judgment. He would tame Alle, or he would sell him to the mines like any other common heathen. But there was nothing to be done about that tonight. Gaius stood up and padded to the serving table for another swig of drink.

"You're suffering the sickness of Aphrodite," said a spooky voice.

Gaius froze, but the wine continued to pour out of the jug until the burgundy liquid gushed over the lip of the cup, spilling all over the table. He took a deep breath and slowly turned around, but there was nothing there. The room was dark, lit only by a bronze lamp flickering on the table next to his chair, quiet except for the rapid beat of his racing heart and the crickets chirping outside.

Gaius swallowed the unease clogging his throat. He turned back towards the wall with his shoulders slouched and grabbed on to the edge of the table. "Marvelous. Now I'm hearing voices."

"Your mind's been poisoned by Cupid's passion."

He balled his clammy hands into fists and spun around. "Who's there?"

"Come closer." Whispered a deep voice from the bed, as if the pillows and bedcovers had become strange sirens beckoning him. As he drew closer, a shape materialized on top of the mattress. The pale apparition of something large lay on his bed, a nefarious cloud in the form of a man.

"What are you?" Gaius wanted to ask, but only the first word left his lips before he gasped and jumped back three paces. The specter of a tall figure wearing a golden wreath and a tattered senatorial toga lay across his bed.

"Don't you recognize me, Gaius Fabius Rufus?" The thing stretched its huge arms inviting him to embrace.

"Maximus! Guards!" Gaius shouted while he cinched his summer cloak tightly around his waist and backpedaled towards the exit. Max burst through the door, followed by two sentries with their swords drawn.

"Sir?"

Trying to catch his breath, Gaius pointed. "Maximus, what do you see there?"

"Bedcovers and some pillows, sir. Do you wish me to have the steward freshen your bedding?"

"For the love of all that is holy, you can't see that heinous creature lying on the mattress?"

Max cautiously approached the bed for closer inspection. "No, Commander. I see nothing out of the ordinary, sir."

Gaius rubbed his eyes hard but the ghost remained. It tilted its ghoulish head and smiled; its white teeth glowed brightly against its grey, gloomy visage. Gaius exhaled and dropped his arm. He swayed and staggered until Max rushed over and caught him. "Are you feeling ill, sir?"

"Too much drink, too little sleep. I need to lie down and rest."

"Let me help you to the bed, Commander."

"For fuck's sake, I'm not staying here. I'll retire to a spare bedroom."

"Take my arm, sir," Max urged as he extended his left forearm and wrapped his other arm around Gaius's waist. "There's a guest room down the hall. Hold on to me, Commander."

Together they toddled down the wide vaulted corridor, past the closed doors of two rooms and a series of paintings of Ulysses' treacherous voyage decorating both walls of the grand hallway.

"I'm drunk," Gaius garbled. "This is disgraceful."

"You'll feel better in the morning, sir. A pitcher of water and a good night's sleep is all you need."

"But I actually heard it, Max. I've sensed the presence of ghosts in this haunted house before, but that—that manifestation fucking spoke to me."

Gaius abruptly stopped in his tracks. After he'd shrugged off Max's arm, he muttered in fury, "I will not be driven out of my master chamber in my own fucking house by some monstrous phantom of my imagination." He turned around, marched back to his suite, and slammed the door shut behind him, leaving Max dumbstruck out in the corridor.

His nostrils flared as Gaius motioned to the terrace and slurred, "Be gone, whatever the fuck you are!"

"I've been waiting for you, Lion of the Lucky Fourth."

Again, that eerie voice, but now it sounded more familiar.

His trepidation tempered by determination, Gaius staggered to the bed and climbed onto the mattress on all fours. As he crawled closer to the headboard, the apparition grew more visible, more defined. As if a thick fog were lifting, the illusion became more real. The dark ghostly hollows beneath its heavy brow gradually transformed into light blue eyes sparkling with hints of life.

"Greetings, my gorgeous soldier. Did you miss me?"

A sound close to a whimper escaped Gaius's lips. "Lucius?"

"In the flesh—well, not flesh exactly." The phantom took hold of

Gaius's hand and squeezed. The thing was all hard bone and scaly skin and so fucking cold. Freezing.

Gaius jerked his hand out of the ghost's frightful grasp. "How is this possible?"

"You daft, adorable man." Some invisible force playfully ruffled Gaius's curls. "At the tomb of my ancestors you made a most generous offering."

"I sacrificed pigs in your honor as is customary. We celebrated your memory with a feast."

"Yes, and you poured that refreshing Chalkidian wine into the lead pipe to Hades. After I'd lapped up every drop of that reviving elixir, I found myself here. I've been patiently waiting to chat with you in private ever since."

The spirit lowered its deep baritone voice to a hush. "Are you aware your mansion is packed to the rafters with angry ghosts, Gaius? Your dead father wanders about these halls in extreme distress, mumbling all sorts of rants and curses. Shit, he's bloody scary."

"Old dead and disgraced Quintus frightens you? Ha! Wait until you encounter my bitter ancestral ghosts who rattle chains and scream. But how—why are you here, Lucius?"

"I was released from the dreaded underworld to exact revenge, of course. Most of the departed who return or never leave do so because vengeance burns in their lifeless hearts. Tell me, how do I look? Am I more handsome than you remembered? Younger?"

Gaius's shock gave way to incredulous laughter. "You vain son of a bitch! How do you look? You look—dead. You're a living corpse, despite the fact your body burned to ash on the funeral pyre." Gaius scrambled off the bed and stood with his arms crossed, swaying back and forth. "So solve the mystery for us, oh carcass of Narcissus. Who killed you?"

The spirit sighed as it stretched its wraithlike limbs. "I don't know. They struck and disappeared before I knew what had happened."

"Assassins, I suspect. What information did you uncover during your investigation of the treasury embezzlement, counselor?"

"I—I don't remember."

Gaius dropped his arms in exasperation and belched. "Brilliant. Blasted Pluto sends me the grisly spirit of my dead conceited lover, and the bastard can't recall a bloody thing!"

Ghost Luc slid off the mattress and trudged across the room to the serving table. He lifted an ornate bronze jug and sighed. "Alas, there's no wine save graveside offerings in the underworld. Drink as much Falernian as you can stomach while you're alive, darling." Lucius turned around and wagged his finger at Gaius's groin. "Now, let's discuss your little problem."

Gaius cupped his genitals and snarled. "A temporary affliction, I assure you. I consumed too much grape and ale."

"Rubbish. I've seen your sloshed prick fuck a harem of camp whores raw. Your impotence has nothing to do with drink." The phantom of Lucius tapped its head with its skeletal finger. "Your inability to fornicate is a result of your twisted desires, darling. The prostitute you just dismissed resembles that Dacian beauty you had me purchase for you at Decius's auction. You tried to fuck a substitute, but your cock wasn't fooled. By the most blessed gods, Gaius Fabius has fallen in love. Admit it! You've lost your heart to that furry barbarian slave of yours, haven't you?"

Gaius lurched, snatching the wine jug from the ghost's hand, and swallowed three generous gulps. He wiped the drops from his lips and growled. "Is that why you're fucking here, Luc? To mock me?"

"Changing the subject, hmm? I told you—I've returned for revenge."

"I promise you your killers will be hunted down and executed. Marcus has his men scouring the city for those fuckers."

"You don't understand, love. I don't give a rat's arse about whoever murdered me. I'm dead. It's done. No, I'm here to avenge the mutilation of Bryaxis. I will kill everyone in this shithole city who took part in the castration of my pet." Lucius sobbed as he rested his cold hand on Gaius's shoulder; an icy shiver sliced through Gaius's gut. "How—how is my sweet Bry?"

His finger shaking, Gaius gestured towards the door. "Go and see for yourself, Luc. He's here in a cell in the slave quarters. As we agreed long ago, I'm guarding him until the inheritance magistrates unseal and read your testament."

"Alas, I've already seen him," the apparition of Lucius confessed; his eyes were glassy with sorrow as he sat down on the edge of the serving table. "I visited him late last night. He was reading Homer." When Lucius paused, his ghostly glow dimmed. "Bry wasn't able to see me or hear my words. He couldn't feel my touch or taste my kiss. He just sat there, cold and detached, oblivious to my presence. My heart fucking shattered, Gaius."

As the room started to spin, Gaius groaned and sat down beside the specter. "I'm sorry I arrived too late to prevent his injuries. But your Caledonian will recover and his wounds will heal. I promise, as long as it is in my power, he'll live a long life. Did you bequeath ownership of him to me or Titus?"

"To you, of course. Titus and Gallus already have enough mouths to feed. Neither of my brothers needs another financial burden."

"Oh, fortunate me!" Gaius laughed as he scratched his scalp. "Your despicable widow advised me to sell Bryaxis on the eunuch market."

"Aurelia is a spiteful bitch. She'll suffer dearly for what she did.

But heed my words: if you sell my Bry, you will have no peace. I'll haunt your dreams for eternity, Gaius Fabius."

"You already are—you and that Dacian rascal of mine. And I am not in love with the barbarian. I'm merely fascinated with him. Call me intrigued by his contradictions."

The apparition snickered. "You're an imbecilic, smitten fool. Barbarians know nothing of true love. He'll only deceive you and break your heart."

"Bryaxis is a fucking barbarian, is he not? Enough of this nonsense! Lucius, I have to leave Rome. The Emperor has ordered my departure from the capital. I'm traveling down to Campania after the inheritance proceedings are over, and Bryaxis will accompany my escort to the villa. There's plenty of space in the stable house. He'll be safe there, and there's work to occupy him." Gaius rested his elbows on his knees and took a deep breath. "Come with us, Luc. Leave this wicked city and join me."

"I can't." Despite his soft chuckle, Luc's specter was fading. "I tried to visit you at your villa after the attack. I couldn't get past the door of the mausoleum, let alone across the sacred boundary of the city. I may be free of my sepulcher thanks to your gift of revitalizing nectar, but I'm still trapped in Rome like a rat in a dank cistern."

"Perhaps not." Gaius turned to face the pale vision of his dead lover and cocked his brow. "There's an old legend about a distant ancestor of mine—a Cornelius—a fantastic fable my Avia use to recite with a gleam in her eye. Memmia Cornelia has lived a long life. She knows about the possible impossibilities of this world."

"I would never underestimate your grandmother, bless her crotchety soul. Is she well?"

Gaius stood and stumbled to the bed. With a pained grunt, he slowly lowered his arse on the mattress. "Yes, she's as healthy as a bear—a hungry, ornery old sow. Luc, I want you with me in Puteoli. Perhaps you'll remember some details if we chat there. If there's any truth to Avia's tale, there may be a way for you to travel to Campania. Are you willing to break the law, my dear counselor?"

"I'm dead. There are no laws to uphold anymore."

Gaius fell back on the plush mattress and stared at the ceiling. He clenched the thick bedcovers to try and force the room to stop spinning. "Ah, but there's a catch. I must also be willing to believe in the powers of our inattentive gods."

"Then we'll both make sacrifices. What's your plan?" Ghost Luc asked as he lay down beside Gaius.

"Do you remember what happened to the nymph Daphne when golden Apollo laid his filthy divine hands on her chaste body?"

"Metamorphosis. Her father cast a spell and turned her into a laurel tree. I always adored that lusty tale. I have a sculpture of Apollo and Daphne in my library, but it's a myth. It's only a story, Gaius. It's not real."

"Says the fucking ghost of my dead best friend. Luc, we all know there are ancient truths buried deep in our myths. Did you know the sorceresses in Diana's groves practice powerful rites with rare plants and potions? They chant archaic incantations and control the unnatural. But if we attempt this, we'll risk incurring the wrath of our most holy Lares. The gods may condemn our spirits to damnation."

"So we're going break the law and fuck with the household divinities, then? Are you sure this is wise?"

"No." Gaius rubbed his temples and cackled as his words slurred into one another. "May every fury and grace of the heavenly immortals protect and forgive us."

"Shit, you are plastered. Do you know where to find one of these formidable herb witches?"

"Yes, right here. I fucking own her. Do you remember Simon's mother, Callidora?"

"That spiteful old whore?" Ghost Luc's shook its head. "You are mad."

"Deranged and as drunk as a piss-pickled squid. Gods, this bloody room won't stop fucking whirling. I'm so damn tired, Luc."

No sooner had Gaius's eyes closed than he began snoring. Ghost Lucius pulled the covers over his half-draped companion and brushed a rogue auburn curl off of Gaius's sweaty forehead.

"Pleasant dreams, my handsome troubled soldier. And whether you care to admit or not, you are in love. I recognize the signs. I only pray cruel Aphrodite grants you more solace than agony, more joy than pain, my darling."

With a despondent sigh, the ghost of Lucius rose from the bed and extinguished the lamp. As wisps of smoke from the smothered flame dissipated into the night air, he looked up at the waning moon and disappeared.

⇶⫷⫸

9

"PEOPLE OF ROME, MAKE way for Gaius Fabius Rufus, Lion of the Lucky Fourth! Clear a path!"

Everyone scrambled off the paved street as Gaius, dressed in full military parade gear, marched down the Sacred Way. His eyes remained focused on his destination, the majestic building ahead on the left. Behind him marched over fifty of his veteran followers, their weathered faces hardened by war, their loyalty guaranteed with Dacian gold. Like an army of worker ants, their boots clattered in martial rhythm across the shiny basalt pavers. Tied bundles of rods and axes propped against their shoulders, eleven strapping body-guards surrounded him at the head of the procession. Gaius had held the office of consul twice; his proconsular status afforded him all the legal trappings of Rome's supreme magisterial office, including a gang of brutish lictors charged with protecting him.

Where had Luc's official state bodyguards been on the night he was murdered? He'd served as consul three times in his short thirty-seven years. Had Lucius foolishly dismissed his lictors as unnecessary for a casual stroll to an informal dinner party?

With soldierly determination, Gaius approached the arches of the great Julian basilica; the ancient civic building soared two stories high into the cloudless blue sky. Bright morning sunbeams reflected off its white marble blocks and red-orange terracotta roof tiles as inky shadows filled every archway. Magnificent and sublime, the Basilica of Julius Caesar housed Rome's famous Court of the Hundred. Today, ten of those inheritance judges would preside over the unsealing of Luc's will in front of as many people as managed to cram inside the massive hall. Boisterous crowds jostled as they waited for the guards to permit entrance. A fistfight broke out, soon quelled by a blow from a sentry's heavy shield. The entire city was anxious for the final spectacle of death.

Who would be the heir to Lucius Petronius's substantial estate?

As Gaius began the short climb up the broad steps to the main entryway, he spotted a group of boys standing huddled together in the shade of a nearby archway. In the center of the forest of spindly lad legs sat two prepubescent urchins. One tossed a handful of knuckle-bones up into the air over a gaming board incised into the marble step; his companions cheered when he caught four of the playing pieces.

"Who's winning?" Gaius asked as he removed his polished silver helmet.

"Tiberius, sir. But he's a cheater," answered one lad with a scowl, his mop of dirty blond hair hanging down past his nose as he pointed to the smaller of the two players.

"That's a serious allegation. How do you know he's playing unfairly, scamp?"

"Because he always cheats. He's a right trickster. Fast with his hands and all."

"Ah, a young Sisyphus in the making, then?" Gaius leaned down and ruffled the dark-haired boy's locks. "Be mindful of the rules, son. At the end of his life, even the trickster Sisyphus suffered dearly for his clever deceptions. The gods are vengeful, and they're watching you."

"The only gods watching me are my father's household spirits, and those shitheads are back home in their shrine." The boy spat back with a sneer, mischief twinkling in his light blue eyes—the same color and shape as Lucius's eyes.

A dainty hand snaked its way between the boys' bodies and slapped the young lad across the back of his head. "Tiberius! Watch your language! You're not some foul-mouthed street dog," a woman scolded before she withdrew her arm.

By Minerva's saggy tits, Gaius hadn't heard that voice in years. And yet there she was, standing beside her husband, Titus Petronius. She turned to Titus and tugged his elbow. "You shouldn't allow your son to gamble with this low-born rabble. It's—it's unseemly."

"He's not gambling, darling. They're merely playing a harmless game. These common boys could grow up to be soldiers and, if they're lucky, serve under our son's command. It's important for Tiberius to be streetwise and understand the ways of the proletariat. Isn't that right, Commander Fabius?"

"Don't drag me into your marital squabbles, Governor Petronius. Antonia, my dear—it's lovely to see you."

Antonia pushed away a strawberry-blonde curl stuck to the sweat on her flushed cheek. "Greetings, Commander Fabius. We appreciate that you've agreed to serve as Lucius's executor. Such a despicable tragedy. Is your wife attending the ceremonies?"

"Alas, no. She's resting at home. This heat and these crowds are unwise given her condition."

"Yes, of course. Titus shared the wonderful news about the baby. Please do give Marcia my congratulations, won't you?" Antonia paused. "And to you as well. Um, I mean… both of you must be so happy."

Like her husband, Antonia struggled to hide her discomfort over

Gaius's intimate friendship with Luc. Salacious relations between two Roman men—worse, two aristocratic peers—were unseemly, after all.

"Thank you, Antonia." Gaius forced a polite grin as he twirled Lucius's gold signet ring on his finger before gesturing towards the stately door. "The proceedings should begin soon. Shall we go inside?"

Holding back the excited mob with their shields and spears, the guards positioned before the enormous bronze door allowed Gaius, Titus, and Antonia passage through the portal. Once inside, the bright sunshine of the Forum gave way to the dim light of the cavernous interior. On the left side of the wide central aisle, ivory chairs for the imperial household sat empty atop a grand dais. In the center of the basilica's nave, a low platform had been constructed for the ten toga-clad judges who sat chatting like fidgety hens. Rows of folding stools, some empty but most occupied, filled the available space on the first floor. State-owned slaves stood along the walls, fanning the restless crowd with palms leaves, but the heat was still stifling.

Lucius's domestic servants were gathered together in the far back corner of the basilica. Resigned to whatever fate awaited him, Bryaxis stared down at the elegant floor, his hands clasped together over his tunic-covered, emasculated groin. Beside him stood Euphronia and that freckled kitchen girl, their eyes bloodshot and swollen. Citizens and slaves alike were drenched in sweat, but the proceedings couldn't begin until the imperial couple arrived in a flourish of colorful fabric and pomp.

While Titus escorted Antonia to her seat beside Aurelia, Gaius weaved his way through the assembled attendees to the open area in front of the judges' platform. The other five witnesses were already lined up, shuffling their feet. Pliny appeared to be comforting Luc's distraught youngest brother, Gallus. Meanwhile, Luc's client from the Quirinal, Gnaeus Decius, wiped his sopping brow as he spoke to the lawyer, Gellius, and that greasy-haired fart, Asinius. As Gaius drew closer, all five men acknowledged him with courteous nods before stepping aside to make room.

Gaius squeezed Pliny's shoulder. "Is everyone present, then?"

"All save Titus Petronius. I'd heard he'd arrived from Greece, but I haven't seen him anywhere in the city."

"Have you seen my—my—my brother, Commander?" Gallus squeaked. Despite his thirty years, Gallus had never managed to overcome his debilitating stutter. "An infantile mind trapped in a grown man's body," Luc had often lamented. Both Lucius and Titus were fiercely protective of their disadvantaged youngest sibling, even more so after their parents died.

Gaius gently tapped Gallus's forearm and pointed. "Titus is here, Gallus. See? He's right over there, tending to Antonia."

"My brother's here! Antonia's here!" Gallus softly clapped his hands in relief.

Gaius approached the other three men. "Gnaeus Decius, you filthy hog! I haven't seen you since that auction at your estate. By Asclepius's snake, you're pastier than wet plaster, old boy. What ails you?"

Decius threw his hands up in the air. "My most noble and generous patron is dead. My future livelihood—the destiny of my entire household—is written down in those sealed tablets. Have pity on me, cruel Fates!" Gnaeus blew his piggy nose into a fold of his toga and glared at Pliny. "But I count my blessings, Commander. At least Counselor Petronius didn't die on *my* doorstep."

Pliny's eyes grew furious at the accusation. "Choke on shit-covered grape, Decius. Counselor Petronius was not murdered in my home!"

Gaius draped an arm over each man's shoulder. "Now, now—let's not engage in petty plebian bickering on such a solemn occasion." He pulled Pliny over to the side. "Your insults are quite colorful these days, old friend. Listen, when these proceedings are over, go home and pack your travel bags. I'll send guards to collect you."

"Collect me, Gaius?"

"You recall Emperor Trajan ordered me to leave Rome for the duration of his investigation, yes? I have decided you will accompany me to Campania and enjoy a relaxing but brief holiday at my villa. No wives, no children. You and I have matters to discuss."

"I—I…"

Gaius narrowed his eyes. "You'd be wise not to decline my invitation, my dear Pliny. I rarely invite associates to my private seaside estate."

"Yes, sir. It's a great honor. Your generosity humbles me."

A few moments later Titus strolled over, hugged his little brother for what seemed an eternity, before facing the other witnesses. "Greetings, gentlemen. My family thanks you all for fulfilling your duty to my late brother."

Pliny rushed forward and shook Titus's hand like a guilt-ridden lunatic, refusing to let go. "Warmest greetings to you, our esteemed Governor Petronius. Please accept my condolences for your loss. It's a grievous tragedy, and justice will be served. I do hope your sea journey from Athens was pleasant."

"Lucius's death is a great loss for all of Rome." Titus bit his lower lip. "Despite our swift and uneventful voyage, we made landfall after my brother's funeral rites had been concluded. I pray every morning my departed brother's spirit forgives my absence."

Pliny scratched his chin, unable to muster a quick, thoughtful reply. Just as he opened his mouth, the trumpeters blew their horns to announce the arrival of the emperor. The crowd rose to its feet while Marcus, in the company of the Praetorian Guard, ascended the dais, guiding his wife to their chairs in the front row. Publius and Sabina stepped onto the stage and took their seats, followed by other members of the imperial family. Everyone appeared appropriately glum and stern-faced, which Gaius found comical given each wore bright, festive attire. No doubt there would be another lavish banquet at the palace tonight. Thank the gods' balls he'd be far from Rome on the road to Campania long before the first course was served.

Gaius scanned the faces of the Praetorians. Livianus appeared to be absent, again. He took a deep breath and closed his eyes.

Had they gained access by now? Could Max steal the statuette without incident? What if Aurelia had stationed additional guards to monitor the house during the proceedings?

Wringing his hands, Gaius exhaled.

They were both armed, he reminded himself. Varius was a loyal bull and Max a talented thief. They'd be fine. His plan would work.

Shit.

The emperor banged his bronze scepter on the wooden floor of the dais, and all conversations buzzing throughout the hall quieted to a low hush. Even the mob of rowdy spectators looking down from the second balcony lowered their voices to faint whispers.

The eldest inheritance judge cleared his throat and began. "Our most esteemed and glorious Emperor Trajan, noble Senators, dutiful witnesses, fellow magistrates, priests, and people of Rome: we are here today for the reading of the last testament of Lucius Petronius Celsus, the most illustrious chief counselor of the imperial court, a proud son of Rome viciously cut down in his prime."

Gallus tried to muffle a guttural sob by coughing into his fist. Titus shuffled closer to comfort him.

The judge continued. "It is time to unseal the testament. Gaius Fabius Rufus, as executor of Counselor Petronius's estate, can you affirm all the sanctioned witnesses are present?"

"All are present," Gaius answered as he slipped off both his signet ring and Luc's ring from his fingers.

"Please bring your signet rings forward, gentlemen."

One by one, each man climbed the platform stairs to place his ring on the table. Gaius carefully laid down his and Luc's gold bands side by side. After the judges had matched the design on each ring to the emblems stamped in the wax, they broke the large red seal and opened the tablets. The court herald stepped forward, and the entire audience took a collective breath of anticipation.

"I, Lucius Petronius Celsus, son of Tiberius Petronius Longus, hereby offer my last will and testament."

Gaius winced; the herald's nasally voice was high-pitched and scratchy, completely unlike Luc's delicious booming baritone.

"I have lived an honorable and fortunate life, a life devoted to my family, my emperor, and above all to Rome. Faithful friends have been many; precious loves sweet and everlasting."

Gaius couldn't help but glance over his shoulder. Staring straight ahead, Bryaxis sucked in his cheeks as he wiped away streaks of tears. When Gaius turned back to face the judges, agony choked his throat. He bit his tongue to prevent the crushing sorrow drowning his eyes from cascading down his face.

"To my dearest and most beloved Tiberius Petronius Gallus, I offer my declaration of adoration. Juno herself blessed our family on that day you were born, little brother. For all of your life, you have been an honest and compassionate man. To you, my gentle Gallus, I bequeath the sum of 20 million sesterces and my profitable Sabine vineyards. I wish you a healthy and joyous life and only ask you continue to be both just and noble. Do not listen to detractors, fools, or liars, and be mindful of our brother's sage advice. Remember my words in times of sorrow and fear. Even in death, I will protect you. Be strong, my kind-hearted Gallus, and honor my memory with generous sacrifices at our family tomb."

Nodding, Gallus rubbed his eyes as he leaned against Titus.

"To my dearest and most valiant Titus Petronius, I offer my declaration of admiration. You are brave, virtuous, and trustworthy. You are the very best of men, and I have been most honored to call you not only my brother but also my faithful friend. Do not be excessively proud in your offices or foolhardy on the battlefield. Cherish your wife and children, and protect our family's reputation above all other concerns. Honor me, my courageous Titus, with proper and regular sacrifices at our family tomb."

When the herald paused for a sip of water, the vast hall grew eerily quiet as every ear waited for the next words.

～

LUCIUS PETRONIUS'S HOUSE, THE QUIRINAL HILL, ROME

HE KNOCKED THREE TIMES. The grand door swung open, and Max nodded to the sentry. "Greetings, Calvus, sir."

"Greetings, friend. You've visited this home before with Commander Fabius, yes?" Calvus queried as he motioned for Max to enter the vestibule.

"That's correct. My name is Maximus, freedman and client of Commander Fabius. The commander believes he's left his favorite cloak somewhere in this home. He's asked me to collect it."

"I haven't seen your patron's cloak, but perhaps the steward knows its whereabouts. He should be pruning the roses at this hour."

"May I speak with him?"

"Of course, but I can't leave my post, I'm afraid. We're short on staff, given the proceedings taking place down in the Forum and all.

Can you find your way to the garden alone?"

"I'll manage. Thank you." Max nodded one more time and strolled towards the large entrance hall. The house was nearly deserted; only a handful of lamps lit the rooms and corridors. When Max entered the atrium, he pulled out a bundle of red fabric from beneath his cloak and shaped it into a tight pile on the floor behind one of the large columns surrounding the shallow pool. After he'd stepped back to make sure the crimson heap was reasonably well hidden, he surveyed his surroundings. The small altar for the household gods should be close by, nestled in an alcove off of one of these hallways. But which one? During all his visits to this home, Max had never noticed the location of the domestic shrines. Should he try the left hallway first or the one on the right?

This whole mission was fucking mad. Steal Counselor Petronius's Genius statuette while everyone was attending the ceremonies at the Julian Basilica? Even Varius, who decided he preferred to stand guard out on the street, thought the Commander's orders preposterous. Thievery was illegal.

Shit, this scheme was worse than criminal—it was fucking sacrilegious. Would the gods curse them?

He rubbed his temples. Years earlier, he'd overheard Euphronia mention sacrificing honey cakes fresh out of the oven to her master's protective spirit. Max drew a long breath and entered the barrel-vaulted hallway on the left leading to the servants' quarters and the kitchen. He trotted through shadows, the patter of his sandals echoing through the corridors. He turned one corner and then another and there it was: a brightly painted altar in a large semi-circular niche. Within the tiny temple shrine stood three bronze statuettes, but there were no traces of a recent fire or a libation or a cereal offering. Counselor Petronius's household spirits had been forgotten and neglected. Max lifted a small ceramic jug sitting on the altar and peered inside; drops of thick rancid wine clung to the bottom. After he'd shaken the dregs onto the altar, Max covered his head and recited the traditional prayer for the household deities. Bryaxis would be pleased Max had fulfilled his duty and honored his late master's spirit.

The sounds of heavy footsteps came from the hall behind him. Max snatched the small image of a toga-draped man from the shrine and shoved the Genius statuette under his cloak until it was cradled deep within the folds of his tunic. The metal was cool and hard against his perspiring skin.

"Who trespasses there?"

Not recognizing the man's voice, Max backed away from the altar and turned around with both of his palms open. "I am not trespassing. I received permission to enter."

"Is that right? Wait, I recognize you. You're Fabius's Ethiopian slut, aren't you?"

"My name is Gaius Fabius Maximus, freedman and client of Gaius Fabius Rufus, the executor of Counselor Petronius's estate."

"Gaius Fabius Maximus? Oh, that's a bloody priceless play on names! Who knew Fabius was a fucking punster, the arrogant prick. Why are you here? Shouldn't you be supporting your witty patron down at the basilica?"

"I'm afraid I don't understand the joke, sir. I'm here because Commander Fabius misplaced his cloak during his last visit. He'll be leaving the city today and that garment is his favorite—a lucky souvenir of the last triumphal parade. Have you seen a red mantle with gold trim?"

"No, I haven't seen it. I don't bloody live here, you idiot. I'm guarding the estate at the request of Petronius's widow. Come, let's find Fabius's special cape so I can wipe my arse with it."

When the man reached for his elbow Max pulled back and asked, "Pardon, but who are you?"

"Tiberius Claudius Livianus, Prefect of the Praetorians. We'll search for this fancy rag of yours together. I can't have you wandering about the house alone nicking the poor woman's silver cups."

"I'm not a thief. I'm here on the orders of Commander Fabius."

Chuckling, Livianus playfully punched Max's side. "Settle down, lad. This is Rome—everybody's a fucking thief. Lo, what's this you've stashed under your tunic?"

Shit.

"Um… It's, er…" Max blabbered as he withdrew his knife from its scabbard. "It's my dagger. See? The neighborhoods at the bottom of this hill are dangerous."

"You're carrying a weapon for protection? Understandable, since that area of the Quirinal is hazardous, a breeding ground for miscreants." Livianus returned Max's dagger and marched towards the atrium. "All right, let us start this quest for Fabius's missing frock in the assembly hall. A red cloak, right?"

~

THE JULIAN BASILICA, OLD FORUM, ROME

THE COURT HERALD PLACED his bronze cup of water on the table and cleared his throat. A child up on the balcony cried out for its mother; an elderly man in the back of the hall fainted from the heat and fell to floor with a thump.

"I, Lucius Petronius Celsus, entrust Titus Petronius—to whom I owe my deepest loyalty for the great affection he has borne me—to be my heir. I bequeath to Titus Petronius 50 million sesterces, my properties in Latium and Etruria, joint guardianship of my surviving children, the allegiance of my clients and all associates named here within, and all rights to our family estate on the Quirinal."

The crowd erupted in a raucous chorus of cheers and applause. Aurelia may have impressed the mob with her expensive funeral pageantry, but Titus Petronius was a military hero, a favorite son of the common people.

As Luc's words rolled off the herald's tongue, Gaius smiled so broadly his dimples danced. With one hand peeking out from beneath his crimson cloak, he flashed Aurelia an obscene victory gesture. She covered her face and collapsed in a torrent of tears. Seated beside the hysterical widow, Antonia gasped and turned away, no doubt grumbling about Gaius's unseemly behavior.

"To my dearest and most esteemed associate, Gaius Fabius Rufus, I offer my declaration of everlasting affection."

Gaius took a deep breath. No matter what followed, this was going to hurt.

"You, Gaius Fabius, are the noblest and most loyal man I have ever been honored to call my friend. Together we stumbled through our youthful studies, shared honest opinions, debated the finer points of viticulture, and fought alongside one another in battle. Be patient and gentle with those who love you, cherish your family, and above all trust the truth in your heart. To Gaius Fabius Rufus, I leave the contents of my office and library as well as the obligations of my client, Gnaeus Decius, and my estate guards. I trust your integrity above all others. Therefore, I also bequeath to you my devoted personal slaves along with the sum of 500,000 sestertii for their maintenance. Honor me and our memories, Gaius Fabius Rufus, with regular sacrifices and libations at my family tomb."

Despite Gaius's best effort, a breath escaped his lips as a soft, mournful moan. It was over. They were over—finally and forever over.

The herald continued to read out loud the remainder of Luc's last will, but Gaius found it difficult to concentrate. Much of the rest of his testimony was formulaic and predictable. Lucius praised his clients for their allegiance and bestowed appropriate sums of money. To his widow, Aurelia, he bequeathed a modest sum for a dowry and joint guardianship of their daughter, Petronia, on the condition Aurelia prove herself innocent with respect to the circumstances of his death. Luc's testament concluded with generous praise for the emperor and substantial gifts to the imperial family and the people.

Proper duty and all.

Pleased with the testimony, Marcus stood and raised his royal staff. "People of Rome, in honor of our most esteemed Lucius Petronius Celsus, I grant every citizen five baskets of grain and three amphorae of wine. Return to your homes and celebrate the memory of our noble and generous counselor."

As the whoops and hurrahs subsided, people filed out of the great hall into the sun-drenched streets of the Forum. After bidding his farewells to the other witnesses, Gaius approached Luc's slaves. For better or worse, they were his property now. Wearing thankful smiles, Euphronia and her kitchen girl bowed low and blessed him. Bryaxis remained stoic, his strong jaw set firm, as he dropped to his knees and pressed his forehead to the colorful marble floor. His voice cracked with heartache as he addressed his new master.

"Dominus."

Gaius ignored him. "My guards will escort you all back to my home on the Caelian. In three days time, you will accompany my wife to her Alban villa and tend to your new Domina's needs—all of you, that is, except for you three."

In unison, the slaves lifted their chins and waited.

"Euphronia, you and your kitchen girl will travel to Campania with my retinue. It's high time I enjoyed better fare down there. Bring your cooking pots and spices."

"Yes, Commander Fabius," Euphronia answered with joy as she wiped her nose.

Gaius cupped Bry's jaw and lifted his face to look into his sorrowful eyes. "And you will also join me for the journey south, Caledonian. There are mountains of Luc's papers still waiting for you to examine. When you return to the Caelian, repack all his letters and legal documents and prepare the crates for travel. I'll decide your future when our investigation is complete. And before you leave the hall, retrieve my signet ring from the inheritance judges. Luc's oak ring now belongs to his heir, Governor Petronius. Do you understand, Bryaxis?"

"I understand." Bry blinked once, slowly. "Dominus."

Did Luc's castrated whore sound more defiant than defeated?

"It's an arduous trip down to Puteoli. We'll depart after the midday meal. By the gods, I can already fucking smell the fresh salt air." Gaius clapped his hands once and took three steps towards the exit before turning around. "And, welcome—all of you—to my family."

10

As the procession of horses and wagons ambled southward down the road, Gaius snaked his hand under his cloak and rummaged through his travel sack until he found the cool bumpy surfaces of the small bronze statuette. With sweaty fingers, he rolled the Genius image over a few times, rubbing its miniature face, stroking the spot of its non-existent genitals. Perhaps the warmth of his hand would stir the talisman to action.

Nothing.

Had she botched the spell? As Avia had instructed in her letter, Callidora purchased specific, rare herbs and assorted nasty animal bits from shops in the back alleys of the city. She'd boiled the noxious concoction, sacrificed a frog and a rooster, and recited the long incantation to chaste Proserpina and fruitful Ceres five times in a row, carefully enunciating each archaic word.

Five fucking times she repeated that peculiar magical charm while Gaius sat in a chair and stared at the figurine, waiting for any movement or subtle indication of life.

Nothing.

He couldn't fail Lucius again.

"How much longer until we reach your villa, Commander?" Pliny whined through a yawn as his horse trotted up alongside. At least the talkative lawyer had kept his tongue quiet for much of the trip. Thank the gods for small favors.

"We'll arrive well before nightfall, old boy. Arse getting sore then?"

"I need to invest in a more comfortable saddle. My tailbone is on fire."

"Take a rest in the second wagon, Pliny. Maximus and Bryaxis will keep you company."

Pliny raised his right eyebrow and lowered his voice. "You want me to ride alone in a wagon with two catamites?"

Gaius tossed his head back and laughed. "Would you prefer my girls entertain you instead? Callidora and Delia are in the third wagon. My wife's loaned me her nimble Arabian nymph until we return to Rome. I tried to buy the girl from her, but Marcia refused. Stubborn woman. Tell me, which wagon would you prefer?"

Pliny removed his sunhat and wiped his brow as he considered the options. "No doubt my wife would prefer I ride in the second wagon with your lads. She's a jealous woman."

"By Vulcan's cuckolded balls, has every senator in Rome become a spineless twat? Listen, I granted Maximus his freedom. He's now my trusted and dependable client. The lads won't assault you. You'll be fine." With a gentle nudge, Gaius sped up his horse to a fast trot and hollered over his shoulder. "I promise your tender plebian bum will remain unsullied, Pliny!"

∿

PLINY JERKED HARD ON the reins until the second wagon caught up with his irritated mount. "Halt, driver! Stop the carriage. I'm riding in this cart for the remainder of the trip."

The haggard driver grumbled curses under his breath while Pliny slid down to the ground with a thump and readjusted his dislodged sun hat. After he'd handed his horse off to one of Gaius's guards, he climbed into the covered travel wagon through the back door. Seated with their backs against a stack of crates, Max squinted as he nudged his companion awake.

"Senator Plinius? Greetings, sir! We weren't expecting another traveler. Allow me to prepare proper seating for you."

"Thank you, Maximus. My aged backside will appreciate the padding." Pliny rubbed his arse while Max shook an old blanket before spreading it over the wooden floor. Pliny happily accepted a flask of water from Max and gulped it down. As he dabbed his mouth with his tunic, he said, "Commander Fabius tells me he's awarded you your freedom."

"Yes, sir, but it's conditional. We haven't formalized my status before the manumission magistrates yet. Dom—um, I mean Commander Fabius has been occupied with more urgent matters of late."

"Alas, the unfortunate death of Counselor Petronius has disrupted all business in the city. The backlog of cases will take months to grind through the courts."

"Pity his murder couldn't have been more convenient for you." Lucius's assistant snarled with one eye cocked open. "Sir."

"I've seen you with Counselor Petronius at the basilica and the archives."

"Yes, sir. I was his legal assistant—and his bed warmer."

"Then more's the pity your late master didn't grant you your freedom in his last testament. To be honest, I was shocked he didn't. Prominent patriarchs are expected to show mercy and liberate their favorite personal slaves in their wills. Perhaps you weren't cherished by our chief counselor after all."

Every muscle rigid with anger, the slave glared at him. Before the concubine uttered another inappropriate remark, Maximus interjected.

"Bryaxis meant no offense, sir. This long, wearisome journey has loosened his impudent tongue." Max slammed his elbow into the assistant's side. "Apologize to our noble guest, slave. Your new master will not tolerate insolence."

Bryaxis gritted his teeth. "My sincere apologies, Senator Plinius. And you are correct. I meant absolutely nothing to Counselor Petronius. I was merely another piece of property, an expendable object like an old broken chair or a worn pair of sandals. Of course, Maximus here has dutifully licked Fabius's boots like fucking well trained hound for years."

"Bry…" Max warned, but Bryaxis ignored him.

"So you see now why Maximus has been granted his freedom, sir. He's a good dog, loyal to a fault. Perhaps that explains why my dear friend still has his enormous testicles, and I—" The slave lifted his tunic and pulled his limp cock to the side to expose his mutilated groin. "And I do not. Sir."

"Bloody barbaric Cretan!" Pliny averted his eyes, his mouth twisted in disgust when the wagon wheels sank into a large crater in the road. The high pile of crates swayed, threatening to fall. Bryaxis jumped to his feet and stretched his arms to hold them in place as the wagon swayed back and forth.

"Precious cargo, then?" Pliny wondered. "What's in those boxes? They appear heavy."

Bryaxis started to explain, but again Max interrupted him and replied curtly, "These are Commander Fabius's possessions, sir."

Pliny chuckled. "Jugs of imported Spanish grape, if I know Gaius."

Max forced an uncomfortable laugh. "Excellent guess, sir. The Commander often purchases extra stock from his favorite merchants whenever we visit the capital."

"Whores, weapons, and wine—the infamous vices of Rome's Lion of the Lucky Fourth. At least we'll drink well when we finally arrive at this blasted villa. Now, where in this baking box might a respectable man empty his bladder?"

~

ALONE AND LOST IN thought, Gaius rode a good distance ahead of the wagon train. The clip-clop of his horse's hooves across the charcoal grey pavers harmonized with the random patterns of soothing shade cast by clumps of pine trees bordering both sides of the road. With a sigh, he pulled Luc's Genius statuette from his leather pouch and cradled it in his hand, staring at its blank, patina-encrusted expression. Its miniature face looked nothing like Luc, not that a resemblance was to be expected. Artisans fashioned hundreds of these generic figurines in the foundries each year. This one appeared antique, likely passed down from one generation of Petronii to next.

"Are you in there, Lucius?" Gaius whispered and gently squeezed the holy relic. He waited for a sign before wiping away the tear sliding down his sun-kissed cheek.

It must have been a dream, he concluded—a drink-induced hallucination. But the weight of the bronze in his palm was heavy; the idol was a very tangible and comforting connection to his dead friend. He raised the statuette to his lips and kissed its miniscule nose.

"Just in case you are with us, we'll arrive at my villa in another ten miles or so. You remember my delectable blond faun, Nicomedes, don't you? And you'll meet my curly pup, Simon, and..."

Gaius sighed in resignation as he placed the statuette back into his bag. "The Dacian's name is Alle. It's short for Allerix, second son of Thiamarkos. Yes, I know what you're thinking. No, I've not been entirely forthright with you, Lucius. How could I? If I'd been honest and shared the details, I would have made you an accomplice to my crime, and the penalty for treason is death."

Gaius paused when the travel pouch seemed to wiggle against his hip. He retrieved the Genius figurine, but it lay in his palm motionless, cold and lifeless. He was going fucking stark raving mad.

"Despite all my efforts to protect you, you still died a brutal death. I suppose there's no point in hiding the truth from you any longer, Luc."

He took a deep breath and explained, "There was a minor skirmish during the final months of the last war. A handful of Dacian rebels ambushed our supply wagons in the forest. It was a futile, idiotic exercise on their part, doomed to fail, but that's when I first saw him.

By Hercules, I'd never seen such a ferocious and brave young warrior. He fought shirtless, his alabaster skin glistening with sweat, his black hair pulled up into knot tied high on his head. Alle killed three of my more experienced men and injured another five. Inked or not, I knew he was a royal. Only a princeling would have had access to the superior steel of that blade and the training to wield it. As you'd expect, we captured most of the attackers, but Allerix escaped and ran off to the more remote mountains. I had my scouts looking for the gorgeous fucker for days on end to no avail.

After their pigheaded king committed suicide, the war was all but over and I wanted my damn trophy. I sent word to one of my associates in Macedonia, telling him to scour the slave markets for an ebony-haired Dacian youth with heavy hazel eyes and a flawless plump arse. I knew Allerix would be caught eventually. Talented, courageous fighters don't stay hidden in the bushes. It wasn't long before my client found him at the slave market in Amphipolis and sent me regular reports of his condition. I covertly arranged for Alle to be sold to Decius's Egyptian dealer, Septus, and brought to Rome. So you see I knew far in advance my Dacian prince would be dragged up onto the stage at your client's private auction. Little did Allerix, or anyone else for that matter, know I'd been waiting for him."

Down the road, the clatter of hooves grew steadily louder as Varius galloped his large brown gelding in the direction of the wagon train. Gaius lifted the statuette close to his face and confessed, "In my efforts to protect you, I deceived you, my dearest friend. I hope you can forgive me for my duplicity."

"Commander!"

Gaius shoved the statuette back into his pouch and straightened his posture while Varius, disheveled and short of breath, pulled his frothing mount to a stop.

"That flooded section of road, and the damaged bridge at Liternum have been repaired. There's no need for a detour, sir."

"Excellent news, Varius. Fortuna is with us." Gaius kicked his horse as he scratched his beard and smiled. "Come, let's go home."

~

GAIUS FABIUS'S SEASIDE VILLA, CAMPANIA

SMILING, GAIUS LEANED AGAINST the doorpost. Try as he might, all attempts to steady his breaths didn't seem to help calm his racing heart or temper his sweaty palms and trembling fingers. He was finally home, and the young man who'd dominated every one of his recent salacious fantasies was standing a mere twenty feet away. His fierce prince.

His forbidden prize.

Careful not to make a sound, Gaius shifted his weight to his other wobbly leg. Just the sight of the lad dazed him.

Dressed in a belted beige tunic and tall leather boots, Allerix scooped up a forkful of green hay and threw the dusty grass into the feed bin. Any moment now the stallion would spy Gaius's silhouette backlit by the waning afternoon sun. With an excited neigh, Ferox snatched a mouthful of hay and happily munched down his meal, pausing every so often to nuzzle Alle's hand with his nose.

Shit, look at his magnificent boy. While Gaius had been away in Rome, Alle had matured into a strapping young god. The lad's fair skin was lightly tanned, and his once lithe muscles were now solid and defined. A rosy veil of fresh sunburn colored his full cheeks and furry forearms. Fucking breathtaking.

Licking his chapped lower lip, Gaius curled his shaky hands into fists. "Greetings, *căţel*."

Allerix dropped the rake and froze. With a bite of hay still in his mouth, Ferox raised his head and pawed the wooden floor with his massive hoof.

"You're back," Allerix said softly, refusing to look at him.

Gaius stepped over the threshold and marched down the aisle separating the rows of stalls. "Do I need to restart your training from the beginning, Dacian?"

Alle shook his head and slowly sank to his knees; he lowered his chin and mumbled towards the floor, "No, sir."

Gaius pressed his lips together and crossed his arms, but said nothing as he waited. Moments passed, filled by the whinnies of agitated horses shuffling in their stalls. Exhaling, Allerix finally capitulated. "Welcome home, Dominus."

"That's much better. Stand and look at me."

After he'd risen to his feet, Allerix turned his head and gasped, his eyes wide with shock.

"Is my appearance that revolting to you?" Gaius asked.

"No, it's not..." Allerix swallowed. "I mean, well—I didn't think Romans wore beards."

"Ah, yes—this." Gaius chuckled as he rubbed his curly amber-brown whiskers. "Our men abandon the barber's razor whenever a family member or close friend dies. It's a sign of respect, although more and more fools, like my ward brother, now consider it fashionable. These damn whiskers are as itchy as Medusa's snatch, but the beard of mourning is an ancient tradition. I can't wait to having this fucking wool sheared off my face."

"You're not keeping your spectacular beard? Dacians honor full beards like yours as virile badges of supremacy. A warrior must demonstrate expert weapons' skills in battle before he's permitted to wear such an impressive beard."

Gaius strolled over and cupped Alle's cheeks with both hands. "I'm Roman, pet, and I damn well intend to savor every moment of this rare, brief respite from war. This furry rat's nest needs to be removed."

"What a shame." With his finger looped through one of Gaius's red curls, Allerix frowned as he gently tugged on Gaius's beard. "Your copper ringlets are remarkable. Have you finished grieving for your dead friend, sir?"

"Yes, the time for mourning is over. Now I must ensure there's fucking justice for Lucius Petronius. As much as I'd prefer to summer down here in Campania, I must return to the capital as soon as possible."

"Take me with you. Let me help, Rufus," Allerix whispered.

Gaius smothered Allerix's mouth with a long, deep tongue fuck. When Alle kissed him back, he pulled out and rested his forehead against Alle's temple as he fiddled with the bronze fugitive tag.

"Only Fortuna can help me, Alle. My recent visit to Rome was a fucking waste of time. I suffered through unpleasant dinners with my irritating family, received reprimands from both the emperor and my grandmother, not to mention witnessing the pathetic spectacle of your little friend ripped to shreds in the arena."

Alle's strained smile faded as he tilted his head. "What do you mean, my *friend*?"

Gaius held Alle by both shoulders. "The peasant boy, Allethod-okoles. You remember him, don't you? A scrawny, manure-splattered urchin whose ridiculous name you'd foolishly pretended was yours back in the playroom?"

"He's dead?" Alle blinked as his eyes welled up with tears.

Gaius nodded as he pressed his forefinger to Alle's mouth. "Hush, we'll discuss all of this later. Right now, I need wine, a rubdown, and a hot bath. Return to the stable house and eat. When you've finished, wash up and wait for me to summon you. Understood?"

Allerix pushed back and cried, "How could you kill an innocent child?"

Quick as a cat, Gaius grabbed Alle's left arm and twisted it behind his back. The Dacian's musky, masculine scent invaded his nostrils as he pressed his lips against the damp skin behind Alle's right ear.

"Enough! I was not responsible for the boy's death. The emperor orchestrated the execution and then ordered me to leave the capital. Worst of all, I arrived too late to attend my best friend's funeral. His killers are roaming free, and I'm powerless to avenge his murder. Do not test my fucking patience."

Gaius released his grip, and with one hand tangled in Alle's ebony locks, he spun the Dacian around to face him. He traced a finger over Alle's curved eyebrow before scraping Alle's lower lip with his fingertip. "I've missed you more than you can imagine. More than is natural, gods help me. Return to the stable house. I'll call for you soon."

As Gaius walked towards the barn door, Allerix asked, "Did he suffer?"

"Who?"

"Allethodokoles."

"No, it was over quickly. Were you close acquaintances?"

"I barely knew him. Did the boy at least receive a proper burial?"

"Man or child, every savage executed in the great amphitheater is interred in the gullets of Mars' bloodthirsty dogs. I intend to do everything in my power to ensure you avoid the same inglorious misfortune."

"Why?" Allerix grit his teeth. "Why do you care whether I fucking live or die?"

"You're a member of my happy little family now, Alle, and I protect my family. The cruel Fates have dispatched far too many of my kin and my friends to the Underworld. I'll be damned if I fucking lose you as well. Now, obey your supremely whiskered master and go get something to eat."

Alle wiped his brow and spat with contempt. "Yes, Dominus."

"Bloody ungrateful barbarians," Gaius griped under his breath as he sauntered through the grass to the entrance of the main villa house where his servants, new and old, scrambled out of the wagons. Perfumed with the sweet fragrances of oleander and fruit flowers, the courtyard was buzzing with exclamations of relief and amazement. Grinning from ear to ear, Euphronia helped Daphne carry their canvas bags filled with cookware and spices to the side entrance. Max and Bryaxis stood at attention waiting for further instructions while Atticus supervised the staff busy unloading the crates.

After he'd removed his hat, Pliny shielded his eyes and surveyed the lush grounds and colorful gardens. "Lovely estate, Commander

Fabius. By Juno, Campania is glorious this time of year. Do you happen to know if there's prime property for sale in the area?"

"You already own more villas than any man should be allowed, my dear Pliny. Atticus, escort our esteemed visitor to the guest chamber overlooking the sea. You should find the views most enchanting, Senator. Enjoy a bath, relax on the terrace, have a nap. You'll join me for dinner this evening."

After his steward led Pliny inside, Gaius turned to Bryaxis.

"Follow Maximus to the stable house. Get something to eat and rest. Lucius's papers will be stored in my spare office. Your examination of his documents resumes at dawn, Caledonian." Gaius paused and scratched his nose. "Max, tell our sweet curly-haired pup to report to my private baths."

"Simon, sir? But I thought you'd want…"

With a growl-like yawn, Gaius stretched his arms high above his head as he climbed the marble steps to the main door. "All I desire at the moment is a soak in the bath and a deep massage, Maximus. My fucking back is tied up in more knots than a crooked oak. After I unwind and wash off the stench of travel, I intend to deal with my spirited Dacian. I think it's time for our heathen to learn a new skill, don't you?"

"Yes, Commander."

⁓

"Greetings, Simon." Alle nodded as he and Max walked down the corridor connecting the private baths to the Roman's master suite. Refusing to look at Alle, Simon grunted in return, his expression sullen and brooding. Any lingering vestige of their initial camaraderie had vanished since that wrestling match in the muddy goat pen. Simon the Testicle-Masher didn't forgive easily.

"Move along, Dacian. Commander Fabius is waiting for you." Max nudged Alle towards the end of the hallway where the door to Gaius's chamber had been left ajar. No chains shackled to his ankles, no irons binding his wrists, only the solid weight of the silver torque wrapped around his neck.

Seated naked in his chair, a white sheet draped across his lap, Gaius grinned when Alle and Max entered. The shutters were open, and the balcony curtains pulled aside; the edges of the drapes fluttered as cool ocean breezes drifted off the quiet surf into the bedroom. Gaius lowered his handheld mirror and said, "There you are, *câţel.* Come here."

When Allerix drew closer, Gaius patted his thigh. "Put your left foot up."

After hesitating longer than he should have, Alle finally raised his foot and teetered on one leg as Max handed Gaius a thick shackle designed to mimic a gold bangle. Gaius wrapped the hinged band around Alle's ankle and snapped it shut. "Maximus, attach that chain secured to my chair to our lad's shiny new bauble."

"But I thought..." Slack-jawed, Alle protested. "You said I didn't require shackles any longer."

"It's time for a new lesson, and certain lessons demand a measure of restraint, Alle. Here, hold this mirror upright for me so I can fucking see what I'm doing. Maximus, how long have you served as my barber?"

"Almost ten years now, Commander," Max replied after he'd passed a pair of silver cross-bladed scissors to Gaius. Out of the corner of his eye, Alle caught a glimpse of Max sharpening the iron blade of a lion-handled razor with a whetstone as Gaius snipped off a chunk of his beard and threw it to the floor.

"An unfortunate consequence of my generous reward of freedom to Maximus is I'm now forced to find a new barber. I can't ask my dear client here to perform a task far beneath his station, now can I?"

"You want *me* to shave you? You'd hand a Dacian a razor?" Alle let out an exasperated chuckle, and the mirror shook.

"Do not fucking interrupt me," Gaius hissed, grabbing the edge of the mirror to steady it before he cut off another section of his beard. "Have you ever given a shave before?"

"Yes, I have," Allerix answered, his lips downturned as he watched Gaius's clipped copper curls fall to the floor. "And I shaved Nic while Max was away, but—"

"Excellent." Gaius trimmed the remainder of his hanging spirals and held out the scissors. "Max, take these shears and give our lad the razor. Where's my dagger?"

Once Allerix had the ornate razor in his left hand, Gaius pointed the tip of his dagger's blade at the underside of Alle's chin.

"Listen to me carefully, Alle. If you cut me, I will punish you. If you slice my throat, Max will kill you. Shackling your leg to this chair simply makes it easier for him to exterminate you, should you be so foolish." Gaius reached up and grabbed hold of Alle's silver collar, jerking his head down. "I strongly advise you not kill me, understood? Max, fetch the shaving oil."

Gaius pulled the sheet up over his shoulders, oiled the remainder of his beard, and tipped his head back. "Shave close and clean, Dacian."

Allerix leaned over and pulled the skin of Gaius's right cheek taut. The butcher's larynx slid up and down, his thick neck exposed and vulnerable. It would be so easy, so simple to cut his throat—one clean swipe of the knife—but Alle's plans didn't include killing the Roman, not this Roman. Somehow, he would convince this Roman to take him to their capital city, to the vile palace of their merciless demon-king, to his chance for revenge and immortality. First, he had to win this skeptical lion's trust.

Allerix raised his elbow and adjusted his grip on the razor's handle; Gaius glanced at him, the corners of his predatory golden-brown eyes wrinkled in amusement. When Alle's fingers started to shake from nerves, Gaius smiled, which only deepened the creases of his seductive crinkles. He slowly wrapped his hand around Alle's wrist and squeezed gently.

"Steady, *cățel*. Remember to breathe."

With a hesitant stroke, Alle carefully scraped off a swatch of short whiskers beneath the swell of Gaius's cheek. He took a deep breath before he shaved off another patch and then another until he uncovered Gaius's seductive dimple. He'd never been so close to the bastard's face for this long; his gaze darted from the man's tapered amber eyes with their lush fans of brown lashes to his thin but expressive lips, until his eyes lingered for too long on the Roman's well-defined aquiline nose, curved and long and pointed.

"Distracted by my patrician snout?"

"Your nose is, um—conspicuous, sir."

Gaius tapped his nose with the side of his dagger blade. "This is a fucking noble, aristocratic Roman feature, Dacian. An eagle's beak."

"It's very regal, Dominus." Allerix smirked, trying to reposition his hands to better shave Gaius's chin. He shuffled his feet and sighed. "My task would be easier if I were allowed to—"

"I'm not removing your ankle bracelet, pet."

Alle leaned closer and whispered, "Can I straddle your lap to shear the rest of your whiskers?"

"What a brilliant idea, but first remove that blasted tunic. We should get reacquainted, but let's mind that sharp edge, right? We don't want anyone hurt, much less killed, over a simple late afternoon shave."

"I'll be most careful, sir," Allerix replied as he pulled his blue tunic over his head and dropped it onto the cool marble floor. With excitement tinged by trepidation, he lifted his right leg and carefully settled his bare bum on Gaius's muscular thighs. As he shifted his arse across Gaius's sturdy legs, Alle closed his eyes and lost his balance. When he grabbed Gaius's bicep for support, a low, lustful groan slipped off his tongue.

"I'm delighted to hear you've missed me as well, *căţel.*"

Gaius wrapped his fingers around Alle's arousal, enticing him to scoot closer until both of their hardening cocks rubbed against each other in Gaius's strong hand. "Now, focus and get the job done."

Allerix scraped the razor down and under the curve of Gaius's chin. A shower of chestnut bristles gradually blanketed the white cloth draped over Gaius's shoulders. After he'd shaved the other side of his master's face, Alle sat back to admire his work, tilting his head and scrunching his brow. The tip of his pink tongue jutted out between his lips.

"Just one more small patch over here, sir." He gnawed on his bottom lip as he dragged the razor across the skin by Gaius's right ear.

Wincing, Gaius touched his ear. He held up his left hand and snarled. "You cut me."

"It was a mistake, Dominus. The blade slipped."

"Likely story. Clean off my fingers." Gaius commanded as he tightened his grip on Allerix's shrinking penis. As Alle licked the drops of blood from his fingertips, Gaius distractedly grumbled more orders, "Maximus, take the razor from our Dacian, replace this dagger in my hand with a full cup of wine, and leave. My beautiful, clumsy new barber stays."

After Max had closed the door behind him, Gaius offered Alle a drink, which he greedily slurped down. "Despite your mistake, you did well. If you can perform a more demanding task with equal vigor, I won't punish you as harshly as I should. Maximus tells me your mouth's nearly as talented as Nicomedes' pretty gob."

He let go of Alle's flaccid cock and spread his knees apart as he brushed the back of his hand across Alle's wine-stained lips. "Every fucking moment I spent in Rome, I spent starved for your succulent mouth, desperate to feel my heat between your perfect lips. Down on your knees and assuage my aching appetite."

"Ass-what?"

Gaius cupped the back of Alle's neck and stroked his skin with the edge of his thumb. "Suck my cock, Alle."

※》》》《《《※

11

WEARING A HINT OF a grin betraying his unspoken salacious dreams, Allerix slid off Gaius's lap down to the floor. He ran his hands over the man's muscular legs and noticed a ragged scar on the inner side of Gaius's right thigh. Leaning closer, he lightly touched the mark when Gaius mumbled, "An old injury from the First War. I have several scars much more impressive than that minor scratch."

"How were you hurt?"

"The way most soldiers are wounded—I was sloppy and distracted. A rebel I'd thought had been disarmed had hidden a weapon in the folds of his cloak."

"A Dacian?"

"No, one of my junior officers. Or he was until I relieved him of that ill-suited responsibility, permanently. By Pollux, you're excessively inquisitive today. Do I need to bloody shove my sword down your throat to quiet you?"

"No, Dominus."

Allerix clamped his left hand around the base of Gaius's shaft and stared at the Roman's erect length like a devoted worshipper before a sacred idol. The man wasn't enormous like Max—shit, he wasn't even as big as Brasus—but his solid, meaty cock made Alle's mouth water. After he'd closed his eyes, Alle ran his tongue up the underside, pressing hard against Gaius's prominent pulsing vein. What were those secrets Max had divulged before that idiotic escape attempt?

Soft.

Wet.

"Suck slow and soft and wet. Worship him with tenderness, and he'll surrender all command to your mouth."

Allerix slid Gaius's plentiful foreskin down and licked all around the edge of his bulbous head before pulling him into his mouth. Alle relaxed his throat and swallowed him deeper; Gaius entwined his fingers through his hair and moaned.

"Perfect, *cățel*. Gods, your mouth feels…" Gaius untangled his right hand and lifted his chin with one finger. "Keep your eyes open and look at me."

Alle glanced up, batting his eyelashes slowly, and smiled around the girth of Gaius's shaft. When he began to use his whole body, bobbing up and down, sucking gentler and sloppier with each stroke, Gaius threw his head back against his chair. He moaned and gasped as his blunt fingernails scraped Alle's scalp.

"Don't fucking stop!"

If he hadn't had Gaius's length deep down his throat, Allerix would have laughed; he had no fucking intention of stopping. He relished this delicious power, this visceral sense of control. He slowed his already languid pace, sucking and licking until he couldn't curb his urges any longer. The clean, masculine scent of the man's groin combined with the salty taste of his early release aroused every fucking nerve. Alle reached down between his legs and stroked his aching prick in rhythm with his tongue's machinations. His mind was spinning, his senses overwhelmed by the raw strength throbbing in his mouth.

"Oh, gods!" With a final ecstatic groan, Gaius's body went rigid, and he emptied his balls. Wave after wave of semen flooded Alle's throat, trickling down to his stomach with each swallow. After one last spasm, Gaius withdrew and lifted him off the floor to sit in his lap. Caught between catching his breath and laughing like an idiot, Gaius twisted a clump of Alle's hair while he wiped a dribble of cream from the corner of Alle's lip with his other hand.

Alle playfully licked the juices off his finger. "I hope I performed adequately, sir."

"Max undervalued your abilities. Your fellatio skills are exceptional." Gaius flicked the upturned tip of Alle's small nose. "However, my gratification came far too quickly."

"My apologies, Dominus. I was hungry for you. Next time, I promise to curb my appetite and prolong your pleasure." Allerix brushed his hand across Gaius's hairless chest, pausing to roll the man's hard, small nipples between his fingers. With a flirty smirk, he licked his flushed lips and asked, "Are you ready for more, Rufus?"

"You cheeky little slut. Shit, look at your heavy-lidded eyes sparkling with wolfish mischief. I'm tempted to call you *bubo*."

"You want to call me 'little owl'? I think I prefer *căţel*. It's slightly less insulting."

"Oh, is that so?" Gaius asked with an incredulous grin. "By bloody Jove, who could have guessed? I swear you are every-fucking-thing I never knew I wanted until I..." With his confession on the tip of his tongue and his heart poised to betray him, Gaius shut his mouth and shook his head with amusement.

"I may be a cheeky slut, Dominus, but I'm not an owl nor am I a dog. My name is Alle."

"Are you sure this time, Dacian? You're not planning on adopting another alias?"

"I'm sure, Rufus."

Gaius tore off the sheet from around his neck and shook his shorn whiskers off the cloth. With a fold clenched between his teeth, he ripped off a strip and then another, before twirling his pointer finger. "Turn around. Your satiated master may not recover as quickly as he once did, but he's damn ready to indulge that spirited, delectable arse of yours."

Allerix tentatively complied. As Gaius gently nibbled on his earlobe, he loosely bound Alle's wrists together, finishing off the crisscross pattern with an elaborate looped knot. "As tempting as it might be, do not untie this bow, or I'll be forced to administer a far less enjoyable punishment. Do you understand?"

Alle nodded as his cock hardened with anticipation.

"Good." Gaius wrapped his left arm around Allerix's slender waist and pulled him back against his chest. "Now, open your beautiful, talented mouth."

"Sir, I—"

Before he could utter another word, Gaius slipped the second band of cloth between his lips and secured it behind his head. "Too tight?"

Allerix swallowed and shook his head. It was true, neither binding hurt at all. He could've easily wriggled free, which made the flimsy tethers all the more dangerous. The Roman was challenging his self-control, testing him.

"Normally, I prefer my pets scream with pleasure, but we have a guest staying with us at the villa. My dear friend, Senator Plinius, is an uptight prude about carnal desires. No matter what I do, no matter how difficult it is to hold your tongue, you will be quiet. Can you do that, Alle?"

Allerix nodded, whimpering a muffled 'Yes, Dominus' through the gag.

After dropping the remainder of the cloth sheet to the floor in front of his chair, Gaius kissed the back of Alle's neck and unlatched the gilded shackle. He removed the bangle from Alle's ankle before pushing him headlong between his thighs down towards the floor. His legs and arse up in the air, Alle broke his fall with his elbows and avoided slamming his face into the fabric-covered marble floor. Like a pendulum, the fugitive tag dangled from his silver collar, brushing his chin with each pass.

Gaius bent forward and bit down on Alle's left bum cheek. "Gods, look at these ripe peaches. It's my turn to feast on you, Dacian, and I'm starving for your scrumptious arse."

After he'd swallowed a long gulp of wine, Gaius spread Alle's firm cheeks and ran his wet tongue up the sensitive valley between Alle's balls and his hole. When Allerix tried to peek over his shoulder, Gaius dug his fingers into Alle's thighs and warned. "I didn't give you permission to watch. Just feel."

Alle closed his eyes tight as soft breaths of warm air danced over his saliva-coated skin. When Gaius licked circles around the edge of his tender hole, Alle groaned through the cloth gag. He clutched fistfuls of fabric as he pressed his forehead against the floor and arched his spine, reaching back with his bound hands to pull his aching erection.

"You're too clever for your own good." Gaius chuckled before slapping Alle's left cheek hard enough to leave a lingering, pleasurable sting. As Alle silently hoped he'd spank him again, Gaius lifted Alle's hips up into the air and flipped him over onto his back. Dangling upside down, Allerix's cock jerked against his abdomen, dripping with precum and desperate for attention, but Gaius ignored his glistening erection.

"Keep your hands above your head and your *bubo* eyes closed.

You're not allowed to watch me or touch yourself. I'm in control. I decide what you feel and when you feel it. Now, relax and enjoy my mouth as I devour you."

At first the Roman only licked and teasingly poked his hole. Frustrated, Alle raised his hips higher to offer up more of his arse. As his prick twitched and leaked more pearls over his stomach, his ache for release blocked out all other sensations. He couldn't see; he couldn't touch. He couldn't hear anything over the sound of his heart pounding in his chest. Nothing else existed, only the Roman's wet, probing tongue penetrating his body, fucking him senseless. He was desperate to grab his shaft and pull hard, but the bastard had denied him that freedom. All freedom. He'd been seduced by the Roman's desire to pleasure him.

"Do you want sweet release?" Gaius taunted, his lips purring against the damp warmth of Alle's crack. Alle nodded furiously although the cloth gag stifled his low, pleading groans. With rough hands, Gaius pressed Alle's arse cheeks apart even wider and snaked his commanding tongue farther into his tight heat. Alle wriggled as euphoric tears poured from the corners of his closed eyes, streaking down his cheeks until they soaked into the white cloth cradling his head. Snarling like a famished animal, Gaius fucked him with his tongue, his lips, and his proud, patrician nose—over and over, each thrust deeper and harder and hungrier. Allerix teetered on the edge of lust's precipice, begging for release with his entire body. When Gaius cupped and gently squeezed his aching full balls, a surge of semen flowed up the length of his cock. His hands balled into fists, and his toes curled as the blinding orgasm ripped through his body, splattering warm seed onto his chest and face. The cloth restraint barely muffled his tearful cries of pleasure.

"Fucking gorgeous," Gaius muttered against Alle's tender skin as he covered his hairy thighs with soft kisses. He reached down and pulled Allerix up into a fierce embrace. "Let's take this off, shall we?"

After untying the gag and gently removing it from between Alle's quivering lips, Gaius dabbed Allerix's flushed face with the cloth to wipe off sticky splotches of milky cum. "Here, drink," he urged as he offered Alle his cup half-filled with red wine.

Alle slurped two healthy swigs and crumpled, resting his head on Gaius's shoulder. "By the most glorious gods, Rufus."

Gaius held him tight and pressed his cheek against Alle's forehead as he petted his drenched hair. "Most glorious gods, indeed. You're now your master's official cocksucker, my raven-haired wolf."

With a chuckle, Allerix quipped, "My father would've been so proud."

"Smart arse." Gaius lightly whacked the back of Alle's head. "I have another important chore for you, Alle." Gaius continued as Alle's breaths slowed. "I want you to use that incorrigible charm of yours to tame my Thracian stallion. I saw you two at the stables. The animal trusts you. Break Ferox, teach the beast to accept the saddle."

Swabbing a dribble of semen off of his chest, Allerix paused as his eyes crinkled with skepticism. "First the shave, and now you want me to train your prized horse? What about Simon?"

"Simon's a competent rider, but he's twitchy around the creature, and that fucking nag has thrown me off its back more times than I care to admit. From my experiences during the wars, Dacians are excellent horsemen, schooled in the equestrian arts from an early age. Perhaps Fortuna will grant you better luck. Train Ferox, and I'll allow you to ride him."

"Ride him where?"

"To Rome."

His swollen lips parted in a mixture of shock and suspicion; Allerix arched his eyebrows and asked, "Rome?"

"The Fates be damned, I will bloody persuade the emperor to allow me to return to the capital, and soon. I will avenge Luc's murder." Gaius lifted Alle's left hand and licked his sticky fingertips. "I'm inclined to bring your mouth with me unless you give me cause to change my mind."

Allerix brushed his fingers across Gaius's lips. "I won't disappoint you, Rufus."

~

THE JOYOUS RUMBLE OF men's laughter drifted from the stable house as the last golden beams of the day struggled to resist sinking below the horizon. Simon took a deep breath and opened the door, slamming it shut behind him.

"There you are! How was your reunion with Dom, twat?" Seated in Max's lap, Nicomedes snorted as he snuggled against Max's broad chest. Clearly, Nic had already had his arse fucked stupid.

"There was no reunion. I gave Dom a back rub, and he fell asleep." Simon tore off his summer cloak and threw it over a chair. When the cream-colored fabric slithered off and fell to the floor, an unfamiliar man picked it up. He carefully folded the cloth into a neat square, and placed in on the table in front of him.

"Who are you?" Simon scowled, blinking while his pupils adjusted to the dim light of the common room.

"Mind your manners, pup," Max warned before swallowing another mouthful of wine. "Simon, this is Bryaxis. Bry's an old friend of mine. He was Counselor Petronius's favorite bed warmer."

"*Another* fucking whore? Why is he here?"

Bryaxis slowly put down his cup, pushed back his chair, and stood; Simon's mouth fell open. By gods, this man was as tall as a tree, even taller than Maximus, who was until that moment the tallest person Simon had ever seen in his short eighteen years.

After Bry retrieved the jug of wine and filled his empty cup, he walked over and fluffed Simon's hair. "Well, aren't you a darling, foul-mouthed twit. I'm here because our masters were close friends for many years. Unfortunately, my beloved, kind-hearted master was murdered instead of Fabius. In his last testament, Lucius left owner-ship of me to—" Bry swallowed and pointed towards the main house. "To that red-haired, pompous shit bag of a prick! I don't want to be here anymore than you want to compete with the Dacian for your Dom's fickle affections, boy."

Most holy Penates, this Bryaxis fellow had the most mesmerizing voice, not to mention a jawline so sharp it could cut stone. Simon brushed his fingers through his curls and stammered. "Um, how do you know about—?"

Max interrupted. "During our journey from Rome, I informed Bryaxis of all the nonsense going on down here ever since that barbarian arrived. But it's damn good to be home." Max cooed into Nic's long wavy locks as he hugged the blond tighter. "Nic told us all about your wrestling match, Simon." Max raised his cup as he fought to contain his laughter. "A toast to our revered victor—Simon, son of Theodorus, famed winner of the goat shit games."

"To the health of the champion!" Bryaxis chuckled as he lifted his drink and swallowed.

His neck and cheeks flushed to bright red, Simon plopped into a chair at the table and rested his face on his folded arms. "I may have won, but I cheated."

Bry tousled Simon's hair again, weaving his long fingers through his curls. "And an honest champion at that. Honorable lads are hard to find."

"You have a strange accent," Simon grumbled, refusing to lift his head.

"Has this fetching boy never met someone from the far north before, Max?" The tall man bent down to look directly at Simon. Shit, the stranger's golden-green eyes were seductive. "I was born in Caledonia. Do you know where Caledonia is, Simon?"

"Yes, I fucking know where Caledonia is. I've read Pytheas' accounts of his circumnavigation of Britannia. According to the geographies, your region's a mountainous wasteland occupied by illiterate savages."

"Charming." Bryaxis sighed as he stood and turned to Maximus. "So he's a schooled little shit, then?"

"Simon's well educated. He's apprenticed to serve as Commander Fabius's scribe."

"Can he read Greek?"

Simon sat up and snapped, "Yes, I can read Greek—sort of."

"Sort of will have to suffice. This illiterate Caledonian savage needs an assistant." Bryaxis slapped Simon's back. "Get some sleep tonight, lad. There are fucking crates of documents to review come morning. Be dressed and ready to work before the sun rises."

"Max?" Simon protested.

"It appears you have a new chore, pup." Max winked at Bry, before waving over the skittish young servant rocking back and forth on the balls of his feet by the doorway. As he took the rolled note from the boy, Max waggled his brows at Simon. "Your new Caledonian tutor here can teach you all sorts of invaluable skills, pup. Pay attention and learn."

Max unfurled the thin scroll and read the note as he dismissed the messenger with a wave of his hand. "Nicomedes, get dressed. You're to be Dom's cupbearer for this evening's dinner with Senator Plinius.

Hurry up now, and select an outfit less skimpy than you'd normally wear for the task. Dom's esteemed guest is an old-fashioned prig."

"Right! Duty calls." Nic chuckled as he pushed off of Max's lap and climbed the wooden stairs to the bedrooms on the second floor. After he'd disappeared down the hall, the door to the common room swung open again.

"Bryaxis, my dear boy!" Her shrill exuberance nearly cracked the glass water pitcher on the sideboard table. A blur of bright orange wrapped in a green dress whizzed past Simon, as the squat woman pulled Bryaxis into a suffocating hug.

"You're too thin. Is the food terrible?" She asked as she patted Bry's long, bronzed arms. Wearing a dazzling slanted smile that dried Simon's throat and made his dick twitch with interest, Bryaxis gently took hold of her wrists and stepped back. "I'm fine, Euphronia, and the food—well, it's edible. You've spoiled me with your gourmet cuisine. What are you doing here?"

"I ran into this most gallant young man on my way back from gathering blackberries for tonight's dessert. Since he'd offered to carry my heavy basket for me, I decided to stop by the stable house for a visit. On the walk over, I told him all about our situation." She gestured toward the open door. "Isn't he delightful? And so polite."

Alle crossed the threshold, a woven basket laden with dark indigo fruit hanging from his right arm. He extended his hand to Bryaxis as he spoke a garble of words in some bizarre language Simon didn't understand.

Queer barbarian fucker.

Bryaxis hesitated to shake Alle's hand for a moment before capitulating. "I am called Bryaxis. You speak common Celtic?" Bryaxis raised one brow quizzically.

"Greetings, Bryaxis. We call the language Galatian. I learned it as a child, but I fear my pronunciation's rusty. My name is Alle."

"Your pronunciation is quite good, Alle. So you're the infamous Dacian, eh? Strange. I would have expected Fabius to prefer pretty Simon here."

"Simon's his favorite whore. I'm nothing more than a prisoner of war. A temporary curiosity." Allerix replied brusquely, placing the weighty basket on the large wooden dining table.

With his elbows propped on his knees, Max vigorously rubbed his face. "Gods, are you still regurgitating that bloody rubbish? You're not a prisoner, Dacian. You're a fucking slave."

When Euphronia cleared her throat, Max added, "Apologies for my vulgar language, Euphronia. We rarely entertain women here at the stable house."

"Ten years with the general and it's no wonder you've picked up much of his colorful phrasing, Maximus." Euphronia's smile faded as she dragged her finger through a film of greasy dust covering the surface of a side table. "You boys need to tidy up this place. Grime attracts rats. And speaking of rodents, where do you keep the dormice, Maximus? Commander Fabius has requested a platter of tender fellows stuffed for appetizers tonight."

Max rose from his chair when Plautus, grumbling under his breath, shuffled into the room. He spotted their bosomed guest and exclaimed, "By the holiest gods, what a glorious vision have we here!" He bowed before taking Euphronia's small pudgy hand between his. "Forgive me, but are you the mortal twin sister of our fair-faced Venus, dear lady?"

Euphronia laughed so hard two curls broke free from their hair-pins. "Alas, I'm called Euphronia, not Aphrodite."

As she blushed, Bryaxis wrapped his arm around her shoulders. "This brazen flatterer is Plautus, respected war veteran and renowned cook of barely marginal slop, though there's rumor he bakes excellent bread. Plautus, my dear mum is looking for the dormice. Where are they kept, sir?"

Releasing her hand, Plautus backed up to scrutinize them both. "This whore is your son, dear woman?"

"I didn't give birth to Bryaxis, but I did raise him for a good part of his life." Euphronia wrapped her arm around Bry's waist and sniffled. "We're closer than most mothers and sons. For years, we belonged to Counselor Petronius until the cruel Fates took our noble master from us far too soon. Plautus, why don't you show me where to find the dormice, and perhaps I'll share one of my recipes with you, hmm?"

Euphronia reached for her berries when Plautus rushed over and grabbed the basket handle. "Please allow this humble soldier to escort you to the main house, madam. The breeding jars are stored close to the gravel path. There're several particularly plump mice ready for harvest."

Shamelessly complimenting every aspect of her appearance, Plautus ushered Euphronia out of the stable house. Max pushed past Bry and ran to the door, yelling, "Keep your lecherous hands to yourself, Plautus! Commander Fabius adores that woman. Be a gentleman, or he'll slice off the rest of your filthy sausage fingers. Um, sir."

⇶⋙≪⋘

12

THE SOPPING GREEN GRASS squished under the weight of his heavy leather soles. With each hurried step, morning dew seeped in between the woven straps, soaking Max's chilled toes. He'd checked everywhere in the main house—the atrium, the master chamber, the kitchen, both fucking dining halls, the exercise yard, the baths and gardens, and even the playroom—but he couldn't find Commander Fabius. And where was Varius? Surely Max should have run into the veteran oaf making his security rounds at some point during his search, no?

The stables.

If they weren't there, and a couple of horses were missing as well, perhaps Dom had left the estate with Varius for a trip to town, or perhaps he'd gone hunting in the nearby forests. Perhaps they were hunting for quail! Praise Minerva, Euphronia did wonders with a batch of fresh little birds. For that one dinner ages ago, she'd stuffed the quail with figs and cured pork and wrapped them in grape leaves, roasting the packed, juicy chicks in a tasty wine sauce. Gods, he'd sucked an obscene amount of delicious relish off of Dom's fingers that night.

Licking his lips, Max stopped in his tracks and rubbed his forehead. "Not Dom, you fool. Commander Fabius."

As Max marched past the stable house, the lush grass turned to loose dirt dotted with mud puddles. At this early hour, the common room was deserted, everyone off busy with chores. Nic was tending the fish, and the Dacian was mucking the stalls while Simon and Bryaxis were holed up in the spare office reviewing Counselor Petronius's letters and records.

Had Bryaxis had this much trouble when Counselor Petronius had demanded Bry call him Lucius instead of Dominus?

Probably not.

Bryaxis was clever and educated and mindful of small but significant details. And now Bry was here, living and working at the villa. Despite having lost his master and his balls, so far his poor friend didn't seem all that different. He still laughed at dirty jokes, rolled his eyes at daft comments, and launched his arsenal of sarcastic jabs without warning. When would Bry change? Max had never known a eunuch before, let alone lived with one under the same roof. Would Bryaxis become fat and bald like those Egyptian priests who oversaw the shrine of Isis in Neapolis? Would he become a skeletal waif and wear exotic outfits like the self-mutilated followers of the Great Goddess, wandering the streets and telling fortunes to any passer-by with enough coin to spare? Despite his phenomenal talents, Bry was too old now to whore for anyone else. Would Commander Fabius protect him?

Shit.

Perhaps the commander would free Bryaxis just as he'd freed Max and Theodorus. But Max wasn't truly free like Theo, was he? Not officially. When they returned to Rome, he would gently remind his forgetful patron to visit the magistrates, recite the declaration of manumission, strike him with the ceremonial rod, pay the tax, and sign the documents. Once the officials recorded his new status in the state ledgers, Max could put on the floppy cap of a true freedman and celebrate with wine and dancing and feasting.

He would rejoice day and night with Nicomedes by his side.

But when that glorious moment of official freedom finally came, would he have saved up enough money to buy Nic? Would Dom sell Nicomedes to him, as he'd hinted he would?

So many questions. So much uncertainty. Gods, his fucking head hurt.

When he approached the stables, the thundering clatter of hooves enticed him to bypass the barn and take the narrow path that led to the riding arena. And there he was, outside the paddock leaning on the fence, his rich auburn hair reflecting the early morning sun as though his curls were spun from bright copper wire. Dressed in a belted crimson tunic and leather boots, Commander Fabius raised his fist and cheered. Max blinked. Were his eyes failing him? By the immortal gods, was the bloody Dacian on the back of that feral black horse?

"Greetings, Commander."

"Good morning, Maximus. Beautiful day, no?" Gaius smiled, but his gaze remained fixed on the ebony-haired barbarian atop the horse trotting circles inside the fenced enclosure.

"The weather is wonderful, sir. Commander, are you going for a ride? Hunting, perhaps?"

"No, I've made other plans for today, Max—special plans."

"I haven't seen Varius anywhere this morning, sir."

"I've sent him on an errand. Varius should return by sunset. Why were you looking for…?" An excited whinny from the horse inter-rupted Gaius's question. He turned and shouted, "Look at that maneuver! By Mars' saucy balls, my lad's a fierce horseman."

"He's almost as skilled as Simon, Commander."

Gaius scoffed at the comparison. "Simon's never shown the courage or the confidence required to break a wild beast. Alle's fucking fearless. Watch, and you'll see."

Riding bareback, his only equipment a rope attached to a loose training halter, Allerix used his voice and his balance to push Ferox to a fast canter before abruptly slowing the horse's pace to a walk. The stallion protested, kicking up its hindquarters and turning its head to nip Alle's legs, but the barbarian remained calm and focused. He turned the animal around and repeated the gaits in the opposite direction. When the Dacian noticed Max at the fence, he cantered over and spun the horse a full circle before riding up to the railing.

Braggart.

Alle nodded to Max, although he never took his eyes off of his master. As Ferox stomped and snorted impatiently, Alle remarked between rapid breaths. "He should make an excellent hunting steed, Dominus. Very agile."

"But will that unruly nag ever be trustworthy on the battlefield?"

"Too early to tell, sir, but he's strong and damn fast. I'd say the enthusiasm is there. Ferox likes a challenge."

"What that randy bastard likes are your beautiful balls brushing all over his back. Don't get cocky, Alle. You still have to saddle him. All right, that's enough pony play for one day. Get down and wash up. You and I are going on an excursion after the midday meal."

When Gaius turned to head back to the house, Ferox backpedaled and reared before he bucked, each leap into the air more hysterical and violent. Grabbing fistfuls of the stallion's long silky mane, the Dacian held on until the fifth kick. He flew off of Ferox's back, crashing shoulder first onto the ground. Gaius and Max shimmied through the rails and ran across the arena. Dagger in hand and waving his arms, Gaius chased the frightened stallion back towards the barn before racing to crouch next to Alle's dirt-covered, prone body.

"Where are you hurt?" His eyes ablaze with panic, Gaius carefully rolled the lad over and stroked his dust-covered hair. "Answer me! Are you injured?"

"Shit." Alle opened his eyes and coughed, wiping the blood from his nose. With Max's help, he lifted himself up to a seated position. "I'm fine, sir. Nothing's broken except what little dignity I had left. Something must have spooked Ferox, but I didn't see what startled him. Is he all right?"

Exhaling in relief, Gaius tugged Alle's blue tunic down from around his waist, covering the lad's exposed crotch. Rubbing his eyes, Gaius sighed. "I fear my expensive horse may be untamable. You're damn lucky that fall didn't snap your neck. Are you sure you're not hurt?"

"I'm not hurt, sir. I've fallen off many horses, and I always manage to get back on. Trust me—with consistent training, Ferox will be an obedient and dependable mount, Dominus."

"Perhaps the animal will yield to the bridle's bit eventually, but will you ever surrender to your fate, *cățel*?" After fluffing Alle's matted hair one more time, Gaius rose to his feet, wiping the dirt off his hands. "The young believe they're fucking immortal. Max, escort our battered and bruised Bellerophon to the stable baths for a long, hot soak while I check on the preparations for this afternoon's voyage."

"Voyage?" Allerix asked, glancing nervously at Max.

"Despite that unfortunate mishap, I'm damn impressed with your riding skills. Are you game for another, less hazardous adventure?"

"Do I have a choice?"

Smiling, Gaius reached down and brushed the underside of Alle's chin. "No, you do not."

~

"FABIUS CALLS THIS A fucking office?"

Bryaxis threw open the shutters only to discover the window looked out onto the dark brick wall of an adjacent passageway. Shaking his head, he put his hands on his hips and groaned. "Simon, you'll need to light all the lamps you can find if we're going to see a damn thing in these ledgers."

The cramped storage room was stuffed floor to ceiling; narrow aisles snaked their way through mountains of teetering boxes. As Simon scurried through the maze of crates, stopping here and there to light the wicks of the ceramic lamps, Bryaxis unloaded a small container of scrolls and stacked them carefully on the reading table. They pulled up chairs, and Simon blew out a deep breath, wishing like mad that he'd taken his dull Greek lessons more seriously. At least his insecurities were distracting him from the towering Adonis sitting next to him, or they were until the man's knee casually rubbed against Simon's thigh.

"All right. Let's start with this one. What do we have here?" Bryaxis inspected the broken wax seal before unfurling the papyrus. After scanning the document, he chuckled with a sneer. "How bloody ironic. It's a letter to Dom from fucking Fabius."

"Really? What does it say?"

Bryaxis rolled up the scroll and handed it to Simon. "More of the same lies and horseshit. Fabius has never given a damn about anyone other than himself, including Lucius."

Simon scrunched his brows together as he studied the frayed correspondence. He read the first few lines and gasped, tossing the love letter onto the table as if the papyrus were on fire. "Shit, I can't read Dom's letter!" Simon lowered his voice to a whisper. "It's intimate and, um, private."

Bry snickered. "You're a bloody peculiar one, Simon. Let's move on to this document." When Bryaxis reached over to grab another scroll, his muscled bronzed arm brushed across the back of Simon's hand, sending tremors of lust through Simon's entire body.

Fuck.

"Are you shivering?" Bry asked suspiciously, as he put the scroll down and wiped his perspiring brow with his other forearm. "Fuck, it's as hot as Hades' flaming arse crack in here. You aren't with fever, are you?"

Simon stared at Bryaxis' large fuckable mouth, fantasizing how those luscious crimson lips would feel wrapped around his neglected prick. With an eyebrow cocked, Bry stared at him as he waited for an answer. Simon shoved his stiffening member down between his shaking legs and blurted out, "No, I'm not sick. I'm fine."

"Good. You can't afford to get ill. There's too much work to do. And stop gaping at me like some pathetic, deprived puppy desperate for attention."

"I'm sorry, it's just that…"

"What?" Bry crossed his arms. Gods, the man had delicious arms. "What is it, Simon?"

"I—I think you're incredibly handsome. That's all."

"How long has it been since Fabius fucked you?"

"Long before he last left for Rome. It was quick, and—just between us—it wasn't all that pleasant. I had to finish myself off."

Bryaxis grunted, shaking his head. "Well, that explains it. Listen, I appreciate the compliment, but I'm not…"

Twiddling his thumbs, Simon tilted his head, hanging on every word. "You're not attracted to me?"

"No, no—it's nothing like that. Max hasn't said anything to you and the others yet because I asked him not to." Bry rubbed his eyes with the heels of his palms and continued. "I'm not whole anymore. I was castrated after my Dom died."

When Simon jumped to his feet, the legs of his chair scraped across the floor like a witch's fingernails on slate. "Shit, they cut off your dick?"

"No." Bry rolled his eyes. "Just my balls."

"So you still have a dick?"

"For fuck's sake, yes. I have a dick, not that it'll do me any good in a few months."

"Why?"

"Do you know what a eunuch is, Simon?"

"You mean those bald, pudgy priests who stink of incense and cow shit? Most Holy Penates, are you going to lose all of your hair as well? You have such gorgeous hair." Simon sighed wistfully, touching Bry's sun-streaked brown locks until Bryaxis pulled away, snorting.

"I don't honestly know. I've never lost my balls before. But I do know that my prick will stop—working."

"Shit." Simon flopped back down into his chair. "Has it stopped working yet?"

"Not yet. I enjoyed a good wank before this morning's meal."

Simon's eyes crinkled with delight. "Me too. Can I visit you tonight? We're allowed to touch each other, you know."

"Ha! Fabius's generosity knows no bounds, does it? He lets you pull each other's peckers?"

"Yes, as much as we want. And we have toys back at the stable house. All sizes." Simon leaned in closer. "If you're looking for a huge poker, I stashed it away in my room. I'd be happy to share."

"Shit, Maximus was right. You are incorrigible. So you fancy big cocks, eh? Too bad Fabius doesn't have the equipment."

Simon sat back, propping his arm on the back of his chair and exhaled. "Yeah, I know. You'd think with that big nose of his."

Bryaxis held his stomach, tears threatening to spill down his sculpted cheeks. "Oh, Gods! Stop!"

"What did I say? I mean, Dom has a big nose, big feet, and then…" Holding out both palms, Simon shrugged. "He's not a minnow, but he's no eel."

Bryaxis waved his hand as he tried to catch his breath. "I beg you, stop. Damn, I almost thought I'd forgotten how to laugh."

"Do you have a big cock?"

Bryaxis froze, his eyes huge and his hand covering his mouth. "What did you just say?"

"Shit. My apologies. That was a rude and daft question."

"You want to see it, do you?" Bryaxis stood and raised his tunic. "Not a pretty sight, is it?"

Simon looked up, his lips parted, and swallowed. "Holy Vestals! You're fucking enormous. You're nearly as big as Max. Who needs balls when you have a cock the size of an elephant's?"

Chewing the inside of his cheek, Bryaxis glanced down at his mutilated crotch. "I'm nothing more than a fucking discarded mutant."

"Rubbish! You look fine to me. More than fine. Did it hurt?"

"What do you think? I fucking blacked out from the pain."

"Well, you're safe now. We can be friends, right? Eunuchs need friends, don't they?"

After dropping the hem of his tunic, Bryaxis bent down and brushed the long curls from Simon's face, giving him a light peck on his forehead. "We're going to be good friends, Simon, son of Theodorus."

Gods, his lips were warm and soft and—perfect. So Bryaxis didn't have balls. Simon had never been an enthusiastic ball licker in the first place.

"There you are! Atticus told me you were wandering about the main house. Come and give your mother a hug." Dressed in her typical flouncy garb, Callidora stood with both arms outstretched until Simon reluctantly rose and awkwardly embraced her. They rarely touched—shit, they rarely talked—since his poor older brother had been wrenched from their mother's grasp and sold off to some heartless, sadistic bastard.

"Greetings, Mother. Welcome, home. Let me introduce you to—"

Calli took two steps back and pursed her lips in disgust. "Ah, yes, Maximus's castrated acquaintance from Rome. For the life of me I can't imagine why our Dominus has brought this feckless gelding down here to our villa."

"Don't be vicious, mother." Simon glared before glancing at Bryaxis. "Bryaxis is here to examine Counselor Petronius's papers. He's going to figure out who murdered his master."

"And Simon is my overly-optimistic assistant. You're Callidora, aren't you? Max has had much to say about you, none of it flattering."

"Maximus is a spiteful bastard."

"Aside from his devotion to Fabius, he's also an excellent judge of character. You should be thanking me, Callidora. By the time Simon and I finish examining all these documents, your son will be an experienced archivist and scribe, well worth his weight in bronze." Bryaxis stood up and smiled smugly. "I have to admit I'm shocked Fabius has kept an old harpy like you around for so long, but there's no accounting for some fools' tastes."

With waves of colorful fabric flying in her wake, Callidora stormed over and jabbed her breastbone with her thumb. "I am the most valuable member of this family, and Dominus would agree. Watch your disrespectful, forked tongue around me, you useless whore."

Bryaxis stuck out his long tongue and wiggled it in her face, causing a most embarrassing gurgle to erupt from Simon's mouth, something halfway between a gasp and a giggle. With his sleek arm draped over Simon's shoulder, Bryaxis cocked his hip as he pointed to the door. "Leave, sorceress. We have work to do."

"You don't order me anywhere."

"Fine, stay and watch." Combing his fingers through Simon's curls, Bryaxis kissed him on the mouth, urging him to part his lips with the tip of his probing tongue. The toasty room began to spin; for the love of all the gods, the man tasted even better than he looked. When Simon's knees wobbled, Bry pulled him into an embrace and sucked on the soft swell of his upper lip. Simon moaned, and the door to the storage room slammed shut.

Bryaxis pulled back, stroking Simon's cheek, and chuckled before he sat down in his chair. "Is your mother always that malicious?"

Catching his breath, Simon replied, "Unfortunately, yes. She's an angry woman, but she adores Dom. What's your mother like?"

"Dead for all I know. After the soldiers destroyed our village, they put my mother and my older sisters in a separate wagon with the other women and carted them all off to gods know where. The brutes hauled my pitiful arse to Rome. I'll never see my family again, alive or dead."

Simon folded his hands and stared at the floor. "You were born a free person, like Max?"

"My Caledonian birth name was Brendan. Lucius gave me the slave name, Bryaxis. It could have been worse. His other choice was Brocchus."

Simon giggled. "Toothy?"

"I do have a big mouth."

Simon's mirth gradually faded, replaced by that familiar ache of melancholy he'd carried in his heart since childhood.

"I'm a homebred slave, born into this family, but I lost my older brother. I mean he's not dead, I think. He was sold to a different household, but no one knows where he is now. My mother begged Dominus to bring Castor back to us, but Dom couldn't find him."

"Wait, Fabius sold off your brother, and then…?"

"No, no. It was Dom's mother, Julia, who sold Castor to this horrid, despicable monster, or so my mother once told me. I don't remember much from the short time I lived in Rome."

Crossing his arms behind his head, Bryaxis leaned back. "What a pair of sad, sorry slaves we are. Come on—back to work. I need to review whatever's in that stack of crates before sunset, or your master will have me flogged."

"He's your master as well now, Bryaxis."

"Fabius will never be my fucking master. I'll obey him and finish this task, but only because that's what Lucius would have wanted. When I'm done, Fabius will sell me or kill me. Doesn't matter really."

"Dom will protect you. You'll see." Simon scratched his ear and asked, "Bryaxis, um—was Dom responsible for cutting off your balls?"

"Fabius? No, he had nothing to do with it." Bryaxis bit his lower lip and turned away as a tear slid down his face. "It was Lucius's order."

⇶⟫⟩✕⟨⟪⇷

13

ALLERIX TURNED HIS HEAD toward the refreshing breezes blowing off the ocean. The winds cooled his face, a welcome relief from the otherwise blistering afternoon heat. Perched on a wooden plank seat, he swayed back and forth while wave after wave slapped against the sides of the boat. Despite the queasy feeling churning his stomach, he enjoyed riding the sea swells as they lifted and rocked the small vessel forward to some unknown destination.

As the sun sank lower in the sky, its intense rays weakened, and the waves turned into gentle ripples. Two of the crewmen pulled their oars out of the water, placing them on the broad lip of the vessel with a splashy thump-thump.

"We're nearly there," Gaius murmured with a hint of glee.

Allerix tried to ignore him, but he couldn't temper his curiosity. "Where is there, sir?"

"Patience, Alle. You'll see."

"I won't be able to see anything unless you remove this blindfold. Sir."

When he laughed, Gaius's breath tickled the perspiring skin just below the nape of Alle's neck, sending tingles down his spine.

"Soon, but not yet. We need to round one last outcrop in the cliffs."

Gaius pulled him in tighter and rested his chin on Alle's shoulder. "I want you to see this spot as I first saw it and because I'm a selfish prick, I want to experience that moment anew through your eyes."

"Where are we going?"

"To a hidden oasis I've never shared before."

"Not even with your dead lover?"

The awkward silence was broken only by the shrieks of the gulls and the splashes of two oars slicing through the calmer waters. Allerix feared he had pushed too far when Gaius relaxed his grip and sighed. "No, I never did bring Lucius to this spot. I discovered this haven before the First War and purchased the land for a hefty price. I visit when I can, but I've kept her secret all these years, all this time waiting."

"Waiting for what?"

"Waiting for whom, *cățel.*"

"For whom, then."

"For you."

Alle's neck warmed bright red. He tried to say something coherent, but his tongue refused to cooperate. Several moments passed before Gaius untied the loose knot of the blindfold. The black strip of cloth that had covered Alle's eyes since they'd left the villa's stone quay slipped down his face and dropped into his lap.

"There she is." Gaius wrapped his muscular arm around Alle's waist and pointed to the curve of white sand in the secluded inlet. "My secret mistress."

Bracketed by steep rocky crags, an ominous cave dominated the otherwise idyllic, sandy cove. As the boat drew closer, the sea breezes trapped by the bluffs whistled like the deadly serenades of the Sirens that bewitched Odysseus' crew. The vessel jerked when the hull scraped along the bottom of the sea floor; Gaius and his team of oarsmen jumped out and dragged the boat up onto the beach.

"Take my hand and let me show you my grotto. Don't worry about those—the boat hands will unload the supplies."

Fine white sand coated Allerix's bare feet as they climbed the gentle slope to the cave's jagged entrance. Hidden in the shadows sat two plush couches draped in sumptuous fabrics embroidered with gold thread. Surrounding them stood ornately carved tables, marble water basins, and silver lamp holders, transforming the natural hollow into a fantastical stage for a lavish but intimate dinner. Together they stood at the entrance in silence until Gaius exhaled and said, "This is the first time I've seen her adorned in all of her fineries. She's more splendid than I'd anticipated."

Alle spun around, his jaw slack. "How—how did you do all of this?"

"I have copious funds and a fucking army of slaves," Gaius stated, his voice flat and emotionless, before he walked farther into the cave. Suddenly, Gaius exclaimed, "Look here, Alle! Our pugnacious friend, Varius, hauled this hefty oak table to this very spot from way over there on the beach. He carried an entire damn boatload of furniture up to this grotto on his back." His lips pressed together, Gaius tapped the table's surface with his knuckles. "Alone."

Smirking, Allerix scratched his sunburnt cheek. "By himself? But you just said you have an army of slaves."

"The onerous, unpleasant chore was his punishment for striking you. I won't tolerate baseless violence inflicted upon any member of my family, soldier or slave. Varius has a hot temper, but he's an honorable veteran who understands discipline. I disciplined him."

Allerix wandered around in circles, stopping twice to marvel at the irregular, dagger-like rock formations suspended from the domed ceiling. Were they real or carved to appear real? What was the truth, and what was an illusion?

"Varius hates me," Allerix mumbled while reaching up to touch one of the lower hanging rock protrusions.

"The blade of a Dacian falx scarred Varius's face, though to be honest he was never an attractive fellow. He fought valiantly on the battlefield that day, but it was Fortuna who saved him. I was sure the old ox would die from his injuries before nightfall.

For generations, we've fought Dacian incursions across our borders, attacks on our allies' villages, and senseless disruptions of our trade routes. For as long as I can recall, Romans have feared and despised your people, veterans of those brutal wars most of all."

Furrowing his brow behind his thick black fringe, Alle traced circles around a large knot in the table's oak surface with his finger. "Do you hate my people?"

"Dacians are—or, were—the finest warriors I've ever had the honor to defeat."

Before Allerix could respond, Gaius placed his hands around his waist and lifted him, setting his bum on the edge of the table. He took a wicker box from one of the attending boat crew and set it down beside Alle's hip. After dismissing the servant, Gaius lifted the hinged lid and wagged his eyebrows as he rubbed his hands together. "Euphronia prepared a selection of her special delicacies for us. Let's see what we have here, hmm?"

"Why are you doing this?"

Gaius dropped the lid and fiddled with Alle's fugitive tag, rubbing his left hand up Alle's lean thigh. "What exactly is it you think I'm doing?"

Despite the cooler temperature and the sheerness of his gauzy, short tunic, sweat poured down Alle's neck, soaking his back. Between the man's touch and his sun burnt skin, he was on fucking fire.

"Treating me to a feast in your secret cave, this magical place you've never brought anyone to before. Why?"

"You're too young to be so damn cynical." When Gaius laughed, his deep dimples were even more seductive. He cupped Alle's face and cooed, "I can't have a banquet without you, Alle. You're the dessert. Do you see these bottles nestled in straw inside this basket? Each one contains a different, delectable sauce. Close your eyes."

Gritting his teeth, Alle hesitated.

"Would you prefer to be blindfolded again, *cățel*?"

"No." Allerix snapped. After one last, lingering pause, he reluctantly lowered his eyelids when Gaius pinched his earlobe.

"Are we forgetting our manners?"

Alle clenched his fists and grumbled. "No, Dominus."

"And can I trust you to keep those big, beautiful eyes shut?"

"Yes, Dominus."

"Good boy. Self-control is the noblest of virtues, or so that gloomy Stoic philosopher, Zeno, once claimed." Gaius's husky voice nearly drowned out the sounds of straw crunching and wax seals popping off the containers. "Although the tenets of the Stoic school appeal to me, I'm wary to heed convictions spouted by a bedraggled Cyprian. Did you know old Zeno committed suicide by holding his breath?"

Alle opened his eyes and scoffed, "That's not possible."

"Right. Blindfold it is, then." Smiling, Gaius set the glass jar on the table and loosened the yellow linen sash tied around Allerix's waist, pulling it off slowly while he stared into Alle's eyes. Once the make-shift blindfold was snug and secure, Alle exhaled and waited. He rubbed his abdomen when his stomach grumbled loud enough to echo through the cave.

Gaius chuckled. "Open up—and no biting."

Two thick fingers coated with sauce brushed over Alle's tongue, filling his mouth with a sweet syrup lightly seasoned with pepper. After Allerix sucked off the relish, Gaius withdrew his fingers and scratched the late afternoon stubble on Alle's chin.

"Tasty?"

Nodding, Alle forced a smile. "Delicious."

"Why are you scared?"

"I'm—I'm not scared. I'm suspicious."

"That's understandable. I'll have to earn your trust, just as you must earn mine. Now, the concoction in this green bottle smells brilliant. Fucking perfect for pork. Bring the first course!"

Soft footsteps tapped across the sand. Metal scraped against wood and pinged against more metal while liquid splashed into empty cups. Once the table stopped shaking, and the din quieted, Gaius yelled, "Music!"

The performers started to blow their pipes when Alle blurted out, "Dominus, may I ask a question?"

Gaius gently squeezed the tops of Allerix's knees. "You may."

"Are we eating stuffed mice?"

"I didn't order any mice prepared, but I can send for some."

Allerix reached out and happened to catch Gaius's forearm. "No! Please don't. I'd prefer not to eat rodents, sir. Well, that's not entirely true. I do like a well-seasoned rabbit. I love rabbit."

"What a charming smile." Gaius laughed. "It pleases me to see you relax. And you're in luck. I see our dear Euphronia prepared one of her succulent roasted hares. Can you smell it? Lie down on the table and raise yourself up on your elbow like a proper dinner guest. There you go—that's right."

As he lay down, Allerix's stomach growled again. Earlier that day, after he'd stripped off his soiled riding clothes, he'd foolishly soaked his sore muscles in the stable bath for too long and missed the midday meal. Now, his nose greedily inhaled every whiff of the appetizing aromas permeating the air of the cave. With his eyes blindfolded and his mouth watering, he pushed away his distrust in anticipation of that first bite of Euphronia's famed fare.

"By Minerva's tits, what a feast we have here! Open up."

When Gaius pushed a bite-sized morsel of food between Alle's lips, a chorus of perfectly harmonized flavors exploded in his mouth: cooked minced rabbit marinated in a wine broth with chopped berries and nutty spice. Allerix chewed the tender meat and groaned with pleasure; Gaius offered another taste, which he eagerly gobbled down before licking his lips.

"That's divine," he said and opened his mouth wide like a baby bird begging for more.

Gaius placed another bite of food on his tongue. "With more training, Alle, you could be the star attraction at those naughty dinner parties I attend back in Rome. I can picture you now, naked and kneeling on a stool below my couch, your skin adorned with glittering flecks of gold. You'd remain completely still, your full lips parted, obediently waiting for your benevolent master to spoil you."

A tidal wave of nausea ripped through Alle's stomach, souring his appetite. He choked down the morsel and asked for a drink of water, but a bitter hint of revolting bile clung to the back of his throat. The humiliation required to endure these deceitful games was dangerously close to unbearable. He took a deep breath and asked, "Then you'll take me to Rome, sir?"

"As I told you, I'm considering it. First, however, I need to persuade the emperor to allow me to return. If there are notations concerning some crime or nefarious affair tucked away in Luc's papers, Bryaxis will find them. And if Luc's chicken scratch holds promise as a clue to solving his murder, Emperor Trajan should grant me permission to come home sooner than he'd intended." Gaius paused. "Would you care to try a spoonful of this lovely cheese relish? I believe this ambrosia was made with the milk of my prized goats."

Shit, not those damn nanny goats again.

Allerix half-heartedly nodded and forced his lips to open; a smooth, tangy mixture of mild and pungent cheeses danced across his taste buds. At least if he had to suffer these indignities to fulfill his destiny, he'd do so with a content belly.

Gaius brushed his cheek. "It's excellent, no? All right, my turn. Lie down on your back."

After stretching his body along the length of the table, Allerix lay with his arms at his sides, his sight obscured by the dark golden veil of the blindfold. When he moved his right hand to quell an itch, his fingers bumped against a short stack of thin metal objects. Serving spoons, he guessed, before jerking back his hand and flattening his palm on the table's surface.

"Don't let this startle you."

Despite the warning, Allerix instinctively flinched when Gaius poured a thick cold liquid, drop by drop, onto his sun burnt skin. The smooth mixture flowed down to his breastbone, pooling in the hollow at the base of his throat just above the riveted bulge of his silver slave collar. With a satisfied groan, Gaius lapped the fragrant nectar off his skin. After he'd devoured the entire, tiny puddle of sauce, he ran his tongue up and over the knob of Alle's larynx. He sucked and kissed the bony lump before nibbling the side of Alle's neck just below his left ear until Allerix squirmed.

"You're delightfully ticklish here, aren't you?" Gaius chuckled against his neck.

Even though the strip of cloth shrouded his vision, Alle squeezed his eyes shut. Why did the Roman bother with this playful seduction when he could easily take whatever he fucking wanted? What did the bastard gain from this tortuous charade? Suspicion boiled in Alle's gut, his instinct to resist increasing with every beat of his heart.

Without warning, Gaius pulled down the cloth covering Alle's eyes. He extended his hand and said softly, "Let's retire to the couches so we can dine with more decorum."

Staring at the barbed underside of the cave's ceiling, a rush of panic raced through Alle's body. He grabbed one of the metal spoons resting beside him on the table before realizing too late it was a knife. He stared at it, knowing full well he should drop the weapon, but his hand refused to cooperate with reason. Gaius grasped Alle's wrist and squeezed hard.

"This is how you thank me for my generous hospitality?" The Roman's tone was cold and venomous.

Dazed by his irrational decision to snatch the utensil in the first place, Allerix stuttered, "I—I didn't know. I didn't intend…"

He uncurled his fingers, and the weapon fell, ringing like a finger cymbal when it hit the wooden table. After picking up the carving knife, Gaius turned around and lobbed it onto the sand. One swipe of his arm and the rest of the tableware flew to the ground. When he shoved Allerix down onto his back, Alle tried to scramble away, but Gaius climbed on top of the table's sturdy surface on all fours and pressed Alle down with his heavier frame. Their brief scuffle ended when Gaius pinned Allerix's wrists above his head.

Breathing hard, his amber eyes wild and hot, the Roman crushed Alle's wrists and growled. "What did I fucking say about playing with fucking knives without my permission? By bloody Pollux, did you so foolishly imagine you could kill me with a table knife?"

Allerix waited until Gaius caught his breath. "I made a mistake. I don't want to kill you, Rufus."

"Another mistake?" Letting out a scornful chuckle, Gaius rolled off and stood by the edge of the table. Tousled clumps of auburn curls framed the man's face, his thin lips twisted in fury. He withdrew his lion-handled dagger from the scabbard strapped beneath his tunic and raised its lethal blade; his golden-brown eyes darkened to a shade closer to arousal than anger.

"Everyone out of here!"

The music stopped abruptly. The servants scampered out of the cave, leaving just the two of them poised for a private battle, alone together in uneasy silence.

He snatched the hem of Allerix's tunic and pulled the garment taut, slicing his sharp blade up through the fabric.

"Honest mistakes are tolerated, but always corrected. If I'm ever to bring you anywhere, *căţel*, you'll require more discipline. I can't have my slave stealing sharp implements off the serving trays at exclusive dinner parties."

Gaius sliced the tunic open to Alle's navel and pressed the blunt side of the blade against Alle's stomach. "I've always loved to play with knives. You're not squeamish about blood, are you?"

Gaius jammed the point of his dagger into the wood and used both hands to rip apart the rest of Alle's flimsy tunic. "Roll over on your stomach and stay completely still. Trust I will not injure you, at least not seriously."

Allerix swallowed and turned over, fighting his fears, succumbing to his furtive desire to submit. He exhaled and gripped both sides of the table. If he were ever to be allowed to visit their king's palace, he would do so as the Roman's obedient whore. Alle took another deep breath, mindful that every effort to comply would bolster the bastard's confidence in him. Every act of submission was another step towards his ultimate goal.

Revenge.

Immortality.

Gaius ran the flat of his dagger's blade up Alle's right thigh, dragging the steel in a straight line over his sensitive tendon. Allerix didn't move a muscle, but instead pressed his cheek against the wood and concentrated on the steady rhythm of his breathing: inhale, exhale, inhale.

Trust.

The Roman gulped a drink, probably wine. Alle gasped when Gaius touched the knife to his right arse cheek, tracing circular patterns over his tender skin with the blunt side of the blade. Fear gripped his gut; Alle started to shiver and shake.

"Self-control, Alle."

Gaius drew the steel up the furrow between Allerix's shoulder blades, pressing hard enough to scratch. Across his shoulders it trailed and back down the length of his left side before gliding over his left hamstring. In its wake, the dagger's metal left tingling trails of warmth. Was he bleeding? Where was the pain?

He startled at a sudden sharp sound before realizing Gaius had slid his blade back into its scabbard.

"And again, I'm impressed. Take this cup and quench your thirst while I wipe these puddles of sweat off your delectable body."

Trembling, Allerix lifted himself up on his elbows. The crisp white wine drenched his parched throat and warmed his belly. Two more, long swallows and he'd drained the cup. He placed it on the table by his head and glanced over his shoulder. No blood. No damage to his skin except harmless pink stripes.

"You didn't cut me?"

With a smile, Gaius flicked the band of wet fabric, slapping Alle's bum. "No, this time I did not. You have to be fit to ride that mad horse when we return to the villa. But you performed well, Alle—more fearless than those I've been forced to tie down to play this game." Gaius snatched a fistful of Alle's damp hair. "Do not break my fucking rules again. No knives. Understand?"

"Yes, Dominus."

"If you ever pull a knife on me again, I will use the lethal edge of my dagger. There will be blood."

He let go of Alle's locks and stroked Alle's body, gently rubbing the light rosy marks on his skin. "Courage, composure, and obedience are rare and highly valuable traits. You impress me more with every test. I fear, if I'm not careful, I may lose my heart to you, *căţel.*"

Alle swallowed. What was he supposed to say? Was the Roman speaking the truth, or were his words more cleverly shrouded deceptions?

Before he had a chance to navigate the storm of conflicting emotions swirling through his head, Gaius lifted him off the table, pulled his head back, and devoured his mouth in a passionate kiss. With what little strength he had left, Allerix turned around and kissed him in return, running his hands over Gaius's body. He couldn't dampen his urge to taste and smell and feel every inch of the man. Although he could feel the sand under his toes, he was floating, his fears extinguished by desire, by the overwhelming ache to surrender.

Allerix broke off the kiss and fumbled with Gaius's tunic. "Off."

"Was that a bloody order?" Gaius chuckled.

"A request, Dominus."

Gaius pulled his tunic over his head and tossed it over a lamp stand. "Request granted."

After he'd unstrapped his scabbard and thrown it behind him, Gaius spun Alle around and lightly bit the top of his shoulder. "Gods, you're a sweet, sensual boy. My beautiful, brave barbarian."

When Gaius pushed his legs apart with his feet, Alle gasped but didn't resist. He waited, anticipating the initial discomfort of penetration, but the Roman only slathered the insides of his thighs with oil. "I will worship you as Alexander once loved his beloved companion, Hephaestion."

Gaius pushed his hard cock between Alle's quivering thighs before squeezing Alle's legs together, enveloping his heat between Alle's slicked muscles. Whatever the fuck the Roman was doing, it felt damn good. Allerix leaned back, arching his neck over Gaius's shoulder, reaching and pleading for more of Gaius's mouth. With one arm wrapped around Alle's hips and the other hand stroking Alle's erection, Gaius bent his knees and thrust his cock into the tight, slippery space between the tops of Alle's hairy legs. His throbbing shaft slid in and out, rubbing against Alle's full balls while Gaius's right hand pumped Alle's prick closer and closer to orgasm. Alle stood up on his toes and held onto the table, fighting the forceful urge to release his seed.

"Wait—wait for my permission," Gaius growled, his raw lust deepening the tone of his commanding voice. Balling his hands into fists, Alle nodded; rivulets of sweat flowed down his face and neck. Gaius plunged harder and faster until, sucking the back of Alle's neck, he cried, "Now!"

Gaius came first between Alle's trembling thighs; his sticky semen covered Alle's balls and the insides of Alle's legs. While Gaius groaned against Alle's shoulder, Allerix's balls emptied, splattering cords of milky cum over his stomach and the table. Caught somewhere between laughing and sobbing, Allerix gasped for air as his legs shook uncontrollably. Gaius's strong fingers combed through the tangles in his hair while his lips planted sloppy kisses up his neck. Alle swayed to one side, and Gaius caught him, pulling him back to rest against his soaked, broad chest.

"You enjoyed that, *cățel*?" Gaius murmured playfully.

Allerix slowly tugged out of Gaius's embrace to turn and face him. Wearing a grin so broad his full cheeks mimicked a squirrel's swollen with chestnuts, Alle draped his arms over Gaius's shoulders and leaned on him for support. A soft sound resembling 'Yes' was all Alle could manage before he brushed his lips across Gaius's hot mouth and moaned. "Dominus."

"You've never been loved in the Greek manner before?" Gaius asked, his voice sounding so damn pleased it threatened to dissolve into laughter.

"I never knew—" Allerix rested his brow against Gaius's forehead and paused to draw another deep breath. "That was even possible."

"The gods have gifted men a variety of exquisite positions for making love and satisfying our desires, Alle. I intend to see you experience them all." Gaius ran his palm over Alle's abdomen before he stepped back and offered out his hand. "By Hercules' crusty scrotum, we're both fucking covered in gloppy seed. Come, I have something else to share with you."

Alle lifted his heavy eyelids. "Food?"

"Are you still hungry? Soon we'll eat, but let's save the next course of our private feast until after you've seen this. I have another surprise, something unique." Gaius pushed aside rogue strands of Alle's ebony fringe and pressed his mouth against Alle's forehead, whispering, "It's another treat I've never shared."

He clasped Allerix's hand, snatched a bronze oil lamp from one of the lamp holders, and guided him to the dark recesses in the back of the cave.

"We're going in there. Are you frightened of confined spaces?"

"There's little that frightens me, Dominus."

"Good. Fortuna favors the bold. Now mind the jagged rocks and don't let go of my hand."

Naked, they treaded carefully through the narrow tunnel. When the cramped passageway opened wider, Gaius stopped. The thrilling sound of water gushing from somewhere echoed off the rock walls. Gaius loosened his tight grip and pressed a finger against Alle's lips.

"Stay here. I'll light the torches I've had fixed to the walls."

At first, Allerix could see little beyond his outstretched hands. When Gaius lit the first torch, and then the second and third, the rough textured walls and vaulted ceiling of a second, smaller grotto appeared. Every surface sparkled as though coated with gemstones. A rushing stream of steaming water emerged through an opening high up on the back wall before cascading into a wading pool below.

Allerix gazed in wonder at the staggering space. It couldn't be real but yet here it was. He had no words in his language adequate enough to describe this wondrous magic.

"Those are slivers of quartz embedded in the rock," Gaius explained. "The crystals shimmer in the torchlight like bright stars in our night sky. Natural hot springs are common here in Campania. Some fools believe they are the tears of the betrayed god, Vulcan, as he toils at his forge inside the mountain of fire."

Gaius strolled over to Allerix and snorted. "I suspect there's no divine blacksmith crying streams of sorrow, but I'm an incorrigible skeptic when it comes to the priests' fanciful stories. The natural historians tell us the earth's furnaces inside our ferocious volcano heat the spring water. Be careful, Alle! The water's much too hot to touch until after it collects and cools in the basin. Fortunately, the pool's not deep and the temperature's perfect for a brief soak." Gaius took hold of Allerix's hand and added with a smile. "Let's wash off so I can dirty your beautiful, clean body all over again, yes?"

~

STRETCHED OUT UNDER A blanket on one of the couches, Allerix rubbed his eyes and yawned, his body and mind refreshed from a deep, restful sleep. The first rays of the sunrise peered over the edge of the cliffs, coloring the ocean's surface with an entrancing, yellow-rose hue. He sat up and surveyed the dimly lit cave, only to discover he was unshackled and alone.

After drinking a cup of cool water and relieving himself in the silver chamber pot, Alle scanned the isolated cove as he strolled to the water's edge. Gaius's red tunic lay crumpled on the white sand, discarded close to a smoldering fire pit. Underneath the cloth Alle discovered a folded blanket and an opened travel satchel; the edges of papyrus scrolls peeped out from between the worn leather flaps. Nearby, sat a pile of kindling and a jug of crimson wine.

A pair of footsteps in the sand led to the water.

Shielding his eyes, Allerix stared at the ocean's expanse until Gaius emerged naked from beneath the gentle surf. His skin glistened in the sunlight like the bronze of a divine statue. Poseidon himself had come alive before Alle's eyes.

Memories of the previous night's delicious lovemaking feast flooded Alle's heart. After they'd finished the rest of the dinner courses, Gaius drizzled a mixture of honey and cream over Alle's cock and balls and teasingly sucked off every sweet sticky drop. Afterwards, he rolled him over and poured more honey balm over his arse. Once Gaius had licked his cheeks and crack clean, he turned him over once more, wrapping Allerix's long legs around his waist, and impaled him. Gaius smothered his mouth with his lips until they both surrendered to eruptions of exquisite pleasure.

No one had ever kissed Alle in that manner; no one had ever cherished him so completely and selflessly. His confused heart fell deeper into a toxic swirl of love and resentment. Damn the gorgeous bastard!

Allerix waved from the beach as Gaius trudged through the waves towards the shore. Sopping wet, he kissed Alle's mouth and took the garment from his outstretched hand.

"Greetings, *cățel*. How did you sleep?" Gaius asked as he wiped his face and patted his dripping copper curls.

"Extremely well, Dominus. Have you been awake long?"

"You'll learn I rarely sleep more than four or five hours at most. But I've found there's no better way to start a new day than with a good book and a vigorous swim. By Neptune's shriveled balls, that water's damn cold. Come sit with me. I'll relight the fire, and we'll watch the sunrise."

After he'd pulled on his tunic, Gaius threw a handful of twigs and two larger pieces of wood onto the embers. The blaze grew quickly, its flames twirling up into the breezy morning air. They settled down on the blanket when Gaius grabbed the wine jug and enjoyed a long, satisfying gulp. Wiping his mouth, he said, "Swimming in the ocean is a source of immense comfort. She soothes my soul because she's in my blood. My family has always owned seaside property; my great-grandfather, Servius Cornelius Scipio, spent much of his life in ships traversing her waters."

"He was a sailor?"

"An admiral in the navy."

Allerix snickered. "Of course—an admiral. I take it that's an important job."

Gaius merely smiled and guzzled down another swallow of wine.

"This cove is wonderfully serene, Dominus. May we stay here for the rest of the day?"

"Sadly, no. The boat to bring us back to the villa should arrive soon. I need to check on Bryaxis' progress, and you need to saddle that damn stallion."

Allerix pulled in his legs, resting his cheek on his knees, chewing on his thumbnail. It was time, perhaps his only chance to address the key to all his plans. He had to know.

"Am I your favorite, Rufus?"

Gaius narrowed his eyes at Alle's audacity. "My favorite?"

"Nic explained how it works, the hierarchy and special privileges and all."

"Did he, then? Gods, I despise the daft gossip that flitters about the stable house. Listen, I adore all of my boys. Some nights I prefer to fuck one lad more than I do the others. Other times, I want to play with my girls. And then there are those wicked evenings when I enjoy all of my pets at the same time. You do remember the enormous bed in the playroom?" Gaius laughed and waggled his eyebrows.

Blushing, Allerix confessed, "Yes, I remember."

"Don't listen to Nicomedes. I suspect our dear lamb is worried I won't take him to any more dinner parties in Neapolis, the insecure prat."

"I suppose that's possible, sir. But Nic's a good sort."

"Yes, he is." Gaius rubbed his face and exhaled. "So you want to be the favorite, whatever the fuck that means? Well, you can't be the favorite because only slaves can be promoted to that mythical status. But you claim you're not a slave, Alle. You've declared on several occasions that you consider yourself a prisoner of war, yes?"

Lifting his head, Alle glared defiantly. "I am a prisoner."

Gaius leaned over and kissed Allerix's nose. "Let me know when you've come to your senses and finally accept the wars are over."

Sharing the rest of the wine, they said nothing for a while, comfortably lulled by the crashing waves and the morning calls of shorebirds. Alle took the last swig and smiled. "I enjoyed last night,

Dominus—very much."

"Now *that* pleases me, *cățel*."

"I was surprised you didn't chain me to the couch after I'd fallen asleep."

"If I do take you to Rome, I'll need to trust you won't run away or do something even more idiotic. Prisoners of war are notoriously unpredictable. Tell me, when is your birthday?"

"My birthday?" Allerix laughed in disbelief. "Um, it was few days before the summer equinox. I spent it shackled to the bars of a cage in a hot, stinking slave market."

"Most unfortunate." Gaius reached into his leather bag. "Here, a belated birthday present."

Allerix took the slender scroll secured with a blue ribbon from Gaius's hand. "What is this?"

"I just told you. A gift. Open it."

Allerix unfurled the scroll. His hands began to shake as he read the document. Every nerve in his body told him to jump to his feet and run, but there was nowhere to escape to here on this secluded beach nestled beneath the steep craggy cliffs. Alle read the words a second time, and then a third, his heart threatening to burst from his chest.

His lips trembled as he looked up. "What—What is this?"

"As far as I'm aware, that's the only official record we have of your capture, Allerix. I discovered that addendum stashed away in the state archives, and I stole it."

"You know who I am?" Allerix was close to tears, as he envisioned his entire scheme for revenge disintegrating to worthless dust. He pointed to the letters and asked, "How did you know this was me?"

Gaius tapped the edge of the scroll. "All military missives from Dacia pass across my desk at some point or other. It wasn't hard to put two and two together. And when I realized my Dacian peasant was, in fact, a prince, I found myself in a dilemma. In Rome, possession of a Dacian royal is considered a treasonous act, punishable by death. I could be executed for owning you."

"Then why do you keep me?"

"I'm entranced by you, thanks to our cruel Venus. And your skin is not riddled with royal tattoos betraying your lineage—a wise decision, by the way. Your fiery nature intrigues me, Allerix. I won't have your gorgeous body ripped to bloody bits by the beasts in our great arena. You belong to me. I protect my family."

"You're keeping me and, in doing so, breaking your own laws because you love me?"

"Love? Let's call it enchantment for the time being."

"What am I supposed to do with this?" Alle asked, waving the papyrus.

"It's yours to do with as you wish. There's a good chance that scrap of papyrus is the only evidence proving Allerix, second son of King Thiamarkos, ever existed. Keep it tucked away in your room as sentimental proof of your barbarian nobility, but understand that record could bring death on us both."

Gaius lifted Alle's chin, stroking the side of his jaw with his thumb. "Or you could destroy the damn thing, and only I will ever know who you are. It will be another one of our secrets. Save the record or burn it. It's your choice, Allerix."

After staring at the scroll for a while, Alle crumpled it into a ball and tossed the record of his capture into the flames. He blew air through his pursed lips, fighting back the tears, as he watched his identity and his past burn to ash. Now that everything was gone, there was nothing left to lose. Taking a deep breath, he brushed away a sniffle and gazed into Gaius's amber leonine eyes.

"The wars are over, Dominus."

"Yes, they are, Allerix. Now that you've accepted reality, we can return to the villa and resume your training. Some day perhaps I'll share my other mistress with you, the glorious capital city of the entire fucking world. My home."

14

CROSSING HIS ARMS AS he leaned against a tower of crates, Gaius stood in the narrow passageway and watched Bryaxis and Simon inspect one document after another from the pile of scrolls stacked on the storage room table. When Simon tapped Bryaxis on the shoulder and pointed to a line on a record, the Caledonian draped his arm over Simon's shoulder and spoke softly into Simon's ear. These two rascals had become rather friendly, hadn't they?

He marched over and gripped the backs of their chairs. "Greeting, lads."

"Dominus!" Simon sprang to his feet and clumsily dropped to his knees. Would Simon ever learn to genuflect with a bit more fucking grace? In stark contrast, Bryaxis stayed seated, elegantly folding his arms behind his back, and lowered his chin in deference. Gaius arched a brow and nodded his approval.

"What's your report?"

Bryaxis tapped the carefully arranged collection of rolls on the left side of the table. "We've examined these records, sir, and we'll finish that entire pile by sunset. Those crates by the window were reviewed yesterday. We've found nothing curious yet, I'm afraid."

"You two have been scouring Luc's papers for how many days now? Fifteen, is it? For fuck's sake, the Dacian has nearly tamed that

226

damn feral horse in half that time. What *have* you found, Bryaxis?"

"So far, only trial transcripts and letters, sir. Dom's notations on everything we've examined so far appear routine and insignificant."

"Were any of those letters from me?"

"Yes, Commander. I took the liberty of gathering your letters to Dom and organizing them into a separate batch. They're in the box on the floor here."

"Did you read them?"

"No, sir."

"Liar." Gaius scoffed. With a skeptical grin, he picked up the box to rummage through its contents. "Shit, some of these are ancient. Here's one I'd sent shortly after I'd arrived in Macedonia. And another when Lucius had taken leave from his studies to return to Rome for his mother's funeral."

"Dom purchased me at auction during that visit," Bry added, before quickly shutting his mouth and handing Simon another document to inspect.

"Yes, I remember." Gaius grunted and carried the box of letters over to a chair beneath the window. As he sat down to rifle through the old correspondence, Simon blurted out, "Holy Penates, what's this?" Realizing his audacity, he lowered his head and mumbled, "My apologies, Dominus."

Gaius strolled over and stood beside Simon, fluffing the lad's mop of brunet curls with his fingers. "What have you discovered, pup?"

Simon relaxed and exhaled. "Drawings in the margins, sir. Are these—are these Counselor Petronius's drawings, Dominus?"

Gaius leaned down for a closer look and hollered with laughter. "By randy Jove's purple prick, those are Lucius's sketches! He used to draw all the time, until his tutors, not to mention his parents, demanded he stop wasting his energies and focus on his studies." He carefully pulled the scroll from Simon's hands and brought it over to peruse under a large bronze lamp hanging from a stand.

"You lads need more fucking light in here. I can barely see a thing," Gaius grumbled. In the margins of the document, sections of otherwise blank space were filled with rapid, skillful sketches. "Let's see what you've created to entertain us, my old friend. Hmm, we have animals. He always did prefer to draw animals."

Gaius unrolled the long sheet of papyrus wrapped around the rod in his right hand, rewinding the reviewed sections back around the wooden roller in his left. "And here's more animals: elephants and bears. He's drawn three elephants dancing with three bears."

He unwound more of the scroll. "And here the elephants are wrestling the bears, and finally we have the elephants fucking the bears with their trunks. That's lovely, Lucius."

Gaius grinned and glanced back at Simon and Bry; mesmerized, Simon was beaming ear-to-ear while Bryaxis had his eyes closed, tears running down his face.

Gaius tossed the scroll onto the table and asked, "Is there something wrong with you, Caledonian?"

Bry wiped his eyes before coughing into his fist. "Dom was always doodling pictures right up until the day he was murdered, sir. Back when I was promoted to serve as his apprentice, I was a distracted, squirmy little shit but he was convinced I could learn. He'd sketch all sorts of creatures in the margins of dull law records to encourage me to review every column of writing. At the end of each workday after I summarized what I'd read, Dom would say to me, 'And tell me what happened my story?' And I would recount whatever plot he'd crafted with his silly sketches. He loved how much I enjoyed his indecent fables."

Without thinking, Simon exhaled. "Shit, that's romantic." He snatched another scroll, unfurled it and exclaimed, "Here's another one with drawings in the borders! Is that—is that a dog?"

Bry leaned over. "It appears to be a dog and an eagle." Bry cocked his eyebrow and chewed his lower lip. "I've never seen these sketches before, sir."

Gaius circled around behind them to peer over their shoulders. "That's not a court transcript. It's a financial ledger. You see the numbers." Gaius pointed to the text and bent down lower; his eyesight wasn't nearly as sharp as it had once been. He scanned the writing, scratching his scalp. "This is a treasury record, an official tally of palace expenditures. I thought I told you to review those first?"

"I did, Commander; I reviewed every one I could find before that nervous imperial freedman came to the Caelian to collect the documents. Gods, he was a twitchy codger, babbling non-stop about how he had to return the ledgers to the palace archive storehouse as quickly as possible." Bryaxis rubbed his chin before touching the edge of the scroll. "That's odd, sir."

"What?"

"This is a copy, not an original like the scrolls I reviewed in Rome, sir. You can tell an original from a reproduction, Simon, by the poorer quality of the papyrus. It's thinner, more brittle. Dom must have obtained a set of facsimiles from the palace archivists."

Gaius rubbed the papyrus between his thumb and forefinger, before conceding, "Yes, you're right. It's a copy. He never told you about obtaining a set of replicas?"

"No, sir. Why would he want a replica when he'd been given access to the originals? And why did Dom separate this record out from the other expenditure lists? He was always fastidious about organizing his papers."

"Unroll the damn thing, Simon. Let's see what lewd zoological adventure our dear counselor left for us this time."

Simon slowly unwound the document and revealed a similar scenario of lively animal drawings populating the margins:

A large-eared dog stalking an oblivious eagle;

The dog and the eagle boxing before a small crowd of spectators;

The dog and the eagle fighting as gladiators with a sword and a trident;

The dog, now accompanied by a peacock companion, chopping off the sorry eagle's head.

"This tale's a bit more gruesome." Bryaxis noted while Gaius sat back down in the chair by the window, carding his fingers through his hair.

A dog, a peacock, and an eagle?

As Simon continued to unfurl the papyrus, Bryaxis shouted, "Stop!"

Gaius glanced up. "What is it?"

"An unusual notation, sir." Bryaxis placed his pointer finger on a smudge of writing. "Right here. It's letters, I think. Greek letters, though they're nearly illegible."

Gaius rushed over to the table and pressed his face close to the scroll until his beaked nose was a hair's breadth from the papyrus.

"Pi. Alpha. Alpha. Is that a judicial abbreviation?"

Bryaxis shrugged. "I've never come across it before, sir. Perhaps Counselor Plinius could be of assistance? He's had much more experience with both legal and financial records, sir."

Gaius rested his knuckles on the table and glanced in the direction of the doorway. "Gods know Pliny hasn't been much help yet. Bloody old tramp can't remember a damn thing from that dinner party save the menu and that absurd fish story. Roll that ledger up. I'll see if he can shed light on the letters' significance before he departs for

Neapolis."

"He's leaving so soon, sir?" Bryaxis asked.

"Not soon enough." Gaius snatched up the scroll and snaked his way halfway across the room when he stopped and said, "Simon, wash up after you finish here. We're having a party in the playroom tonight."

Simon mumbled a curt, "Yes, Dominus."

What had happened to the pup's spastic, randy enthusiasm? Gaius mulled it over for a moment and added, "You as well, Bryaxis."

Over the stacks of crates, he overheard Bryaxis whisper a disgruntled, "Wonderful," as Simon clapped softly. Gaius shook his head with amusement and headed for the guest suite.

~

"GAIUS PLINIUS, ARE YOU comfortable? Should I have a servant fan you, or are the ocean breezes sufficient to cool your indolent plebian arse?"

Lying on a plush couch at the edge of the spacious terrace overlooking the white-capped, azure waters, Pliny pushed up the brim of his straw sunhat and smiled. "Commander Fabius, I can't thank you enough. This unexpected seaside holiday has been both vivifying and relaxing. I fear I may never leave."

"Oh, trust me. You are leaving. The horses will be ready for your departure to Neapolis after the midday meal."

"Oh gods, Neapolis. Remind me again exactly why I'm dragging my old senatorial bones to that crime-infested sewer of a city?"

"You have business with the decurions at the civic assembly hall tomorrow—a meeting concerning the harbors, as I recall. I, on the other hand, plan to enjoy a more licentious affair this evening. Dionysian revelry with bountiful refreshments and the exquisite company of my lusty, limber fauns."

Blushing like a callow maiden, Pliny jerked himself up to a seated position and waved his hand. "No, no. That's very generous of you, Commander, but I'll be on my way shortly."

"That wasn't an invitation to the bash, old boy. You're leaving long before the sun sets, but before you do I need your assistance."

"Gaius, I've already told you everything I can recall about the dinner party."

Gaius dragged over an ornate stool and sat down, handing Pliny the unfurled scroll. "Have a look at this document from Lucius Petronius's office. It's a copy of a palace ledger he must have acquired during his embezzlement investigations."

"Hmm? Yes, it's a facsimile." Pliny unrolled the papyrus and laughed. "By Castor! What are these depraved drawings in the margins?"

"Lucius fancied himself an artist in his leisure."

"He was talented. Are you looking for my assessment of their artistic merit?"

"No, read on. There's a curious scribble likely made by our dear Lucius. I don't recognize it, and Lucius's legal assistant has never seen it before. I thought, given your years in the courts, perhaps you might understand its significance."

Pliny unrolled the ledger, scanning column after column, until Gaius jabbed his finger at the scrawled Greek letters. "There."

"Pi, alpha, alpha?" Pliny scratched his temple before taking another sip of wine. "This is not a legal notation. Since these are financial records, perhaps it's arithmetic? Greek letters can also be read as numbers, as you well know. Could there be some meaning associated with eighty-two, or perhaps eight hundred and eleven?"

Gaius shrugged. "Anything's possible, I suppose."

"What's the text here by these account numbers? Ah, it identifies a substantial withdrawal from the Treasury as a maintenance expense."

"Maintenance for what?"

"Doesn't specify. Perhaps costs related to a road project or aqueduct repairs or a temple refurbishment? These funds could have been used for anything, Gaius. Our esteemed Emperor is obsessed these days with putting his marble signature all over our fair capital."

"I've noticed his zeal for building. He's restless. Peace bores him."

"Well, I for one am basking in this rare cessation of hostilities. The campaigns against those heathens across the Danube were glorious but costly. And for what?"

"You know very well for what, Senator. Dacian gold."

Pliny sighed. "Yes, and more mines, more grain, more territory. By the most revered gods, one day this empire will crumble under the weight of its ungovernable expanse. Gaius, did you hear our gracious Emperor is considering me for the governor's post in Bithynia? What on earth am I going to do in that remote wilderness?" Pliny whined as he continued to unfurl the remainder of the scroll.

"You'll manage, counselor. There are far worse places to be assigned than that Greek region on the dark sea. Be grateful he's not shipping you off to the fucking bowels of the Carpathian Mountains. Wait! Stop there. What are those notations?"

Pliny lifted the papyrus closer to his nose and squinted. "Now these comments I understand. Here, our dear Lucius had jotted down cross-references to two more documents. See? And again, there's those curious Greek letters, or numbers—pi, alpha, alpha. The citations I do understand refer to the tag identifiers attached to the scrolls. Do you have the records he's referenced amongst that slew of our dear departed counselor's papers?"

"I'll have the slaves search for them." Gaius plucked the scroll from Pliny's fingers and stood, gesturing towards the door. "Thank you, Counselor Plinius. You've been helpful. Come, let's enjoy one last stroll through my garden before we eat, hmm?"

"Splendid idea, Commander. A bit of exercise should rouse my palate. What are you serving if I may be so rude as to inquire?"

"Lampreys from my ponds."

Smacking his lips, Pliny rubbed his palms together. "A superlative delicacy. And perhaps your cook might prepare a platter of stuffed dormice to whet our appetites?"

～

"FOLLOW ME."

When Allerix reluctantly took his hand, Gaius detected trepidation tingling up through the lad's fingertips.

"Are you sharing another one of your secrets with me, Dominus?"

Gaius tightened his grasp and led Alle down the corridor away from his master chamber.

"My sexual proclivities are hardly secret around here." Gaius chuckled before adding, in a more serious tone, "This time we're not enjoying a private picnic, *cățel*. We have guests waiting for us in the playroom."

Caressing Alle's twitchy hand, Gaius pushed the heavy door of the playroom open half way. Silver and bronze oil lamps of all shapes and sizes, some crafted to resemble birds, hung from elaborate stands positioned in the far corners of the spacious room. The flickering light of the flames darted across the red frescoed walls, illuminating the Cupids crafted in stucco cavorting on the ceiling and the plush burgundy fabrics covering the enormous bed. Before Gaius crossed the threshold, Alle jerked his hand out of his grasp, his heavy-lidded eyes dark and defensive.

"You had me beaten in this room."

Gaius took a deep breath and closed the door, leaving them standing alone in the hallway. "You were punished. Tonight is not about punishment, Alle."

"Is this another test?"

Cupping Alle's jaw with his hand, Gaius grazed his thumb across Alle's lips. "No tests—only ecstasy and celebration. Will you join me or would you rather I have a guard escort you back to the stable house?"

Allerix sucked in his upper lip and asked in a tone more worrisome than was warranted, "Who are these guests, Dominus?"

Rubbing his brow, Gaius smiled and sighed in exasperation. "My handsome freedman, Maximus, and three delectable pleasure slaves. You know everyone behind that door, some quite well I imagine."

"Oh, I thought…"

"Yes?"

"Then the guest isn't that gaunt, older man with the strange hat who's visiting from Rome?" Allerix wrinkled his nose, but Gaius ignored him. He had more pressing desires than to frighten the cub further by reprimanding him for his disrespect towards a Roman magistrate.

"Gods, no. Senator Pliny's of a different inclination; he wouldn't know how to enjoy one of my boys, let alone all of them. The old coot was put on his horse and trotted off to Neapolis earlier today, *cățel*. It's just us. Are you coming?"

Gaius held out his hand, and Allerix took it, his grip more firm and confident.

When they entered the room, Simon and Nicomedes were down on their knees, their foreheads pressed against the marble floor, gold bangles hugging their taut biceps. They both wore ivory linen skirts tied around their waists with string, the curves of their round bums on blatant display. Behind them stood Max and the Caledonian, ivy-leaf wreaths adorning their heads, short staffs tipped with pinecones in their hands. Max's bulky ebony arms sparkled with silver jewelry. Smudges of charcoal encircled Bry's stunning, golden-green eyes. In the glittering lamplight, the lot resembled a pack of wanton satyrs waiting to start a salacious bacchanalia.

Tugging on his heavier blue tunic, Allerix leaned over and whispered into Gaius's ear, "I'm overdressed."

"We'll take care of that soon enough." Gaius placed his hand on Alle's shoulder. "Kneel, *căţel.*"

After Allerix knelt, Bryaxis gracefully sank to his knees. Max glanced around and began to lower himself when Gaius shook his head, wagging his finger.

"Maximus, freedmen do not kneel. Ah, look! Splendid! You've prepared our entertainment."

Gaius strolled over to the canvas and leather sling suspended from iron hooks on the ceiling and caressed the tightly woven straps of hide between his fingers. Smooth and supple, but sturdy. He'd had it crafted based on his recollections of a similar toy back in Athens.

"By Pollux, we haven't brought out this exquisite contraption in far too long. But before we succumb to its delights, fetch wine for everyone, Bryaxis."

Bryaxis rose to his feet and gathered up the silver cups on the side table, placing them onto a tray with a pitcher of wine. After he'd served everyone a full cup of drink, Gaius inhaled the grape's fragrance. "An excellent dark, dry Falernian, the prized fruit of our fertile mountains and a rare treat for you lads. Rise to your feet and drink to sacred Eleutherios, the giver of many joys. Cheers!"

"To Dionysus! Cheers!" They all replied in unison except for Alle, who appeared bewildered but intrigued.

Gaius tossed back a swallow and roared, "Let golden Aphrodite's festivities begin!"

Simon guzzled down his wine in three slurps before snuggling his glistening body between Bryaxis and Max. They took turns kissing him, rubbing their experienced hands over his gyrating arse and sleek torso. Max and Bry performed like seasoned dancers, anticipating each other's every lustful maneuver. When Max devoured Simon's mouth, Bryaxis latched onto Simon's neck, sucking his skin, pulling loose the string holding up the lad's skimpy covering. Simon moaned as the thin fabric clung to his erection before fluttering to the floor.

"They are beautiful, aren't they?" Cup in hand, Gaius draped his arm over Allerix's shoulder and smiled. He pointed to the leather apparatus and asked, "Would you care to try Venus's divine swing, Alle?"

Transfixed by the playful threesome fondling one another a few feet away, Allerix swallowed a hefty mouthful of wine and wiped his lips. "What does that device do?"

Gaius laughed and tossed back another swig. "Nicomedes, come here! Explain to our dear boy what the swing does."

His golden brown balls swinging to and fro beneath the hem of his short skirt, Nic sashayed over and wrapped his arm around Alle's other shoulder, purring into his ear, "The swing doesn't do fucking anything, Dacian, except cradle the lucky slut the rest of us worship with our cocks and mouths. Have you ever been fucked by a group of generous, talented companions before?"

Allerix's spine stiffened. He glanced sideways at Gaius before shaking off Nic's arm. "No, I haven't. The only companions I've been forced to endure were savage animals."

Gaius squeezed his cup until his knuckles turned white. Have patience, he reminded himself. Titus Petronius wouldn't fail him. He'd deliver a list identifying the rogue scouts who'd raped Allerix, who'd discovered his royal birth name. No matter who they were or where they were, the Lion of the fucking Lucky Fourth would hunt them down one by one. The lethal point of Gaius's sword would be the last bloody thing those soldiers would see before they crossed to the Underworld. Allerix would be safe.

Nic held up his hands. "Easy there, Dacian. No need to be prickly. We're all friends here, except for Dom cause, well—Dom's our master."

Gaius slapped Nic's partially exposed bum. "Shut your luscious mouth and refill my cup, lamb."

"Yes, Dominus."

After Nic had slipped away, Gaius kissed Alle softly on the mouth to reassure him. "Relax, *căţel*. The swing is simply a shrine for pleasure, but you needn't experience it until you're ready. Perhaps you'd enjoy a demonstration?"

Allerix tried to disguise the thrill creeping into his voice with a disinterested, "As you wish, Rufus."

Gaius yanked on the twisted coil of Alle's silver collar, pressing his finger against Alle's lips. "None of that fucking 'Rufus' nonsense, not while we're in the company of the other lads. Permission to refer to me by that absurd nickname of mine is a liberty I grant only when you and I are alone. Understood?"

"I understand, Dominus."

With a quick pat to Alle's cheek, Gaius ambled across the room to the rollicking threesome and carded his fingers through Simon's soft, honey-brown curls. How the boy loved to be loved. Nic handed him a second cup of wine; Gaius took a sip and pulled Simon away from Max and Bry's greedy affections. "You're overdue for a delicious, eye-watering fuck, aren't you? Let's not delay our starving pup's gratification. Lift him into position."

Nodding simultaneously, Bryaxis and Max each took one of Simon's arms and carefully guided him backward to the edge of the canvas seat. Bry leaned over and asked with concern, "Do you want us to secure these bindings, Simon?"

His green eyes aflame with excitement, Simon nodded furiously. "By the Holy Penates, Bryaxis! If you don't strap me in, I'll fall out and crash onto the fucking floor."

After Simon had lowered his bum into the seat of the swing, Bryaxis fastened the padded straps around his wrists and, with his palm pressed against Simon's chest, pushed him downward. Simon's legs lifted up into the air. Max grabbed Simon's feet and buckled the second set of leather bindings around his ankles. With a gentle shove from Max, Simon swayed back and forth, his limbs splayed as if he were a young Ixion strapped to the fiery wheel.

"Comfortable, pup?" Max asked, tickling Simon's toes, his hardening cock protruding under the sheer fabric of his white tunic.

Maximus had always fucking loved the swing.

"Comfy cozy, sir. Dominus, can they blindfold me?"

Gaius grinned. "Bryaxis, blindfolds are kept in that storage chest in the alcove. And grab the spare jars of oil as well. Atticus will restock the supply come next market day."

"Yes, sir."

When Bryaxis had finished tying the soft black cloth around Simon's head, shielding the boy's lust-filled eyes, Gaius pulled Nic closer and relayed his orders to the entire group.

"Nicomedes, attend to Simon's neglected cock while I encourage Alle to relax. I suspect our sheltered barbarian has never experienced an orgiastic party. Caledonian, fuck Simon's fetching mouth if you can still manage an erection without your balls."

Bryaxis opened his mouth to say something but clearly thought better of it and nodded once as Gaius continued. "Simon's arse is yours to plow, Maximus. Make the pup sing for us, yes?"

His lips parted in anticipation, Simon groaned and squirmed, gripping the swing's tethers.

"With pleasure, Commander." Max tipped his chin, his hand under his tunic stroking his member fast and hard. Gaius rubbed Max and Nic's shoulders before marching over to the bed to view the spectacle. He patted the mattress and leaned back. "Alle, replenish your wine and join me."

"There's a sweetness to it that tastes peculiar. Is this wine tainted?" Alle asked, licking his lips as he sat down.

"A splash of honeyed aphrodisiac never hurts. It's mild and harmless. Stop worrying and enjoy the show."

"Do you ever participate, sir?"

When Gaius stopped laughing, he stroked Alle's cheek and whispered, "I've played the leading role on occasion."

Blushing, Alle looked down and rubbed his thumb across the floral designs on the surface of his metal cup as Simon's moans and gasps filled the smoky air.

Gaius lifted Alle's chin. "Tonight, my affections are focused on you, Alle. Given the prudish traditions of your people, I'd wager you've never experienced polyamorous play with a chorus of lads. By the gods, little compares to having every erogenous spot on your body stimulated at the same time by a gaggle of beautiful boys. I want to bask in your first impressions. I confess I have a deep fondness for novel escapades."

Allerix forced a half smile. "Novelty is fleeting, Dominus."

"Then I'd better hurry. Stand up and peel off that tunic, Alle."

Gaius commanded with a smile and a flick of his finger before scooting his arse up the mattress for a more panoramic view.

Alle lifted his tunic over his head, slowly. When Simon cried out behind him, he froze. Gaius spread his legs and tapped to the section of bedcovers between his thighs. "Come here, *căţel*. You'll appreciate their performance better from this vantage point."

Allerix crawled onto the mattress and settled between his legs, his round bare bum nestled against Gaius's crotch. His crack was hot and tight and far too tempting. Gaius took a deep, steadying breath, wrapping his arms around Alle's waist.

"Well, look at that. Luc's whore can indeed get his pecker up. Impressive, though his virility won't last much longer. Such a shame—the Caledonian has one spectacular purple spear. I've always been envious."

Alle scoffed. "He's a slave. How could you ever be jealous of a slave?"

"Bah! To the eyes of the gods, we're all fucking slaves. Fortuna's fickle temper determines what roles we play in this ever-changing game of survival." Gaius dropped his voice to a whisper, "Allerix."

Alle gasped, pressing his cheeks harder against Gaius's groin. Gaius pulled him closer and smiled; he'd have to call the Dacian by his full proper name more often. As Alle's breaths became more rushed, Gaius nibbled on his earlobe. "Keep your hands latched to my hips, beautiful. No touching your cock until I grant permission. Tell me, which excites your more? Penetrating or being penetrated?"

Alle clenched his fingers around Gaius's hipbones and fell back against his shoulder, his eyes half shut. "Both excite me, though I've never penetrated anyone."

"Mmm, yes. Both are exquisite," Gaius murmured against his black hair as he glanced over at the swing. Bryaxis' impressive cock was halfway down Simon's throat; the lad was having difficulty taking all of the Caledonian's length, saliva dribbling from the corners of his stretched lips, but Simon smiled around Bry's girth. The lad had always loved substantial tools.

"Our sweet Simon loves being the center of the attention." Gaius chuckled against Alle's neck. "Are you enjoying yourself, *cățel*?"

"They're tantalizing to watch." Allerix groaned and dug his fingers into Gaius's flesh. "Please, Dominus. Please touch me."

"Patience, Alle. An arduous journey makes the destination all the more delicious."

While Bry fucked Simon's mouth, Max poured oil onto the lad's chest and dipped the pinecone tip of his mock satyr's staff into the puddle of viscous liquid. After he'd coated its leather surface with lubricant, he brushed the slippery bulbous toy up Simon's crack and over his full balls.

"It's been a while since I've ploughed your tight bum, Simon," Max groaned. After making several more passes with the pinecone, he tossed the toy to the floor and bathed his fingers in oil before slowly inserting two thick digits into Simon's heat.

"Still as tight as a Vestal maiden, I see." Max smiled at Bry and pushed his fingers in further, combing Nic's silky waves of sandy hair with his other hand. "Does he still taste like a sweet cherry picked fresh off the tree, lamb?"

Nic groaned a low, slobbery 'uh-huh' around Simon's cock; Simon gasped louder and squealed as the swollen crown of Max's cock penetrated his tight ring of muscle.

"Pummel him, Maximus. Give our randy faun what he needs." Gaius growled from the bed, his hands roving over Alle's chest and abdomen. "Up on your knees, Alle." After Allerix had repositioned himself on the mattress, Gaius reached around from behind, pinching and pulling Alle's fleshy brown nipples until they hardened under his fingertips. Allerix writhed and moaned, but kept his arms at his sides.

"I adore worshipping a lad who's sensitive," Gaius murmured, lowering his hands to Alle's crotch. He latched on to Allerix's mouth, snaking his tongue between his lips, as his skilled hands lightly stroked Alle's stiff prick with teasing, upward motions. Alle's desperate mewls for more harmonized perfectly with Simon's guttural, muffled cries.

Without warning, Gaius broke off the passionate, deep kiss. "Such a damn gorgeous cock you have, *cățel*. Stay right here and do not touch yourself."

Alle protested with a confused whimper when Gaius removed his hands and rose from the mattress. In one smooth motion, Gaius lifted his tunic over his head and dropped the garment to the floor. The warm, perfumed air of the playroom sent shivers up and down his aroused, naked body. He strolled over to the swing and lifted Nic mouth off Simon's engorged cock. "Come play with us on the bed, my naughty Nicomedes."

Nic wiped the spit from his lips and smiled. "Yes, Dominus."

Gaius turned to Max. "Give our Caledonian slut a turn pounding Simon's scrumptious hole, Maximus." Gaius leaned closer and whispered, "And after Bryaxis buries his prick deep, fuck his barbarian arse. Gods know our poor eunuch must need a good hard thumping after all this time, hmm?"

Max arched a brow and grinned wickedly. "I'm sure that's true, sir."

Gaius gave Max a peck on the lips before, he and Nic held hands and approached the bed; Alle watched in awe as Gaius unfastened the scrap of fabric tied around Nic's waist. Gaius caressed the curve of Nic's arse and commanded, "I'll fill your delectable mouth while our dear Alle fucks you with his lovely cock."

Allerix's eyes widened with shock and disbelief. "Dominus?"

"You'd said you've never speared another lad's bum. Is that true, *căţel*?"

Alle swallowed and nodded, sputtering a hushed, "Yes."

"Do enjoy Nic's arse, but be gentle—at first—and, more important, be aware that playing the role of lustful Jove is most addictive." Gaius chuckled, brushing Alle's sweaty face with the side of his hand. Gaius gently shoved Nic forward. "Up on the bed on all fours, lamb."

Nic snickered as he climbed up onto the mattress, positioning his body to afford Max a clear view of the action, and raised his bum high. Standing at he edge of the bed, Gaius lifted Nic's chin and slipped his aching cock through Nic's flushed, swollen lips. After a deeply satisfied groan, Gaius gestured toward the side table. "Use a good amount of that oil in the bottle there, Alle."

Allerix nodded, his hazel eyes turning coal-black with lust, unable to free his gaze from Nic's tempting arse crack. After he reached over and fumbled with the jar, he doused his cock with the slippery lubricant, spilling glops of oil onto the bedcovers.

"Careful with that costly oil." Gaius laughed, shoving his cock farther down Nic's talented throat.

Alle looked up and stammered, "I—I'm sorry, sir."

"No more talking. Fuck Nicomedes."

When Allerix pushed his shaft into Nic's tight hole, he closed his eyes and roared the filthiest groan Gaius had ever heard. Gaius bent down and grabbed Alle's collar, pulling his face up for an indecent kiss. Their tongues wrestled as their cocks slammed over and over into Nic's compliant body.

Panting, Gaius murmured into Alle's ear, soft enough so only Alle could hear his confession, "You and I are much alike, my sweet Prince Allerix."

Alle gasped and screamed, "Gods, yes!"

One final ferocious thrust and Alle emptied his balls into Nic's intoxicating heat. Catching his breath, ecstatic tears running down his reddened cheeks, Allerix brushed his small nose across Gaius's lips and whispered, "Thank you, Rufus."

❯❯❯❯❯✦❮❮❮❮❮

15

GAIUS FABIUS'S SEASIDE VILLA, CAMPANIA

KNEELING BEFORE THE STATUETTES housed inside the small shrine built into an alcove off of the kitchen garden, Nicomedes placed a garland of flowers on the altar and recited the prayers.

"Take this garland—oh, Lares, oh, Penates, oh, Genius Spirit of our Paterfamilias, oh, Genius Spirit of Counselor Petronius—and protect this household. Bring all who dwell here good fortune, happiness, and prosperity. May you all be strengthened by my offering."

After he'd lit the incense and the ceremonial oil lamp, Nic poured a stream of wine into a sacrificial bowl on the altar. Once the offerings had been made, he pulled off his hood, lowered his head, and finished the invocation to the household gods. "Blessed may it be."

Gazing at the boy's back, Max added in his deep booming voice. "You forgot to ask for good health, lamb."

"Shit!" Nic recovered his head with his thin cloak and blurted out, "And bring good health as well, divine Penates and everyone else." Nic rose to his feet, turned, and grinned that sublime smile he only shared with Max. He pushed back the hood before flinging his long blond braid over his shoulder.

Gods, even after six years, the man still took Max's breath away.

"How long have you been standing there, sir?"

"Not long. I'm headed to the kitchen, but your beauty distracted me from my task. Haven't you already offered the morning prayers to our household divinities, Nicomedes?"

"Yes, sir, but I thought another demonstration of devotion couldn't hurt."

"One can never show too much devotion, sweetheart." Max cupped Nic's face with his huge palms and planted a soft kiss on Nic's forehead. "Are you purposefully avoiding your chore, Nic?"

Nicomedes raised his pinky and confessed, "One of those nasty, slimy lampreys latched onto my finger yesterday, Max. I know Dom finds them tasty and all, but I hate those fucking eels. They're mean and ugly."

"Stop sticking your hands in that damn pond, you adorable imp." Max chuckled against Nic's hair and gave his arse a hard pat. "Now, off with you and feed those fucking fish, yes?"

"Yes, Hercules." Nic pursed his lips in a mock kiss and flashed a coy smile before trotting off towards the villa fisheries stocked with an exotic array of sea life. Gods forbid those repulsive lampreys perished from hunger. The Commander adored them fresh and well fed, grilled over a wood fire and smothered in a vinegar and honey sauce.

As Max turned to cross the herb garden for the kitchen, the flames of the torches attached to the walls of the alcove simultaneously flared up and blew out. Only the ceremonial oil lamp on the altar remained lit.

"Maximus." A voice hissed.

"Who's there?" Max asked as he cautiously took three steps towards the tiny, temple-like shrine. He nearly peed his tunic when the small toga-clad statue of Counselor Petronius's Genius waved him to come closer. Max crouched and stared at the bronze image bouncing on his toes amongst the lifeless statuettes of the other domestic deities.

"Thank venerable Juno, you can hear me! Greetings, my dear Maximus."

"By the most unholy Furies!"

His eyes as wide as wagon wheels, Max backpedaled, looking to his right and then to his left. He was alone, except for the wee bronze man strutting back and forth atop the altar.

"Counselor Petronius, is that you? You're—you're alive?"

"Alas, no. I'm quite dead."

"I—I don't understand, sir. You're talking? Why are you speaking to me, sir?"

"Because you, my dear fellatio trainer, performed the traditional rites before the shrine in my home. My household gods had been woefully neglected. Our dear Gaius might imagine his old harpy's magic caused my reawakening in this statuette, but he'd be wrong. It was you, darling."

"Me?"

"Thank you, Maximus. You are a most pious and honorable fellow."

"Um, can everyone hear you, sir?"

"Apparently not, nor do they seem to see me. I've been jumping, screaming, and waving my arms like a crazed idiot, but no one has noticed me. Even Gaius walked by with nary a glance in my direction. Max, I can't get down from this blasted shelf. Lend me a hand, won't you?"

Max held out his large hand, and little bronze Lucius vaulted down into his palm. When Atticus appeared on the opposite side of the garden, Max gently wrapped his fingers around the statuette and hid it behind his back. Shaking his head, Atticus toddled past him, grumbling about the disarray of the playroom and the cost of imported orchid oil. When he was out sight, Max opened his hand

and stared at the statuette's tiny face. He nearly dropped the bronze idol when it reclined in his palm, raising itself on one elbow.

"Ah, it's damn good to be away from those insipid figurines in the lararium shrine. They're spooky, just standing about, doing nothing. Max, how's my Bry? Gods, I've been sick with worry. He's all right, isn't he?"

Max swallowed and whispered, "He's fine, sir."

Max desperately wanted to ask the man why he'd ordered Bry's gelding, but he was fairly certain he didn't want to know the reason, whatever it was. Best to not to bring up the indelicate matter at all. And besides, even in miniature form, Lucius Petronius intimidated the crap out of him. He always had.

"Bry's here at the villa, sir. Dom—I mean, Commander Fabius has boarded him at the stable house with the rest of us. It's not the sort of accommodations he's accustomed to, mind you, but he's managing. Bryaxis is resilient—he's a fighter, Counselor Petronius."

"Thank the gods he's safe. Can I see him? I suspect he won't be able to hear me. I only want to look at him. I beg you, please take me to Bry. I've missed him more than I can bear, Maximus."

"Of course, sir." Max choked back a sob, carefully tucking the figurine safely into a fold of his cloak. He glanced over at the marble sundial in the center of the garden. The hour was close to midday; perhaps Bryaxis was back at the stable house. As Max walked down the gravel path, he questioned his sanity, but reminded himself that the cosmos contained all sorts of miracles and strange wonders. There were omnipotent gods most never saw, bizarre events no philosopher could explain. Perhaps Counselor Petronius's spirit had been revived not by piety or spells but by his devotion to Bryaxis? Was love that powerful?

It was another scorching day, the fruits on the lemon trees nearly ready for a second summer harvest. Max froze in his tracks and wiped his brow.

Gods, what the fuck was Dom going to say when he learned of Lucius Petronius's resurrection? Dom had said he'd sensed the presence of his ancestors' ghosts back at his mansion in Rome, but what would he think when he learned about an animated idol that acted and sounded like Counselor Petronius?

Shit.

Max rubbed his temples and picked up his pace, imagining the possible scenarios. Perhaps after his tragic death, Lucius Petronius hadn't crossed the River Styx like most departed souls. Or perhaps he'd come back from the Underworld, bent on revenge? Was Bry's former master stuck in the eerie shadows separating the world of the living from the Elysian Fields of eternal happiness? Max touched the statuette through the fabric of his cloak and exhaled. Perhaps if the counselor saw Bryaxis, his spirit would feel comforted and finally traverse Charon's waters?

When Max entered the common room, he discovered Simon scarfing down his midday meal. He and Bry must have been allowed an early break from their tedious work in the spare office.

"Greetings, pup. Where's Bryaxis?"

His mouth stuffed with food, Simon glanced up through his floppy curls and garbled an incoherent string of words as he pointed to the wooden staircase leading to the second floor.

"Is he in his room?" asked Max, gripping the metal figurine hidden in his cloak.

Simon nodded and smiled, bits of bread falling from his lips onto his plate. Max climbed the steps two at a time and tapped lightly on the wall by the open door so as not to startle his dear friend.

"Enter."

Bry sounded tired and sad. Shit, he always sounded glum these days.

"Greetings, Bryaxis."

"Max? What a pleasant surprise. Greetings! Tell me you've come to skewer my arse again."

Laughing, Max cleared his throat. "I'm afraid not."

"Pity, but thank you for last night. My bum is still tingling. Gods know I needed a good fuck."

"Give thanks to Commander Fabius, not me. I was just following orders."

Bryaxis flashed his familiar grin and gestured for Max to sit. "Ever the devoted, obedient soldier. How may I help you, mate?"

Max dragged a stool over and lowered his large frame onto the curved seat. The wood creaked under his weight. "Bryaxis, do you believe in ghosts?"

Bry frowned. "Ghosts? No, I don't. After witnessing the rape of my sisters and the destruction of my village, I don't believe in anything but the certainty of death and despair. Lucius is gone, and someday I'll be dead as well. Soon, if Fortuna is merciful."

Max covered his mouth and momentarily closed his eyes. Gods, would Bryaxis ever recover? Would he ever again find happiness?

"I don't believe in ghosts either, Bry. Or I never did until a few moments ago."

Max reached down and poured himself a cup of water from the pitcher on the floor next to Bry's bed. After a long, fortifying gulp to loosen his tied tongue, he placed the cup on the floor beside his seat and exhaled.

"Listen to what I have to say and don't interrupt. Your Dom is still here, Bry, and he's asking for you. I know it sounds bizarre but his spirit hasn't gone to Hades. It's in his Genius statuette. I don't understand why, but it seems I'm the only one who can hear him. Bry, he jumped off the altar right into my fucking hand! Counselor Petronius pleaded with me to bring him to you." Max withdrew the Genius idol from his tunic and laid it on Bryaxis' thin mattress.

Bry stared at the lifeless object for several moments before lifting his bewildered gaze. His eyes were glassy, his expression skeptical.

"Are you mad, or have you become a cruel fucker, Max? I thought—I thought we were friends."

Max leaned forward and put his hand on Bry's thigh. Bryaxis was trembling. "I'm sorry. I know it sounds impossible and absurd, but you have to believe me."

"Is he talking now because I can't hear a fucking thing? I know, why don't you ask him why he had my fucking balls cut off?"

Max cleared his throat. "Counselor Petronius? Bryaxis is here. Can you see him? Do you want me to tell him something?" Max leaned down, lowering his ear to the statuette and waited for what seemed an eternity, but nothing. Not a word or a flinch of his wee bronze limbs.

"Doesn't feel like chatting with his old, mutilated whore?"

Bry's sarcastic demeanor darkened to rage. He snatched the metal statuette off the bed and stared into its blank eyes. "Nothing to say at all, eh? Well, I have a couple of things to tell you, Dominus. You bloody said you loved me, over and over until I was fooled enough to believe it. But the chief counselor of the courts, our most noble Lucius fucking Petronius, never loved his halfwit barbarian slave, did he? Was it another one of your jokes?

Fuck you, Lucius! Fuck you for having me castrated! Fuck you for saying you cherished me when you never did, you heartless, deceitful Roman prick! You're no better than Fabius."

Bry paused to catch his breath and chuckled in disgust, scrubbing his face. "No, that's not true—you're far more vile. At least Fabius's arrogance is honest. He never pretends I'm anything more than dispensable property. You and all the other aristocratic cunts you called your associates are nothing more than sadistic, selfish bastards, and you're the worst of the lot. I hope you fucking rot, Lucius!"

Bryaxis pulled his arm back and hurled the idol across the room; it smashed against a thick beam and dropped to the floor. Its miniscule arm broke off but otherwise the figurine remained intact. Max ran over and squatted to scoop up the two pieces. "I swear this thing talked to me, Bry. I'm so fucking sorry. I—shit, can you forgive me?"

Max looked up to find Simon standing in the doorway, his brows drawn together in confusion.

"What's the matter? I heard shouting," he asked.

Bry jumped to his feet, breathing heavily, his face flushed and sweaty. "Everything's fine. Max and I had a minor dispute over a useless little doll. The fucking thing's worthless, Max, just like me. Come, Simon. It's time for us to return to work. Let's go."

Close to tears, Bry pushed past Simon and bounded down the stairs.

"Max, sir?"

Max pressed his teeth into his bottom lip as he slipped the statuette and its severed arm under his cloak. "Keep an eye on him, Simon. Bry's suffering, and I fear I've made matters even worse."

Simon crouched down and rubbed Max's shoulder. "Oh, Max. Shit, I don't know what happened, but everything will be all right. I promise, sir." Simon rose to his feet and raced after Bryaxis.

Max retrieved the broken statue body and glanced down at the figurine's face. Droplets of water rose from the concave hollows of the Genius's lifeless eyes; Max blinked, and the tears were gone as if they'd never been there in the first place.

He sniffled and stood, straightening his spine. "Perhaps I have gone insane. But you're in there, right? You fucking spoke to me, Counselor Petronius. I bloody well know you did."

Nothing.

Max took a deep breath and looked out the small window. "Commander Fabius is off hunting in the forests with Varius and the Dacian. When he returns later this afternoon I will ask to speak with him. If he grants me an audience, I'll tell him exactly what I saw and what I heard. Bry thinks I'm insane, but by the gods of my homeland, Dom will believe me.

Max laid the damaged bronze statuette on the mattress and collapsed onto Bry's bed, holding his head between in his hands. He blew out a long breath and mumbled, "Shit, what if Dom doesn't believe me either?"

~

THE DOGS GROWLED AND gnashed their sharp teeth, drool foaming from their muzzles. Like a swarm of vicious gadflies, the pack barked without pause, charging and retreating, taunting the large beast they'd trapped in a cavity between the rocks. Whenever the animal rushed one of the brown hounds, the others would attack it from behind, nipping its bristly hide, dodging to avoid the pig's deadly tusks.

"Aim higher, slave."

His arm pulled back, the fingers of his left hand wrapped deftly around the spear's shaft, Allerix slowly blinked and turned to glare at Varius, who was standing right beside him. Gaius smiled at Alle's fierce reprimand.

But Alle didn't berate the veteran; unperturbed, he focused on his target and hurled the pike at the wild boar.

From atop his grey gelding, Gaius leaned forward in his saddle. The spear sliced through the air and hit its mark, plunging deep between the boar's ribs. The wretched animal squealed in agony, thrashing and staggering, but it was doomed to die. Its brief battle for survival was all but over.

"Excellent shot! Call off the dogs, Varius, and tell the men to put that filthy swine out of its misery before the meat becomes tough. Haul our catch back to the villa. The field slaves are preparing a roasting pit. By Flora's wooly twat, we're going to feast like vulgar tyrants come the holiday tomorrow, lads!"

"Yes, Commander," Varius grumbled, bumping his shoulder against Allerix's head as he pushed past him. His hands balled into fists, Alle grimaced and turned to glare at Varius's broad back.

"Mind your temper, Alle. He'd pummel you to a pulp. Come and retrieve your horse. We're taking a different path home. There's a place I want to show you."

Allerix grabbed Ferox's long onyx mane and swung himself onto the stallion's back. The Dacian's consistent training had indeed paid off. Ferox stood saddled and compliant, clearly attuned to Alle's every move and command. Together they ambled their horses down a dirt trail, leaving behind the men and howling dogs and the slaughtered boar. As they entered the solitude of the verdant forest, beams of bright sunshine pierced the heavy canopy of leaves, dotting the ground with swatches of orange-golden light.

"You're skilled with a spear." Gaius noted as he kicked and clucked, frustrated his dawdling mount couldn't keep pace with the black stallion's long-legged strides. "Did you hunt often as a boy?"

"I hunted as often as I was allowed—deer mostly, sir."

"You've taken down a buck with a spear?"

"I used a bow for deer hunting, Dominus"

"By Hercules, you're a bowman as well? What about a slingshot?"

"No, I've never handled one of those."

"Slings are marvelous weapons—cheap, easy to carry, and fucking deadly once you learn to throw a lead bullet accurately. I keep a couple of well worn favorites of mine back at the villa. I'll teach you how to use one. They take practice to master."

Alle smiled and pulled on the reins to slow Ferox's naturally swift gait.

As they continued down the path, the dirt surface switched to a poorly paved road. Gaius's horse stumbled over a dislodged block but caught its balance. Gaius cursed, sputtering, "Bloody shoddy construction! I paid good coin to have this road built through my estate. Remind me to hire engineers from Rome if I want work done correctly."

Gaius patted the side of his gelding's neck, praising Glaucus for his sure-footedness. His brow arched, an amused smirk lit Alle's face.

"Alle, there's a meadow up ahead beside a stream teeming with fish. We'll stop and eat. A successful hunt always sharpens my appetite."

"We're going to catch fish? With what?" Alle chuckled. "Um, sir?"

"With whatever works. We'll fucking improvise."

A mile down the road, the trail veered closer to the hills; through the trees on the right appeared a lush green field, the grass waist-high in spots. The gurgling sound of a rushing stream nearly drowned out the songs of the birds and cicadas chirping high up in the trees. Gaius pointed and said, "There it is. Let's dismount and lead the horses down for a drink."

"It's pastoral, like something from a poem." Alle commented, as he slid off Ferox and readjusted his blue tunic. A small flock of sparrows flew up and away from the forest.

"Do you hear that?" Gaius asked, turning in his saddle to survey the dark woods on the left side of the road.

"No, I don't hear anything, Dominus," Alle mumbled as he loosened the cinch of his saddle.

"Exactly. It's too quiet. And something startled the birds."

From the shadows, a barrage of barbed missiles, one after another, whistled past them. Most scraped tree trunks or bounced off rocks, but one arrow pierced Gaius's hip, striking him near the bone.

He cried out through clenched teeth, "Shit!"

Allerix ran over and helped him down off his horse. "Seems we have company, sir."

"Bloody bastards shot me in my fucking hip. Let's take cover down there." After draping his left arm over Alle's shoulder, Gaius pulled his sword from the scabbard strapped to his saddle before slapping his horse's flank to shoo both animals to safety. As the horses trotted away, Allerix wrapped his arm around Gaius's waist; they scrambled down the gentle slope to a clump of large trees.

"Who's attacking us?" Alle asked between rapid breaths as he lowered Gaius to the ground.

"Common robbers would be my guess. They likely outnumber us, but chances are they're poorly trained. Here, take my dagger." Gaius withdrew his prized weapon and handed it to Alle. Grunting and groaning, he twisted his torso for a better angle, trying twice to break off the arrow shaft protruding from his ivory tunic.

"Let me do that," Allerix insisted.

"No, leave it be." Gaius exhaled and leaned back against the tree. "I can manage."

Allerix gave the shaft a whack with his palm. "You can manage?"

The pain seared through the left side of Gaius's body. The reddish-brown stain around the puncture hole in his tunic grew larger as more blood seeped into the fabric. Alle squatted and snapped the shaft in two, leaving only a short rod of thin wood jutting out from the wound. He pressed a finger to Gaius's lips; men's sinister voices echoed through the woods above them.

"I hit one of them!" cried a squeaky voice from the road.

Allerix whispered, "They're coming closer. I need something besides this posh knife of yours, pretty as it is." He scanned the area around their hiding spot and picked up a long, sturdy branch to assess its weight and balance. "This will have to do. Can you fight?"

"If I don't, I'm as good as dead. You can't fend off a gang of miscreants with a bloody stick." Gaius muttered as he used his sword to push himself up to his feet. "We'll hold the lower ground and force them to come to us. I'll stay here. You move behind that rock over there."

A voice bellowed from above. "Come now, friends! Let's not make a simple robbery messier than need be. Surrender your coin and we'll be on our way."

When a lanky fellow with a bow slung over his shoulder slid down the slope and peered around the rock, Allerix hollered a savage war cry. With one brutal blow, he smashed the man's head with the thick branch, crushing his skull against the boulder. As blood dripped down the curve of the mottled stone, Alle tossed the branch and snatched the robber's sword from his limp hand.

"Poorly trained was a generous assessment, Dominus." Alle chuckled and ducked back behind the rock.

"Don't get cocky. Stay down and wait for the others."

Two more men approached Gaius's hiding spot behind the tree. Pointing, Alle shouted. "On your right!"

Using his good leg to pivot, Gaius inelegantly jumped out and thrust his blade into one man's stomach as the robber's companion circled around the other side of the trunk. Alle sprang to his feet and threw Gaius's dagger, hitting the poor sap squarely in the furrow of his spine. As the bandit screamed, collapsing to his knees, Gaius jerked his sword out of the first robber's belly and sliced the second bastard's throat. Blood sprayed from the fatal gash, soaking Gaius's shins and riding boots in crimson warmth.

"That's three." Gaius snarled as retrieved his dagger from the corpse's back, wiped off the blood on the dead man's cloak, and slid it back into its scabbard. Allerix nodded and tightened his grip around the hilt of his borrowed sword.

A commotion of footsteps rustled through the brush; another wave of bandits were attacking in unison. When they drew close, Gaius stepped out again from behind the tree and challenged the nearest pair.

"You're on my fucking property. Trespassing is a crime, gentlemen." He snarled, limping forward, his sword raised and his nostrils flared.

Despite the blatant fear in their wide eyes, two robbers rushed forward. Three precise, lethal stabs of Gaius's short sword and the men fell to the dirt, bloodied and dead.

Gaius glanced over. Alle had dispatched the shorter of two more attackers, but a mountain of a man had the lad pinned to the rock, the giant's blade hovering dangerously close to Alle's face. Gaius hobbled over, slipping on the damp leaves, and grabbed the back of the lout's tunic. He pulled the large assailant off balance while simultaneously impaling his blade into the man's lower back. The robber reached around and nearly grabbed Gaius's leg. Unlike his companions, this ox wasn't going down without a struggle.

"Roll!" Gaius ordered. Allerix shimmied out from under his attacker's grasp, slid off the rock, and picked up another discarded sword. He stuck the blade into the man's torso and jerked it downward; a gruesome tumble of twisted intestines spilled out of the giant's severed abdomen.

Gaius shoved the robber's lifeless body toward the stream; the disemboweled corpse rolled down the slope, finally splashing into a waterlogged ravine at the bottom. With a groan, he leaned against the rock, pressing his finger to his lips. They both remained quiet, listening for any signs of more attackers.

Not a sound, save the babbling of the brook below. Moments later, the birds began to sing again.

Gaius threw his sword to the ground "So much for a fucking peaceful picnic in an idyllic meadow. Are you hurt?" he asked.

"No. Not a mark."

Allerix stood up, the sword in his left hand pointed at Gaius's heart. If there was ever a moment the Dacian could kill him with ease, it was now. Gaius raised his hand. "That's merciful of you, *căţel*, but there's no need to put me out of my misery just yet. Chances are I'll survive this minor injury." Clutching his hip, Gaius's sarcastic grin twisted into a grimace. He slid down to the ground, exhausted and covered in blood.

"Shit." Allerix lowered the tip of the blade, a wave of concern washing over his face. "You need help."

"Run to the villa and bring back assistance, Alle."

"I'm not leaving you here, sir. There could be more of those fuckers out there."

"Listen to me! I can't walk that far and you can't carry me. I'll stay put and wait here. Get some damn assistance now before I bleed to death."

"Don't be dramatic. You're not losing much blood, sir."

Allerix stuck his thumb and forefinger into his mouth and blew. His piercing whistle reverberated through the dense forest. From out of nowhere, Ferox trotted through the trees and down the slope, snorting and pawing the earth near Alle's feet. When Allerix grabbed the bridle and fed the stallion a treat from the pouch tied to his belt, Gaius laughed and shook his head.

"That's a useful pony trick, my dear Prince."

"Let's get you home, sir." Allerix retightened the saddle's loose cinch and intertwined his fingers to form a step. After a bit of clumsy jostling, he hoisted Gaius onto the stallion, all the while muttering gentle commands to soothe the agitated horse. Alle climbed up on the rock and settled onto Ferox's rump behind the saddle, wrapping his arms around Gaius's waist to steady him.

Alle made a smacking sound with his lips and nudged Ferox forward with his toes. Once they'd ascended the slope and were back on the road, he mumbled into Gaius's ear, "Comfortable?"

"I'm fine—in fucking blasted agony, but I'll survive. As soon as we get back, Felix will extract this fucking arrow point from my hip."

"The blacksmith?"

"Felix was also a field medic in the army, and a damn good one. Shit, it's a pity we didn't bring along any wine for our little excursion."

Allerix reached into a leather bag strapped to his saddle and pulled out a leather wineskin.

"Have a drink, sir."

Leaning back against Alle's chest, Gaius guzzled a long swallow and closed his eyes. "By Pollux, you've thought of everything, haven't you?"

Allerix chuckled and pulled Gaius into a tighter embrace, brushing his lips over the shell of Gaius's ear. "Maximus packed the wine, sir."

"Remind me to thank him."

"Yes, Dominus."

~

Eavesdropping on Max's conversation with Felix and a physician from Puteoli, Allerix hid in the shadows of the corridor outside Gaius's master suite.

"Felix skillfully removed the point," the emaciated, olive-skinned doctor explained. "And, by Fortuna's grace, the laceration was simple to stitch. He's lost some blood, but he'll recover. Unfortunately, the missile hit the bone. He'll have difficulty bearing weight on his left leg for some time."

"The Commander's survived far worse battle injuries than that pansy little wound." Felix retorted with a grin. "The general will be back on his feet in no time, as good as new come the autumn festivals."

"Thank you, sirs. Is he alone in there?" Max asked, his deep voice cracking. He was fidgety, repeatedly touching an object stashed in the folds of his tunic.

"No," Felix conceded. "That witch, Callidora, is playing nursemaid. The Commander developed a fever early on. It was mild but worrisome. She applied cool compresses soaked in one of her foul brews and lowered his temperature to normal. Bitch seems to know what she's doing."

Max nodded and glanced through the open door. "We should let Commander Fabius rest then. I have your payment prepared, doctor. Let's settle our business in the atrium."

Once they'd left, Allerix crept closer to the doorway and peered inside. Gaius lay on his back on the bed, fast asleep and tucked safely under the covers. A cascade of copper curls encircled his face, his nude chest rising and falling in a steady, relaxed rhythm. He looked older, and vulnerable. A woman with long dark hair and full breasts wiped his brow with a white cloth as she hummed a soft, soothing tune. Could that be Simon's mother? Simon had described her once, but Alle had never seen her with his own eyes.

Alle took two more steps forward, stopping before his sandal-clad foot crossed the threshold. He rubbed his eyes and when his pupils refocused, Gaius's entire body was contorted in a violent seizure, thrashing about and gasping dreadful, inhuman noises. The woman gently rolled Gaius onto his side and stroked his hair, but the convulsions continued. Alle ran over and crouched by the edge of the bed.

"What's happening? He was fine a moment ago. What the fuck are you doing?"

Callidora glared, her large brown eyes huge and defensive. "Who are you? Oh, you must be the infamous Dacian whore. By Juno, you are more striking than all of Dominus's girls stacked together.

The strange woman leaned closer. "There's something mystical about you, though—your eyes change color without warning, and that intense spark shimmering through your pupils grows and wanes so quickly it's hard to discern. I see it clearly, mind you. Was your mother a sorceress, Dacian?"

Flustered, Allerix refocused his gaze on Gaius's face. "No, my mother was a revered high priestess, not some meddling, loathsome witch."

"Priestess, sorceress—we're all sisters reawakening the ancient truths dwelling in sacred plants and venerated groves." Calli wrung the cloth over the bronze bowl. "Dominus is temporarily incapacitated. In a short while, he'll recover and slip back into a restful slumber."

"Stop touching him!" Alle snarled between his teeth. "Is this the fever? Is it back?"

"No." Callidora dipped the cloth into the bowl. "Dominus has suffered from a sickness since childhood. He must have forgotten to imbibe my medicine according to the schedule. I should have reminded him."

"Medicine? You're not a doctor. You're poisoning him, aren't you?"

"Lower your voice, barbarian. I'm his savior, you imbecilic cur. Years ago when our Dominus was a young boy, I discovered there was a potion that could calm his illness."

Allerix pinched her shoulder until she winced. "Can this disease be cured?"

"No. Only managed. I've been charged with managing it. This time, I failed him." Calli's strained words cracked as Gaius's spasms gradually subsided. He inhaled sharply as if he'd just emerged from under water, and collapsed into sleep. Calli brushed his soaked, chestnut curls.

"There—the fit's finally over." She sighed and turned Gaius onto his back, wiping his forehead again. "Dominus requires absolute discretion concerning this affliction." Callidora's eyes bore through Alle's skull. "This is not a subject for gossip at the stable house. You will say nothing about what you've seen."

Alle tore his eyes away from her bewitching glower. He snatched the rag from Calli's fingers and swiped the cool cloth across Gaius's cheek and down his jaw. "He's not as strong as he pretends."

"Nonsense. He's a champion. His illness is a nuisance, an unfortunate complication. Nothing, including you, will prevent Dominus from succeeding to the throne. It's his destiny. Now, listen to me. Dominus won't recall this terrible seizure at all. He rarely does. We'll both act as if you were never here. Do you understand?"

"If I find out you're poisoning him, I'll kill you."

"Kill me?" Calli cackled. "Oh, you silly, stupid slut. If you kill me then you'll destroy him as well. Is that what you want? To destroy your benevolent master?"

Breathing hard, Allerix rose to his feet. "No, that's not what I want."

"Then leave, and keep your pretty heathen mouth shut. Don't speak of this to anyone, especially not to Maximus. This unfortunate spying of yours will be our little secret."

>>>><<<<

16

GAIUS FABIUS'S SEASIDE VILLA, CAMPANIA

NICOMEDES STUCK HIS HEAD into Allerix's room at the stable house, wiggling his eyebrows, with a silly grin plastered across his handsome face. "Lo, Dacian. Want to see something?"

"If it's another dildo, Nic, you've already shown me all of them."

Laughing, Nic sauntered over and sat cross-legged on the floor next to Alle's bed. Nodding a curt hello, Simon remained in the doorway, leaning on the jamb.

Nic lifted the lid on the small wooden box in his hand. "Achilles woke up from his summer's nap. He's frisky and starved for treats. Would you like to see some of his daft tricks?"

Seated on his mattress, Allerix leaned over and peered into the box. "Does this mouse perform tricks, Simon?" Alle was desperate to end the tiresome tension between him and the brooding pup. Indeed, everyone had grown weary of Simon's surly, uncharacteristic demeanor.

Fidgeting with his golden bracelet, Simon hesitated but finally flashed a forced smile. "Nic claims the little fellow's learned a new stunt. Let's see it then."

"It's brill! Out you go, clever mousey." Nic tipped the box, and Achilles scampered down. His back foot was misshapen, contorted and twisted, but otherwise the small fluffy rodent moved around well.

"We'll start with an easy one, the first trick I'd ever taught him." Nic touched two fingertips to the floor and walked his fingers forward one after the other; Achilles weaved between them for several inches until Nic rewarded his pet with a plump seed.

"That's impressive," Alle remarked, glancing over at Simon. When Simon noticed him, he stopped smiling, clearly trying his damnedest to appear only mildly interested in the rodent show.

"Let's see if he remembers the trick from this past spring." Nic pulled out a small wooden bead and gently rolled it across the floor. Achilles scurried after it on three legs, picked up the tiny ball in its mouth and brought it back, dropping it into Nic's open palm. Simon laughed; after some hesitation, he padded into Alle's room and sat on the floor beside Nic.

Nicomedes rolled the sphere two more times, and twice Achilles returned it to his waiting hand. "Do you want to try, Simon?" Nic asked.

"Yes, please." There was Simon's sweet smile forcing its way through his stubbornness. He tossed the bead, and again the tiny dormouse fetched it for him like a well-trained dog.

"What else can he do?" Allerix asked.

Nic made an open ring shape with his fingers, and the rodent jumped through his handmade hoop three times. He then pulled out five bronze coins and laid them side-by-side on the floor. "Here's his new trick. Hush, though. Don't tell Max I borrowed five of his bronze bits for this stunt, right? I'll put them back in his jar when we're finished."

Alle and Simon nodded in unison.

"All right, Achilles. Time to pay the magistrates for your freedom. How many coins have you saved up, little slave?" Nic put the small box on the floor; the mouse grabbed the cumbersome metal discs, one at a time, and dropped them into the empty container.

"Oh, my! Is that five shiny new sestertii?" Nic playfully gasped with boyish exuberance. He offered the mouse a small swatch of cloth; Achilles squirmed under it, holding the fabric on his head as if it were the official cap of freedom. "You're free, Achilles, the freedmouse!"

They all fell into laughter as Nicomedes scooped the mouse up and petted its tiny, adorable head. After Simon and Alle had taken turns stroking the mouse's soft stomach, Nic put his pet back into the travel box beside a pile of seeds as his reward.

"How much does it cost to purchase freedom, Nic?"

"I have no idea, Dacian. More coin than I'll ever see."

"Do you know, Simon?"

"No." Simon rose to his feet. "I told you—I never want to be freed."

"Why?" Alle and Nic both asked.

"C'mon, Nic. You fucking know why. I'm safe here—well fed and cared for. I'm a proud member of a powerful and wealthy family. Dom's family. If I were free, I'd have to work some shitty job and find a place to live and purchase my own food. I want to stay here and be what I was fated to be."

"So you're scared of freedom," Allerix mumbled as he twiddled with the edge of his bedcover. When Alle was younger, he'd experienced Simon's dread of leaving his family, his fear of loneliness, his fear of independence.

"Bugger off, barbarian." Simon spat at him before hurrying out of Alle's room.

"Don't listen to him, Alle. Max was thrilled when Dom freed him. And now he spends more time with Dom than any of us, and he earns coin."

Allerix sighed and said, "Can I try that trick with the bead, Nic?"

Nic snickered. "Sure, but I've no more seeds." Nic pulled out the tiny wooden ball again and rolled it over to the wall. "Go and fetch the bead, Dacian, and afterwards we'll sneak into the kitchen. It's Plautus's naptime. There's bound to be leftover wine somewhere."

~

TURNING THE SMALL BRONZE statue over and over in his hand, Max walked through the open door into his patron's chamber. Sitting on the bed with his arms crossed behind his head, the commander stared at the fluttering curtains separating the master suite from the sunny balcony, his attention lost in some far-off place. Jumbles of scrolls, a wax tablet, and a stylus were strewn across the mattress. Dom was restless; days confined to bed rest didn't sit well with any man, and certainly not with this ornery, red-haired soldier. Max coughed into his fist; Gaius slowly turned his head and smiled.

"Maximus! Thank the fucking gods you've come to entertain me."

"Sir?" Max tentatively stepped into the room. Whiffs of sweat, wine, and tedium hung in the air. "May I have a word with you, Commander?"

"You may, but only if you make me laugh. Have you a dandy joke for me?"

"No, sir."

With his fingers interlaced, Gaius groaned as he stretched his arms in front of his chest and cracked his knuckles. "Gods, I'm bored shitless. Where's our dear Lucius when I desire I daft pun or two, hmm?"

Max took a deep breath, and before nerves tied his tongue, he blurted out, "I've come to talk to you about Counselor Petronius, sir."

Gaius's amused expression darkened. "Have Bryaxis and Simon discovered another odd notation in Luc's papers?"

269

"Not that I'm aware of, Commander."

"Maximus, come and sit. Your handsome face is riddled with doubt and—what is that I see? Fear?"

Max lumbered over and settled into the chair nearest Gaius's grand bed. He retrieved the Genius statuette from his tunic and stood it up on the side table. Together, they stared at the little figurine until their eyes met.

"Why is Luc's Genius not in the shrine as it should be, Max?" Gaius picked up the idol and inspected it. "And why is the damn thing broken? Where's its fucking arm?"

Sheepishly, Max pulled out the battered fragment of the statue's bronze arm and laid it on the table.

"I suspect you have an interesting tale to tell."

"Sir, I've gone mad."

Gaius shrugged. "Sanity is simply a matter of perspective, Maximus."

Max laughed nervously and pointed at the bronze idol. "Counselor Petronius is in that figurine."

"Yes, he is. The priests purport that a man's Genius—his life spirit—dwells in his idol. Little statues such as this symbolize a man's essence, his dreams, his past achievements, and his desires. We offer daily prayers and sacrifices to the Genius statues of our ancestors and our heads of households to ensure prosperity and good fortune for the entire family. I explained all of this rubbish to you ages ago, Max."

"Yes, sir. I understand all of the rites."

"But?"

Max's pointer finger shook as he exclaimed, "He's bloody in there! He spoke to me, and he even moved. I mean, the statuette moved. That thing jumped into my hand, Commander." Max swallowed as Gaius gaped at him, unblinking.

"Go on."

"Counselor Petronius claimed I revived his spirit through that statue when I'd recited the traditional prayers to the Lares in his home. He hasn't crossed the river to Hades, sir."

Gaius blinked and scrubbed his face before asking, "When did you offer these rites at Luc's shrine?"

"Right before I stole the idol as you commanded, sir—that day when you attended the reading of Counselor Petronius's testament at the basilica. I know it sounds impossible, and I may very well be deranged, but I swear it talked to me. I heard the counselor's voice."

"And what else did it say?"

"Um, first he told me that my solemn prayers before his household shrine had reanimated his Genius, not Callidora's bizarre witchcraft. I'm sorry you went through all that trouble with those spells and disgusting sacrifices. Anyhow, for some reason, I'm the only one who can see or hear him. He—he asked about Bryaxis. He's worried about him and, to be honest, so am I."

"He's concerned about Bryaxis, hmm? That shouldn't surprise me. How was this figurine broken? Did you fucking drop it?"

"No, sir." Max chewed on his fingernail. "But it was an accident."

"I see. Has Lucius's spirit spoken to you since its arm was lopped off?"

"No, sir."

"You know I value your honesty, Max. You're tired and burdened with many additional responsibilities these days, but do not worry. We'll have Felix patch this little metal fellow back together. After it's mended, this Genius statuette remains in the lararium shrine. It's not to be taken about the villa grounds on risky adventures. This talisman is not a child's doll. Understood?"

"Yes, Commander."

"Leave tiny Lucius here, and return to your chores. And close the door on your way out, Maximus."

After Max had departed, Gaius picked up the bronze figurine, rubbing his thumb over the break where the arm had detached. "Chatting with my freedman but not with me, old boy? You, of all people, know what a jealous prick I can be."

Gaius scoffed, tossing the statue to the foot of his mattress. He pressed the heels of his palms against his eyes. "Talking dolls! For fuck's sake, I need to get out of this bleeding room before I truly do go mad."

He glanced down at the wax tablet resting by his elbow and picked up his silver stylus. He'd already scratched two sentences about the last war into the soft indigo wax surface, colorful details he'd recalled from the final days of the great siege. As he reread his shorthand, the wax surface gradually smoothed over, as if an invisible hand were wiping the tablet clean with the stylus' scraper. But the stylus was right there, dangling between Gaius's fingers. He watched, stupefied, as his scribbles mysteriously disappeared.

He looked over at the figurine on the table; little Luc hadn't moved one iota. Gaius rubbed his eyes again and glanced down for a second time. Stroke by stroke, large letters were scratched anew into the wax.

TELL

HIM

Gaius leaned down. Perhaps his eyes were playing tricks. He chuckled suspiciously. "Tell whom what?"

Faster than was possible, the writing was smoothed away, quickly replaced by more.

BRYAXIS

TELL HIM

"Lucius? Shit, are you here?" Gaius scanned his room, but he was alone. "It is you, isn't it? You're still skulking about, haunting me. Max hasn't gone mad, and I wasn't hallucinating that night back in Rome, was I? For fuck's sake, your spirit managed to cross the sacred boundary and leave the capital. You're down here in Campania."

Gaius raked his hands through his hair before he grabbed the wine jug off the table, gulping slurps until dribbles of wine spilled from his lips. "All right, my spooky wee friend. Let's play this poltergeist game of yours. What is it you want me to tell Bryaxis? Would you have me eulogize your undying love to the Caledonian in iambic pentameter?"

NOT ME

TELL HIM

Gaius threw his hands in the air. "What, by the monstrous Gorgons, does that mean? Not you? I need more information. A complete fucking sentence would be most useful."

More letters were scraped; this time gouged with such deep and aggressive strokes that Gaius caught the scent of burning wax.

NOW SOLDIER

TELL HIM

As if heated by some unseen flame, the scratched wax melted, smoothing back to its pristine, glossy surface. All evidence of Luc's curious commands had disappeared.

"Wait, Luc! Those Greek letters—what do they mean?" A strong, noxious breeze blew in from the balcony, and the leaf of the wooden tablet lifted off the mattress and slammed shut. Gaius dropped his stylus and hollered, "Guard!"

The door swung open. "Yes, Commander?"

An icy chill gripped Gaius by the balls. "Have my freedman, Maximus, and the slave, Bryaxis, report to me now. Immediately!"

~

"ENTER!" GAIUS BARKED FROM his bed.

Together, Max and Bryaxis crossed the wide threshold and shuffled to the center of the bedroom. Max stood at attention while Bryaxis lowered himself to his knees.

"Maximus." Gaius lowered his right leg to the floor and held his hand out. "Bring my mantle and help your crippled patron over to that chair. I'll be damned if I hold an audience from my fucking bed like some decrepit old tramp."

"Yes, Commander."

After he'd hobbled over with Max as his crutch, Gaius belted his crimson cloak around his nude torso and sat down. Tipping his chin towards the table beside his bed, he asked, "Now, how was that Genius statuette broken? Tell me the damn truth."

Without looking up, Bryaxis mumbled, "I broke the figurine, sir."

"How? Why?"

"I threw it at the wall. I was angry, sir."

Snarling, Gaius pushed himself up and limped over to Bry. He snatched a fistful of Bry's sun-streaked brown hair, yanking his head back, twisting the clump between his fingers until Bryaxis flinched.

"You were fucking angry, slave? Angry because your former master had the audacity to be murdered?"

Bry's teary eyes burned red, his hushed voice ragged with steely resentment. "I will mourn Dom's brutal assassination until the day I die."

"Mind your impudent tone!" Gaius raised his hand, poised to strike, but dropped it with a sigh before stumbling back to his seat. Max rushed to offer him a drink; Gaius pushed the cup away and scowled.

"What, by the gods, is going on here? Why did this slave assault the Genius of his master, the life spirit of my departed friend? Explain this baffling horseshit to me, Maximus."

Max squatted beside Gaius's chair and glanced up. "Sir, Bryaxis suffers from overwhelming sorrow and confusion. It was an accident. Surely he didn't intend to break the idol, sir."

"That's a damn lie, Maximus," Bryaxis snapped and started to weep. "Tell him the truth. Go on, tell him."

Gaius lifted Max's chin and softened his voice. "Tell me, Maximus."

"Bryaxis has been hurt, but the temporary anger he harbors is unwarranted. If a master orders his slave tortured, killed, or castrated, then so be it. The laws permit a master to discipline, eliminate or mutilate his property. Bry's been pampered concubine for much of his life. He'd forgotten what it meant to be a slave, sir."

Gaius pressed his lips together and nodded. "The last bit is certainly true."

He snatched the cup from Max's hand and tossed back a swallow of wine, swiping his forearm across his mouth. "Wait one fucking moment. Maximus—surely I'm misunderstanding you. Did you just imply Lucius was somehow responsible for this Caledonian's gelding?"

"Um, he gave the order, sir, did he not?" Max stuttered as he rose to his feet, backing up a step.

"He most certainly did not! Whatever gave you that preposterous idea? Lucius Petronius is an honorable, civilized gentleman—or he was—most of the time." Gaius struggled to his feet and pointed at Bryaxis. "How could you believe that Luc...? By Pollux's prick, now that damn tablet nonsense makes sense."

"Tablet, sir?" Max asked.

"Never mind. Bryaxis, come here." Gaius commanded as he lowered his arse onto his chair. Bry stood up and slowly knelt at Gaius's feet.

"Listen to me, Caledonian." Gaius glanced over at the statuette. "And you as well, counselor."

He stared into Bry's eyes as he cupped the slave's jaw. "Lucius would never hurt you. He would've rather suffered the Furies' most dreaded curse than see you injured in any way. He loved you. I'll grant you that reality took years to sink into my stubborn heart, but it's the truth. He did not order your castration, for shit's sake. That fucking weasel, Aurelia, is responsible for your heinous mutilation, not my Luc."

Pulling on his hair, Bryaxis' tearful whimpers turned to hysterical sobs. "Oh, gods! How could I have believed Domina?"

Gaius let go of Bry's chin and sat back. "Because she's a practiced liar. That cow had the gall to pretend she had a letter from Lucius instructing her to sacrifice your testicles on his funeral pyre. She forged a fucking letter! By the gods, does the wretched woman have no scruples? Why on earth Luc ever married that shrew boggles my mind to this day."

"Oh, most holy gods! Forgive me, Lucius!" Bryaxis cried. His eyes rolled back in his head and he blacked out. His chin hit the floor, rivulets of blood spilling from where his teeth had cut his full lower lip.

"Another bloody thespian. My life has always been complicated by the theatrics of others." Gaius grumbled and struggled to hobble over to the bed. "Maximus, find Varius, and the two of you haul this giant twit back to the stable house. All this wailing has given me a headache. And from now on, have Bryaxis offer the morning prayers alongside

Nicomedes at the lararium. Perhaps regular visits from his melodramatic slut will appease our restless ghost."

"Ghost, sir?"

"Yes, the ghost of Lucius Petronius Celsus." Gaius plopped onto the mattress and waved his hand. "You're not insane, Max. I confess Luc's spirit has visited me as well, twice now if I don't count the nightmares. I suspect our beloved specter won't quit his haunting until he gets what he wants—retribution. Ghosts' cravings are frightfully predictable." He pulled the bedcover over his wounded hip. "Go and find Varius. Little Lucius and I will watch over eunuch Endymion until you return."

17

"WELCOME TO MY OFFICE," Gaius announced with a wave of his arm.

The room was more spacious than Allerix had anticipated from out in the corridor. On the soaring painted walls, vibrant gods danced alongside lively mythical creatures within delicate geometric borders on a pale cream background. Above them, an array of shields hung from pegs high on the cornice. Cupboards, large and small, wooden and bronze, stood in tight formation around the perimeter of the room. Scrolls and boxes jammed the shelves while an enormous carved desk dominated the center of the workplace.

"Where are Simon and Bryaxis?"

"On the opposite side of this wing in a cramped hole packed to the rafters with crates. I must remember to have Atticus supply more lamps for those two."

Beneath a pair of large windows along the far wall of the room sat a plush couch. Outside in a sunny courtyard, surrounded by greenery, marble benches, and statues, a fountain in the shape of a colossal vase gushed water into a shallow pool. Through the columns, Alle spied grand views of the gravel paths, rolling pastures, and the orderly orchards of Gaius's seaside estate.

Speechless at first, Alle finally asked, "What do you do in here all day, sir?"

"Read, review correspondence, compose letters, and when I find the time, I write down my recollections of the wars. Mostly, I read. A man's office is his gymnasium for the mind."

"Sounds like school to me. What was up there in the empty niche?"

"Always curious, aren't you? That shelf held a portrait bust of my father, Quintus Fabius. I smashed it recently. I should have cast him out of the villa years ago."

Alle raised an eyebrow but kept his mouth shut. Hostility between a man and his father wasn't uncommon. He'd only wished he could have shared a final farewell with his beloved patriarch; Thiamarkos had been strict and often disenchanted, but he'd been a devoted if not affectionate father. The old man had an infectious laugh hearty enough to warm winter's chill.

Like an animal drawn by some irresistible but invisible phero-mone, Alle's eyes converged on a large wooden cabinet against the far wall.

"That cupboard contains my other toy collection." Gaius retrieved a key from a drawer in his desk. Running his hand up and down Alle's back, he boasted. "I've been acquiring foreign weapons since I was old enough to swing a sword. Their variety of designs and embellishments has long fascinated me."

Gaius unlocked the cabinet and pulled open both doors.

Allerix failed to contain his astonishment. "This is where you store the falx?"

Gaius reached up and grasped its long handle, dislodging the le-thal, curved blade from its bracket. With both hands, he offered the falx to Alle. "Go on and take it. This weapon deserves leisurely study. Rumor has it this blade once belonged to your dead king, Decebalus."

Alle extended his hands. The falx was lighter than it appeared and its balance was uneven. Now that he'd been allowed a close appraisal, he noticed the designs etched onto the blade, although well executed, were unfamiliar and meaningless.

"Your fighting skills back in the forest betrayed experience and training, Allerix. Tell me—why did you spar with such blatant incompetence during our initial swordplay in the courtyard?"

Alle turned the falx over as he explained, "I was playing the part of an inept peasant boy, Dominus."

"Calculated trickery, was it?"

"Survival, sir." Alle swallowed and handed back the weapon. "This is a forgery."

"Yes, I know. If we did capture Decebalus's regal falx, I suspect Emperor Trajan kept it for himself, the greedy old bastard. Marcus always was piggy about his trophies," Gaius explained as he returned the weapon to its display rack. "I keep this fake to remind me my collection lacks a genuine Dacian falx."

Deliberately changing the subject, Alle pointed to a dagger. "What is that?"

"Ah, now this is authentic." Gaius beamed as he lifted the Celtic weapon with the sea monster headed handle. "A ceremonial dagger, Celtic manufacture. This precious antique is at least three hundred years old." Gaius gloated with a grin as he placed the knife into Alle's open palms.

"Gorgeous," Alle muttered, studying the intricate metalwork design of the hilt. "Remarkable craftsmanship." When he'd finished marveling over the dagger, Allerix gingerly placed it back on its shelf. As he paused for one final look at the weapons inside the cupboard, he said, "Thank you for showing me your splendid collection, Dominus."

"Few appreciate my insatiable fetish for exotic treasures, *cățel*." Gaius pulled open a bottom drawer in the cabinet. "Ah, here's what I'd promised to share with you, my old set of slingshots. Shit, I've owned this leather rascal for years now. Back when I was a boy—a young, precocious little monster, mind you—I would sneak out to the gardens at dawn with this slingshot and knock the peckers off of statues."

With sparkling eyes, Allerix laughed with delight. "You did what?"

"Todgers were my favorite targets. When my nursemaid finally discovered it was me vandalizing my parents' costly artworks, I received a severe flogging." Gaius brushed Alle's cheek with his hand. "The next day still striped and sore, I woke up before sunrise and shot off three more. I hid the dismembered marble knobs under her pillow just to spite the tattling bitch."

Alle chuckled and asked, "Can we practice? You said you'd teach me how to hurl sling bullets."

"It's been two months since I was injured during our eventful hunting trip. The arrow wound has healed, thanks to Felix and our divine Asclepius, but my left leg still drags a bit. When I fully recover, we'll have a go with these in the field behind the stables."

"I look forward to that day, sir."

The leather cords of his childhood vandalism dangling from his fingers, Gaius pulled Alle into an embrace and kissed him softly on the mouth.

"Take my hand. There's a picturesque view from the couch."

Gaius interlaced his fingers with Alle's and walked with him to the windows. The distant landscape revealed autumn's approach, the fading pastures clinging to summer's last heat, another orchard ready to relinquish its ripened fruit. The familiar smell of dying leaves wafted through the air.

"How long have you lived in this paradise?" Alle asked as Gaius wrapped his arms around Alle's stomach, resting his cheek on his shoulder.

"I inherited this property or a small part of what I now own when my father died. He'd acquired the land through a cousin of his. It was a hovel when I first arrived, grossly understaffed and overgrown. I doubt Quintus had ever visited the place. As soon as I graduated from military training, I started buying as much land as I could convince my neighbors to sell. She's a healthy size now and well tended. Her farmland, pastures, and woods supply much of our food in addition to a small yield of inferior grape. I still haven't persuaded her to bless us with fruitful vineyards."

"Your world is unlike mine. Your land is controlled, fenced in and shackled to your appetites. The mountains and forests of my homeland are wild and unpredictable, not easily tamed or harvested."

As the words tumbled out, Allerix's heart ached. Was Silva still alive, roaming free with a pack of her kind through the Carpathian woodlands? If he ever saw her again, would she even remember him?

When Alle sighed, Gaius pulled him closer. "Unlike Dacia, Rome is lumbering, unstoppable machine. We move our legions over mountains and across oceans, build cities, transport water, and feed the masses. We subjugate nature, and the fertile earth in return thanks us with seasons of bounty." Gaius rubbed his nose behind Alle's ear and whispered against his skin, "The difficult part is laying down arms long enough to savor her fruits."

Allerix took hold of Gaius's wrists and pulled him down to lie on the couch. Caressing the nape of Gaius's neck, he softened his gaze and smiled. "May we lay down our arms for a while, Rufus?"

Gaius cradled Alle's face and kissed him at the corners of his lips, teasing him with soft nibbles that promised much more. He lifted himself up on his elbow and brushed a few strands of black hair off Allerix's forehead. His groin aching with desire, Alle craned his neck and kissed Gaius's right dimple. When Gaius captured Alle's mouth with his tongue, the clamor of boots and frantic shouts interrupted their silent, seductive conversation.

"Watch out! Clear the way!"

Gaius sat up, pulling Allerix up with him. Outside, several stable hands were running along the path closest to the house, hollering and waving their arms in panic. Allerix jumped off the couch and raced over to a smaller window on the adjacent wall. "It's Ferox. He's galloping away from the barn."

"Wait for me!" Gaius yelled, his voice fading as Allerix sprinted down the corridor in the direction of the servants' entrance.

~

"GODS, WHAT A FUCKING beautiful day!" Nic shouted as he raised his arms above his head to the heavens. Twelve strides or so ahead of Max, he pranced down the path bordered on both sides by large, leafy boxwood hedges. Nicomedes paused and twirled round in circles, the hem of his tunic hovering like the flimsy dress of a wood nymph dancing through Diana's sacred groves.

Max cupped his hands over his mouth and hollered, "Careful with that basket of figs, scamp! If you damage those fruits, you'll face the wrath of Euphronia. She may appear meek, but that woman has a fierce temper!"

Nic grabbed a fig from the bulging basket, lobbed it up into the air and caught it. Max shook his head, laughing. How he loved watching Nic frolic; how long he'd waited to see this damaged former brothel whore so filled with unabashed happiness.

Since that night Dom had freed him, Max had ferreted away his wages, accumulating close to five hundred pieces of bronze stashed in ceramic jars in his room. Would it be enough to buy Nic when the day of Max's official manumission arrived? Surely, Nic was worth a higher price; Max could only hope Commander Fabius would be charitable and accept his paltry offer.

Thunder rumbled, but there wasn't a cloud in the sky. Max stopped; voices screaming from somewhere grew louder and louder.

"Max?" Nic's voice was so soft Max could hardly hear him.

From a cloud of dust the black beast emerged, its eyes ablaze, its long mane flying like a boat's sail, charging full speed down the bounded gravel walkway on a course straight for Nicomedes.

"Nicomedes! Get out of the way!" Max yelled.

Mesmerized by the horrific power of the barreling horse, Nic froze in place and dropped the basket. It tipped over at his feet; ripe purple figs rolled across the pebbled ground.

"Nicomedes!" Max shouted until his voice broke. "Nic, run!"

Nic looked over his shoulder at Max, pleading for help with his terrified eyes.

"Run towards me!" Max cried, racing to Nic with his arms spread wide. "Now!"

"Max!" Nic screamed as he stole one last look at the stallion charging him. He turned and stumbled over the large basket and fell to the ground. As he scrambled to his feet, Nic tripped again, crawling to Max on his hands and knees.

With panic choking his throat, Max jumped to one side of the path, pressing his back into the dense, prickly hedges. All he saw was a blur of dark fury race past him before a thick veil of dust rose up. He didn't want to look, he couldn't believe any of this was real, but he forced his eyes open. The dust settled. Nic lay face down on the ground, silent and still, surrounded by the gooey red flesh of crushed figs, his blood seeping into the gravel path.

~

WHEN GAIUS ARRIVED AT the ghastly scene, Varius and Felix by his side, Max was cradling Nicomedes in his arms, sobbing and trembling. There was no sign of the stallion; only the carnage the beast had left in its destructive wake. Allerix was nowhere to be seen. The foolish barbarian must have chased after that damn horse.

Gaius limped over and crouched down. "Maximus. Move away and let us tend to Nicomedes." Max looked up, broken and confused, his face soaked with tears. He said nothing, only nodded, releasing his hold and moving back to allow Gaius room.

"Nicomedes," Gaius whispered as he brushed a strand of hair from Nic's face. Nic's back was broken, his legs crushed and mangled. The boy was alive, barely, and suffering.

Choking back a sob, Gaius shouted, "Varius! Ride to Puteoli and fetch the doctor!"

"Commander." Felix's voice was low and sober. Gaius glanced up, and Felix shook his head with a wrinkled frown. "These injuries are fatal. I have opiates to blunt the worst of the pain, but there's nothing I or anyone can do to save him, Commander."

"My poor, sweet lamb," Gaius cried. Holding Nic's limp hand, he raised his eyes to the sky while Varius and Felix solemnly bowed their heads. "Jove and Feronia, hear me and may all bear witness to my words. I, Gaius Fabius Rufus, award liberty to Nicomedes, a man without a father, a compassionate caretaker of animals, and my beloved boy. From this moment forth, I declare this man free. He shall enjoy the full status of a freedman and client, with all the privileges and rights granted by law."

"We bear witness," Varius and Felix muttered.

"Be free." Gaius released Nicomedes' hand, completing the archaic ritual of manumission. Nic cracked open his bright blue eyes and tried to speak, but no words came out, only a dribble of blood. He closed his eyes, groaning as a final spasm of pain shook his arms, and exhaled his last, torturous breath.

"Dominus?" Max whimpered and covered his face with his hands. "Oh, gods, no! Don't take him from me. Please, no."

Bryaxis and Simon rushed to Max's side and embraced him, whispering words of comfort he couldn't or wouldn't hear. Max was uninjured, but he would never recover either. The Fates had irrevocably altered his world.

Everything had changed.

"Suffer no more, my beloved Nicomedes." Gaius pushed himself up and crouched over Nic's corpse. "I swear this oath before every fucking god anyone has ever believed existed: I will honor your noble spirit with proper funerary rites, sacrifices, and interment. You will be worshiped as an honored member of my family, forever. Come, let's have you washed and dressed for your journey, lamb."

Gaius picked up Nic's slack and battered body and carried him towards the main house. A few feet before he reached the stairs to the main entrance, Gaius's broken heart shattered and his knees buckled. He drew a deep, fortifying breath and straightened his spine before climbing the steps, clutching Nic's lifeless body tight to his chest.

～

TWO BY TWO, THEY carried torches as they followed the mule-drawn cart carrying Nicomedes' body through the fallow fields at the edge of the estate. Nic's corpse lay stretched on a funerary bed, dressed in his treasured diaphanous golden tunic, his arms and ankles adorned with bejeweled bangles. The slave girls pulled their hair and wailed laments for the deceased young man as musicians blew their mournful pipes. Grief and loss and disbelief weighed down on every mourner like the heavy, dark cloud of an ominous omen.

Gaius led the procession alone, his head covered with the folds of his cumbersome wool toga. With an arm around his friend's waist, Bryaxis held Max's elbow as they stumbled along, second in line. Several positions back, Allerix walked beside Simon. He glanced down at the cloth in Simon's outstretched hands. In the tan fabric was little Achilles, rolled up into a tight ball. Simon had discovered Nic's pet dormouse dead in its clay jar in Nic's room the day after the terrible accident. Now this sorry furry fellow would join his doting master in the afterlife.

When they reached the square pyre constructed of wood and scraps of papyrus kindling, the wagon stopped. Gaius reached down and scooped up a handful of earth. Reciting a prayer to the gods of the Underworld, he threw the dirt on Nic's corpse and withdrew his dagger. Max closed his eyes while Gaius severed Nic's pinky.

Shocked, Alle asked Simon, "Why did he cut off Nic's finger?"

Simon wiped his eyes and whispered, "It's custom to bury a piece of the body separately. You're supposed to be quiet. Stop fucking talking."

Carefully, Gaius dropped the amputated finger into a crimson pouch held open by Atticus. The funerary couch was lifted and placed on the pyre; Gaius opened Nic's eyes and raised his hand.

"Offer your gifts."

One by one, each member of the family placed a small token beside the body: homemade jewelry, pots of honey, flowers, ribbons, incense, fruits, and nuts. Max offered a jar overflowing with bronze coins; Alle placed Achilles' wooden bead toy on the fabric by Nic's hand. Lastly, Simon approached and, with tears streaming down his face, offered the stiff remains of Nic's pet dormouse. They would journey together across Charon's waters.

Everyone stepped back and, at Gaius's signal, recited the final farewell in unison.

"Gaius Fabius Nicomedes, freedman of Gaius Fabius Rufus, may your spirit cross the river to everlasting bliss in the glorious Fields of Elysium."

All fell quiet, save the errant sniffle and muffled sob when Gaius placed his hand on Nic's freshly washed hair. "Rest in eternal peace, lamb."

He rubbed his face before gesturing to his veterans who held the ceremonial bronze torches. "Light the fire."

The blaze caught quickly and roared up, crackling through the early autumn night sky. After the fire had consumed the corpse, Gaius accepted a large jug from Atticus and doused the dwindling flames with wine.

"It is done," he muttered to no one. After removing his hood, Gaius limped through the crowd of mourners before stopping in front of Allerix.

"At dawn's light, Maximus and I will return to collect Nic's charred remains and place them in a cinerary urn for interment. Walk with me back to the house, *căţel*."

In silence, they plodded through the barren planting rows and low weeds, leading the solemn procession homeward. Allerix glanced back at the smoldering pyre. When the silhouette of the main villa residence grew clearer, Gaius hollered, "Varius!"

The veteran jogged to the front of the sober parade. "Yes, Commander?"

"Prepare the horses and wagons for departure. We leave for Rome in two day's time."

"Rome, sir?"

"It is my sacred, inviolable right as his patron and as the head of this family to place Nicomedes' ashes in the tomb of my family's freedmen on the Appia. I want everything packed and ready before tomorrow's nightfall."

"How many travelers, sir?"

Gaius thought for a moment. "Eight. I should return Marcia's girl, or my covetous wife will banish me to the vestibule."

After Varius had left, Gaius exhaled. "Curse the Fates, I'm going to miss my dear Nicomedes."

"So will I, sir. We'd become good friends. Nic didn't suffer long, did he?"

"No, he didn't. Gods, his last moments must have been terrifying. The lad was scared of horses, especially that black beast. Alle, I've made a decision. I will bring you to Rome, but not until that fucking horse is dead. Dispatch the stallion or stay behind with the field hands."

Allerix's voice quivered in disbelief. "You want me to kill Ferox?"

"The horse is dangerous. I want it exterminated."

"But?" Alle took several deep breaths as Gaius continued to march towards the house. Catching up with him, Allerix stammered, "I will do as you order, Dominus. May I ask when you'd received permission from your king to return to your capital?"

"Unfortunately, I haven't. Fortunately, I don't need his blasted permission, not for this dreadful duty. By custom, I am allowed to deposit my freedman's cinerary urn in my family's columbarium and perform the final rites. Marcus is a traditionalist. He won't undermine my sacrosanct authority as head of the patrician branch of the Fabian clan. On our journey to Rome, we'll stop and call on my wife and grandmother. The Alban Hills are serene this time of year. I regret I never took Nicomedes for a visit. My sweet lamb would have loved the ponds stocked with pretty, ornamental fish."

Bewildered, Allerix said nothing for a while until he muttered, "I hope I am permitted to meet your wife, sir."

"Obey my order and perhaps you shall." Gaius pulled Alle to a stop. "By Hercules, I haven't told you yet, have I? Despite this horrific tragedy, I have good news to report. I'm going to be a father."

18

GAIUS FABIUS'S SEASIDE VILLA, CAMPANIA

To my dearest Marcia Servilia

May this letter find you in good health. With heaviness of heart, I deliver tragic news. My beloved slave, Nicomedes, was trampled by a horse. Before he died, I granted him liberty. I am returning to Rome to complete his rites at the freedmen's tomb of my family. On our trip to the capital, I will pay you and Avia a visit at Aricia.

TWO SOFT KNOCKS ON his office door interrupted his thoughts. Gaius laid down his stylus and propped his elbows on the desk, resting his chin on his clasped hands.

"Enter."

When Bryaxis and Simon reached the round mosaic on the floor in front of his writing table, they dropped to their knees.

"Stand up. What's your report?"

"We haven't been able to locate the two scrolls Counselor Petronius referenced, sir," Bryaxis explained, his gaze cast respectfully downward.

Leaning back in his chair, Gaius crossed his arms. "That's curious."

"We've checked every crate and canister multiple times, Dominus.

The documents aren't here." Simon's voice had grown deeper and more confident. Archival work suited him; soon a promotion would be justified.

"Then we have three possibilities." Gaius lifted his right hand and raised his fingers one at a time. "Our dear Lucius scribbled nonsense, or the records no longer exist, or the fucking scrolls do exist and are still in Rome. The last option is my only hope to confirm whether or not Luc's mysterious scrawls mean a damn thing. Box up the relevant papers for transport to the capital. We may need to consult them once we're there."

"Yes, sir," they answered.

Bryaxis was halfway to the door when he paused. "Commander Fabius, may I have a word with you, sir?"

Gaius nodded once. "Return to the spare office, Simon, and begin packing."

After Simon had closed the door behind him, Bryaxis approached and once again lowered himself to his knees.

"As tall as you are, I can't fucking see you over my desk, Caledonian. Get up, sit in that chair, and speak."

After Bry had settled into his seat, he exhaled. "I thought it best to reveal another discovery I'd made outside of Simon's presence, sir. Several of Dominus's registers for household expenditures are also missing."

"His financial accounts?" Gaius leaned forward in his chair. "All of them?"

"Not all, sir, but I haven't found any record that dates after the last Saturnalia. A couple of recent bundles are absent."

"That's disturbing. He must have given copies of his personal accounts to his financial advisor as security." Gaius poured wine into his cup and swallowed half of it. "I can't recall—who is his procurator?"

"Gnaeus Decius, sir."

"Is that right?" Grinning, Gaius narrowed his eyes like a tomcat spying a tidy sparrow. "Gnaeus Decius, my new, pasty-faced and nauseatingly obsequious client who frolics with his overfed birds?"

"Yes, sir. Dominus's previous procurator, Sextus Pomponius, had died from consumption during the last war. Decius volunteered to serve in a temporary capacity until Lu—Dominus could appoint someone more suitable."

"Once we've completed the funerary rites, I'll pay a visit to our smarmy Birdman up on the Quirinal. We'll investigate these missing records if I have to pry the duplicates from Decius's clammy fingers. Tell me, Bryaxis. You've been offering the morning prayers at the garden shrine for a while now. How is Luc's clobbered statuette coping these days? Is its arm holding up?"

Bryaxis' ears flushed pink. "Felix reattached the broken arm, sir. Thank you for allowing me to make sacrifices before Dom's Genius, Commander."

"Do you find it comforting?"

"Yes, sir. I can only hope he's forgiven me for assaulting his sacred figurine."

"And you've had no—how should I phrase this—no unusual encounters with our little bronze man?"

Bryaxis stared at him, perplexed but clearly not entirely surprised. "Before Nicomedes' terrible accident, Maximus had claimed the statuette spoke to him and moved, sir. I've not heard or seen anything unusual. I assumed Max had been having a lark with me."

Gaius rose from his chair and ambled over to the large window overlooking the garden. His hip was close to healed; only minor twinges of discomfort bothered him, and rarely during the day. He stared out at the autumn scenery and said, "Maximus wasn't lying or playing pranks with you. Lucius's ghost has visited me as well, Bryaxis."

Bry gasped. "He has? How—how is that possible?"

"I have no idea. Perhaps we're all a bit mad. I admit the notion of an afterlife—of someplace that exists beyond this—is a tempting belief."

He walked back over to the chair and continued. "Lucius first visited me in the form of a grotesque phantasm. I'd consumed too much drink that shitty day and dismissed the strange incident as a hallucination.

The second time happened here at the villa. His specter was invisible, but its desires and fury abundantly clear." Gaius rubbed his face. "I spent my early years growing up in a house haunted by ornery ancestors. When the dead are angry, their displeasure lingers like smoke in the air. Lucius's ghost demands vengeance. Gods, if only he'd divorced that rapacious gorgon after she provided a child."

"After his daughter was born, Dominus prohibited conflict at home, sir. He avoided unpleasantness instead of confronting it, bottling up his wrath until he erupted."

Gaius turned to see Bryaxis gazing at him with that lop-sided, melancholy smile. The Caledonian already had proven his worth, even if the slave's temperament still bristled his nerves. He'd have to make a decision about Bryaxis, and soon. Wearing a warm grin, Gaius said softly, "Lucius did have a tempestuous streak, didn't he?"

"Yes, sir. Dominus had said you'd once called him the Vulcan of Vesuvius."

"Ha! Indeed I did. Believe it or not, he was worse back in Athens. Despite the fact he'd always been a star student, Luc nearly throttled a teacher for misquoting him in front of everyone in the lecture hall. I found out later the old tutor had insulted Lucius months earlier. Count your blessings our dear counselor mellowed with age."

"Yes, sir." Bry's smiled faded. "May I ask a question?"

"Go on."

"Why didn't Dominus free me in his will?"

Gaius took a long, deep breath and released the air slowly as he gathered his thoughts. "It might be difficult for you to understand, but the reason is quite simple. Given the circumstances, he knew you'd be safer as my slave than as the freedman of dead man."

Rubbing his fidgety hands back and forth, Bryaxis sighed while Gaius continued. "Before his murder, Luc had been charged with investigating a bloody dangerous case of embezzlement involving the imperial coffers. He had adversaries in the courts and the palace—shit, we all do. If he'd granted you freedom in his testament, you would have been a freedman without a patron. You would have had no fucking protection from his enemies. That's why he transferred ownership of you to me. Gods know that bitch Aurelia had no intention of safeguarding you. Do you understand?"

"I think so, sir." Bryaxis fought back his tears. "Do you believe Domina was involved in his murder?"

"She's a candidate, but then again Luc left her a pittance in his will, so why murder him? Was she so stupid to believe he'd allow an outsider—someone he'd never loved—to inherit his family's fortune and ancestral home? She must have known he'd bequeathed the Petronii estate to his brother, Titus. That rapacious weasel married him for status and for a luxurious lifestyle, and she realized her desires tenfold. Shit, Lucius was worth more to her alive than dead."

Gaius massaged his furrowed brow and exhaled. "Whatever her part in his murder, Luc's ghost wants Aurelia and her pack of mutilators punished for gelding you. I will see to that, but our dear ghoul can't savor revenge from Campania, can he? Pack the figurine carefully, and guard it. Keep it on your person for the time being. Lucius may or may not reside in his Genius, but we'll take his rambunctious little idol to Rome for another adventure."

Just as Bryaxis opened his mouth, there was another knock on the door.

Gaius slammed his fist on the table. "For shit's sake, I might as well be in the bloody packed center of the fucking Forum. Enter!"

Max marched into the office, his eyes slightly swollen and blood-shot. "Sir, a courier has just arrived. He's brought a missive from Rome."

Waving his hand, Gaius grumbled and sat behind his desk. Dressed in barely used travel garb and dusty riding boots, the messenger cautiously bowed and offered a scroll. "Correspondence from Governor Petronius, Commander Fabius. I was instructed to deliver it to you personally."

After setting the scroll on his desk, Gaius wrote a couple of more sentences to Marcia and rolled up his letter, pressing his signet emblem into the soft wax seal. "Are you familiar with the lakeside estate of the Marcii at Aricia, their larger property on the Mount?"

"Yes, Commander Fabius." The wiry-haired lad's voice quivered, as he stood there, wringing his hands.

"For how many months have you served in the imperial courier service?"

"I was appointed on the Kalends of Martius, Commander."

"An auspicious day not that long ago." With a skeptical arch of his eyebrow, Gaius handed him his letter. "Deliver this correspondence to my wife, Marcia Servilia. Tell the emperor's guards I'd sent you and show them my insignia in the wax. Use the fast route and be sure to present her with this note yourself. Do not get fucking lost."

Nearly tripping over his clumsy feet, the fledgling courier genuflected and jogged out of the room.

"Let's hope that letter arrives before we do." Gaius inspected the
signet mark on the delivered scroll and broke the wax seal. A smug
smile stretched across his face as he leaned back in his chair. "I can
always rely on our efficient Tribune Titus."

"Good news, sir?" Max asked with no emotion, his voice cracking
from despair and fatigue.

"For me, yes—most advantageous news. My dear Maximus, are
you able to work or should you rest until tomorrow? You seem
preoccupied and exhausted, understandably."

Max looked up, startled. "Rest, sir? No, I'm well. I much prefer to
work."

"Very well. See that Euphronia and Callidora have packed ample
supplies for our trip and then spend some time in the baths, by gods.
Refortify your spirit. We have much to accomplish in Rome and I
need you fit for the tasks. I've given Bryaxis his orders. You both may
leave."

After they'd departed, Gaius drained the wine from his cup before
unfurling Titus's report once more. Rubbing the scruff on his chin, he
chuckled as he stared at the name. "So you're the only survivor of that
scouting troop, my vile, piggy-eyed friend. You're a fucking disgrace
to your noble Eagle. How marvelous our wise Fortuna has relin-
quished your sorry fate to me."

∼

STANDING IN FRONT OF Ferox's stall inside the stables, tears welling up
in his eyes, Allerix exhaled as he took the sharpened short sword from
Felix's outstretched hand.

"In the neck, right there." Felix pointed with an amused sneer.

"The cleaner you strike, the quicker it'll be over."

Allerix took two steps closer to the horse, its black eyes glowering distrustfully. The damn beast could smell the Dacian's apprehension. He stroked Ferox's long forelock, tangling his fingers in its silky black hair.

"I'm sorry, Ferox. I—I have no choice. You're a damn fine horse, best I've ever ridden," Alle mumbled to the stallion and raised the blade.

"Put the sword down."

Alle exhaled and cast the weapon to the ground, bending over as he clutched his stomach. "*Măcelar*," he spat under his breath.

Gaius emerged from the shadows. "A butcher would demand you slaughter this feral beast. I consider myself a merciful man." Gaius strolled over to the stall door and gently tapped the horse's muzzle with his knuckles; Ferox snorted and shuffled to the far corner of his box, his rump facing outward in defiance. "Merciful men don't kill animals for behaving like animals. It's uncivilized."

"I'm a barbarian. I don't know how to play your civilized games, sir."

"I had to know how far you'd go. But if you blindly obey a blatantly idiotic command, chances are you'll die young and for no good reason. We don't want that now, do we?" Gaius grabbed Alle by the shoulders while Felix picked up the discarded sword and stepped back. "I'm pleased you understand the gravity of a direct order, *căţel*. And, given what I've just witnessed, apparently you're desperate to visit Rome, so much so you'd slay a horse for being a fucking horse."

Gaius pressed his lips tight and smiled as he patted Alle's cheek. "I find your obsession with the capital charming but curious. Go assist Maximus and Varius. They're in the courtyard loading the wagons. You'll ride to Rome in a cart with Bryaxis and Simon and a shitload of crates."

"Yes, sir," Allerix grumbled, a resentful scowl spoiling his lovely face.

"Don't pout, Alle. There'll be other opportunities to wield a sword. I may not reprimand animals for their bestial actions, but I do punish men who behave like animals." Gaius hollered at his back as Allerix stepped over the threshold and out into the courtyard lit by the setting afternoon sun. Alle turned and looked back but said nothing, his expression hard and bitter. Their fragile, burgeoning trust had cracked.

When he was out of earshot, Felix asked, "What is the Dacian's purpose in Rome, Commander?"

"I don't know. The only way to find out, save torture, is to take him along and allow him to reveal his intentions through his actions. I'll keep a close eye on him."

Gaius pinched the bridge of his nose. "You're in charge while I'm away. And if that damn stallion hurts anyone else at the villa, kill it. Animal or not, I will not have a fucking horse disrupting the serenity of my seaside retreat."

Felix nodded. "Understood, sir."

～

AMIDST THE DUST AND noise and servants dashing to and fro, Allerix stood to the side and observed Varius diligently inspecting each packed crate before the men loaded it onto one of the wagons in the courtyard. Max stood beside an adjacent supply cart, an unfurled list dangling from his hand, his dark eyes blank and aloof. Preoccupied or perhaps just disinterested, neither man seemed to notice when Alle casually strolled past them toward the rows of the veterans' homes.

It was the perfect chaotic opportunity; his only chance to retake what had once belonged to him.

Another thirty feet from the courtyard and no one was in sight, except for a stray dog curled up in a ball asleep on the gravel. He'd seen the mangy mutt before, prowling the perimeter of the villa grounds for food scraps. Allerix sidestepped the brown lump of fur and crept down the narrow street between the small buildings erected to house the Roman's employed staff. At the far end was a large brick bath building; smoke poured from its chimneys.

"Which one belongs to that scar-faced prick?" Alle mumbled to himself as he scanned the structures.

Near the end of the row, a larger house on the right with a pitched tile roof stood out from the other domiciles. Allerix dashed from shadow to shadow until he scooted through a narrow passageway to a large window on the side of the house. Up on his toes, he peered through the iron bars: a table, two chairs, a bed, and a cupboard. In the far corner, a battered leather breastplate and a practice shield had been propped upright against the wall. The place appeared empty.

Allerix scrambled back out onto the narrow street and pulled on the iron door handle; it was locked. He circled around back and noticed another window without security bars. The opening was high up on the wall and small, but worth a try. He climbed the wooden end beams projecting from the exterior walls and squirmed through the window, only to drop down onto a cantilevered storage platform.

After several moments, he was certain he was alone. Alle jumped down to the floor and studied the room. Like the Roman, Varius would keep his valuables in his cupboard. When he opened its cabinet doors, a face stared back at him, a visage so lifelike he recoiled and gasped. It was a painted portrait of a woman with dark, curly hair and bright eyes. She beamed an attractive, friendly smile. On either side of the round picture frame sat a pair of smaller paintings: a boy with long, brown ringlets and an older girl holding a dove.

It was Varius's poignant, private memorial for his dead wife and children. Well, at least he'd trespassed the correct house.

Allerix steadied himself and searched the cupboard shelves below. In the far back he found a tool wrapped in a tan cloth. After opening the fabric and staring at the gold-handled dagger, he turned the blade over. The distinct wolf design etched into the metal caught the orange glow of the afternoon light and sparkled.

"Mine," Alle whispered before rewrapping the dagger and shoving it under his belt. Outside, a dog barked as heavy footsteps crunching the gravel-covered ground grew louder. Alle surveyed the home for a hiding spot. Without doors or much of anything to hide behind, he grabbed a blanket and crawled beneath the bed. Sweat poured down his neck, his fingers clutching the dagger handle.

"Clear off, you filthy, flea-infested cur!"

The dog yelped in pain, followed by men's laughter.

"Have a drink with me, Varius!"

"It would be my pleasure, Felix. First, I need to shit."

Shit! The bastard had to shit? Alle wiped his neck and scooted closer to the wall. He winced when his head hit a large metal bowl on the floor.

Keys rattled, and the unlocked door handle creaked as it turned. When the door opened, a stream of golden sunshine lit the room.

Before they crossed the threshold, Felix said, "Varius, wouldn't you prefer to empty your bowels in the veterans' spotless latrine where we have sponges and running water rather than use your old chamber pot and stink up your home?"

"Hmm, you do have a point."

"Come! I see the baths are open, and the furnaces stoked. We'll visit the latrine and afterwards enjoy a cup of wine and a soak in the hot pool."

"Felix, my wise friend and comrade. Yes, let's be civilized Roman men. Lead the way!"

The door closed with a bang; the lock clicked. When the veterans' bawdy laughter faded, Alle crawled out from under the bed and closed the cupboard, glancing one last time at the striking painted likeness of Varius's pretty departed wife. He grasped the concealed handle of his dagger before climbing up to and through the small window. Alle landed on the ground outside, half-hidden by the long shadows of the approaching dusk, and snuck back to the courtyard.

~

THE VIA APPIA

"TELL US MORE, BRYAXIS," Simon pleaded as the covered travel wagon rocked back and forth up the paved highway. "Is the city as grand as they claim?"

"Don't you recall anything about your birthplace, Simon?" With one eyebrow arched in jest, Bryaxis snatched the flask of water from Simon's hand and gulped a swallow.

Two more days' travel and they'd arrive at Aricia, wherever that was. Somewhere close to Rome, Allerix surmised, but he'd never heard of the town or the Alban Hills for that matter. Despite his anticipation to proceed with his plans for revenge, his nerves were frazzled, his heart distracted. What if the Roman truly loved his pregnant wife? What if his wife disliked Alle? Would she have him castrated?

Alle opened his eyes and stared at the pile of crates stacked against the wall of the wagon compartment. He'd managed to hide his dagger in a box of scrolls, scratching an identifying mark into a wood plank of the crate. And there it was, bottom row, the storage box on the far right. Somehow, before Bryaxis and Simon had a chance to unload its contents, he'd find a way to retrieve his weapon.

His birthday gift to Brasus.

Alle sighed and thought back to his capture. A prince died that day in the field, and a slave was born. Slave Alle or Paulus or whatever fucking name they called him had only one purpose now, one goal. If he were fortunate, this wagon would carry him to his glorious death and the eternal afterlife. Would his dead kin welcome him as a hero, as the savior of Dacia's pride and prestige?

"The last time I was in a cart headed to Rome, I was shackled to the floorboards alongside other pitiful wretches," Alle muttered, expecting no one would hear him over the rumble of the noisy wheels.

"And look at you now!" Bryaxis mocked. "Returning to the famous capital of the world as a whore of the Lion of the Lucky Fourth."

Alle swore the nastiest Celtic curse he could remember; Bryaxis cackled. "Oh, thank you for that gem, Dacian. No one has called me a bumfuckled donkey cock slathered in pig shit since I was a wee boy."

"My pleasure, eunuch." His smile sarcastic, Alle tipped his head. "Like Simon, I remember little about this famed city. Tell us all about it, Caledonian."

Bryaxis took another drink and handed Alle the water. "Rome is more spectacular than any place you could imagine. Seven hills straddle a broad river spanned by stone bridges. Everywhere are colonnaded streets, tall apartment buildings, lush public gardens, and towering marble temples to all the gods. Gilded colossal statues and monuments so enormous you'd think Titans must have constructed them. Food, wine, fabrics, and spices—anything you desire, if you have the coin."

Simon unfolded his crossed legs and scooted his bum closer. "What's Dom's house like?"

"Fabius's mansion on the Caelian is posh, much larger and more luxurious than his villa house. Even the slave quarters are spacious and comfortable."

"And what about his wife?"

"Jealous already, Alle?" Bry snickered. "I met her once, perhaps twice, in passing. She seemed pleasant enough—aristocratic and rather attractive for a noble matron. She's a friend of Lucius's bitch widow. Gods, I hope Domina isn't visiting Fabius's wife up in the Alban hills."

"What will you do if she's there?" Simon's bright eyes widened with concern.

"Stay out of sight. She fucking hates me, always has."

"What happens when we arrive in Rome?" Allerix asked, nibbling on his thumbnail.

"I suspect you'll spend most of your time attending to Fabius's prick. Simon and I have investigative work to do. We've been charged with finding those missing scrolls."

"Where do you think they are?" Simon asked, his arse bouncing up and down.

Bryaxis stroked the small leather pouch attached to his belt. "If they still exist, I'd wager they're stashed somewhere in Lucius's home. Dom's brother owns the property now, so we should be allowed to scour every corner of the place. If they're not there, then we'll search the state archives. And if that's for naught, perhaps Fabius can convince the court scribes to permit us access to the palace depositories. They're bloody massive, a labyrinth of shelves and records. There must be all sorts of secrets hidden the there."

"Gods, this is brill!" Simon rubbed his hands together. "Fuck, I wish Nic were with us."

Allerix mumbled, "Nic had never wanted to go to Rome."

Simon glanced at him and sighed. "You're right, Alle. He never wanted to leave Campania, and now we're carting his ashes to the capital. Gods, I miss him."

All three sat in silence, the wagon rocking back and forth until Simon confessed, "But I've always wanted to go on a real adventure."

"And an adventure you shall have." Bryaxis assured. "Strap up your sandals, Simon. Rome's also home to criminals of all shapes and depravity. The filthy alleys are full of shit and piss, decayed bodies float down the river, and everyone—and I mean everyone—carries a fucking knife. We don't go out on the streets after dark, mind you."

"Oh, a scary, dangerous escapade then?" Rubbing his palms together, Simon squirmed with excitement.

Snickering, Bryaxis rolled his eyes. "Only the best for you, pup."

19

MARCIA SERVILIA'S COUNTRY ESTATE, THE ALBAN HILLS

As THE HORSES AND supply wagons slogged up the steep dirt road, little by little her ancestral retreat came into view. Not since before the first war, soon after they'd married, had he visited Marcia's country estate up in the Alban Hills. The sprawling villa sat atop a ridge overlooking Lake Albanus, the water's dark sapphire surface as smooth as glass. On the southern edge of the estate, tantalizing glimpses of her sacred little sister, Lake Nemorensis, peeked through the dense thickets of trees. Soon a smattering of this year's leaves would wither and fall, carpeting the ground in shades of vibrant ochre, revealing panoramic views of the mystical landscape. Like many aristocratic Roman clans, the Marcii sought refuge from late summer's heat in the hills close by the ancient, hallowed groves of the almighty huntress, Diana.

When they reached the summit, the drivers pulled their vehicles to a stop in front of the house, and he slid down from his tired mount. Unclasping the pin on his riding cloak, Gaius trudged up the steps and past the palace guards stationed at the portal. After tossing his crimson mantle at the doorkeeper, he found Marcia's steward and her favorite nymph waiting for him in the well-appointed entrance hall.

"Greetings, Dominus."

"Greetings, Melissa," Gaius answered, acknowledging the thin steward standing beside her with a brusque nod. "Where is Domina? Did she receive my correspondence?"

Her sleeveless, cream-colored dress cinched tight at her waist, Melissa rose to her feet but kept her eyes fixed to the polychromatic mosaic floor. "Yes, Dominus. Your letter arrived four days past. At the moment, Domina is resting in her chamber."

"Inform her of my arrival. I'll visit her suite after I've washed off the dust and stench of travel."

"I'll make sure the baths are prepared, sir." Melissa bowed and scurried off.

"Steward, show my personnel to their temporary quarters. We'll be staying one night." Gaius hollered over his shoulder, "Maximus!"

Max ran into the atrium. "Sir."

"This slave will escort you and the lads to your accommodations while I refresh in the baths. And I've decided Alle will serve as cupbearer for tonight's dinner."

Max's mouth dropped. "Cupbearer, sir?"

"If he can saddle an unbroken stallion, our Dacian should be able to pour some damn wine without spilling it. Bryaxis has little time to train him, so tell the Caledonian to be expedient but thorough. And have Alle dressed appropriately, something formal and blue. Domina and I will dine with my grandmother, assuming our dear Avia is still in residence. Make sure my cub understands proper protocol."

"Yes, Commander."

⁓

"THIS ISN'T BAD," SIMON said, scratching his scalp as he wandered around the large stockroom attached to the kitchen area. "We have some old chairs and a table, but um—no beds."

"Looks like we're kipping on the floor. Ah, but we can fashion mattresses from these vegetables," Bry grumbled as he picked up a handful of greens from a produce crate.

Allerix opened the shutters. Cool breezes rushed in, freshening the stale air trapped in the dank space. Glittering specs of dust swirled in the bright beams of sunshine flooding the room. He drew a deep breath and studied the landscape. The Roman hadn't exaggerated; the hills were picturesque and the winds revitalizing. As he surveyed the unfamiliar but scenic terrain, it dawned on him he'd never again see the rocky peaks and dense forests of his Carpathian Mountains. If his plans came to fruition, he'd die in a foreign city far from home.

"Dacian!" Max stuck his head through the doorway. "Come with me to the servants' baths. The Commander wants you to play Ganymede tonight."

"What exactly does that mean?" Allerix glanced at Bryaxis, who patted his shoulder and smirked.

"Fabius has promoted you to cupbearer for the evening, barbarian, and in front of the wife, no less. That's an important step to attending posh parties in the capital. Well done, son."

"Dom wants *him*?" Simon pointed at Alle.

Max ignored his protest. "Bryaxis, you're to train the Dacian. Arrange a mock dinner setting with this scrap furniture and find a jug of water and cups. Simon, you'll assist me. Follow us to the baths to groom this grubby peasant."

"Bring back your appetites, lads." Bry jested, as Max marched Alle down the corridor. "I'll be serving stinking cabbage and leek soup!"

"Did you pack that blue tunic I'd given you back at the villa?" Max asked.

He wouldn't look at Allerix. Shit, Max had barely spoken to him since Nic's death. Did Max blame him for what had happened? Alle replayed the niggling question in his mind over and over as he trotted to keep up. "Yes, sir."

"You'll need proper footwear, not those soiled, ratty work boots. Simon's new pair of sandals should fit your heathen feet."

"What!" Simon squeaked.

Max stopped and grabbed both boys by the collars of their beige tunics, lifting them up on their tippy toes. "Listen to me. We're guests here at the estate of Marcia Servilia. She is our most treasured Domina, the Commander's noble wife! I won't tolerate any childish antics from either of you while we are guests at the home of our gracious and generous mistress. Understood?"

They both closed their mouths and nodded.

After a quick but painfully rigorous scrub in the warm bath, Allerix sat pink and naked on a stool while Max shaved his face. "Remove every bit of grime from under his nails, Simon, and clip them short. A cupbearer's hands must be immaculate."

When he'd finished dousing Alle's face and neck with lubricating oil, Max scraped the razor's blade across his thick, black stubble. The creases around Max's eyes and mouth seemed deeper and harsher than Alle remembered as the freedman leaned closer to barber his neck. Despair had aged him. After he'd finished the last stroke, Max swathed Allerix in a clean woolen mantle and led him back to the storage room, Simon jogging alongside them down the hallway.

"Welcome home, friends. Time for our bountiful feast!" Bryaxis bowed with a dramatic flourish of his long, sculpted arm, gesturing to the wooden chairs pushed up against one another to mimic dining couches. "You, Maximus, will play the head of the household for our extempore etiquette class. Simon, you'll sit here as our esteemed guest."

After they'd reclined across the chairs, Bryaxis handed them each a ceramic cup and turned to Alle. "Get dressed, Dacian. Tonight's affair will be a formal dinner with noblewomen present. No naked oiled bums at this sober bash."

Alle retrieved the blue tunic from a travel sack and pulled it over his head. "All right, what now?"

"Don't grumble. You want to attend parties in Rome, don't you?" Bry motioned Allerix to join him behind the chairs and handed him a pitcher filled with a clear liquid. He leaned over and whispered with a wicked grin, "I couldn't find water. That's vinegar."

After he'd cleared his throat, Bry explained, "When the guests call for wine or simply raise their vessels, quickly tiptoe to the couches and replenish their drink to a thumb's width from cup's lip. Don't say a word, don't look them in the eye, stay as invisible as possible and, whatever you do, don't spill the fucking wine. After you've finished pouring, wipe the edge of the pitcher with this cloth and withdraw. When your services are not needed, put your back against the wall. Keep your eyes open and your ears closed."

Alle sniffed the acerbic fluid in the water pitcher and grimaced. "How am I supposed to close my ears?"

"It's quite simple. Unless you're summoned for service, do not react to the diners' conversations, no matter what is said. A cupbearer is selectively deaf and always dumb."

An elegant, elderly woman appeared in the doorway, a pastry clenched in her slender, bony fingers. "What do we have here!" she shrilled. "I recognize our dear Maximus, of course, but who are these other charming sprites?"

Max bolted from his makeshift couch contraption and dropped to his knees, pressing his forehead to the floor. The grey-haired woman sighed as she shook her head. "Maximus, you're a freedman now, aren't you? By gods, stand up tall like a citizen!" The slender matron took a bite of her sweet treat and mumbled, "You lot must be my grandson's boys. Tell me your names."

"Greetings, Matrona." Max kept his eyes averted. "This is Bryaxis, Lucius Petronius's legal assistant, and former personal slave."

Bry knelt while she looked him over. "I remember you from our feast at the tomb of the Petronii on the Tiburtina. Lucius Petronius was an honorable man. I'm confident the emperor will execute his murderer, after a fair trial of course. And who's this yearling?"

"The slave's called Simon, Matrona."

"For the love of Minerva, is this Callidora's spawn? My, he's grown up nicely, hasn't he? He looks just like his father. And that dark-haired one?"

"My name is Alle," Allerix declared, stepping forward and offering his hand. Max ran over and slapped it down.

Memmia laughed. "Rather bold, aren't we? You have an unfamiliar accent. What are you?"

Allerix waited until Max nodded. "A barbarian, madam."

"Yes, I know that! You're all bloody barbarians. Where in our great empire were you born?"

"Dacia, madam."

"Well, pinch me purple! So Gaius has found himself a Dacian distraction, has he? By gods, my grandson is appallingly predictable. Maximus, which of these boys will be serving wine this evening?"

Allerix moved forward another step, bowing with his hands clasped behind his back. "I have the honor to serve as your cupbearer, madam."

"Marvelous! Be sure mine is always filled to the brim, and stop calling me 'madam.' I am Memmia Cornelia, a patrician daughter of the renowned Cornelii. I'm also your master's paternal grandmother. You may refer to me as Matrona, although I'm not the woman in charge here at this country hovel, technically speaking." She gnawed another mouthful of her pastry.

"Yes, Matrona."

Memmia snatched the empty cup from Max's hand. "Let's see your talents, Dacian. Pour me some of that wine there."

Alle glanced nervously at Bry, who only smirked and nodded. Alle tipped the pitcher of vinegar until her cup was full. She took a deep draft and pursed her lips. "By Castor, this swill is dreadful. I'm not surprised, however. For as long as I can recall, the parsimonious Marcii have served substandard libations."

She threw the ceramic cup to the floor, shattering it. Vinegar puddled on the brick, filling the air with its biting reek. Smacking her lips in disgust, Memmia lifted the hem of her voluminous dress and sauntered out of the room, leaving a trail of crumbs behind her.

～

GAZING AT THE CALM, shadowy lake, she stood near the balcony of her bedroom, backlit by the bright cloudless sky. Melissa knelt at Marcia's feet, her eyes focused on the floor.

"Greetings, Domina," Gaius said softly with a smile.

"You're here," she practically whispered, her words bursting with relief and hints of affection. She turned around, holding out her arms. "And there's your handsome face. Thank the gods you shaved off that barbaric beard."

By gods, the woman was as plump as a ripe pomegranate!

Gaius exclaimed, "Marcia, are you wearing some hideous contraption under your dress to fool Avia? It's most convincing." He approached, gaping incredulously at the large lump protruding from beneath the folds of her loose, lavender gown.

Marcia extended her hand. "It's not what you think. Gaius, come closer. Touch."

He took a step back. "I'd rather not."

"Come on, now. Don't be frightened."

"I am not fucking frightened of a sack stuffed with feathers or straw or whatever it is strapped to your abdomen."

"Place your hand right here," she insisted, cradling her stomach as she approached him.

"Marcia?" He gently ran his hand over her swollen curve. The protuberance was firm and smooth and—shit, it twitched under his fingers.

"By Jove's porphyry prick, it moved! What sinister sorcery is this?"

Chuckling, she grasped his reluctant hand and flattened his palm over her womb. "The baby's often awake and stirring this time of day."

Gaius jerked his hand away, lowering his voice. "That's not a stage costume? There's a baby in there? You're—you are with child?"

"Our child."

"But—but how?"

"Really, Gaius? How?" She raised her delicate, brunette brow, shaking her head while Melissa covered her mouth to stifle a giggle. "We've been blessed with a baby because I worshiped before the Aventine shrines on every damn festival day. As thanks for my generous offerings, Juno and Artemis acquiesced to my prayers and granted you an heir. You should venerate our fair goddesses more often, you know. Of course, Avia's tickled silly and rarely gives me a moment's peace. She's convinced the baby is a boy—a Cornelius. What's the matter with you, Commander? Are you at a loss for words once in your life?"

"I'm—I'm overwhelmed. After seven years of trying to produce an offspring, I never thought..." He blubbered, pulling her into an embrace, pressing his left palm against her bulging abdomen. "Shit, I am going to be a father."

"Twice over. Your mouse, Zoe, is even larger than I am. Melissa, be a dear and fetch your flabbergasted Dominus some wine."

His eyes wet, he lifted her chin. "Are you well? Has a physician examined you?"

"Yes, I'm fine. Those bouts of nausea we'd both attributed to indigestion or illness turned out to be nothing of the sort. Thank Juno, my stomach quieted soon after we'd arrived in Aricia. The doctor has proclaimed our baby a healthy, energetic little soldier. I confess I've been eating without pause. By Minerva, I've become as gluttonous as vile Vitellius."

He chuckled with tenderness. "Our long dead swine of an emperor had no excuse for his piggish behavior. As long as you're not snatching the sacrificial cakes off of the gods' altars, you should indulge, Domina."

"Speaking of unwelcome sows, both Plotina and Sabina traveled up from Rome for a brief visit during the last full moon." Marcia lowered her playful voice. "I do believe they were on a mission to confirm the veracity of my condition."

"The spying bitches."

"Had the Fates and our gracious goddesses not interceded, Gaius, it would have been impossible to deceive them. Plotina brought a doctor from the palace to examine me. You should have seen our dear empress' face when she realized I am in fact with child! She perspired and twitched until her cosmetics melted down her neck."

"I would have fucking loved to have been witness." Gaius cupped her face with his hands. "My dearest wife. You're giving me an heir—a legitimate, patrician heir."

After planting a peck on the tip of his thumb, Marcia beamed. "Remind me what the oracles foretold. On the day when the Marcii and the Fabii produce an offspring…"

Gaius adopted a silly, high-pitched voice. "Rome will enter her greatest golden age, a glorious era of bountiful riches and renewal."

"Yes, yes! That was the prophecy!" She laughed until tears streamed down her cheeks.

"Marcia, why didn't you send word to me down in Campania? I would have raced up here immediately."

"I'd hoped to share this splendid news with you face to face, and—lo and behold—Fortuna granted my wish. I did have a letter written awaiting a courier, but your melancholy message arrived before he did. I'm terribly sorry about the loss of your beloved slave boy. I remember you telling me all about your sweet, naughty Nicomedes."

Gaius pulled back and exhaled, rubbing his brow. "The accident was horrific—there was nothing I could do to save my lamb—and Maximus is devastated. He and Nic had been bedmates for years. I'd planned to gift Nic to him for the Saturnalia."

"Our poor, unfortunate Max." She wiped her eyes. "Please excuse me, Dominus. Gods, I've little control over my emotions under these conditions."

He hugged her again, tighter, mumbling into her hair, "Hush. Your condition is miraculous. Bloody drown me in tears for all I care. I hesitate to ask but is Aurelia still lurking about?"

"No, she returned to the city. Gaius? By Mercury's staff, have you not heard? Lucius's murderer was apprehended. There's to be a trial after the Great Games."

"What? Why didn't the emperor send word to me?" Gaius moved farther back, gripping her slender shoulders. "Who's been charged?"

"The Praetorian Prefect, Livianus. As you'd suspected, he and Aurelia are adulterers. It wasn't exactly the evisceration I'd planned, but I did almost manage to pry a confession from her. One night after she'd consumed more wine than she should have, Aurelia hinted Livianus was somehow involved in Lucius's murder. Nevertheless, she was most distraught when news of his arrest arrived. Aurelia and her noisome cousin left for Rome the following day."

"Livianus?"

"You seem surprised. Given his illicit entanglement with Aurelia, he's an obvious suspect, no?"

Gaius took the cup of wine Melissa offered on a tray and sat down on the couch. "Yes, quite obvious."

He took a long, slow swallow, mulling over the situation. "My stay here will be short, unfortunately. I must finish the rites for Nicomedes and, given this curious Livianus development, I need to visit the palace and speak with Marcus. Will you journey back Rome with us, Domina?"

She sat next to him and gripped his knee. "The physician's advised I not travel. I'm afraid our child will be born in the Alban Hills, not in Rome."

"Very well, but I want a doctor from Rome up here. Archigenes will arrive before Jupiter's festivals are over. As long as you and the baby survive the ordeal, the birthplace is irrelevant. There won't be a more Roman or more patrician child born for generations."

"The Virgin huntress will protect us. You'll stay the night though, won't you? Dine with me and your grandmother before you depart for the city?"

"I'll gladly stay with your permission, Domina. I must confess I've brought along my boys, including my latest acquisition. He'll serve as cupbearer for tonight's dinner."

Marcia's eyes widened as she chuckled. "Another boy, Gaius? By Castor, you're insatiable."

"This impassioned lad's special, Marcia."

"More so than our dear Maximus? I refuse to believe that."

"Trust me. Alle is—" Gaius hesitated, searching for the right word. "Fascinating."

"That's an odd name. What's it short for? Alexandros?"

Gaius swallowed and blinked. Fuck, fuck, fuck! Why hadn't he thought of a suitable and believable ruse earlier? Despite all his efforts to destroy every bit of evidence for Allerix's existence, revealing his true name to anyone remained far too risky. Alexandros was common enough to suit his purpose—a haughty but popular appellation for provincials.

"You are most insightful, my dear. Yes, yes—his name is Alexandros, as are the names of scores of heathens from the Greek-speaking regions of our ever-expanding empire. And, like the great Alexander, he's a remarkable horseman."

She eyed him suspiciously. "If I didn't know you as well as I do, I'd think you were smitten with this boy. And how generous of you to allow your new slave to retain his birth name, Gaius."

"I'm an indulgent bastard, aren't I?"

"Among other attributes, dear husband."

~

"Who's that little old man, sir?" Allerix asked in a hushed voice from the entrance to the spacious dining hall.

"The grape custodian."

"I thought I was serving the wine."

"You are. That poor codger safeguards the drink. He swallows a hearty gulp before the guests touch the wine to their lips. If the custodian chokes and drops to the floor, the grape is poisoned."

"And here I thought mucking out the stalls was a shitty job."

Max bumped Alle with his shoulder. "Quiet! When I tell you,

stand at the other end of that table with your back against the wall, hands folded behind you. Pour the wine as Bryaxis has taught you."

"Yes, sir." Alle gulped. "Maximus, sir? May I ask another question?"

"If you must," Max grumbled.

"Do you—do you blame me for Nic's death?"

Max bit down on his lip and looked away before confessing, "No, I don't blame anyone but myself. I should have run faster and pulled him out of the path of that mad beast. He was frozen with fear and there was time to save him, for fuck's sake, but I panicked and..." Max's deep voice cracked. "I failed him, and I lost him."

Alle struggled to find comforting words when the grandmother sauntered into the palatial room and reclined on one of the three plush couches.

"Quick, stand by the table." Max hissed and shoved Alle over the threshold. He trotted over to his spot and assumed the correct posture moments before the Roman and a short, attractive brunette dressed in a richly embroidered green dress entered the room. He was holding her hand.

"Greetings, our most honorable Avia!" Gaius roared, stealing a quick glance at Allerix. He nodded to him, his dimples deep and seductive, as he led the demonstrably pregnant woman to her couch. He helped her lay down on her side, fussing with her voluminous gown until the folds covered her legs and feet.

"Ah, there you two are. Greetings, grandson! And don't you look divine, Marcia. How is our expectant mother managing tonight?"

"Greetings, Avia. I'm starved, as usual. I've had my cooks prepare a scrumptious feast," Marcia replied, as Gaius stretched out on the couch between her and Memmia, propping himself up on his elbow.

Memmia leaned over to her grandson and muttered, "I hope it's more palatable than her foul wine."

With a baffled look on his face, Gaius looked over his shoulder at Alle. "I'm sure all will be splendid, Avia."

"Don't count your sacrificial chickens. Well, at least your new cupbearer is comely and well trained. But a Dacian, Gaius? Not that I'm surprised in the slightest, mind you. You've always succumbed to your lust for trophies and other war trinkets."

With effort, Marcia pushed herself up. "Is that your new concubine? You didn't tell me he was a Dacian. I've never seen one up close. Let's have a look, then."

Fiddling with his empty silver cup, Gaius sighed and relented. "Alle, stand before the couches and present yourself to your Domina, Marcia Servilia."

When Max nodded from the doorway, Alle approached and gracefully dropped to his knees on the stool in front of Marcia's couch.

"Let me see your face, slave. By the gods, are all Dacian boys this alluring?"

"No," Gaius responded curtly.

"What astonishing eyes he has, like those of a foal. I must admit he's more androgynous than I'd expected considering your usual tastes in companions, Gaius." Marcia squinted and leaned closer. "What's that curious disc hanging from its collar?"

"A fugitive tag. He tried to run off, once. I've since discovered the lad's too bright to attempt a second escape, but a deterrent seems prudent."

"Why does the tag say Paulus?"

"That was the slave name the dealer had assigned. At first, I'd thought I might keep it, but I've decided it doesn't suit his nature."

"That's a rather costly torque you've collared him with," Memmia interjected. "Why didn't you simply abide by tradition and brand his damn forehead? A stamp seared into the skin is both permanent and inexpensive."

"And that's enough tedious questions from the both of you. My throat is bloody parched. Custodian, sample the grape!" The Roman's discomfort was endearing; Alle covered his mouth to smother his grin.

The little old man scuttled over and poured a cup, handing the pitcher to Alle. He swallowed one long gulp while everyone watched and waited.

Nothing.

Gaius led the applause. "Good show, old boy!" He raised his cup and explained, "Wife, I've brought three amphorae of exquisite nectar grown on the fertile slopes of Vesuvius as gifts for your indulgent hospitality. Fill our beakers to the brim, Alle."

"Campanian wine? Thank Dionysus and his entire entourage of whore maenads!" Memmia rejoiced, thrusting her cup in front of her.

Marcia shook her head and smiled. "I humbly accept your lavish gifts, Dominus. To our gracious Juno Lucina!"

"To good health and prosperity!" Gaius and Memmia responded.

After he'd finished filling Gaius's cup, Alle hurried back behind the couches and stood against the wall, waiting for the next signal, trying but failing to keep his ears closed.

"Let's discuss my favorite topic—the baby. If the child is a girl, will you award her a nickname, Gaius?" Avia wondered as her aged, glassy eyes filled with pride. Her cranky demeanor and penchant for tactless remarks reminded Allerix of Istros. Gods, he'd never see his beloved old tutor again either. Perhaps they'd reunite in the afterlife.

Gaius hesitated before answering, "Yes. I'll name her Marcella, my little warrior maiden. Fabia Marcella."

The old woman's smile lit up like a torch. "Brilliant choice, Rufus."

Marcia leaned over and asked, "And if the goddesses bless us with a boy, dear husband?"

"Lucius, of course. Lucius Fabius. I'll decide his nickname after the sprog has a chance to be more than his bloody hair color."

"Splendid." Marcia sighed, rubbing her stomach. "But Lucius Fabius Marcius, I think."

Gaius pressed his lips tight. "We'll discuss the specifics at a more appropriate time, Domina."

"I think we should discuss it now," she retorted, her lip curled in defiance.

"More wine?" Alle stepped forward and immediately backpedaled, his eyes downcast. Shit, he wasn't supposed to talk, let alone ask a question. Allerix peeked up from under his thick fans of lashes, trying his damnedest to appear demure and contrite.

"Yes, my foolhardy *cățel*. Quench my thirst." Gaius beamed gratefully, hoisting his cup, seemingly unperturbed by Alle's unsuitable outburst.

"Cat-sul?" Marcia garbled, her pronunciation painful while Alle refilled their cups.

"It's a Dacian word and none of your damn concern, dear wife." Gaius wiggled his finger, blatantly annoyed. "I'm fucking famished. Where's this feast you've promised, hmm?"

As though on cue, a flock of servants carrying trays laden with sizzling meats and succulent sauces scurried into the spacious hall. Allerix couldn't identify most of the food, but everything smelled delicious.

"We need entertainment. Does your Dacian boy sing?" Marcia wondered.

"I don't know." Gaius turned around. "Can you sing, Alexandros?"

Allerix cocked his head, his brow scrunched.

Alexandros?

"Um…"

"Yes or no? It's a simple question."

"Yes, Dominus."

"Wonderful. Put down that pitcher and serenade us with a song in your heathen tongue."

Allerix scratched his chin and smoothed his tunic before returning to stand in front of the couches. When he opened his mouth and sang a battle tune he'd learned during the first war, Marcia exclaimed with glee, "For the love of Apollo's dulcet lyre, he's a barbarian Orpheus! What a beautiful voice your new boy has, Gaius."

"I had no idea he had this talent either." Gaius grinned and gestured for him to stop. "Lovely, Alle. But next time be sure to choose a song that does not describe in vivid detail the maiming and beheading of Roman soldiers."

"Cheeky bugger," Memmia cackled through her mouthful of food. "You should keep this pretty savage, Rufus. I like his pluck."

"And you should swallow before you speak, my dear Avia." Wiping off a speck of food from his cheek, Gaius waved his other hand. "Back to your station, my plucky Alexandros."

>>>><<<<

20

MARCIA SERVILIA'S COUNTRY ESTATE, THE ALBAN HILLS

AFTER THE SUN HAD set, and the plates of fruits and cakes picked over, Marcia and Memmia bid their farewells for the evening while servants hurriedly cleared away the dishes. Given all the clatter and chatter during dinner, the grand dining room turned eerily quiet. Gaius strolled over to the serving table, the echoes of his footsteps filling the stillness and poured a cup of wine.

"You do have a most captivating voice, Alle, and you even charmed Avia. My tetchy grandmother rarely pays any notice to the slaves, let alone a compliment. Here, a well-deserved drink."

Allerix accepted the cup and glanced around to be sure they were alone before mumbling, "Thank you for not branding my forehead, Rufus."

"Disfiguring your exquisite face was never an option, Allerix." Gaius unbuckled Alle's belt and caught the leather strap before it fell to the marble floor.

"Why did you call me Alexandros, sir?"

"Ah, yes—that. Earlier today when I'd visited Domina, I referred to you as Alle. My astute and ever curious wife immediately inquired about your full, proper name. No doubt others in the capital will question your nickname as well, so I've decided to call you Alexandros when we're in public. Do you like it?"

"Does it matter?"

"It fucking matters to me, yes."

"It's fine, I suppose." Alle shrugged. "Alexandros is a common name."

"True. It's quite popular and a tad haughty for a Dacian farm boy, but it serves my purpose. Learn to answer to it. Your life depends on a consistent and credible alias."

Allerix lowered his chin. "Yes, Dominus."

"Despite your inexperience, you performed well tonight. Marcia was impressed, as was I. However, cupbearers never speak unless asked a direct question. I'll have to punish you—a few sharp swats to redden your brazen arse." Grinning, Gaius slapped the leather belt against his palm, once and not hard.

Allerix's balls ached as blood rushed to his prick. When he noticed Alle's arousal tenting his tunic, Gaius's grin broadened into a smile. "Alas, discipline will have to wait. First, I must say something to you. Pay attention. There's a good chance I'll never say these words again, so listen and remember this moment." Gaius snatched the silver cup from Alle's grasp and swallowed a gulp of wine before handing it back. "I owe you an apology."

Alle raised his eyebrows but kept his mouth shut.

"Back at the villa when I demanded you kill the horse. I needed to measure your resolve to obey my orders, but my test was ill conceived and unfair. I was a sadistic prick and for that, I am sorry."

Allerix blinked slowly before taking a long draft of drink. "May I speak?"

"Yes."

"The wars are over, sir. You are the victor, and I am your subject, your slave. I accept my fate, and I will strive to obey all of your orders, even the daft ones. But, Dominus—you don't owe me an apology. I'm the one who must beg you for forgiveness."

Gaius brushed his hand over the blue fabric covering Alle's round bum before caressing the hollow at the small of his back. Confusion tempered his seductive smile. "Forgive you for what, Allerix?"

"For Nic's death. I trained Ferox, so all blame for the horse's lethal actions falls on my shoulders."

"That's noble of you, but complete fucking rubbish. Stallions are always unpredictable, trained or not. The entire disaster was an unforeseeable accident. No one is at fault, Allerix."

Alle glanced at the empty doorway. Although Max had left long ago, he lowered his voice to a whisper. "Max believes he's to blame for Nic's death."

Sighing, Gaius took the cup from Alle's hand and set it on the table next to Alle's belt. He pulled him into an embrace, lifting the hem of Alle's tunic to caress his bare arse with his warm, strong hands. "Considering he witnessed the tragedy, I'm not surprised he's carrying unwarranted guilt. Maximus loved Nicomedes as much as I've grown to cherish you."

"You cherish me?"

"Worse. I fear I'm falling in love with you."

"Don't be afraid, Rufus." Alle purred while brushing his lips across Gaius's smile. Gods, if he wasn't mindful, he might damn well trick his own heart into believing his feigned passion was real.

Gaius nudged him back and grabbed his chin. "In his final testament, Lucius advised me to trust my heart, but I wonder if I should trust you, *cățel*? Do barbarians honor the fragile bonds of love? Will you break my heart one day?"

"Never underestimate a Dacian—isn't that what you'd once said to me?" Allerix jested.

Gaius chuckled. "Indeed, I did. But does a Dacian's love or loyalty have any value?"

Taken aback, Alle fumbled to explain he was only joking when a beautiful and heavily pregnant young blonde entered the dining room. Her face flushed to a charming shade of pink after she'd spotted them embracing by the table. "Most holy Minerva! My apologies, Dominus. I'd thought this hall deserted, sir."

Gaius patted Allerix's backside before extending a hand towards her. She shuffled over to him and lightly kissed his knuckles. Unease churned in Alle's gut; the girl was frightfully beautiful.

"Zoe, my nymph. No, no—don't kneel. I'd been planning on visiting you in the morning before I depart, but here you are. This young wolf is my new bed warmer, Alexandros."

"Greetings, Zoe," Allerix said, nodding slowly. She had captivating blue eyes, not quite as sapphire in color as Nic's, but still beautiful. Her alabaster skin looked as though she'd been sculpted from the finest white stone.

"Greetings," she answered modestly and tipped her chin before turning to gaze at Gaius's face. "Dominus, my heart is shattered. Domina told me about our dear Nicomedes and that dreadful black horse. No matter how hard I try, I can't contain this flood of tears."

"Hush, my dove," he replied, pulling her sobbing body into an awkward embrace. "The Fates had been bloody cruel to him, but for the last years of his life Nicomedes enjoyed good food, companionship, and the love of his family. We will all miss him and forever honor his memory." He nudged her backward. "Let me take a look at you. By Juno, girl, you look as though you'll burst at any moment."

She smiled; her ivory teeth were bloody perfect as well. "Your child is healthy, Dominus. He's a kicker, fierce and robust like his magnificent father. Domina's physician estimates I'll give birth soon, sir."

Allerix's mouth dropped. Another child? How many fucking seeds had the Roman sown?

"I have only one child waiting to be born, Zoe. You're carrying an unfortunate accident, a wretched slave without a lawful father. Understood?"

She lowered her eyes, folding her dainty hands over her grossly swollen abdomen. "Yes, Dominus."

"I am delighted to see you are healthy and well-cared for. Obey Domina, but remember you and the bastard in your belly are my property. I'll see you next when I return to celebrate the glorious birth of my patrician offspring and rightful heir. You may leave."

After Gaius had watched her waddle out of the dining hall, he crossed his arms and sighed. "She's a sweet thing, the most pleasant, compliant girl I've ever owned. I pray she survives childbirth."

"Do you love her?"

"Love? No. I do adore her, as much as I'd adored Nicomedes. I often called both of my flaxen-haired pets to the playroom for salacious, three-way games. Gods, those two beauties together were a delicious treat." Gaius sighed wistfully before cupping the back of Alle's neck.

"Now, where were we? Ah, we'd been discussing trust before that interruption, yes? Trust me when I say all I want is you, and only you, in my bed tonight, Allerix. But first, there's the matter of your punishment."

Alle took a deep breath, trying to stay focused on his schemes. "May I confess something?"

Gaius cocked a brow. "You may."

Gods, this was discomfiting, but an admission of the truth might strengthen his chances to bind the Roman's heart and access the king's palace. And he wanted it. Gods, how much he wanted to feel that delicious sting. Allerix parted his lips but stammered as his cheeks blushed. "I—I, um…"

Gaius pushed his fringe to the side. "Look at me. There's no cause to be bashful. Tell me."

"I find spanking more pleasure than punishment." Allerix quickly followed with, "When you do it, Dominus."

Grinning ear to ear, Gaius hushed his voice. "I suspected as much from the very first time I swatted your round rump." He picked up the belt lying on the table and slipped the strap under Alle's silver collar, pulling the end through the bronze buckle to improvise a leash. "Many find it pleasurable. I know I do."

"You do?"

"Indeed, though as I've grown older, I've found I much prefer to give a good swat rather than receive one."

"That's magnanimous of you, sir."

"And there's that seductive sass of yours." Gaius chuckled. "Allerix, you've been schooled for your entire short life to believe your cravings are unnatural, but there's nothing shameful about what you desire." Gaius leaned closer and waggled his auburn brows. "So you would fancy a solid spanking tonight?"

Alle exhaled. "Yes, Dominus."

"Would you prefer I use a strap, cane, or my hand?"

"Your hand, sir," Alle whispered low and deep as he dragged his freshly manicured fingernails across Gaius's palm.

"And again we share similar proclivities." While tugging the belt leash, Gaius bit and sucked Alle's full lower lip until they both groaned. He took a step back and tugged harder, growling.

"On your knees, Allerix. There's to be no screaming here at Domina's estate, not with Avia sleeping down the hall from my guest room. Will you be able to stifle your cries?"

Alle looked up and swallowed. "You'd better gag me, sir."

Gaius laughed. "Wise answer. I intend to spank your fit bum until your fucking toes tingle. And once I've slapped your arse scarlet hot, I'll introduce you to a most wicked device I've brought from the playroom. Do you have any idea how much I love watching a boy squirm in ecstatic frustration, how much I enjoy denying him his exquisite release?"

Alle exhaled loudly but said nothing.

"That was a direct fucking question, Alle."

"Yes, Dominus."

"If I'm satisfied with your obedience, I'll impale your tight heat until my thick, noble cream spills out of your arse and drips down your long, furry legs. And if you beg sweetly, I might suck your gorgeous cock until you come so hard those beautiful eyes of yours roll back in your fucking skull."

A desperate moan escaped through Alle's parted lips.

Gaius reached down and ran his thumb over the luscious swells. "So many delightful possibilities ahead of us tonight. Stand up and let's retreat to my guest suite. Shall we take what's left of this wine with us, my siren prince?"

Alle pressed both hands against his raging erection before cupping his aching balls and gasped. "Gods yes, Rufus."

~

THE VIA APPIA, ROME

"LOOK THERE, MAXIMUS! OUR esteemed guest has arrived earlier than I'd expected."

Gaius pulled his ambling horse to a stop and pointed to a table surrounded by folding stools set up by the side of the road near the entrance to his family's tomb for their freedmen. With little hair and an angular face, a man wearing a crisp, white toga sat on a stool behind the wooden desk, a scroll clasped in his hand. A tall, armed attendant with a slender rod stood at attention by the man's side. A few feet away, Varius greeted Gaius and Max with a nod of his head. A lumpy cloth sack hanging from his hand, Theodorus peeked out from behind Varius's shoulder; his handsome face freshly shaved, Theo's greying brown hair was combed and coiffed.

"Theodorus is here, sir?" Max asked as he dismounted.

"I'd sent word to our dear cobbler inviting him to join us for the occasion. I'm delighted to see he's made it out to the suburbs in time. And it appears he's brought the new pair of stylish sandals I'd ordered. Marvelous!"

Max flashed a quick wave, which Theo sheepishly returned with a daft grin.

Gaius dropped from his saddle to the ground. "I find it increasingly difficult to secure the services of a conscientious and dependable magistrate these days. Once he's completed our ceremony, that fine fellow will receive extra coin for his punctuality."

"I don't understand what's happening, sir. Are we conducting another funerary ceremony before the interment, Commander?"

"No, we're performing a ritual for you, my dearest Max. It's a surprise! Don't you just adore surprises? Welcome to the day of your official manumission. You've served me faithfully and with all your heart for ten wonderful years. As my freedman and client, I pray you remain a member of my family for many more to come. I promise you my support and protection for the rest of your life."

Max's big brown eyes welled up with tears. Before his freedman collapsed into a gush of sobs, Gaius rested his hand on Max's thick, trembling forearm. "We all had expected Nicomedes to be here for this joyous ceremony. Let's carry his cinerary box with us to the judge's table, yes? Afterward, we'll lay him to rest in my freedmen's tomb with great honor and affection."

"Yes, Commander." Max blubbered while he wiped his eyes. "And thank you. Thank you for freeing me, and for allowing Nic to be by my side for the ceremony."

Smiling, Gaius raised his arm high and brushed the side of his hand across Max's cheek. "The gods created you and Nicomedes for each other. Once I understood the divine nature of your love, I never dared keep you two apart for long."

Gaius turned around and shouted to his small retinue of travel companions, "Disembark and celebrate the official grant of liberty and citizenship to Gaius Fabius Maximus!"

Gaius's two guards slid down off their horses and the cart drivers jumped to the ground. Bryaxis, Simon, and Alle exited the first covered supply wagon. Gaius nearly laughed out loud when Alle hobbled along, wincing while he rubbed his spanked, well-fucked bum. From another cart, Callidora and his newly acquired, shapely Arabian girl stepped down into the bright afternoon sun. Marcia had finally allowed Gaius to purchase Delia from her after all, much to Calli's blatant distress. By Mars' balls, women were baffling and disagreeable, and yet undeniably fucking irresistible.

Gaius and Max approached the table; the slender man rose from his seat to greet them. Max cradled the ceramic box containing Nic's burnt remains firmly in the crook of his elbow.

"Greetings, Commander Fabius."

"Greetings, Praetor. A fine day for a manumission, isn't it?"

"Yes, Commander. Splendid autumn weather we're enjoying. Welcome back to Rome, sir. Shall we proceed?"

"By all means. Maximus has waited far too long for this occasion."

"Excellent. Gaius Fabius Rufus, son of Quintus Fabius, do you affirm before our gods and our sacred laws your wish to bestow this slave his freedom?"

Gaius turned to Max and nodded with a smile. "I endorse the grant of liberty."

The magistrate's attendant advanced towards Max and, with the ceremonial rod in one hand, placed his other hand on Max's broad shoulder. The balding official cleared his throat. "I, Servius Laelius, a chief civil officer of our fair capital, declare Gaius Fabius Maximus released from the laws of the Quirites. He is now a free man and a citizen of Rome, with all the privileges and duties his new status dictates and requires."

While the magistrate recited his proclamation, his assistant touched the tip of the liberty rod to Max's bare head. When he'd finished, Gaius gently slapped Max's face with the same hand he'd spanked Allerix's willing arse warm the night before.

"I, Gaius Fabius Rufus, Commander of the Lucky Fourth under the authority of our esteemed Emperor Marcus Ulpius Trajan, declare this man, Gaius Fabius Maximus, released from the laws of the Quirites."

After he'd reached up and grabbed Max by his shoulders, Gaius turned him around and pushed his former slave away from him towards the wagons. "I release you from servitude, Gaius Fabius Maximus. Varius, offer our fellow citizen the cap of liberty."

With Theo on his heels, Varius strolled over and handed Max a floppy cloth hat. Max dutifully pulled it onto his head, clutching the cinerary box to his chest as tears streamed down his face.

Gaius shouted, "All rejoice and applaud this official manumission!"

After Gaius had gestured his permission, Bryaxis and Simon rushed over to embrace Max. Gaius wondered if Simon would recognize Theodorus; he hadn't seen his birth father in years. Now that Simon would reside in Rome for the foreseeable future, it was time for Simon and Theo to reconnect, despite any objections from Callidora.

Gods, Max had been right all along. He should never have sent Theo away from his only child. His son, for shit's sake! Damn Calli and her self-serving, feminine intrusions.

As congratulations were shared, Gaius signed and stamped the official papers with his signet ring and paid the tax in freshly minted coin he'd saved for this specific occasion. After bidding farewell to the praetor and his assistant, he called Allerix over to his side.

"I'm curious, Alle. What were your impressions of the manumission proceedings?"

"Quick and bizarre, Dominus. May I ask a question?"

"Yes."

"Why did you strike Max during the ceremony?"

Gaius scratched the side of his nose. "It's an archaic gesture, a symbolic reminder of his servile past. We have several means to grant liberty, but this formal ritual before the auspices of a praetor is my favorite. The pomp and tradition make the manumission more tangible and personal. Now that that's finished, we must conclude our final task before we pass through Rome's southern gate. Maximus!"

Max rushed over, the soft peak of his liberty hat drooped over his left ear. "Yes, Commander."

"It's time to bid our farewells to Nicomedes. Are you ready, citizen of Rome?"

Max readjusted his dangling hat, straightened his posture, and smiled, the first genuine smile Gaius had seen since the accident. "Yes, sir." Max glanced down at the box. "We're both ready, Commander."

"Varius has unlocked the door to my family's sepulcher. The

rooms and corridors down there house generations of our slaves and freedmen. Tell Bryaxis and Simon to gather up all the lamps and torches. The columbarium is as dark as bloody pitch. Guards, bring my gift for Nicomedes!"

"Gift, sir?" Max asked, an incredulous grin on his face.

"I won't have him interred in that paltry clay box. I'd sent Varius to the Caelian to retrieve a special receptacle, a family heirloom, one worthy of Nic's obedience and devotion. A talented painter decorated it for me. It's my final gift to my dear boy."

Varius passed through the tomb's portal, his blazing torch illuminating the short passageway that led to a steep, stone staircase. Stucco images of garlands, flowers, and songbirds flittering through the sky decorated the walls. After he'd pulled his cloak over his head, Gaius took the bronze lamp from Varius's outstretched hand. In single file, with Gaius at the lead, each person grasped the iron handrail and descended into the cool, musty depths of the vast underground catacomb.

Constructed on three levels connected by stone and wooden stairs, every surface was pierced by row after row of small, man-made hollows, some rectangular in shape, most curved. Each cavity housed a cinerary urn, its inhabitant identified by a simple, painted inscription below the niche noting the deceased's name, status, and age at the time of death. Many of the dead were infants and children who had perished before their fifth birthdays; most of the hundreds of remains had been interred ages ago. Despite their humble rank, every man, woman, and child once owned by the Fabii would be remembered here for eternity. Or for at least as long as the family performed its pious duties and the damn tomb stood intact.

Step by step, Gaius and his retinue descended into the bowels of the earth. After the solemn procession had reached the second level below ground, Gaius stopped in front of a marble altar set beneath a large, empty niche. It was more ornate than the smaller openings surrounding it. Instead of a plain, smooth surface, its concave interior had been carved in a wavy design mimicking the ridges of a seashell. Above the small alcove was a colorful fresco depicting a dormouse playing with a ball of blue and green ribbon.

Max raised his lamp, his teeth shining brightly against his sable skin as he spoke to the cinerary box. "Look up there, Nic! It's a picture of your little pet—that deformed dormouse runt you'd nurtured and taught all those silly tricks. Gods, I will miss you, Nicomedes." Max's final words echoed off the walls.

Fighting to contain his tears, Gaius waved his men over and mumbled, "Open the crate."

Together the two guards lifted the wooden lid and pulled out an elegant, bulbous urn from a nest of straw. On its surface was a skillful painting of a recumbent white lamb, its legs tucked under its wooly body, lying in a field of grass and red poppies. In the flickering lamplight, the golden alabaster vase glowed like the full moon.

"Maximus, place the cinerary box inside this precious jar."

After Max carefully lowered the modest box inside the wide-mouthed urn, Gaius secured its globular lid and set the receptacle on the shelf in the seashell niche. "Here he shall rest for eternity as an honored member of the great Fabii, one of Rome's founding families. My family. Before this shrine, we'll present roses and violets, offer cakes and wine, and feast together every year to honor Nicomedes' memory and remember his kind, loving nature. You're safe here, lamb."

Gaius took a glass jug of wine from Varius's grasp and poured a libation. As the trickle of dark red liquid splashed over the altar's surface, Gaius lowered his covered head and prayed. "May your spirit dwell in blissful peace, Gaius Fabius Nicomedes."

"To the spirits of the departed," everyone recited in response, except Allerix, who stared up at the vertical heights of the massive tomb with a baffled expression on his face.

After lifting the hood of his cloak, Gaius marched over to the stairs and stepped onto the first stone tread.

"Follow me and ascend to the sundrenched world of the living! We'll sacrifice a pig to conclude the formalities, and enjoy an early meal of roasted pork. There will be food and wine for everyone on this momentous day. Let us feast under the shade of the Appia's noble pines and then return to the bosom of our beloved Rome."

21

U P AT THE FRONT of the unroofed wagon, the unfamiliar man
with greying brown hair sat on the bench across from Simon.
Staring at each other's faces as though gazing into mirrors, the two
chatted while they took turns touching a forearm or brushing
fingertips. An astonished grin was plastered across Simon's young
face while the older fellow laughed with blatant joy as he wiped his
teary eyes.

"So he's Simon's father?" Alle asked from his spot near the back of
the cart.

Bryaxis shuffled closer. "Yes, his name is Theodorus. When he was
Simon's age, he belonged to Fabius's father. Fabius inherited him, and
eventually granted him freedom. He's a launderer or shoemaker or
some drudging craftsman now." Bry pursed hip lips and raised his
brow judgmentally.

"At least he's not a slave."

"Trust me, Alle, it's far better to be a cherished slave than a poor
citizen with no protection. Fortunately for old Theodorus, he's a client
of the Lion of the Lucky Fourth. A freedman needs a powerful patron
if he's to survive the perils of living in Rome."

"Is Theodorus a decent fellow?"

"I've never met him before today, but Max speaks of him often and with great affection. They're good friends. Theo and Max shared Fabius's bed at one point."

Alle shook his head. "Who hasn't the Roman fucked?"

Bry shrugged. "Varius? But anything's possible, I suppose."

As they laughed at the absurd image Bry's suggestion had conjured up, the cart hit a rock in the road and lurched, sending Allerix tumbling forward. Before his face hit the floor, Bryaxis grabbed the back of his tunic and pulled Alle up onto the plank seat.

"Careful there! We're nearly home. Hold on, barbarian." Bry warned, a sarcastic lilt to his voice, as he nudged him with his elbow. Allerix hunched down, holding on to the cart's wooden edge for dear life. The wagon hurtled down the road, bumping up and down, rocking back and forth, its squeaky wheels rolling over the paving stones. They must be close to the infamous city; the angular tops of tall buildings pierced the canopy of trees covering the hills ahead.

Cautiously, Alle leaned over the side of the wagon and craned his neck. At the front of the small train of vehicles rode the Roman, his head uncovered, his indigo cloak embroidered with gold threads flapping like a raven's wings in the brisk autumn breezes. With each lively step of his trotting mount, the man's chestnut curls bounced, reflecting the waning golden light. The procession followed a sharp curve in the road; the Roman turned around in his saddle and looked back at Alle. His steely, fierce eyes softened without warning as his stern, thin lips melted into a dazzling, dimpled smile. Before Allerix could catch his breath, the bastard turned back around and pushed his horse to a loping canter.

Allerix, second son of Thiamarkos, was captivated. Would he lose his heart to the Roman before he sacrificed his life for Dacia's honor? At least, perhaps, he would have known love once during his short, shameful life.

As they continued down the broad avenue, the trees along the sides of the road dwindled in number with each turn of the wagon's wheels. After another bend in the street, a densely packed forest of brick, limestone, and marble rose up in front of Alle's bulging eyes.

"Great gods!"

"Bloody impressive, isn't it?" Bry flashed his charming, slanted grin. "Although I've heard Alexandria is even more spectacular than Rome."

To Alle's left, an enormous, multistoried structure crowned the summit of a hill, the building's surfaces shining green, purple, ivory, and gold. Down below, the curved, oblong exterior another edifice consumed the level plain of a narrow valley. Cranes and hobbled mules and pallets laden with materials crowded the structure's perimeter, as bricklayers slapped together walls and masons carefully positioned shaped stones into place.

Shielding his eyes with his hand, Allerix surveyed the bustling activity when Bry explained, "They're rebuilding the markets of the great circus. The old shops were made of wood, but the emperor ordered new ones constructed out of brick and stone to prevent fires. It'll be the grandest racetrack in the world once the refurbishments are finished."

"What do they race there?"

"Chariots, mostly—teams of four-horse carts driven by slaves. When I was younger, Lucius took me along to watch the races. Not often, but we had fun. The crashes are spectacular."

"And what is that building above the racetrack?"

Bry wrapped an arm around Alle's shoulder and flicked his pointer finger towards the hill. "That, my dear Dacian, is the palace. The emperor, his family, and an army of guards reside in its maze of luxurious rooms, formal gardens, and meeting halls. Everything inside is silver and gold and fucking encrusted with gems. There's even a balcony from which the old boy and his mates can watch the races down in the circus without dirtying their posh, purple robes."

"So that's their king's house," Allerix muttered out of the side of his mouth; his eyes fixed on the imposing hilltop palace. He studied the location of every visible window, noting each glimpse of a staircase and ramp, judging the drop distance from one roof to the next. Armed sentries patrolled the exterior walkways and terraces. The sprawling, ostentatious monstrosity appeared heavily guarded and complicated to navigate. As Allerix had long suspected, his chances of escaping alive would be slim at best.

"My death chamber," he whispered under his breath.

"What was that?"

"Um… I'm amazed. I've never seen a royal residence as grand."

Bryaxis tossed his head back, nodding towards the hill. "I've been to parties up there, you know."

"We've all heard about your infamous cock sucking show, Caledonian." Alle turned to watch the palace disappear behind their cart. "That must have been quite an honor, being invited to a palace dinner and entertaining the king's prick in front of the entire court. Your Dom must have been proud of you."

Allerix turned back and stared, waiting for Bry's cheeky response while Bryaxis wrung his hands, clearly irritated with the conversation he'd started. "Lucius put on a stiff mask as he was expected to, but he was terrified of bringing me to the palace."

"Why?" Alle asked before leaning against the backrest of his wooden seat. Out of seemingly nowhere, a towering circular building rose up in front of the wagon. The massive structure quickly filled the sky, dwarfing everything around it. In its arched openings, gilded statues glowed, half lit, half obscured by shadows. At the very top, enormous bronze shields shimmered in the light of the raking afternoon sun. The terrifying structure cast its menacing shadow like a rapacious dragon.

Unperturbed by the change in scenery, Bry yammered on. "Lucius feared the emperor would steal me to serve as his palace whore. He warned he wouldn't be able to protect me. Emperor Trajan takes what he wants without question from anyone." Bry paused and leaned down close to Allerix's face. "You look odder than usual, Dacian. What's bloody wrong with you?"

"What the fuck is that!" Alle cried out.

Bryaxis finally turned his head. "Ah, can't miss the colossal beast, can you? That's the great amphitheater, Rome's dreaded arena—of—death." Bry exaggerated the last two words for dramatic effect.

"Shit, have—have you been in there?"

"Thank gods, no. Lucius never cared for gladiatorial spectacles, beast hunts, or criminal executions. He much preferred the theater, comedies and poetry readings most of all. He enjoyed laughter and beauty more than bloody gore."

The wagon jerked to a stop. Still dazed, Alle opened his mouth to ask what had happened when that luscious, gravelly voice boomed through the air. He startled after realizing the Roman was bellowing from his saddle just five feet from Alle's right ear.

"Welcome to Rome! Varius will escort you all up to my home on the Caelian. Follow his orders. After you've finished unloading the wagons, my steward will direct you to your quarters and have you fed. Maximus! Ride with me up to the palace. I need to pay our esteemed Emperor a courtesy visit."

Max glanced at Bryaxis and swallowed. "Yes, Commander."

～

THE IMPERIAL RESIDENCE ON THE PALATINE HILL, ROME

DRAWING DEEP BREATHS, GAIUS and Max ascended the first marble step of the stairs leading up to the audience hall on the main level of the soaring palace. Unlike his previous visit, the guards were ready and waiting on the landing, sword hilts in their hands. The entire lot appeared twitchy and on edge. Gaius extended his arm to block his freedman from climbing any further.

"Skittish Praetorians can be unpredictable. It'll be simpler if I handle this alone. Wait for me down here."

"Yes, sir," Max replied, his words dripping with relief.

When Gaius approached the top of the stairway, a lanky, pimple-scarred fellow stepped forward. "Greetings, Commander Fabius. Welcome back to Rome, sir. Have you scheduled an audience with our esteemed Emperor?"

"Greetings..." Gaius stepped onto the landing and blinked while studying the man's pockmarked face. "Wait! Is that you, Victorinus? Your new, shiny regalia suggests you've been promoted to a high rank. And to think it was only recently we found you dressed in dull commoner's garb, cowering furtively in the corner of Counselor Petronius's home."

Victorinus's darting eyes grew wide. He shuffled across the marble floor and lowered his voice. "Commander, my appointment is temporary. Given the unfortunate events surrounding our former Prefect, I've been asked to serve as the captain of the guard until a more suitable candidate can be appointed. Sir."

Gaius fought off a smirk and hushed his voice as well. "Where is our former Prefect now, pseudo-captain?"

"Confined to his home on the Esquiline." Victorinus dropped his voice to a whisper. "There's been a terrible mistake, sir. The entire guard believes his claims of innocence have merit. Prefect Livianus would've never murdered an unarmed man without cause, and certainly not the chief counselor of the palace."

"I agree. Livianus is a spineless, incompetent dolt who barely knows how to use a blade. We'll have to wait and see how his claims of innocence measure up against the court's evidence. Where is Emperor Trajan, Victorinus?"

"In the hippodrome garden, Commander. Shall I announce you?"

"That won't be necessary. He's expecting me." He lied and tipped his chin. "My assistant, Maximus, will wait for me down there in the vestibule. We've just arrived from the Alban Hills. Be sure Maximus has something to drink as well as food. Cheese and fresh bread should do. Oh, and he'll need a chamber pot."

Gaius rested his elbow on Victorinus's shoulder and yelled louder than was necessary. "This won't take long, Maximus! Just a quick chat with my unborn child's grandfather!"

Always wise to remind the newer recruits of his status in the family. Five well-armed neophytes on the landing lowered their suspicious gaze and shuffled backward like rats before a fire.

After he'd slapped Victorinus's back, Gaius headed for the garden. Groups of sentries nodded acknowledgement as he marched through twisting, torch-lit corridors and down two more flights of stairs to the palace's private quarters. He peered through the arched entrance to the lush elliptical grounds with their rows of columns and elaborate plantings watered by conical fountains. Dressed in casual attire, Emperor Trajan was strolling down a pathway, deep in conversation with Publius and another man.

Shit, was that Marcus's slimy friend from Spain? Could that be Acilius Attianus, the sly fucker who'd served as Publius's second guardian all those years ago? What, by gods, was Attianus doing here in Rome?

"Gaius Fabius!" Marcus pushed Publius and Attianus out of the way and came charging over. "You're back!"

"Greetings, Caesar." Gaius bowed and glanced at Publius, whose face was a melting, blemished mess of anxiety.

Marcus threw an arm over Gaius's shoulder. "Damn good to have you home, cub. When did you receive my letter detailing the apprehension of that murderous brute, Livianus?"

"I'm afraid your letter never arrived, Caesar. I must have missed the imperial courier in passing. I'd been visiting my wife at Aricia when I learned Lucius's killer had been identified. Do I have your permission to enter the city, sir?"

"Yes, yes—of course! How is our dear Marcia Servilia? Well, I hope. Empress Plotina visited Marcia's estate and noted how stuffed your lovely wife was with child. Gods, I'm thrilled at the thought of finally becoming a grandfather."

"Marcia is in excellent health, and we're both eagerly anticipating the birth. Dominus, is it true Livianus is the only suspect?"

"That's correct," the squat Spanish prick interrupted, once again sticking his stubby snout into a private conversation. "The adulterer Livianus acted alone. It was a crime of passion, a disgraceful act of bestial lust to possess what did not belong to him. The judges have at their disposal piles of written evidence, witnesses' testimonies, and loose-tongued slaves to prove his guilt. I suspect the trial will be brief, Caesar."

"What do you make of this curious matter, Gaius?" Marcus asked.

"Do you want my honest opinion, Caesar?"

"I expect my second in command to be forthright, yes."

"I don't believe Livianus murdered Lucius Petronius and several of his sentries without assistance. Counselor Petronius was no soldier, but he was a robust man who knew how to defend himself," Gaius replied before addressing the intruder from Spain. "In fact, the idea of a single assailant is fucking preposterous."

"Don't you dare use that insolent tone with me, young man."

Marcus laughed. "Come now, Attianus, my old friend. Commander Fabius is merely expressing a critical assessment of your hypothesis, and I agree with his judgment. Gaius and I are soldiers. We've experienced countless battles and skirmishes. A lone attacker seems unlikely given the number of estate guards and the deadly results. Nevertheless, innocent or guilty, I'm glad Livianus is no longer captain of the Praetorians. I've meant to replace him with a more satisfactory Prefect for some time."

"If he's found guilty, Livianus will be relieved of far more than his rank, Dominus."

"Yes, well, what can we do, Gaius? The man's a devious adulterer, the worst sort of villain. The evidence for his illicit affair is solid." Marcus waved Publius over to join the discussion. "And what about you, dear Publius? What are your thoughts regarding Livianus's guilt or innocence?"

Publius stared down at his feet before raising his bearded chin high. "All of Rome knew Prefect Livianus had been bedding Lucius's deplorable wife, Caesar. It was common knowledge. There's the most obscene graffiti on the walls of the porticoes outside Nero's baths, crude stick figures engaged in all sorts of indecent acts. Perhaps Livianus had assistance, but he's as guilty of murder as Medea was mad."

"You see!" Smiling, Attianus raised his arms. "My dear former ward agrees with me, Commander."

"That's one vote out of three, you provincial Spanish clod," Gaius snapped.

Marcus's giant paw clamped down on Gaius's forearm. "I will not permit anyone, including you, to disparage my noble birthplace,

Commander Fabius. We Spaniards are not uncivilized provincials. My beloved mother city of Italica is as Roman as Rome herself."

"Forgive my arrogance, Caesar. I'm but one of very few surviving patrician descendants of our divine Romulus."

While Gaius and Marcus ensnared each other in a pissy staring match, a palace slave ran into the grand formal gardens and scurried over to the happy little group.

"Excuse me, noble sirs, but an urgent message has arrived." The boy nervously offered a scroll to Marcus, who released his grip on Gaius's arm and muttered with a wave of his hand, "My eyes are too old to read anymore. Give the letter to our purple-pricked progeny of Mars here."

Gaius snatched the roll and sighed as he unfurled the papyrus. "Livianus took his life in the bath this morning. Slit both wrists like some fucking cowardly woman, no less. According to this report, he'd left behind a written confession of his guilt witnessed by his steward. He claimed to have acted alone, Caesar."

Publius exclaimed, "Well, stuff me with a three-legged squid. I was right!"

"It was my hypothesis, Publius. You merely agreed with me," Attianus corrected with a sneer.

Gaius shoved the papyrus at Publius's chest and grumbled, "Squids have fucking arms, not legs."

"Gracious Juno! What marvelously tragic news!" Marcus bellowed. "Now we can dispense with a tedious trial and put this nightmare to rest. Justice for our poor Lucius Petronius has been served. Slave, fetch us wine and nibbles. We'll celebrate this most fortuitous turn of events here in the garden. Come, Attianus. You deserve the seat of honor beside my couch."

"I'm most humbled, my esteemed Emperor."

After Marcus and his detestable friend had settled onto their couches, Gaius shook his head and turned to his little brother. "I can't believe that wily mongrel is here in Rome."

"Neither can I. He's staying at the palace, stalking the halls with those meddling, beady eyes of his. His belittling tone still makes me cringe as if I were a pathetic little child all over again. I fucking hate him, Gaius."

"You have more than good cause to despise him." Gaius rubbed Publius's back. "But you survived, Greekling."

"We both survived, Gaius. Oh, gods—I just remembered something! What was it you used to call that shit bag when we were boys?"

"Which one? Marcus or Attianus?"

Publius chuckled. "Attianus, you silly git. Didn't you devise one of your degrading nicknames for him?"

"Shit, I'd nearly forgotten about that. What was that delightful slur again?" Fighting to temper his grin, Gaius glanced up at the sky. "Fox fart! That was it! And, by Hercules, Attianus always was a sly, foul-tempered windbag. He could convince Marcus of any self-serving fantasy. Be careful around him, Publius. He's dangerous."

Publius put on a feeble brave face. "Bah! He was dangerous once, Gaius. Time has aged our despicable fox into a grizzled old cur. His withered winds are harmless."

"Attianus is a vile, decaying carcass, Greekling. I'd wager his gasses are even more fucking fetid and lethal."

"By Hercules! Lower your voice, brother. He'll bloody hear you."

Clinging to each other, they both doubled over and turned to hide their playful, juvenile snickers—rare laughter stolen to soothe the fears of their worst childhood memories.

~

THE FORUM OF TRAJAN, ROME

"DIDN'T FABIUS SAY LAST night we were going to Dom's house this morning? This route doesn't lead to the Quirinal," Bry complained as he, Max, and Simon weaved their way through piles of bricks and stones stacked haphazardly in the central open area of the partially constructed forum. The cacophonous racket was deafening: foremen screaming orders at the top of their lungs, teams of carpenters sawing wood, stonemasons whacking blocks with their chisels, and whips crashing across the bare backs of gangs of state-owned slaves. In the shadows of the half-built arcades, whores shouted to draw attention to their exposed, crab-infested fannies.

Max tipped his chin towards his auburn-haired patron barreling through the construction site ten paces ahead of them. "Commander Fabius desires to speak with the emperor's architect before we ascend the slopes to your former home."

Bryaxis cupped his hand over his ear. "Who?"

"The architect! Apollodorus of Damascus!" Max shouted in response, sidestepping a slave girl pushing a cart of moldy bread loaves. They climbed the shallow, broad steps of a massive but still unfinished basilica, hurried across its partial marble floor, and emerged through the only completed doorway on the opposite side of the half-constructed building. In the center of the next, smaller courtyard, an enormous wooden tower surrounded a tall crane. Brutish workmen operated the machine, lifting round drums of marble onto a massive stone podium, stacking one circular slice of white stone on top of the next. The smooth shaft of marble already reached nearly thirty feet up into the sky.

"What is that thing?" Simon asked.

Bryaxis laughed and draped his arms over Simon and Max's shoulder. "Look at that, lads! Emperor Trajan is erecting a gigantic stone dildo!"

Clenching his fists, Gaius stopped in his tracks. Over his shoulder he growled, "Maximus, did I just hear that foul-mouthed Caledonian whore insult our beloved Emperor?"

Max exhaled. "Yes, Commander."

"Strike his impudent face, and remind our lewd eunuch my protection is contingent upon proper behavior and bloody respect!" Gaius propped his hands on his hips and surveyed the busy scene. "Shit, Apollodorus doesn't appear to be here. Our Syrian friend must be hiding in some damn room in the main construction area we've just passed through. Follow us back there after you've doled out the Caledonian's punishment, Maximus. Come along, Simon."

Simon shot Bry a look of sympathy before scrambling to catch up with Gaius. "Yes, Dominus."

Max pulled back his arm and struck hard enough to send Bryaxis crashing to his knees. While he helped Bry to his feet, he whispered, "Apologies for my fist, but will you keep your damn mouth shut! No fucking jokes about the emperor or his dildos."

"Yes, sir. Oh, mighty freedman." Bry spat back. After he'd wiped the blood off his lip, he frantically patted the canvas sack attached to his wide leather belt. "Shit, where did it go?"

"What?"

"Lucius's Genius statuette. It was right here in this fucking pouch before we entered this building maelstrom. Fabius ordered me to carry it on my person, and it's bloody gone!"

Max rubbed his temples. "Perhaps you dropped it in the larger courtyard." Together, they backtracked through the incomplete basilica, searching the ground with panic-stricken eyes, before returning to the huge open area of the emperor's new forum. Max spotted the Commander off to one side chatting animatedly with the architect in the shade of a large semi-circular portico. There was no fucking sign of the little bronze idol.

~

"AH, THERE'S APPY! SIMON—STAY in this area, but be mindful of your surroundings. Construction sites are hazardous." Gaius strolled over to the nearly finished colonnade. "Apollodorus! I've been scouring this chaotic hive of activity looking for you, and I find you basking idly in the shade. And look whom we have here. Greetings to you as well, my dear Pliny."

"By Hercules, Gaius! You're back!" Apollodorus beamed as he spread his arms for an embrace, his colorful robes dangling back and forth in the breeze. "Wonderful to have you in Rome, sir."

"Welcome home, Commander Fabius," Pliny added with a warm smile, his straw sun hat dangling from his fingers. "You've no doubt heard about Prefect Livianus's arrest. Thank all the gods Counselor Petronius's killer has been apprehended. Now the magistrates can finally put the miscreant on trial for his horrific crime."

"There isn't going to be a trial, Pliny. Livianus bled to death in his baths this morning."

Pliny pressed his fingers to his lips; Apollodorus' brown eyes grew huge as he exclaimed, "By Jove! Was it suicide?"

"So it would appear."

"Do I detect doubt in your voice, Gaius?" Pliny asked.

"The wretched imbecile left a note confessing his guilt, claiming he'd acted alone, which is impossible. The entire mess is all too fucking neat and wrapped up in a convenient, horseshit bow, don't you think?"

Pliny gasped and lowered his voice. "Are you suggesting Livianus was murdered?"

"This is Rome, Pliny. Men are silenced all the damn time. Right, Appy?"

"I am a humble engineer. I honestly don't know what to think, Commander. But I am delighted you're home. Our fair capital shines less brightly when you're not here."

Grinning, Gaius scoffed. "Have you become a shameless flatterer as well, Appy? I've stopped here on my way to the Quirinal to admire your work. Is our emperor's outrageous forum project progressing on schedule?"

"Yes, everything is going swimmingly. Look up there! Those masons are attaching the last of the colossal caryatids. They should have the remaining sculptures in place within a few days." Apollodorus pointed to the top of the portico. Hundreds of enormous, purple-veined marble statues of bearded Dacians were lined up one after the other; their stone hands clasped submissively in front of their sculpted baggy trousers. "They may look identical, gentlemen, but I had each statue carved according to a slightly different design. Each barbarian is distinct."

Studying the massive sculptures, Pliny noted, "They look sad, don't they?"

"Do you think so? I'd asked the sculptors to infuse the savages with sternness and nobility." Apollodorus crossed his arms and remarked wistfully, "But you're right, Senator Pliny. Their expressions are more melancholy than remorseful and obedient. Should I have them recarved?"

"For shit's sake, no." Gaius rested his arms on his friends' shoulders. "They should appear downtrodden. Their gutless king abandoned them, and they lost the damn war. And besides, there's no fucking time to change them if you have any hopes of inaugurating this mammoth complex on time."

"You!" She screamed, running full speed at Gaius, her rodent face twisted in fury. "You killed my poor Tiberius, you red-headed beast!"

While Apollodorus and Pliny scurried off, Gaius stood his ground and yelled over his shoulder, "Bloody cowards, both of you!"

When she drew close enough to punch his chest, he held the hysterical woman by her wrists to control her flailing arms. "Calm down, Aurelia. Are you out of your mind?"

She wriggled out of his grasp and slapped his cheek hard enough to leave a mark. "Tiberius had nothing to do with my late husband's murder. Nothing! And now he's dead."

Gaius rubbed his face, wincing more from embarrassment than from any pain. "You mad bitch."

"I swear I'll haunt you for the rest of your days, Gaius Fabius Rufus. I'll pay sorceresses to plague you and your entire family. I'll have my slaves bury lead tablets scribbled with curses under the arena of the circus. I'll poison your precious milk goats. I'll…"

Gaius grabbed her by the throat. "Stop this idiocy, woman. For fuck's sake, I believe Tiberius Claudius Livianus had been coerced."

"You what?" she choked.

"Will you calm down?"

"Yes," Aurelia whispered with a nod.

He released his grip around her neck. "Even if Livianus had participated in the attack, he didn't act alone, and he certainly didn't orchestrate Lucius's murder. I suspect our incompetent Prefect had been forced to write a false confession of guilt before he or someone opened his veins."

"Yes, that's what must have happened. Someone forced him to write that letter and use the knife. My dearest Tiberius was innocent."

"Innocent? That's doubtful since I detect the unmistakable stench of conspiracy." Gaius tapped the side of his nose before wagging his finger in her face. "You, however, are completely fucking guilty. Did Livianus also take part in your atrocious crime?

She pushed back and squealed, "What crime have I committed?"

"Your repugnant mutilation of Lucius's property. Remember? His beloved concubine?"

"I told you—Lucius ordered the castration!"

"Now that, my dear harpy, is a slanderous fabrication no one has ever believed."

~

"DID YOU FIND IT?" Max asked, sweat dripping down his furrowed brow.

On the verge of tears, Bryaxis whimpered, "No."

Simon wandered over. "What are you looking for?"

"My Dom's Genius figurine. I had it right here in this bag before we'd entered through the forum portal, and now it's fucking gone. Fabius will have me flogged bloody. And Lucius will never forgive me."

Simon clasped Bryaxis' elbow. "I'll help you find the idol. Where haven't you looked?"

While Bry and Simon jogged towards a far corner of the grand courtyard, Max watched Commander Fabius argue with Counselor Petronius's widow. He glanced up and noticed a tiny dark shadow struggling with a knotted rope attached to one of the colossal statues.

Max uttered under his breath, "Shit, what the fuck is that thing? Gods, is that Counselor Petronius's Genius?"

After it had managed to untie the cord, the statuette swelled in size, transforming into a towering, fuzzy impression of a man. He jumped up and down, screaming, "Maximus! Move Gaius out of the way!"

While Max tried to digest what was happening, the specter banged itself hard against a gigantic statue of a bearded barbarian. Over and over, the large silhouette of a man threw himself against the stone until the statue tottered and wobbled. The blurry shadow pushed and shoved with its arms and shoulders until the carved stone block threatened to tip over.

Max's hushed voice soared to a dire shout. "Oh, gods! No! Dominus, move! Get out of the way!"

Unable to hear his screams over the loud construction noise, the general continued his quarrel with the distraught woman. Max ran faster than his feet had ever moved and grabbed his patron, dragging him away from the path of the falling statue. Together, they stumbled backward and fell to the ground; the commander landed on his back, hitting his head on a paving stone. Propped up on his forearm and panting, Max looked to where his former master and Counselor Petronius's widow had been standing.

She lay dead under the stone, crushed like a clay doll by a colossal marble effigy of a Dacian captive. A flood of blood gushed from between her taught, painted lips. Most of her skull had been smashed beyond recognition. Max fought not to vomit. When he looked up at the spot from where the colossal figure had fallen, the shadow man was gone. He rubbed his eyes and exhaled.

Shit.

"Commander, are you all right? Wake up, sir."

～

"EASY THERE, SOLDIER. OPEN those fierce, feline eyes of yours."

Gaius struggled to sit up. He squinted into the bright sunshine as he rubbed the back of his skull. Gradually, a large hand extending down towards him came into focus.

"Take my hand, Gaius."

He blinked a few more times until he could make out the man's face. Shit, he looked exactly the same, exactly as he'd looked back when Gaius had first laid eyes on him all those years ago: tall, tan, and muscular, batting those intoxicating light-blue eyes under that mop of nearly black hair.

"Lucius?"

"Stand up, love," the handsome young man ordered as he pulled Gaius to his feet.

"Gods, I'm dead, aren't I?"

"No, you're very much alive, just unconscious for the moment." Lucius laughed and pointed. "My abominable widow, however, didn't fare as well. I'm afraid Aurelia has splattered all over Emperor's Trajan pristine portico. Just punishment for mutilating my Bry, don't you think? Ah, I must admit revenge is barbarically satisfying."

Gaius looked over at the gruesome scene and let out a sound somewhere between a horrified gasp and an inappropriate snicker. "My fucking gods! How did that happen?"

"You said it yourself—construction sites are dangerous. Accidents happen, stone blocks fall." Grinning, Lucius clamped Gaius's shoulders. His strong hands were warm and comforting. "We only have a few moments, darling. It's time for me to leave."

"Leave? Where are you going?"

"My anger has been avenged. I must cross the River Styx now. Our impatient ferryman is waiting. Gaius, I won't return again, not as a ghoulish specter or an invisible stylus or a spirited figurine. It's time for me to depart the world of the living forever."

"I don't understand. If you're leaving for good, why are you spooking me and not your beloved whore, you bastard?" Gaius flinched at the unintended bitterness of his query.

"You always were a fucking jealous prick. But not to worry—I'll see my Bry again, and soon. We're destined to spend eternity together.

You and I, on the other hand..." Lucius lifted his hands and took three steps backward.

"Lucius?"

"I'm not sure if we'll see each other again, soldier. Perhaps our paths won't cross in the afterlife."

"I'll search the entire Elysian Fields for you, you plebian ox. With whom else will I debate the finer qualities of grape and when best to prune the vines? Who else will force me to listen to his horrid jokes?"

"By gods, we did have fun, didn't we? I adored you, you know. If this world had been different..."

Gaius scrubbed his lightly whiskered face. "Back in Athens, we were allowed to fuck, not fall in love. We both knew the bloody rules."

"I seem to recall we rarely followed the rules, my rebellious patrician."

Gaius looked around; everything and everyone appeared blurry and motionless except for him and Luc. "Are you sure I'm not dead?"

"Positive. You've many more years of joy and tears ahead of you."

"You know what's going to happen, don't you?"

"I've seen foggy glimpses of what might happen, nothing more. The Fates and Fortuna govern the future. Live righteously and with honor, Gaius. Trust your heart and you'll die a man who has loved and been loved. True love, not a young man's prohibited passion." Lucius looked down at his embellished blue tunic and asked, "Indulge your old lover one last time, darling. How do I look?"

Gaius smirked as he stepped back to appraise Lucius's appearance. "For a dead man, you're extremely handsome. And you look young—not a day over twenty-one. You will always be the most gorgeous boy ever born in Rome, my vain *Erastes*."

"Why thank you, *Eromenos*. You, on the other hand, look like shit. Go home, soak in the bath, and make love to your beautiful barbarian.

But first, will you please return my damn Genius idol to my shrine on the Quirinal. It's a precarious, violent world out there for a tiny bronze fellow."

"I'll return the sacred statuette to its rightful home. I promise."

As the substance of his image faded, Lucius reached out to cradle Gaius's face and whispered, "Farewell, Gaius Fabius Rufus, Lion of the Lucky Fourth."

Tears spilled over Gaius's sun-kissed, freckled cheekbones. "Can you pardon my failures, Luc?"

"Only if you can forgive my egregious errors, Gaius."

Lucius brushed his thumb pad across Gaius's sorrowful smile and turned away. After he'd walked past the sickening remains of Aurelia's body crushed beneath the marble statue, he turned back one last time, smiling, and waved. "Don't forget to drink fucking buckets of Falernian for me, soldier!"

Little by little, Lucius's sublime specter vanished into the cool, autumn air.

Gaius bit his lip, his watering eyes fixed on the nothingness that had been his best friend, his first infatuation. "Farewell, Lucius Petronius Celsus, my narcissistic, naughty plebian. May you revel in eternal bliss, counselor."

If there had ever been a Gaius and Lucius—two precocious Roman lads eluding adulthood and its burdensome, preordained realities, lost in lust and whispers of love not allowed—they were no more.

Their forbidden, beautiful game was over.

Forever.

⟫⟫⟫✕⟪⟪⟪

22

"COMMANDER FABIUS, ARE YOU hurt?" Max cried, gently combing his thick fingers through Gaius's curls. "Dom, please be all right!"

Bryaxis lifted his palm from Gaius's chest. "He's breathing, Max. He's alive."

"Why won't he fucking wake up? Look! See? His eyes just flickered behind his lids."

"Perhaps Dom's dreaming?" Simon wondered as he chewed on his fingernails.

Everyone jumped back when Gaius's eyes shot open. Agitated and disoriented, he jolted upright and stared at his hands. "What happened? Did I suffer a fit?"

"A fit?" Confused, Max cocked his head and pointed to the grisly sight some twenty feet away. "You were almost killed, sir. That statue fell from the top of the portico and crashed onto the pavement."

A crowd had already gathered, pushing and shoving to gawk at the horrific spectacle. Stray dogs sniffed and lapped up splatters of blood while a group of loincloth-clad construction slaves tried unsuccessfully to lift the battered statue off her flattened corpse. Pulling their long, matted hair, two prostitutes shouted prayers to Proserpina between solicitations.

"Shit." Gaius let out a long breath and glanced around the court-yard, trying to regain his bearings, when Apollodorus and Pliny rushed to his side.

"By thunderous Jupiter! Are you injured, Gaius?" Pliny asked frantically.

"I'd been standing right fucking where that damn block fell. How am I alive?"

While Pliny inspected the back of Gaius's head, he explained, "Your Ethiopian freedman pulled you out of the way."

Simon tentatively touched Gaius's shoulder. "Max is a hero, sir. He's a fearless Hercules."

"I remember now. I'd been arguing with that madwoman." Gaius's words were void of emotion.

"The widow's dead, Commander," Apollodorus replied flatly.

"Aurelia's dead? Thank the gods he's finally realized his venge-ance," Gaius mumbled before he shook himself out of his trance and grabbed Max's wrist. "Shit, I owe you my life, Maximus. For a second time as both we know."

Wiping his eyes, Max ducked and smiled as Pliny stood up. "We'll get you home to the Caelian, Gaius. There's no laceration, but your physician should examine that lump on your head." Gesturing toward the entrance to the forum, Pliny barked at Simon. "Slave, tell my servants over by the portal to bring my sedan carrier here. The Commander shouldn't walk."

"Nonsense. I don't need a damn litter." Gaius insisted as he strug-gled to his feet, rubbing his scalp. "It's only a blasted bump, for fuck's sake. And I can't return to the Caelian, not yet. First, I have to visit the Quirinal. I'm in possession of Lucius's Genius statuette, and I need to return the damn thing to its proper abode."

"Why on earth do you have Counselor Petronius's Genius figurine, Gaius?" Pliny wondered.

Before Gaius could concoct a plausible fib, Max interjected, "We'll return the statuette for you, sir. You need to go home and rest, Commander. You hit your head hard, sir."

"Carried home on a bier like some fucking cripple," Gaius grumbled but acquiesced, rubbing his scalp again. "But I admit I'm lightheaded. Where's Luc's idol, Max?"

Bry anxiously snaked his hand into his pouch and gasped as he pulled out the small bronze image of a man wearing a toga. "Gods, he's right here!"

"Keep an eye on that little troublemaker, Bryaxis. Here, Maximus, take this." Gaius pulled off his signet ring and handed it to Max. "Go to the Quirinal, show my seal to Titus Petronius, and recount what has happened here. Tell my former Tribune I ordered you to return the Genius and ask his permission on my behalf to search for those two scrolls. And don't lose my fucking ring."

"Yes, sir."

After a gaggle of servants carried over the ornate, curtain-draped litter, Gaius wrapped his arm around Pliny's torso. "Do you happen to have any wine stashed in this effete woman's vehicle of yours, Senator?"

"Wine?" Pliny laughed, shaking his head. "Of course I do, Commander. A flask of a most exquisite Mamertinum."

"Excellent. My throat's parched."

"Should we inquire about Counselor Petronius's widow, or—I don't know—do something?"

"The Urban Prefect's men will clean up that ghastly mess." Gaius dismissed his friend's concern with a flick of his figures. "Ride and imbibe with this fortunate bastard up the hill to my estate, my dear Pliny."

~

GAIUS FABIUS'S MANSION, THE CAELIAN HILL, ROME

DESPITE THE IRRITATING BULGE throbbing at the back of his skull and the swirl of questions nagging his mind, Gaius awoke from his short nap refreshed and rested. Sitting up on his mattress, he threw back a swallow of cool water and rubbed his temples before hollering, "Varius!"

The veteran brute pushed open the heavy bronze door to his master chamber. "Yes, Commander."

"Have Maximus and the others returned from the Quirinal?"

"Not as yet, sir."

Gaius glanced at the light streaming in from the balcony. "What time is it?"

"It's after the eighth hour sir, but the air is still unseasonably temperate."

"Since when do you fucking deliver weather reports, soldier?"

Varius swallowed a chuckle. "A finer appreciation for the gods' gifts is a reward of retirement, sir. How's your head, Commander?"

"Pounding and sore. Tell the steward to prepare the baths."

When the veteran reached for the iron door handle, Gaius added, "Where's the Dacian?"

"I've assigned two of your estate sentries to monitor him, Commander. Last I'd heard the collared heathen was mucking about the formal gardens, basking in the lovely sunshine and revealing his barely-clothed wares. It seems even barbarians can appreciate this most delightful afternoon, sir."

"I suppose I should experience this glorious sunlight personally, then," Gaius grunted, trying not to grin.

"It's wise to move rather than sleep after a head injury, Commander."

After he'd waved Varius off, Gaius snatched his mantle from the chair closest to his bed and threw the ivory cloth around his shoulders. Slipping his feet into his fashionable new sandals, he tied the leather laces up his calves. The entrance to the estate's grand yard of ornamental hedges and flowering rose bushes was down the hall from his bedroom. In his large garden, gilded bronze statues of Muses, half-draped nymphs, and woodland animals decorated the spaces between the columns and around the gurgling fountains. Intrigued by the loud sounds of splashing, Gaius stepped off the paved garden path and popped his head through the arched entry to a walled courtyard.

"Most alluring Adonis," he muttered before ordering his guards to leave with a quick swish of his hand. Back and forth through the crystal clear waters of the rectangular swimming pool, the Dacian swam one lap after another, his lithe body gliding beneath the water's surface. Gaius crossed his arms and leaned against one of the pillars to appreciate the splendid view.

When Allerix stopped to catch his breath, Gaius observed, "You look even shaggier when you're wet, my furry boy."

Brushing back his soaked, ebony hair, Alle stood and smiled. "Greetings, Dominus. Have you recovered from your morning's adventures, sir?"

Gaius resisted the urge to touch the lump on his head. "I feel fine. The weather's a tad chilly for a swim, *cățel*. Aren't you cold?"

"In Dacia, we have bottomless mountain lakes as dark as night and as cold as ice. When I was a young boy, and we had one of those rare hot summer days, I'd sneak off to a lake for a swim. And every damn time I'd freeze my balls and lips blue. This glorious shallow pool of yours is a treat."

"I'm pleased you're enjoying it."

"I'd enjoy it even more if you'd join me." Allerix flirted, lowering himself until his chin sunk below the water's surface.

Gaius untied his leather and fur sandals and removed the ivory woolen mantle wrapped around his nude torso. Alle's heavy-lidded hazel eyes darkened with approval as he blew bubbles across the water's surface. A short gentle ramp led down into the oblong pool; Gaius waded over and hooked his arm around Allerix's waist, pulling him close. While he brushed his other hand through the tufts of black hairs trailing down Alle's abdomen, Gaius mumbled, "The water's much warmer than I'd expected."

"But not nearly as hot as your body burned last night." Alle grinned as he carded his fingers through Gaius's locks. "You're blushing, Rufus. How's that bump? Ah, it's much smaller now."

Gaius removed Allerix's hand from his hair and shoved it beneath the water, rubbing Alle's palm against his lust. "The swelling's moved lower."

Allerix snorted. "Perhaps I can alleviate your discomfort, Dominus." He turned around and wiggled his round rump against Gaius's engorged cock. Gaius snatched a fistful of Alle's dark, wet locks and pulled his head back to murmur against the boy's neck.

"Have you ever had your arse plowed under water?"

Alle closed his eyes and squeezed Gaius's throbbing erection between his cheeks. "You already know the answer to that question, sir."

"It's not as pleasurable as you might imagine," Gaius warned, releasing his grip before he dove to the side and swam to the opposite side of the pool. After he'd lifted himself up on the ledge, he said, "On the other hand, having your bum impaled while in a bath enhanced with slippery fragrant oils…"

When Allerix arched his eyebrow with interest, Gaius curled his pointer finger. "Come here, Alle."

Allerix submerged and paddled under the water, his delectable arse bobbing up and down, his lean muscles rippling in the sunlight until he rose between Gaius's legs. His thick fans of eyelashes pressed against the top curves of his wet cheekbones as he peppered light kisses all over Gaius's heavy balls.

"Now I finally appreciate depraved Tiberius's fondness for tiddlers." Gaius snorted softly.

Mesmerized, he watched Alle's full, wet lips kiss a path from his scrotum to the base of his cock. In long, languid strokes, the Dacian's tongue ran up the length of his shaft, over and over until a groan escaped Gaius's throat. "Gods, you're a fucking beautiful tease."

With an appreciative smile, Allerix wrapped his fingers around his meaty girth and swallowed the head of Gaius's cock, slowly taking him deeper into his mouth, moaning against his pulsing heat. All the while, Gaius watched, his eyes narrow from pleasure, his breaths speeding up with an intensifying ache to release his seed. When Alle flicked the tip of his tongue across Gaius's gaping slit, Gaius pulled the lad's tormenting mouth off. He held Alle's head steady and cried out in ecstasy as surge after surge of his salty cream splattered across Allerix's amused face. Catching his breath, Gaius wiped a generous splotch of semen off Alle's cheek and slipped his coated finger between Allerix's parted, compliant lips.

"So bloody gorgeous," Gaius whispered. After Alle had licked his finger clean, Gaius hooked both his hands under Allerix's armpits, lifting him up for a deep, demanding taste.

A sound somewhere between a groan and a cough erupted from beneath the arched entrance behind them.

Gaius peered over his shoulder. "Maximus, how fucking long have you been standing there?"

"I was waiting for you to—um, finish, sir."

Gaius rolled his eyes as he pulled Alle tighter, stroking his back; Allerix nestled his head in the crook of Gaius's neck and chuckled as he wiped his lips.

"I'm finished, for the time being. What news do you bring from the Quirinal?" Gaius asked while cleaning off Alle's face with the edge of his cloak.

"Counselor Petronius's Genius statuette is home where it belongs, Commander. And Simon found a scroll."

"Marvelous, but only one?" Gaius rose to his feet and grabbed Alle's bicep, pulling him up and out of the pool.

"Yes, sir. One of the documents referenced had been wedged between the wall and a cupboard in Counselor Petronius's office. We searched the entire property—with Titus Petronius's permission, of course—but found nothing else."

"Toss me that white mantle. Where's the scroll now?"

"Simon is safeguarding the document, sir. He and Bryaxis have started unloading the crates stored in the room next to your office, sir."

When Allerix started shivering, Gaius yelled, "Guards!"

Two estate sentries ran over and immediately lowered their gaze as they stood at attention before their exceptionally naked employer.

"Escort my raven-haired pleasure slave to my suite." Gaius wrapped his mantle around Alle's dripping body, adjusting the loose cloth until he was modestly covered, and embraced him, whispering into his ear, "Go to my room, Allerix—peruse my library and help yourself to some wine. There's a pitcher of Sabine grape on the table. I'll join you and that divine mouth of yours soon." Gaius caressed Alle's face and kissed him one more time—soft and lingering—before turning him around to face the guards. He opened his right hand and gave Alle's draped arse one firm slap for good measure. "Off with you, faun."

After Alle and the two guards had crossed the garden, he unfolded his arms and turned to Max. "Let's see what my dear ghoulish friend has in store for us this time."

Max unclasped his cloak and offered it to Gaius, who shook his head and pushed it away.

"I'm in my damn home, Maximus. I'll walk around bloody stark naked if I so desire, which at the moment I believe I do." After he'd retrieved his sandals, he stretched his arms above his head and growled while strolling to the house. "By gods, what gloriously warm weather for an autumn day in Rome!"

~

CAPITULATING TO PROPRIETIES, GAIUS pulled a fresh, gold-threaded green tunic over his head before barging into the storage room adjacent to his office. "Report."

"Here's the scroll I'd found fallen behind a cupboard, Dominus. It's crushed but intact, sir." Wearing a proud smile, Simon held out the scroll as he glanced sideways at Max and Bryaxis. Along the wall behind them stood stacks of crates packed with Luc's papers carted up to Rome from Campania.

"Fallen or purposefully concealed? Whichever is the case, excellent work, Simon. I'm officially promoting you to the honorable position of scribe."

"Scribe, Dominus?" His neck and cheeks flushing bright red, Simon gasped and dropped to his knees more gracefully than he'd even genuflected in his entire damn life. "Thank you, sir."

"Get up off the floor, pup, and unfurl your discovery."

All four men gathered around the large worktable; Simon carefully unrolled the crumpled papyrus. No animal drawings in the margins this time, but the curious combination of Greek letters were there, hastily scribbled next to five separate passages of text.

"And we have yet another ledger from the imperial treasury."

"Yes, sir. Another facsimile." Bryaxis answered, pointing at an entry. "Compared with that scroll we'd discovered back at your villa, the amounts noted in this register are much larger. For example, this entry alone lists one withdrawal for over two million sesterces."

"And again, no description of its purpose other than 'expenditures.' Lucius's fucking notations are deliberately oblique. Why?"

"I don't know, sir. He was a lawyer." When Gaius cast a disapproving glare, Bry dropped his grin. "Perhaps Dominus tried to protect someone from allegations of thievery?"

"Or he's accusing someone of pilfering the coffers." Gaius scrubbed his face and exhaled. "Forgive my egregious errors."

"What was that, Commander?"

"Nothing, Max—just strange words Lucius once said to me. Gods, he knew how much I despise riddles! Roll the damn thing up and give it to me. These mysterious notations must fucking mean something."

Max nodded and handed the rolled scroll to Gaius. "Here you are, Commander."

"We'll search for the other missing scroll in the archives, but it's been a long, arduous day. You three must be hungry. Tell the cook to give you two jugs of our better wine to accompany your meal." Gaius fluffed Simon's honey-brown curls and strolled over to the piles of wooden storage boxes. "Give thanks to our generous Bacchus, raise your cups my recurring savior, Maximus, and celebrate Simon's promotion."

As they were about to cross the threshold, Max mumbled to Bry, "Where's the Dacian?"

"He's in my suite, Maximus," Gaius remarked off-handedly while lifting the lid of a wooden crate. He peered down at its contents and, with one brow arched, chuckled. "Our mischievous peasant is spending the night with me."

~

ALLERIX PRESSED HIS FINGER to his lips as he scanned the impressive collection of Greek and Latin texts. Given the number and variety of books the Roman had acquired for his personal library, it was damn difficult to choose just one. Alle's former tutor, Istros, had once had a wonderful array of books, but rarely did the old man allow Allerix to touch them. After he'd spotted the tag for Ovid's *Amores*, Alle gingerly extracted the scroll from the canister. Book in hand, he lay down on the large, luxurious mattress with Gaius's white cloak bunched over his calves, and unwound the papyrus. It smelled like he'd always imagined the Nile grasses smelled at harvest.

So captivated by the mellifluous words, so enthralled by the rhythm of the elegiac couplings, he hadn't noticed Gaius enter the suite until the man's silky voice caressed the air above him.

"What are you reading?" he asked, standing at the foot of the bed.

"A book of poems, sir."

The Roman examined the wooden tag attached to the scroll's rod. "Ah, Ovid's playful ditties on love. I adored this entertaining rubbish back when I was a schoolboy. My grandmother gifted me that volume. It's a rare edition."

"It smells rare. Your grandmother was kind to me. She seems a remarkable woman, Dominus."

Gaius sat on the edge of the bed and lightly stroked the firm curves of Alle's bare arse. "Avia's a tough old bird with a soft heart she rarely reveals to anyone. She survived the civil wars and the murderous reign of that despotic monster. When I was sixteen years old, she rescued me from my guardian, brought me back home to Rome, and gave me that scroll your holding in your hands for my birthday. I owe her everything."

Alle gripped the scroll tighter. "Why did you need to be rescued from your guardian? Did he mistreat you?"

Gaius hesitated before explaining, "He was ill-equipped to safeguard fatherless boys. It's all in the distant past, Alle."

"What happened to him?"

"Marcus became the most powerful man in the world."

Gaius removed his hand to scratch his scalp. Drawing in a sharp breath, he brushed his finger across the words neatly copied on the sheet of papyrus and deliberately changed the subject. "My dear grandmother has always enjoyed the writings of this exiled fool. I admit she infected me with her affection for Ovid's writings, although now I prefer the *Metamorphoses* more than his erotic poetry."

Alle pointed to a stanza and asked, "Is he comparing lovers to soldiers in this poem?"

"Yes, and not all that well. His rhetoric is heavy-handed and bloody lazy. But I suppose falling in love can resemble going to war. It's a common trope."

Propped up on his elbows, Alle opened his mouth when light taps on the door interrupted his next question. Gaius snaked his fingers under the silver torque encircling Alle's neck and tugged possessively.

"Enter!"

"Your meal, sir."

"I'll dine out on the terrace."

"Yes, sir. The cook hopes the food exceeds your expectations."

The steward bowed before shuffling into the bedroom, followed by several servants carrying heaping trays and dinnerware and jugs of drink. They slid past the gossamer curtains draped between columns and arranged the platters on the low silver table beside a couch.

Paying no attention to the group bustling about on the balcony, Gaius rolled Allerix onto his back. With one hand, he held Alle's wrists together above Alle's head and murmured, "I have very few expectations of this world other than the unconditional loyalty of those I choose to protect, Allerix."

Trying to read the curious expression on the Roman's face, Alle cautiously teased. "Some say expectations are luxuries only enjoyed by free men, sir."

"True, but expectations often lead to disappointment. Freedom has its disadvantages."

Gaius stood up and slowly stripped off his green tunic. As he removed the empty scabbard strapped to his bare torso, his predatory eyes studied Alle's face without blinking.

Unnerved, Allerix asked, "Where's your dagger, Dominus?"

"I must have left the damn thing in my office." Gaius flung the leather band along with the ornate scabbard onto the bed. "Take a look at the craftsmanship, Alle. After I'd acquired my ivory-handle dagger during my deployment in Africa, Lucius gifted me that treasure to shelter the blade. The dagger and scabbard complement each other well, no?"

Allerix inspected the silver ornaments attached to the crimson-dyed leather. A violent scene of a man strangling a lion decorated the large plate affixed to the top of the sheath. "Bloody exquisite, sir. This metal plaque shows Herakles wrestling the lion of Nemea, yes?"

"Yes, it does: Hercules' first labor, his first victory, and our randy hero's first proper fashion accessory." Gaius's intense expression suddenly softened to silly; he propped one of his sandal-clad feet on the edge of the mattress, pointing to the lion head design crafted from leather and fur adorning the top of his calf. "The Gatekeeper of

Olympus has his lion-headed cloak, and now I have my ferocious, leonine sandals. Grrr!"

Allerix laughed in relief, so hard snot bubbles came out of his nose. Gaius reached down and lifted his chin, scratching his fingernails across Alle's shadow of thick, black whiskers. "May the gods shield my battered heart, but how I fucking love to hear you laugh. I want to protect you, Allerix. Help me shelter you from the perils of Rome."

Unable to fabricate a reasonable response, Alle blabbered, "Thank you for taking me to your city, sir. Rome's spectacular."

"Perhaps you'll see more of her." Gaius exhaled and bent down, brushing his lips over the sensitive shell of Alle's ear. "Don't disappoint me, Allerix."

Alle swallowed and lied. "I won't, Rufus."

"Come here and love me." Gaius slid his hands under Alle's bum and lifted him for a kiss before carrying him over to the wall, pushing his back against the polished plaster. Before Alle could utter a word, Gaius pressed his body close, his lips and tongue engulfing Alle's mouth. Alle gripped Gaius's hips with both legs; without breaking the kiss, Gaius extended his hand, wiggling his fingers. The steward rushed over and poured a stream of oil into his cupped palm.

Alle broke off the kiss and pulled back, his brow cocked. "Dominus? Those slaves—they're watching us."

"They're witnesses." Gaius chuckled as he slathered his stiff cock. No hesitation, no fucking preparation. Gaius impaled him hard—one continuous, delicious drive into Alle's bum until he was buried up to his balls. He bit Alle's shoulder; Allerix wrapped his arms around Gaius's muscular back and dug his trimmed nails into his skin as he rode his punishing thrusts. Just when Alle thought he would explode, Gaius lifted him off his cock and lowered him feet first to the floor, pivoting him to face the frescoed wall. When Gaius spread his legs apart with his sandal, Allerix braced his trembling hands against the cool plaster. Gaius flattened one palm on the wall next to Alle's head while his other hand stroked Alle's aching prick. Allerix's legs began to shake; Gaius pounded his arse harder, stroking his shaft faster and faster until Alle groaned in ecstasy.

"You have my permission," Gaius whispered in choppy breaths. "To empty your beautiful balls all over my fucking bedroom wall."

Alle nearly passed out when the blinding orgasm finally ripped through his groin, his milky semen covering sections of the frescos. A blob of cream slithered down the painted face of a frolicking Cupid; another slid across the bared breast of a snarling Amazon. His damp cheek pressed against the wall, Allerix collapsed into uncontrollable post-coital laughter.

Gaius turned Allerix around to face him. Staring into Alle's blissful damp eyes, he commanded, "Hand me the carving knife, Steward."

The stone-faced slave handed Gaius the sharp, serrated tool handle first. Adjusting his grip, Gaius took hold of the torque with his other hand and twisted the pliant metal.

"Lean your head back and do not move."

Inhaling through his nostrils, Allerix lifted his chin high and pressed his skull as flat against the wall as possible. Gaius scraped the edge of the knife's blade against the squat bulge of the rivet until the fastener broke. The dangling, bronze fugitive tag came loose and dropped to the floor with a clang.

"You are no longer a runaway. You are no longer Paulus."

The tip of his tongue visible between his tightly pressed lips, the Roman twisted the metal until the hinge at the back of the collar snapped. While Alle stood completely still with his mouth gaping, Gaius removed the broken torque and tossed it the floor.

"Like the counterfeit Dacian falx, that pretty but worthless collar was a hasty but otherwise persuasive reproduction. Wouldn't you fucking agree?"

Alle glanced down at the twisted hoax that had weighed down his neck for months. "That's fake? But Varius and the blacksmith said it was a precious, antique silver neck ring."

"My clients say what I order them to say." Gaius's stern lips melted into a warm grin. "Of all the trophies I've collected thus far, the real Celtic torque that inspired that forgery is one of my most cherished treasures. Someday perhaps I'll show the authentic artifact to you. But there's no need for you to be collared any longer, *cățel*."

Why?"

"Because you are now officially the favorite concubine of the Lion of the Lucky Fourth, Alle."

"I am? But back at your beach cave, you said…"

"Yes, I know what I fucking said." Gaius tossed his hands up in a huff. "No more damn questions. Hold your delirious tongue and quench your thirst." His dimples deep, Gaius hoisted the gold cup the steward had just placed in his grasp to Alle's s lips. Closing his eyes, Allerix swallowed a gulp of smooth red wine; Gaius picked up a second full cup from the tray and barked at the crew of servants shuffling their feet, "Leave!"

~

OUT ON THE TERRACE, the two enjoyed a leisurely, scrumptious meal as they reclined side by side on the couch. Gaius reached over Allerix's shoulder to feed him bites of seasoned lamb, poached snails, and green olives; neither man had bothered with clothes. As the night wore on, the air grew chilly, and the stars' lights twinkled brightly. Gaius brushed his lips up Alle's long neck and whispered into his ear,

"Are you cold?"

"No, sir, but I can't eat another morsel. Did the meal exceed your expectations, Dominus?"

"Euphronia's cooking is impossible to surpass, but this spread was tasty."

"Why didn't you transport Euphronia to Rome along with the rest of us?"

"She requested to remain in Campania. I suspect she fancies our dear Plautus. The woman asked me a couple of curious questions before we'd left: his age, whether he'd ever married, and other such trifles. Perhaps romance will blossom while we're away." Gaius grinned as he popped the last succulent snail into his mouth, tossing its empty shell to the floor.

"Plautus? The grumpy, portly cook at the stable house?" Alle snorted, mocking Plautus's rotund girth with exaggerated arm gestures.

"Everyone wants love, Allerix—slaves, barbarians, and plump, haggard veterans most of all. They crave a lover to hold at night, someone who'll tolerate and appreciate the fantastic tales of their battle heroics. All men desire to share their hearts and their stories. And speaking of desires, let's light the braziers and retire to the bed. My damn feet are freezing."

Alle smiled after he swallowed his wine. "Let me warm your toes with my mouth, Dominus."

"You're an incorrigible little slut, aren't you?" Gaius laughed as he stroked Alle's cheek with his thumb. "It's my new sandals, isn't it? They're sexy, aren't they?" Gaius wagged his brows.

"Those glorious sandals inflame my unnatural lust to revere your noble Roman feet."

Gaius threw his head back, shaking with hysterics as tears of mirth rolled down his cheeks. He rose to his feet and held out his hand. "Will you join me, my provocative prince?"

As they pushed their way past the curtains, Alle stopped when he noticed the crumpled scroll on the table. His hand slipped out of Gaius's hold. "Is that the scroll Simon found?"

Gaius nodded, glaring at the document. "Lucius's cryptic scribbles and doodles are driving me mad."

"May I have a look?" Alle asked, adding a quick, "Sir?"

"Why not. Perhaps you'll have better luck deciphering Luc's bizarre notations."

Obeying Gaius's eyes, Allerix reclined on the bed while Gaius retrieved the scroll. The Roman scooted across the mattress, pressing his hips against Alle's and slouched as he unfurled the register. "Here's an example of his odd chicken scratch. These three characters appear in the margins without explanation."

"Are those Greek letters?"

"Yes, although they could stand for numeric values."

"Right. I always forget that. Pi, Alpha, Alpha. What does it mean?"

"I don't fucking know. A symbol for something? A sum of funds? A wager on a damn chariot team?"

Allerix's furrowed brow slowly relaxed while he lips stretched into a smile. "I have an idea."

Squinting, Gaius folded his muscular forearms. "Tell me what you're thinking, my learned barbarian."

"Three letters." Alle lifted three fingers, lowering them one at a time as he said, "Gaius. Fabius. Rufus. Gamma, Phi, Rho, right? Perhaps it's an abbreviation for a name—a Roman name."

"A name?" Gaius's frown slowly disappeared. "That's quite possible, although Luc never used an abbreviation of this sort in any correspondence to me. But it's an intriguing idea. You're quite clever, *căţel.*"

"Do you know a person whose name fits those letters?"

Staring at the scribbles, Gaius nodded his head. "I might. Shit, Lucius was investigating some fucking brazen crimes. If these letters do indeed refer to that wily prick, Luc had been in more danger than even he'd realized." Gaius traced Alle's lips with his thumb. "But that's enough sleuth work for tonight. The hour is bloody late, and my balls are ready to burst. I need to make love to you."

Alle kissed his thumb pad and brushed a curl away from Gaius's heavy eyes. "Allow me to untie your sexy lion sandals, Rufus."

～

WHEN ALLE AWOKE WELL before dawn, the thick silver chain was looped around his fingers. The favorite's token bauble, as Nic had once described the gift of jewelry. Shit, he missed Nicomedes.

For much of the night, the Roman had devoured his body, every quaking muscle and sweat-filled crevice. He'd fucked him hard and possessively, ordering Allerix up on his hands and knees, impaling his arse relentlessly until Alle's bum ached with a tingling burn that still lingered. He'd rolled Alle over on his back and spread his legs wide and high to fuck him slowly, worshipping his mouth and neck with his lips and tongue. Gods, the man's stamina was inexhaustible. Allerix came again, launching his milky seed over both their stomachs as the Roman roared in ecstasy through his own ferocious orgasm. Afterward, exhausted and satiated, they'd bathed and shared cups of wine, kissing each other tenderly between sips and laughs. Before they'd settled down to sleep, Gaius reached into the drawer of the side table next to his bed and offered Alle a carved ivory box.

"Proper adornment for your gorgeous royal neck, Prince Al-

lerix. I had this chain made just for you. Solid silver links with an onyx cameo pendant."

"A carved lion's paw?"

"The same design as my signet ring. Behave, cub, because I'm sorely tempted to order my leonine insignia tattooed onto your perfect arse as well."

Alle pressed his head into the pillow, his fingers gripping the necklace tighter, as he pressed his morning erection into the mattress.

He had new collar now, another false identity.

The favorite concubine of the gorgeous, red-haired lion he'd once feared and despised, the Roman whose heart and trust Alle was destined to break.

Soon.

Allerix, son of Thiamarkos, would assassinate the Roman king and receive immortality and everlasting honor for his bravery.

Revenge was within his grasp.

A rumble drifted over from the other side of the mattress, the fluttering snore of an exhausted man buried deep inside a dream. Allerix hesitated for a few moments before finding the courage to lift the bed covers, slip on one of the Roman's tunics, and tiptoe out of the master suite. The vestibule was empty; the Roman had foolishly dismissed his guards.

Alle scratched the stubble covering his chin. What had Max remarked back by the pool? He'd said the crates were in a storage room next to the Roman's office, hadn't he? Alle glanced down the corridor to his left; rays of moonlight flooded through the colonnaded entrance to the garden. Allerix had already explored that part of the mansion; there was no office in that direction. He turned right, his bare feet gliding silently across the mosaic floor until he spotted a room at the end of a wide passageway. The doors were grand and pompous.

"There." Alle mouthed and ran to the smaller door to the left, turning the handle and pushing it open with his shoulder. Stacks of wooden storage containers lined the walls. The box with his scratched marking stood alone in the center of the room; its lid was gone. His heart stuck in his newly bejeweled throat, Allerix rushed over and dropped to his knees before frantically rummaging through the scrolls jammed in the stuffed crate.

His fingers found the dagger's distinct handle at the same moment a curse escaped his lips. Bemused, Alle pulled the weapon out from between the scrolls and stared at the blade.

The Roman's African dagger with its lion-paw grip.

Shit.

"Never fucking underestimate a Dacian."

With his wrinkled woolen mantle clinging to his shoulders, Gaius leaned against the doorpost, Alle's gold-handled knife dangling from his fingers. Alle remained crouched, panting as he held the Roman's prized dagger in his left hand. His eyes and mouth hard with determination, Allerix pointed the blade's tip and said, "My father awarded that dagger to me before the Second War. I didn't steal it. That knife belongs to me, sir."

Gaius shook his head and snickered. "How can this blade be yours, Alle? My soldiers recovered this pretty trinket from a captured Dacian princeling during the Second War?"

"I'd gifted my knife to a friend for good fortune."

"Ah, yes. Your poor, pathetic friend. Didn't bring him much luck, did it? You know, I had a brief chat about this pretty knife with my veteran client earlier this afternoon. Varius told me all about the fucking groveling barbarian who'd been in possession of this sentimental knife of yours. Was that attractive, blue-eyed young man your lover? Is that why you fucking stole this trophy from Varius's cupboard, Allerix?"

The Romans jealous eyes were impenetrable and cold. Alle swallowed and blinked. "I don't understand, Dominus."

"Don't you? Isn't that why you've so desperately desired to travel to Rome? Are you scheming to reunite with your beleaguered comrade, Allerix?"

Allerix choked back an incredulous chuckle.

He'd been underestimated.

"Yes." Alle exhaled in relief. "When I'd heard Varius boast about possessing my dagger and transporting Dacian prisoners to your capital city, I hoped my friend was still alive somewhere in Rome."

"I suspected as much. You're a hopeless, daft romantic, aren't you? Listen, there is a chance your inappreciative companion is indeed alive. Emperor Trajan has detained scores of miserable Dacian nobles as sacrificial fodder for his triumphal games. He's incarcerated the wretches at the barracks of the Praetorian Guard. Perhaps you and I should visit your friend. What's his name?

"His name is Brasus, sir."

"We'll ride out to the Praetorian's camp and see if we can locate this Brasus fellow. I want to gift you the opportunity to bid farewell to your former lover before he's ripped to shreds in our arena."

Alle lowered his head. "That's most generous of you, Dominus."

"I'm a benevolent man, *căţel*." His nostrils flared, the Roman sauntered toward him. "Now hand over my fucking dagger. Do not dare fight me, Alle."

Allerix loosened his grip; Gaius reached down and carefully plucked the weapon from Alle's hand. His voice ragged, Gaius sighed. "I'm postponing punishment for your unfortunate miscalculation. My head hurts, my groin aches, and I'm too fucking tired to discipline anyone tonight. Let's lay down our weapons, my foolishly heroic prince."

The Roman dropped both daggers into the crate and lifted Allerix to his feet. Rubbing Alle's biceps, Gaius rested his forehead against Alle's right temple and whispered, "I've endured enough bloody drama for one day. Come warm my bed, Allerix."

EPILOGUE

BUZZING ON VIBRATE MODE, my cell phone rattled across the metal bistro table like a drunk, robotic mouse. I glanced at the incoming number and smiled while pressing the button.

"Hey. I'm just about to pay the bill at this tourist trap and head over."

The grumpy waiter stopped at my table and shoved a piece of paper under my empty glass. A flock of screaming school kids kicking soccer balls lingered a few feet away; I pressed my palm over my other ear.

"Wait, say that again. How late?"

Shit.

I hadn't seen in him over six months and now he couldn't arrive to dinner on time?

"All right, I'll be there. Just hurry, ok? Yeah, me too."

After I'd settled my cafe bill, I walked the short distance to the Piazza della Minerva just down the street. Teenagers loitered around the baroque sculpture in the center of the cobblestone-paved square, sharing smokes and jokes as they sat on the stepped base of Bernini's squat elephant holding up an Egyptian obelisk.

After buttoning my sports jacket and straightening my posture, I climbed the shallow steps of the fancy hotel and pushed the ornate, heavy revolving door. The colored glass ceiling and rich marble floor of the hotel's sophisticated atrium lobby never failed to take my breath away. The pricey suites at this place were way out of my league, but the restaurant and bar were usually open to the proletariat. A quick ride up the claustrophobic elevator took me to the rooftop where Antonio greeted me with his usual pat on the back and tight but quick hug. He asked how I'd been; I asked about his family and the business.

"Are you dining alone tonight?" he inquired before escorting me to my table.

"A friend's joining me as soon as his meeting ends."

"You don't eat enough, Carlo. You're too skinny." Antonio frowned as he squeezed my bony shoulder.

I chuckled. "I'll order antipasti *and* dessert this evening."

"Bravo!"

While Antonio scurried off to personally greet the next customers, I sat down and sighed. His work meetings never ended early. Shit, I'd probably wind up eating dinner here alone while waiting for him. Maybe if traffic died down, he'd arrive in time for dessert. Maybe.

But here I was, at the same table we always reserved on those infrequent occasions we were both in Rome. The perfect rooftop bar, even more crowded with beautiful couples laughing and flirting than it had been that evening three years ago. I settled into my cushioned iron-wrought chair and gazed at the curved exterior of the Pantheon's massive domed rotunda. Filthy pigeons perched on rooftops cooed as music drifted up from the street performers entertaining crowds below. A soft-spoken waitress interrupted my brief reverie when she deposited bowls of olives and bar snacks on the table. After she'd left with my drink order, I pulled out my pen and notebook.

$\sim$

30 JULY 2007

IT TOOK ME AN entire fucking week to get up the nerve to pick up the phone and call the number so elegantly written on a handmade envelope sent by that handsome, mysterious dark-haired stranger. Our busy schedules made arranging a drink together difficult, but finally I was here. I'd heard about the trendy rooftop bar overlooking the Pantheon, but I'd never had the nerve to come up to this swanky place on my own. And yet here I was—riding by myself in this firetrap of a puke-green elevator; my heart was racing a mile a minute as I chewed two breath mints.

No escape now.

Calm the fuck down, Hughes.

Despite the fact that I'd showered that day—twice—I still couldn't resist the urge to raise my arms and sniff my pits through my short-sleeved seersucker shirt. When the elevator door opened, I wiped my clammy palms on my best pair of jeans, combed my fingers through my hair, and took a deep breath.

He was alone at a table for two near the balustrade of the terrace, sheltered from the late afternoon sun by the canvas shades flapping in the warm breezes. When he'd spotted me, he stood up and smiled. Unlike the first time I'd seen him two weeks ago at that restaurant with Stefano, my admirer wasn't wearing a formal suit. Instead, his trim, athletic torso filled a crisp white dress shirt, neatly rolled up to the elbows, and his long legs were draped in pressed, navy blue slacks. A red pack of English cigarettes lay on the table, along with a half-filled glass and a bottle of carbonated spring water.

My Frenchman didn't look nervous in the slightest.

Shit.

I drew another deep breath and walked over, careful not to trip over my size twelve feet. He gestured to the chair across the table from him.

I extended my hand. "Hi. I'm sorry I'm late."

"You're not late. I'm early." His grip was firm and electric. "I'm glad you called, Charles. I was beginning to think you'd tossed my number into the rubbish bin."

God, I loved his accent—the way he said *Charles*, as though his tongue were polishing my boring name into a smooth, precious gem.

I pulled out the folded piece of paper I'd kept in my pocket for two whole weeks as if it were a lucky talisman. "Nope, still have it. See? How could I resist an invitation delivered in such a perfect little envelope?"

Jesus, did I just say that out loud! Blood rushed to my cheeks, as beads of sweat rolled down my back. "Wow, this is an amazing place."

"One of my favorite bars in Rome."

The short, balding waiter took our cocktail orders; Yves ordered to a plate of appetizers to nibble on. Who the hell would have ever thought Charlie Hughes, nerd extraordinaire, would ever have a date with a sophisticated, sharp-dressed guy named Yves.

"Forgive me for ordering hors-d'oeuvres, but I'm starving. I worked through lunch."

I held up my hands. "Hey, I'm hungry too. So what do you do, Yves, that forced you to miss your lunch?"

"I'm in finance. I work for an investment firm based in London, but I spend two, sometimes three weeks in Rome on business almost every year. What about you?"

"I conduct research in Rome."

"Can you elaborate, or is it secret spy work?"

Shaking my head, I laughed harder than was appropriate. "I'm an archaeologist."

He poured us both glasses of water. "You study dinosaurs?"

"No, I analyze ancient Romans' garbage, not dinosaur fossils. Sometimes I'm lucky, and we uncover a building or a mosaic floor or a ceremonial dagger. When we're unlucky, we find a skeleton or two."

Yves raised a perfectly groomed brow. "Excuse my ignorance, but is that an actual job someone pays you to do?"

"Ha! Believe it or not, someone pays me to play in the dirt and dig up dead people's junk. I don't make much money, but it's enough. It's a good gig."

Our drinks arrived: his fizzy gin and tonic; my glass of Montepulciano I'd ordered having forgotten how terribly red wine stains my teeth.

Shit.

I raised my glass. "Salute! To investment!"

"Cheers! To good gigs!"

We chatted about our work some more and our experiences of Rome between bites while we scarfed down the delicious spread of cheeses and salami like two ravenous wolves. His sexy blue eyes sparkled in the sunlight reflecting off the white walls of a nearby building; his eyes complemented his broad, refreshingly genuine smile and his low, husky laugh. As the wine warmed my stomach and loosened my nerves, not to mention my tongue, my first date in a fucking very long time turned into one of the most fun evenings I'd ever had. Crap, I desperately craved a second date with this gorgeous Frenchman. I rarely ever wanted a second date with anyone.

Then my damn cell phone rang. I looked at the number and sighed before apologizing for the intrusion. "Sorry, this will only take a moment."

Nodding, Yves waved one hand as he popped another morsel onto his tongue with the other. My dick twitched when he smiled through his mouth full of food. Just take me to wherever the hell it is you live and fuck me stupid, I thought.

"Stefano, I'm out to dinner. What is it?" I asked more curtly than I'd intended as I meandered away from our table to a quieter spot on the opposite side of the torch-lit restaurant terrace.

"What? That's great news! When can we return to the site?" I yelled loud enough to stop conversations at the closest tables. I might have even bobbed up and down on my toes a bit.

After explaining the ministry's change of heart, Stefano described in excruciating detail the preliminary report from the forensics lab. When he finally revealed the conclusions, my mouth dropped. "Really? Wow, that's interesting. I sure as hell didn't expect that to be the case, but this revelation presents some new possibilities. We should get together to discuss all this."

Stefano and I planned to meet the next afternoon to map out our next steps, and I shut off my phone.

"I'm sorry. That was my partner and..."

Yves gave me a strange look as he leaned back; his folded forearms were muscular, covered with the perfect amount of black hair.

"Partner?"

"What? Oh, no, no. I don't have a boyfriend. What I mean is my work partner—my painfully straight colleague who can barely pay his alimony. Anyhow, he shared some amazing news." I took a healthy sip of wine and explained, "The archaeological ministry wants us back on the project. They're asking to collaborate. Apparently fistfuls of American dollars are more important to the bottom line than they'd realized. They've redrafted the permits, and all we need to do is sign on the dotted line."

"Congratulations, Charles! So you'll stay in Rome a bit longer?"

"I will." I grinned and downed the last of my wine. "And we received the initial analysis of our skeletons. We couldn't be sure during the two times we examined them since the light was shit."

"Skeletons? I'm on the edge of my seat." He smirked as he swallowed another gulp of his drink.

Shit, he was charming.

"Two weeks ago, we found two Roman skeletons in an underground corridor adjacent to a medieval well. It turns out that one skeleton is male, the other female."

"Ah, a crime of passion, perhaps? Do you know who these ancient Romans were?"

"No, just their gender and, with more testing, we'll know their ages and general health, which might indicate whether they were slaves or not. I doubt we'll ever learn their names or their stories."

"Why are you perplexed?"

"Huh?" Shit, he could already read my face. "Well, given the extraordinary dagger we'd found near the bodies and the likelihood of violence and even murder, I was expecting them both to be male."

"Women can be as dangerous as men, sometimes more. The lioness is more lethal than the lion when the cubs are in danger."

"Good point." I stretched my arms over my head and leaned back; when I realized I was flashing my pit stains, I jerked my arms back down and crossed them over my chest. "Jesus, what a gorgeous night. Would you like to take a stroll around the neighborhood?"

"Fantastic suggestion." Yves threw back the last of his drink. "And I know the perfect gelateria in Piazza Navona for dessert." He pulled out his wallet and placed a generous pile of euros on the table.

"Um, why don't we split the bill?" I protested as I fumbled to retrieve my ratty canvas wallet.

"My treat. I also have a good gig, as you say." He flashed me a dimpled smile. "You can pay for the ice cream, yes?"

"And afterwards, let's get some Limoncello. It's not as fancy as this bar, but I know a great place in Trastevere." I insisted, touching the back of his hand.

THE END OF BOOK 2

About the Author

When she doesn't have her nose stuck in a dusty history tome, JP Kenwood relishes reading and writing plot-packed erotic m/m fiction with strong romantic elements sprinkled with humor and angst. Her alternate history saga, *Dominus*, features an ensemble of memorable characters—masters and slaves, senators and soldiers, lawyers and freedmen, wives and whores—who live, laugh, and lust during the Golden Age of Imperial Rome.

The second book of this series, *Games of Rome*, follows our auburn-haired protagonist, Gaius Fabius, and his Dacian captive turned pleasure slave, Allerix, as they struggle to overcome heartache and hatred while searching for justice, vengeance, and love.

All of her books are available on Amazon and Createspace. Her fiction works to date include:

Dominus (2014)

"Bashir," in the *Kickass Anthology* (2014)

Games of Rome (2015)

February and December (Dominus Calendar Series I) (2016)

JP spends most days writing fiction and non-fiction, researching historical curiosities, traveling the world, cooking gourmet fare for her handsome husband, and relaxing with a good glass of wine, or two.

Connect with JP Kenwood Online:

JP's writing blog:
jpkenwood.com

Facebook:
facebook.com/jp.kenwood

Twitter:
@JPKenwood

97254188R00240

Made in the USA
Columbia, SC
12 June 2018